by nancy thayer

Family Reunion
Girls of Summer
Let It Snow
Surfside Sisters
A Nantucket Wedding
Secrets in Summer
The Island House
*A Very Nantucket
   Christmas*
The Guest Cottage
An Island Christmas
Nantucket Sisters
A Nantucket Christmas
Island Girls
Summer Breeze
Heat Wave
Beachcombers
Summer House
Moon Shell Beach
*The Hot Flash Club
   Chills Out*

Hot Flash Holidays
*The Hot Flash Club Strikes
   Again*
The Hot Flash Club
Custody
*Between Husbands and
   Friends*
An Act of Love
Belonging
Family Secrets
Everlasting
My Dearest Friend
Spirit Lost
Morning
Nell
Bodies and Souls
*Three Women at the Water's
   Edge*
Stepping

family
reunion

nancy thayer

family
reunion

A Novel

Ballantine Books
New York

Family Reunion is a work of fiction. Names, characters, places,
and incidents are either the products of the author's imagination or
are used fictitiously. Any resemblance to actual persons, living
or dead, events, or locales is entirely coincidental.

Copyright © 2021 by Nancy Thayer

All rights reserved.

Published in the United States by Ballantine Books,
an imprint of Random House, a division of
Penguin Random House LLC, New York.

BALLANTINE and the HOUSE colophon are registered trademarks
of Penguin Random House LLC.

Hardback ISBN 978-1-524-79878-9
Ebook ISBN 978-1-524-79879-6

Printed in the United States of America on acid-free paper

randomhousebooks.com

2 4 6 8 9 7 5 3 1

First Edition

Title page photo: iStock.com/RodrigoBlanco
Book design by Alexis Capitini

For my sister
Martha Wright Foshee
The heart of our family

Acknowledgments

W hat a year 2020 was! I hope you all made it through safely, with the help of good books!

This year, I want to thank Nantucket Cottage Hospital's chief medical officer, Dr. Diane Pearl; her physician's assistant, Annette Adams; nurse Janet Chaffee; and winner of the 2020 Seinfeld/ Hartmann Prize for Compassionate Medical Care, patient service coordinator Diane Cabral.

Our island is small and thirty miles away from the mainland. Around twenty thousand people live here all year. Around thirty thousand summer residents and guests arrive during the summer. Our health workers had much to cope with and did it with excellence. Not only this year, but especially this year, I was grateful to know that this first-class medical team was on the island.

This past year has taught me how fortunate I am to live on this island, in this community.

Jill Audycki, Ken Knutti, Alan Bell, Joanne Skokan, and Ive Nakova at Nantucket Pharmacy: What would we have done without you? You were all so efficient and such a pleasure to see, if only for a moment. Thank you!

I'm grateful to all the FedEx, UPS, and USPS drivers who brought the world to our door during these strange and difficult times. As always, I'm glad to know that Velma and Robin are at the post office counter, and Tita, you have no idea how much I'll miss you. Are you sure you want to retire?

Tim Ehrenberg, you're a genius at creating brilliant ways to sell books at our island's own Mitchell's Book Corner. Plus, you're so handsome. Thank you, Mitchell's staff, for leaving the back door open so I could slip in and sign some books! As a reader and a writer, I'm grateful for Mitchell's Book Corner and Nantucket Bookworks. It's remarkable that this small, faraway island is home to so many fabulous writers: Nathaniel Philbrick, Elin Hilderbrand, Blue Balliet, and Leslie Linsley, to name a few, and also home to the Nantucket Book Festival every June. Titcomb's Bookshop on the Cape, I can't wait to walk into your shop again. I send so much gratitude to independent bookstores everywhere!

This year I really missed seeing—literally—my agent, Meg Ruley. Meg grew up on the island, and often comes here, but we didn't get to have lunch at the Downy Flake this year. Next year, two lunches! Thanks to all at the Jane Rotrosen Literary Agency.

A big hug to my virtual assistant, Sara Mallion, who has been amazingly helpful, clever, and creative with social media. I look forward to laughing with her in this new year. Chris Mason and Novation Media, thank you for your reliable assistance.

We all complain about screens, but I'm glad we have the technology that made it possible for me to see friends and family with FaceTime and Zoom. The first thing I do in the morning—after I make coffee—is to open Facebook and check in with my friends. They keep me in touch with the wide world. It's such fun to see their pets and their babies and grandbabies and to "talk" to them. Thank you all for your conversation and your encouragement!

During this closed-in year, I've been delighted to speak with many wonderful bookshops and libraries and readers through Zoom. I'm sad and probably a little bit insane because I haven't been able to set foot in my beloved library, the Nantucket Atheneum, but I learned about Libby, the online library, and it's been a great help.

I continually find inspiration for books in my own family. This year my daughter, Sam, and her partner, Tommy, added one more to their family. Welcome, little Arwyn, or as my sister insists on calling her, Junebug. (*Is* there a Junebug? My sister is a nurse, and strong-willed, so there is a Junebug *now*!) My sister, Martha, my daughter, Sam, and my granddaughter Junebug are all Geminis and power-houses, but I think Ellias, Fabulous, Emmett, and Annie are power-houses, too. Maybe even power *castles*! I'm grateful to my son, Josh, and his husband, David, for their clever phone calls, videos, and views of gorgeous hiking trails and the Botanical Gardens in Arizona. I'll see them someday.

Charley, I love you more every year and even more during this Covid year. I often felt like we were bears from a children's story, curled up together in our nest with our books, magazines, and fat little Callie the cat. And some chocolate.

In 2020, I was even more of a hermit than usual, and, to be honest, I liked it. I wrote, and read, and occasionally Zoomed or Face-Timed with friends. Hearing someone's voice on the telephone was *brilliant*! I was like a teenager lolling on the bed, having profound conversations. Thank you to Jill Hunter Burrill, Merry Anderson, Tricia Patterson, Deborah and Mark Beale, Sofiya Popova, Antonia Massie, Dinah Fulton, Mary and John West, Melissa and Nat Phil-brick, Janet Schulte, and my OYP (official young person), Sara Manela. Curlette Anglin and Tanieca Hosang, you're our super-heroes!

Robb Forman Dew and I met in Williamstown, Massachusetts, around 1978, when our children were the same age and we were both writing our first novels. Mine was *Stepping;* Robb's was *Dale Loves Sophie to Death,* which won the National Book Award. We criticized each other's work, usually while drinking strawberry daiquiris, talked endlessly every day, and shared our deepest secrets. Robb adored her husband, Charles. I met and married Charley. When I moved to Nantucket with Charley, we stayed in touch and talked on the phone and planned to meet in the middle of Massachusetts in a beautiful B&B and talk about books and life. Robb died this year, not from Covid, and I can't believe she's gone. I keep her last message in her beautiful Southern voice on our answering machine.

Books—reading and writing them—have kept me sane this year. Okay, that's true every year. It's a joy doubled to be working with an editor like Shauna Summers. It's as if we're together in a raft, and when I eagerly paddle toward the rapids, she carefully steers me away. And she doesn't hit me in the head with her paddle. Thank you, Shauna.

Books have kept a zillion people contented during this unprecedented and difficult year. I'm grateful to Gina Centrello, Kara Welsh, and Kim Hovey for keeping the great pleasure yacht of Penguin Random House going full speed ahead. Lexi Batsides, Allison Schuster, Karen Fink, Jennifer Rodriguez, and Madeline Hopkins, thank you for all your help.

I'm writing this on the first day of January 2021. Ahhh. Here at last. I wish you all a safe, healthy, and book-filled year.

family
reunion

One

Summer was almost here! Eleanor Sunderland sat on her deck looking out at the eternal Atlantic, savoring the view. Above in the sky, diamond-tipped stars were appearing, one by one, and Eleanor could hear the gentle shush of the waves on the shore far below her. The scent of long, sunny days drifted in with the light, salty breeze from the sea.

It was late May, and if she tilted her head, she could scan down the row of houses on the bluff. She could see which ones had lights on, which summer people had arrived early. She felt both invaded in her happy seclusion and grateful for the company. The winters here could be lonely.

This summer might be lonely, too.

The air was chilly. She wore a long-sleeved dress, but still she shivered, and when her cat flicked his tail against her leg, she knew it was time to go inside, to give Shadow his treat, to prepare for bed. She had never liked going to bed. When she was outside by the ocean, Eleanor felt no age at all, but in her house all the new and necessary bits of technology made her feel very much her age.

She stood up—too fast. Her blood pressure had trouble rising, her doctor told her, because she was so tall. Never one to enjoy being told what to do, it was a nuisance to be seventy years old and bossed around by her body. She waited, and the dizziness faded, and she went through the sliding glass door into the kitchen to give Shadow a small clump of Feline Feast. She checked the lock on the back door, out of habit, and made her way through the large house, turning off lights as she went. Upstairs, she brushed her teeth and changed into her light cotton nightgown and folded back the light quilt and settled against her pillows.

"Shall we watch some television, Shadow?" she asked the cat, who had eaten and now sat purring at the end of the bed.

She picked up the long black remote control, which made her think of the black monolith in *2001: A Space Odyssey*. It was magical, but it was surely going to give her carpal tunnel syndrome or whatever it was called. Her thumb hurt from pressing the buttons. Yes, she *knew* she could use voice commands to get to a certain channel: PBS. CNN. She knew about the ridiculously named Xfinity, another sign that the English language was being hijacked by idiots, but once she was on the channel—or what was it called now? Stream?—then she had to push a button to go up and down and across the rows of offerings, often accidentally landing in a Japanese anime series like *The Legend of Korra*. She pressed the blue button that allowed voice commands. It made a strange, unpleasant noise. The television screen said, *Something is wrong.* Well, she knew that!

"What are we going to do, Shadow?" Eleanor asked.

Shadow continued licking his beautiful dark fur. At least he didn't run on batteries.

"My hair is still as thick as yours," Eleanor told the cat, who obviously didn't care, but it was true. She had been graced with thick dark hair, and so far age had not thinned it out, even though it had streaked the black with white and wreaked havoc on the rest of her body.

A pile of books lay on the bed next to her in all their glorious colorful jackets. New books she'd bought at Mitchell's, because she loved that bookstore dearly, and also a few books from the library.

She always gave herself some time to browse the library shelves to check out new reads she hadn't heard about and wasn't sure she would want to stick with. Like agreeing to only coffee on a first date, rather than an entire meal.

But she'd spent much of her day reading, and she wanted the effortless zoning out that television provided. She couldn't tolerate being with her own thoughts for one more minute. She needed distraction.

Earlier today, she had walked from her house on the bluff to Martha's house in town. Martha was her best friend. They'd gone through weddings, childbirth, adolescence, and empty nests together. Martha's marriage had been as happy as Eleanor's was miserable, and it was Martha's laughter and advice that had gotten Eleanor through life with her wildly handsome, indescribably tense, strict, virtuous husband, Mortimer Radcliffe Sunderland. Now deceased.

Three years ago, Mortimer died suddenly, in his sleep. During the reception after the funeral, Eleanor had whispered to Martha, "I'm surprised Mortimer would do anything *suddenly*," and they had covered their mouths with their hands and giggled like little girls.

But this morning, over coffee, Martha announced, "Eleanor, guess what! Al and I are leaving this week to take a three-month cruise of the Mediterranean!"

Eleanor felt faint. The floor seemed to slip beneath her feet. "What?"

"I know it's a surprise. I didn't mean to spring it on you like this."

Eleanor sat there, quietly, furiously, trying not to feel she'd just been stabbed in the heart by a traitor. After a moment, she regained her self-control.

"Gosh, what a surprise," Eleanor said in her normal voice. "I had no idea you were planning a cruise."

Martha blushed. "We didn't really *plan* it. We sort of decided on the spur of the moment. We've splurged on first-class tickets. First-class everything, because Al will turn seventy in June, and we decided it's time to spoil ourselves."

"How wonderful," Eleanor announced, lying through her teeth.

"I know! Eleanor, let me show you our ship! Our itinerary! Hang on, I'll get Al's laptop."

So Eleanor had to sit there going "Ooh" at the shiny photos of Greek islands rising out of deep blue seas, elegant staircases to posh first-class suites, and a formal dining room with white tablecloths, floral centerpieces, waiters dressed like naval officers in handsome uniforms, and buffets of food from around the world.

"Al has to take a tux," Martha whispered in awe. "I have to buy some gowns. *Gowns,* Eleanor! One night we'll sit at the captain's table!"

"You're going to gain weight," Eleanor predicted, like the black fairy at Sleeping Beauty's christening.

"Actually, I won't!" Martha pulled up shots of the ship's fitness center, complete with bikes, weights, and yoga mats. "Also," Martha crowed, "ta-da!" A turquoise swimming pool filled the screen. "No salt, no sand, just clear water."

Full of chlorine and other people's pee, Eleanor almost said, but bit her tongue.

Instead, she said, "The ship must be enormous if it has a swimming pool."

"Oh, it is," Martha agreed, and babbled on.

Eleanor stopped listening. She was happy for her best friend. She was simply sad for herself. Summer was always a difficult time on the small island, when thirty thousand or more summer people arrived to share the pleasures of Nantucket. Contractors honked at any car with a New York license plate, families on bikes pedaled blithely past stop signs, and you never saw anyone you knew in the crowded grocery store. Complaining with Martha was one of her few summer joys, and this summer she would be deprived of that.

"*Now* you're going to have to get a cellphone," Eleanor said triumphantly. Martha was kind of a technophobe, using a landline telephone and her old Kodak camera.

"Well, I thought of that," Martha said. "But you know how I hate those things. We've decided that, if necessary, I'll use Al's, but really we'll only need to check on the children, and they're all grown up so we don't even need to do that."

"I'll miss you," Eleanor admitted.

"I'll send you postcards!" Martha told her.

Eleanor restrained herself from rolling her eyes—did anyone even send postcards anymore?

"Please do." Forcing herself to be cheerful, she said, "Oh, Martha, I hope you have a spectacular time!"

She had been sad and hurt and angry when she left Martha's house, because it didn't seem like Martha not to tell Eleanor about something so important before.

Now she tossed the remote control on the quilt. "Alexa," she said, "play Bob Seger."

As his rough and growly voice filled the room with "Against the Wind," Eleanor snorted, because if anything was against the wind it was her old house on the bluff.

Then came the words: "We were young and strong," and Eleanor couldn't help it. She burst into tears.

She'd been young and strong, once. She'd spent all her summers in this beautiful house. Her grandparents had owned it, and then her parents, and now Eleanor. She was an only child, and this house, with its eccentric creaks and uneven floors, was like a living companion to her. A friend. She could walk through the house with her eyes closed and know what room she was in. The house had been built long before fast ferries and UPS, back when islanders made do with what they had or could scavenge, so the doorknobs were all different—porcelain, brass, glass, metal latch—and Eleanor had always thought that made the house friendlier, somehow.

She could put her hand on the wall in the guest bedroom and feel where a door into another room had been removed and the space plastered over. At a casual glance, you wouldn't see it because it had been so carefully done and painted. But Eleanor remembered when the door was there, connecting her bedroom to her grandparents' room. When she was a small child and the night was howling with rain and wind, she would leave her bed to hurry across the cold wide-planked board floors to her grandparents' bed. Her grand-mother would lift Eleanor up, tucking her in beside her. Even now Eleanor could remember the warmth of her grandmother's body curled around her, the protection of the heavy quilt over her, the snores of her grandfather on the other side of the high, wide bed.

She felt affection for the small crack in the window of her bed-room because it reminded her of that long-ago summer night when Kay, her island friend, roused her by throwing pebbles at the win-dow, just like in stories. Eleanor had snuck out of the house, biked down to the beach with Kay, and together they'd gone swimming in the dark waves, something they'd both been forbidden ever to do, swim at night. Oh, they'd felt wicked and brave! Now Kay was living with her husband in California, both of them doing yoga and drink-ing almond milk, and Eleanor was widowed.

At the end of the downstairs hallway, the wall was marked with not one but two indentations, both by Eleanor's son, Cliff. One summer when Cliff was three, he had a small plastic tricycle. Zoom-ing around on that was his favorite activity. The house was large, with many rooms, so on rainy days Cliff was allowed to ride his bike inside. Eleanor could remember his fat legs pedaling furiously as he whizzed around, laughing maniacally. Only once did he crash into the wall. Cliff wasn't hurt nor was his bike but the accident caused a zigzag fissure in the wall. It was minor. They painted over it at some point and forgot about it until Cliff was eleven and bored out of his mind on another rainy summer day. He was throwing a football at his older sister, Alicia, who kept rolling her eyes and saying, "This is stupid." One time he threw the ball too high and too hard, so it slammed into the wall, causing a section of the old wood to splinter and cave in. When Eleanor saw it, she shook her head and hugged her son. "What do you have against that poor old wall?" she asked. A carpenter came to repair it, but the wall never looked the same.

One time, Ari, Eleanor's three-year-old granddaughter, had terri-fied them all when she disappeared from the house and never an-swered their calls. Eleanor's daughter, Alicia, Ari's mother, had been at the point of phoning the police when Eleanor opened the kitchen cabinet and discovered the child curled among the baking tins, her baby doll neatly tucked in a bread loaf pan. The doll's eyes were open, but Ari was sound asleep.

"Ari?" Eleanor had asked gently.

Ari had opened her big blue eyes and smiled. "Hi, Gram," she'd said, and yawned.

Memories were everywhere. Five generations had summered in this fine old house on the bluff. The house was beloved, and so very old. Eleanor knew she was not keeping up with the repairs on the house. When her parents were alive, her father did most of the maintenance, but Eleanor's husband, Mortimer, an insurance executive, was very much *not* DIY, and besides, they were mostly there in the summer, and who wanted to think about power drills and saws in the summer? After her husband died, Eleanor had had a new roof put on the house.

It had always been a tradition for the family to spend summer weekends on the island. Some years the mothers and their children had stayed the entire week and the fathers came down Friday night. After Eleanor's parents died and Alicia married Phillip, the tradition continued. Mortimer and Eleanor's son, Cliff, often came, too, and the family was all there, together, sleeping under one roof. Eleanor loved this custom. She was happiest when her family was with her in the summer. She'd delighted in the shouts of Cliff, Phillip, and Mortimer playing tag football in the yard, and the sudden musical splashing of the outdoor shower when someone returned from the beach. And the casual, messy lobster dinners eaten outside on the long wooden table on the deck, where Eleanor put two large bowls at each end of the table, one full of nutcrackers and picks, the other for people to discard the shells. Smaller bowls at each place held melted butter. Or the rainy summer nights when they sat in the dining room, eating clam chowder and hot rolls, drinking a not very good champagne, telling tales on each other, and laughing.

When her husband died three years before, Eleanor had sold her Boston house and moved to the island to live year-round. She already had friends here, and she'd quickly constructed a routine of social events. When she went to church, she sat with Bonnie and Donnie Hamilton, retired year-rounders who'd been bridge partners with Eleanor and Mortimer. After church, the three often went to lunch at the Seagrille, where within the relative privacy of the booths they discussed all the town issues and who was joining what community committee and how delighted they were that Muffy Andover had joined the board of the Hospital Thrift Shop, even though Muffy (that name!) tended to flash her wealth about. Clarissa Lourie was on the board of Ocean Matters with Eleanor, and they had lunch at least once a week to discuss books. Even after Mortimer died, the Andersons and the Andovers and the Hamiltons always invited Eleanor to their cocktail parties, and when Eleanor became brave enough to give a dinner party herself, it was the Hamiltons, Andovers, and Andersons who were her guests.

And, of course, Martha and Al Clark.

The children—she still thought of Alicia and Cliff as "the children"—came down for the weekends and for the entire last week of August, and after Mortimer died, they all came to the island to spend Christmas with Eleanor. Sometimes Ari, Alicia, and Phillip would arrive early, loaded with bags of decorations and presents. Cliff would surprise them with extravagant gifts. He could afford to. He sold real estate in Boston and had no family of his own. Eleanor would throw caution to the winds and turn the thermostat up to a toasty seventy degrees, Cliff would help her bring in the logs, and they'd build a fire in the living and dining room fireplaces while Alicia and Ari twined laurel all around.

This past Christmas had not been quite so much fun, and Eleanor was worried about the summer. About her daughter, specifically.

Alicia had always been such a very girly girl, even though early on Eleanor and her husband tried to go with the wisdom of the times and occasionally dress her in overalls and give her train sets so she wouldn't be limited by her gender. But by the time she was four, Alicia insisted on clothes with ruffles and frills. She would play only with dolls, and she had so many tantrums when she didn't have the much-discussed Barbie doll that Eleanor and Mortimer surrendered and gave her a Barbie for Christmas. After that, there was no stopping her. She wanted her bedroom to be all pink, she wanted to wear sparkling bracelets and bows in her hair, and when she was older, she saved her allowance to buy *People* magazine.

Her daughter was a mystery to Eleanor. Alicia never seemed *content*. Alicia, fortunate (spoiled?), always wanted *more*. Eleanor talked it over with her husband and her friends, finally deciding that it was Cliff's birth, seven years after Alicia was born, that tangled the family's relationships. Also, twined into Alicia's life—and gene pool— Eleanor's own mother had been fluffy and feminine until the moment she passed away. Audrey had worn lace and pastels, sparkling earrings, and several "signature" scents. Alicia had gone to stay with her grandparents during the two difficult times when Eleanor suffered miscarriages. Alicia had been in heaven with her frilly grandmother and had returned home reeking of French perfume and carrying velvet boxes full of costume jewelry.

When Cliff was born, hale and hearty, Eleanor had wept with joy. Mortimer had made a fuss over having a *son* and for a while Alicia might have felt slighted. Alicia had never been charmed by her baby brother. She nicknamed him Stinky for the first two years of his life, shocked at what his diaper could contain. Cliff grew into a boisterous, mess-making, rowdy little boy, so it was probably true that Alicia had felt ignored or slighted while Eleanor was occupied with saving Cliff from danger or the house from Cliff. There was, Eleanor remembered, the summer when Eleanor had arranged a Cinderella-themed birthday party for Alicia, only to have to rush off to save Cliff from rappelling down the 'Sconset bluff using the ties of Eleanor's robes and scarves.

Alicia had been an indifferent student (but so had Eleanor). Alicia had been terrible at sports in high school (but so had Eleanor). On the other hand, Cliff had excelled academically and on the basketball court, winning full scholarships to several Ivy League colleges. Alicia had begged to go to boarding school when she was fourteen. It was, she told Eleanor and Mortimer, the only thing she wanted in all the world. So they had coughed up the tuition fees and sent her to an all-girls school in Massachusetts, and Alicia had come home on holidays desiring even more. A trip to the Caribbean for Christmas, diamond ear studs, a canopy bed, a Tiffany signature gold bracelet—whatever the poshest girl in her school had.

Alicia was exasperating, but there were times when she sought Eleanor out and wept in her mother's arms. Alicia was beautiful, but she didn't believe that, and the boys she met at the yacht club in the summer flirted with her, but never the boy Alicia had a crush on. Alicia was thrilled when she got to invite a boarding school friend to stay for a week on Nantucket, but she was furious, in private, after the friend left, that Eleanor didn't have a housekeeper and had expected the girls to help carry bowls and plates to and from the kitchen.

Where had she come from, this pretty, demanding, commanding girl? In her heart, Eleanor knew she favored Cliff, even when he broke a chair or was caught smoking at ten or broke a window or showed up with Alicia's lipstick scribbled all over his face. Maybe she shouldn't have asked Alicia to bring her a diaper or washcloth, or to sit alone watching *Sesame Street* while Eleanor cuddled and rocked Cliff when he was teething. Eleanor could understand how her glee and pride when Cliff started walking might have made Alicia jealous. After all, *she* could walk, talk, sing, *and* do cartwheels. Eleanor tried to give Alicia special attention and praise but Alicia often gave her mother a dead-eye stare, as if she knew Eleanor's praise was forced. Cliff was big and strong, knockout handsome like his father, and naturally sweet. If he wanted something, he worked for it, experiencing no wounded pride when he mowed the lawn or raked the leaves or even stacked dishes in the dishwasher, a chore Eleanor seldom asked him to do because he was so clumsy and clashed the glasses together. Alicia always balked at doing chores, sulking if she had to put a load of her brother's laundry in the dryer or carry in the groceries.

Alicia attended Northeastern University, and for a while Eleanor thought her daughter might develop an interest in teaching or business. Alicia did work for the first time in her life, as a salesgirl at

Shreve, Crump and Low, which sold silver ice buckets and other necessities of life. Alicia worked there, she told her mother, because she hoped to meet the *right* man, and, miraculously, she did. Phillip Paget was a resident at Harvard Medical School. He wasn't handsome, but he was kind. He wasn't wealthy, but he was brilliant. Phillip thought Alicia was the most beautiful woman he'd ever met. Their wedding was a stupendously complicated and expensive event that caused Mortimer to retire to his bedroom with a cold cloth on his forehead.

For the first few years, Eleanor was relieved. Both Alicia and Phillip were happy. Phillip became a surgeon who focused fiercely when he worked but couldn't find his car keys when he was at home. Alicia blossomed as a wife, decorating their house, holding cocktail and dinner parties (with temporary help), and after two years of marriage gave birth to their daughter, Ari. Ari's difficult birth had ended in a C-section and a hysterectomy. Alicia was glad she was relieved of the burden of pregnancy. It had not been a state she'd enjoyed. But she was a good wife and mother, happy in her life, even blissful when the family came to the island most summer weekends to relax. Alicia met old friends, played tennis, sailed, and was thrilled to have Eleanor in charge of Ari.

Ari.

Eleanor adored Ari. Ari adored Eleanor. For years, everyone was happy. Now Ari was graduating from college, and Alicia was forty-six, worrying about her age. Alicia was obsessed with money and the status she thought it could buy.

This Christmas, here at the Nantucket house, Eleanor had given Alicia a check for a thousand dollars. Alicia had spotted the amount and her face fell with disappointment.

"Sweetie," Eleanor had asked, "don't you like your gift?"

Alicia was almost at the point of tears. "It's nice, Mom. Thank you. It's just . . . I was hoping for more so I could buy a Birkin."

Ari spoke up, rolling her eyes. "Mom. You can get an Hermès Kelly online for a thousand dollars."

"Yes, *used*. Or a *knockoff*," Alicia shot back.

"I have no idea what you're talking about," Eleanor had said. Her daughter made her feel weary.

Eleanor also worried about Cliff, amazingly handsome, brilliant, hardworking, and wealthy, just like Mortimer had been. Cliff was thirty-nine, and still not married. With his good looks, women had flocked to him in college, but no one stuck. He came to the island most weekends in the summer, but he never brought a woman with him.

"Cliff," Eleanor had asked him one summer, "don't you have a special someone in your life?"

"Yeah, Mom," Cliff had answered. "You." He hugged her as they both laughed.

"Cliff," Eleanor had asked him this Christmas, "are you dating anyone special?"

Cliff grinned and shook his head. "So many women, so little time."

When Cliff was younger, she'd taken him and his sister to all the best plays, musicals, and ballets in Boston and often in New York. After Mortimer died, Cliff invited Eleanor up to Boston, put her up at the Chilton Club, and took her to plays and operas and out to dinner at posh restaurants where he ordered expensive wines. When he began selling real estate, Cliff often emailed Eleanor photos and information about the gorgeous houses he was selling, and Eleanor responded, glad to have this connection with her son. It was fun to see the interiors of houses, even though she wouldn't change a board in her own. Because of the weekends and emails, Eleanor felt much more attached to her son than she did to her daughter, who was, even in her forties, worried about her figure and whether or not to have her forehead Botoxed. It took Eleanor months to realize that the closeness she felt with Cliff was about his professional life, not his personal life. But she had tried to stay close. Weren't men supposed to adore their mothers?

In her most bitter moods, Eleanor blamed her husband for their son's and daughter's obsession with money. But even then, she admitted to herself that she'd influenced them, too. In the early days, she'd left them with a nanny while she tried to be the perfect wife for

Mortimer. She'd furnished their Ipswich house luxuriously and elegantly. She went to a gym to keep herself trim, had her nails and hair done weekly, held the requisite cocktail parties for his colleagues, attended other requisite parties. Because Mortimer expected it, she'd forced her children to attend the appropriate after-school activities: tennis, swimming, archery for Cliff. Tennis, swimming, and ballet for Alicia. She'd taught them manners, yes, and sent them off to boarding schools when they were fourteen, because they'd asked to go.

Still, when they were small, she *had* curled up with them at bedtime, reading to them from the classics. She *had* cuddled them, praised them, tended to their occasional cuts or bruises. And every summer she'd brought them here, to her family's summer home on the east coast of Nantucket Island.

Here, on the island, Eleanor had let the kids run free. Mortimer disapproved of skateboards and especially of any sign of sexual awareness. So Eleanor hadn't told him when she'd sat her embarrassed teenagers down and talked to them about sex. She allowed them to go to beach parties in trucks driven by older teenagers. She didn't mention it when they came home smelling of weed, and she held Alicia's hair the night she came home so drunk she was sick. She put Alka-Seltzer in the medicine cabinet. She didn't mind when they blasted Guns N' Roses or Aerosmith.

Her children had turned out just fine.

Regardless of her parenting, Alicia and Cliff were who they were; they were done, like baked gingerbread cookies. The only family member Eleanor had any chance of being close to was her granddaughter, Arianna. Arianna, who asked people to call her Ari, was graduating from Bucknell University in a week, and she planned to continue her education, starting a master's in early childhood education at Boston University.

Where would Ari be for the summer? Eleanor wondered. She knew Alicia complained constantly about the sky-high tuition for boarding school and college, plus all the extras, clothing, textbooks, trips with friends. In fact, now that Eleanor thought about it, she remembered the atmosphere of tension and anger lying just below the surface of her family when they were on the island for Christmas.

Alicia had wakened Eleanor the morning after Christmas Day. She'd tapped on Eleanor's door, which made Shadow swiftly disappear under the bed, and slid into the room carrying a tray with two cups of coffee. Alicia had bumped the door shut with her hip.

"Good morning, Mommy," Alicia had said sweetly.

Dear God in Heaven, Eleanor had thought, was her daughter not aware that calling her "Mommy" was a dead giveaway that Alicia was going to ask her for money?

Eleanor had been awake, reading, trying to put off the moment of rising and facing her family. She slipped her book beneath her covers and sat up, shoving pillows behind her back. "Good morning, darling." She *did* love her daughter, and wished she knew what in the world would ever make her happy.

"It's a cold day," Alicia said. She set the tray on Eleanor's bedside table. "Phillip is building a fire in the living room. I brought you coffee to warm you up before you come down."

"Thanks." Eleanor took a sip. "Mmm. Nice and hot."

Alicia settled on the bed near Eleanor. "This has been such a wonderful Christmas, Mommy. Phillip loves his Fitbit. And your check was so generous."

"Well, I know it wasn't as generous as you'd hoped for," Eleanor said bluntly.

A stab of guilt pierced her heart as she spoke. Why could she never be tender with her grown daughter?

"I'm sorry if I offended you," Alicia said, pouting, shrugging into herself. "It's just that these past four years, Phillip and I have been stretched financially. Ari's tuition is around sixty thousand dollars a year. Imagine! And now—I don't know if she spoke with you about it—*now* she wants to get a master's in early childhood education."

"Phillip's a surgeon," Eleanor reminded her daughter. "He must make a substantial salary."

"Oh, you would think so, wouldn't you, but recently the insurance companies have absolutely *strangled* all the doctors and hospitals. I can't even talk about it, I get so upset." Tears welled up in Alicia's gemlike blue-green eyes.

"I'm sorry, Alicia, but I can't help with the tuition. I've given you all I can afford to give."

Alicia wiped the tears from her eyes, rose from the bed, and stalked to the window overlooking the Atlantic. Today the ocean was a surly gray.

Without looking at Eleanor, Alicia said, "You could if you would sell this house."

It wasn't the first time Alicia had raised this possibility, and Eleanor kept her anger in check. She said what she'd always said before: "I am not selling this house. It was my mother's house, and now my house, and I intend to live in it until I die, which I hope will not be soon."

Alicia was not defeated. "Maybe you could get a reverse mortgage? Have you heard of that?" She beamed at her mother as she walked back to the bed.

"I've heard of it, and I would be insane to do it," Eleanor said.

"Then I don't know what we'll do," Alicia said sadly, sinking back down on the quilt. "Even if we resign from our Boston club—which is so important for both Phillip and me—" Alicia paused, waiting for her mother to speak.

"You could get a job," Eleanor suggested.

"A *job*?" Alicia looked horrified, as if her mother had told her to drink poison.

"It's not a stain on your character to work," Eleanor said gently.

"Really? Like you would know? Because you never worked in your life!" Alicia's lovely face crumpled. Tears spilled from her eyes. She strode from the bedroom, slamming the door behind her. She had forgotten to take the cups and tray.

Ah, Eleanor had so many memories like that one, when Alicia lost all her charm when charm didn't get her what she wanted.

But Alicia had given Eleanor one miraculous gift: Ari, her granddaughter.

Eleanor and Ari had been like human magnets from the moment Ari was born. As an infant, when Ari wailed inconsolably, Alicia would either wring her hands or rock the baby so quickly she only cried louder. Eleanor would pick her up, hold her to her shoulder, and whisper sweet nothings into her ear. Ari would relax, sagging against her grandmother, sobbing a little less, then a little less, and finally falling asleep. Eleanor had walked miles carrying the little girl. Alicia had been grateful to her mother for the help, and had been delighted for Eleanor to visit for weeks at a time during Ari's toddler and "terrible two" years. But when Ari turned three, Alicia sent her to what she considered *the* preschool, and Eleanor was less useful. Next came school plays, ballet lessons, piano lessons, and playdates with the *right* girls.

Fortunately, Nantucket was *the* place to be in July and August, so Eleanor and Ari continued to enjoy each other's company, especially on rainy days when Alicia had lunch dates. Then the two played cards and board games and read aloud to one another from *Harry Potter*. For a couple of years, grandmother and granddaughter became obsessed with making clothes for a pair of adorable small toy mice.

Those had been heavenly days. But when Ari turned ten, she took sailing and tennis lessons and met friends her own age who came over to hole up in Ari's bedroom, listening to bubbly tween music while trying on clothes and playing with their increasingly sophisticated phones. Two years later, Ari was on the island for only a few days in the summer. Instead, she attended an all-girls New Hampshire camp where she learned to paddle a canoe and a kayak, play volleyball, softball, and soccer, shoot arrows into targets, and run relay races. It would help Ari learn about team spirit, Alicia said, and Eleanor knew she was right. Still, Eleanor was sad to be separated from her granddaughter, even if it was natural and to be expected.

After that, when Ari came with her family to Nantucket, she was affectionate with Eleanor, but she was always racing out the door to go to the beach with a pack of friends.

"Remember what you did when you were her age," Eleanor said

out loud as she sat in her bed. "Now stop being silly and make a plan for yourself in your fortunate old age."

After a moment, she took up her iPhone and texted a message to her son, her daughter, and her granddaughter.

Please come to Nantucket and help me celebrate my 70th birthday on June 3! Party favors and cake for the guests!

She tapped "Send" and found herself smiling. This would give her something fun to think about. She'd ask her cleaner, Penny, to help freshen the bedrooms—well, the entire house, actually. She'd take them all out to Le Languedoc for an extravagant champagne dinner. As for party favors, well, that would take some thought. She'd go exploring in town to find the perfect gift for each person.

Eleanor snuggled down beneath her quilts—even now, at the end of May, it was cold in the house, but she was too much of a New Englander to turn the heat on. It was meteorological spring. She lay on her side and smiled as Shadow crept over and folded himself against the bend in Eleanor's knees. Reaching out, she turned off her bedside lamp.

She closed her eyes, let herself sink into sleep—and had a thought that made her eyes fly open. What if her family thought that by "party favors" she meant giving them the house?

Two

It was Ari's last day at Bucknell University. Her roommates and most of her friends had already left. Her Subaru Forester was almost packed. Her room was empty, down to a few plastic hangers abandoned in the closet.

Ari was dressed casually in a sundress and sandals, her long dark hair tied back. No jewelry, no makeup. She wanted to be plain, plain, plain, unequivocal and understood. She had tried doing this before, as early as the beginning of their final semester, but Peter had been anxious about keeping his grades up and she didn't want to wreck it for him. She really had tried, in so many ways, to give him hints, to back away. Peter should have guessed something was wrong. He should have been at least partly attuned to her. But he was excited about graduation, parties, celebrations with friends and family.

And their engagement to be married.

She'd met Peter Anderson when they were fifteen years old, swimming relay races at their summer camps on Lake Winnipesaukee in New Hampshire. Ari's mother had sent her to Bird Bell Camp for Girls every summer since she was thirteen. The camp was named in honor of two female British explorers, Isabella Bird and Gertrude Bell, and its mission was to teach girls independence, self-control, and mastery of sports. Ari loved being at the camp. She returned every year, thrilled to see her camp friends, to spend all her hours in nature, to run down the trails beneath towering evergreens. When Ari was fifteen, Miss Kiltenbarr, the head counselor, announced that there would be a one-day festival with the boys' camp across the lake. It included races, sports, charades around the campfire, but most of all, it included boys.

Ari was a strong swimmer. She'd learned to swim in the Atlantic, with its salt and its waves. The clear, sweet water of the lake offered little resistance, and she often won races. The day of the co-camp, she led off in a relay race across the lake. She was neck and neck with the boy when she handed the baton off to M. J. Clark and treaded water, catching her breath.

"Hey," the boy said. He was treading water, too. Like Ari, he was tanned, with a sunburned nose, and his long, thick eyelashes were clumped together with water, and his red hair stuck out in all directions.

"Hey," Ari replied. Her own long dark hair clung to her skull and her forehead, dribbling drops of water down her face.

"I'm Peter," he said.

Peter, she thought, *not Pete. Interesting.* Like her father was Phillip, not Phil. "I'm Ari."

"Let's swim to the island," Peter said.

The island was only a clump of rocks with a few hardy evergreens sticking out, but it was a favorite place to rest and watch the other races.

They sat side by side in the shade of the evergreen clumps, looking out over the other campers participating in water sports. Peter was from New Jersey and went to a boarding school in Connecticut. Ari was from Boston and attended Dana Hall in Wellesley, Massachusetts. His family skied in Aspen. Ari's family went to the Bahamas in the winter. Peter thought his camp was fun, but it was starting to get boring. Ari felt the same way about her camp. Peter pitched small stones into the water as they talked, and Ari was hyperaware of his maleness, his hairy arms and legs, his muscular chest, his deep voice. She was wearing her old navy blue Speedo, approved camp-wear, and she wished her nipples would stop sticking out against the fabric, it was embarrassing, right up until the moment Peter said, "I'd like to kiss you."

"Okay," she replied calmly, as if this happened to her all the time.

Peter put his arms around her, brought his mouth to hers, and kissed her for a long time. Ari found herself *analyzing* the kiss—she'd never been so thoroughly kissed before—while at the same time she censured herself for not giving over to the experience completely. She did put her arms around him. She did allow him to ease her back onto the ground, but when he attempted to move on top of her, she put her knees up to prevent him.

When she did that, Peter stopped kissing her. He smiled at her. "I like you," he said.

"I like you," she said back.

"Let's meet at the cookout tonight," Peter said.

"Okay." She kissed him quickly, briefly, on his mouth, feeling sassy and daring as she did. Then, to be extra cool, she stood up and dove back into the lake.

Before they left camp, they put their phone numbers on each other's phones. During the winter, they kept up a texted conversation. The next year they met again on the co-camp day, and again the year after that. She decided to go to Bucknell University without talking it over with Peter, so she was amazed that Bucknell was his choice, too. Were they destined to be together?

Ari joined a sorority at Bucknell. The delight and friendship and rituals kept her from spending all her time and thoughts on Peter. They argued about this and finally decided to allow themselves to date other people. It was actually, Peter argued, part of the college experience. Ari went out with other guys and enjoyed being with them, but she knew Peter was having much more of the *college experience* than she was. Ari's life was too busy with coursework and deep, meaningful discussions about life with girlfriends and washing cars for a charity with her sorority to feel sad or threatened by Peter's other girls. Maybe that should have told her something about her feelings for him.

Ari majored in early childhood education. Peter took pre-law. In their junior year, Peter told Ari he wanted them to be a couple, now and in the future. He wanted them to be exclusive.

"We're on such different paths," Ari reminded him.

"Ari," Peter said, "you and I have been on the same path since we kissed on the island in Lake Winnipesaukee."

Ari gave him points for that. Peter wasn't often romantic, but that night at the end of their junior year, he was very romantic. Very persuasive. That was the first night they made love. The first time Ari had ever had sex. Not, obviously, Peter's first time. She didn't ask him about it.

Once they became exclusive, they spent all their time together, and much of it they spent studying. They were both ambitious. Peter wanted to become a judge. Ari wanted to run a daycare for single mothers, paid for by the donations of people like her parents. They talked endlessly about their plans over the summer when they didn't go to camp. Instead, Peter came to stay with Ari for two weeks on Nantucket in her grandmother's house. In separate bedrooms, of course.

The fall of their senior year, Peter asked her to marry him. Caught up in the moment, she said yes. Peter was admitted to Harvard Law, an impressive accomplishment that made Ari's mother rapturous. Ari was admitted to the graduate program in early childhood education at Boston University. He took her to his home for Christmas. Ari took Peter to her house for New Year's Eve.

If, sometimes, Ari wondered if she *really* loved Peter, her friends made fun of her doubts.

"You've been together for so long, you're like an old married couple already," Katie Warren said.

"You are so obvs meant to be together," insisted Sophia Brannagan.

"I'll tell you the exact truth," Laura Hunter said. "You want gooey love to come all at once, at first sight, in some blinding fiery revelation that makes your little red heart pound. But that's only infatuation, and you know that leads to disappointment. What you have with Peter is true love, the daily kind that allows you to be mad at each other and still make love at night."

"You're right," Ari agreed. She conjured up an image of the lodge on the shores of Lake Winnipesaukee that she and Peter had reserved for the last Saturday in August. They would be married there, on the shore, even if it rained. The lodge had rooms for their families and several friends, and the owners catered. Ari would wear a ring of fresh flowers in her hair.

Now all that had to be canceled.

Before going out, Ari checked herself in the mirror. Long brown hair, blue eyes, five foot ten and slender, she'd been compared to Kate Middleton often. She and Peter were exactly the same height, as long as she didn't wear high heels. Today was one of those freak spring days that acted like summer, hot and humid, and as Ari walked toward the bench by the Malesardi Quadrangle, she went slowly, telling herself she didn't want to get all sweaty. But really, she was dreading this meeting, even though she was determined to get it done. Fortunately, the campus was empty. The students had left, except for a few stragglers like Ari.

As she neared the half circle of benches, she saw that Peter was already there. Of course he was. Punctuality was important to him. With him, over the past four years, she'd been rushing through every moment, not being late for classes, studying for tests, partying with friends. Even making love with Peter had always happened in a rush. As much as he wanted her, Peter was terrified of being caught in the act. Ari had joked with her best friend Meloni that having sex with Peter Anderson was like wrestling with a nervous puppy. Ari was certain that when Peter felt safe in his life, he would settle down and take things more slowly. She had learned during their time together that while Peter presented a cool, unflustered façade, in his heart and mind he was harried by insecurities.

Peter was at his best when he was at home with his family, although of course Ari and Peter never made love when they were there. He played driveway basketball with his younger brother and his dad and hugged his mom all the time. He would be a good husband and father, Ari decided. He liked being part of something, liked teamwork, liked making his sister laugh and his father praise him and his mother force one more piece of her special chocolate cake on him. The Anderson family was so unlike Ari's, it made her envious. When she took Peter home to celebrate New Year's Eve, her mother had been unusually sweet and attentive, no doubt thrilled that Ari was with a man who intended to go into the law. Ari's father was welcoming in his normal vague way. Phillip Paget was a surgeon, which impressed Peter and his parents, but when he was at home, he seemed to melt. It was as if all the energy had been drained out of him by his exacting work. Ari privately thought her father was simply exhausted, *defeated,* from living with his social-climbing, money-hungry, seldom-satisfied wife. Ari was certainly wearied by her mother.

But Ari had never felt madly, crazily, hopelessly in love with Peter. Each year, each *month,* Peter grew bossier, more arrogant, and less pleasant. She was quite sure she didn't want to spend her life with him. She didn't want to hurt him, but she didn't want to live in misery.

Ari needed to break up with him now. She had to be quick and decisive, kind but unyielding. She'd tried several times to do it gradually, and that had never worked.

There he was, standing beneath a cherry tree, smiling.

Peter caught sight of her. He ran a few steps to catch Ari in his arms. "Hey! We're almost outta this burg."

She shook off his hands and stepped back. Thank God no one else was within hearing distance. Her heart thumped hard with anxiety, and when she spoke, she was almost breathless. Her words flew out in a hurried flutter. "Peter, listen to me. I have to tell you. I can't marry you, Peter. No—I *don't want* to marry you. I've been thinking and thinking, and we're wrong for each other. I'm breaking up with you."

Her hands were clasped in front of her as if she were Queen Elizabeth giving a speech. She didn't want to touch him.

Peter froze. After a moment, he grinned. "This is a joke, right?"

"No. No joke. I'm sorry. I don't love you, Peter. I don't want to have a life with you." She knew him so well. She could see how he clutched his hands into fists at his sides, as he always did when something was unfair. "I never meant to hurt you."

"Well, I never meant to be hurt," Peter replied, without a hint of sarcasm. "Ari, come on. I can't believe what you're saying." He shook his head. "We . . . we're going to get married."

Peter reached for her hand. Ari moved away quickly, sitting sideways on a bench, drawing her legs up to her chest, making herself as small and as untouchable as possible. "I'll take care of canceling the wedding arrangements," she told him.

"That's certainly big of you. I feel much better now." Peter paced up and down the bricks, running his hand through his thick red hair. He stopped in front of Ari. "I had no idea. You gave me no warning."

"But I *did*, Peter. You just never listen to me."

"Come on, Ari. Don't be like this."

"Please, Peter, you *know* I've been wanting to tell you. I've told you I needed to talk to you, but you always said 'later' or that you don't have the time."

"You do realize it's rather normal to be busy and distracted during the month you graduate from college." He had slipped into his *terribly superior, I'm better than you are* mode of speaking.

"Peter, get real. You know you never gave me a chance to talk with you."

"So we're talking, and this is what you have to say?" Peter's voice went bitter. "What's happened? Have you met someone else?"

"I haven't met someone else. I just know I don't want the life you envisioned."

"*We* envisioned."

"No. It was all you. Law school, living in New York City. I don't want that kind of life. I don't want that *speed* of life. Cocktails and social climbing and competition. The terrible pressure. The lack of sleep, working twenty-two hours a day, trying to be, oh, I don't know, *cunning*. I've told you that so many times, Peter."

"You've been worried about it, yes, but I promised you it will be okay. More than okay—it will be great!"

"Peter, listen. I don't want to be married to a man who's always plotting, conspiring to win at a corporate battle, greedy for more money, a bigger office—all of that."

Peter sat down on a bench across from her. He was thinking, she knew. He was trying to turn this to his advantage. "You're just afraid."

"Oh, God, Peter." Ari started to laugh at how he'd come up with a way to twist her words. But she stopped herself. Let him have it. Let him believe she was too shy, too unsophisticated, to tolerate living in the city with a husband who was working for a top-notch corporate law firm. "I suppose you're right," she said softly.

Now she could go. Now she could leave him, and he would feel that somehow he had won.

To her surprise, Peter came over to her bench and lifted her hand. "Ari, we all get nervous. We all get stage fright. But you can do it, I know you can, and I'll help you. You're halfway there. Your father is a surgeon. Your family has a house on Nantucket. You're beautiful, and smart—you underestimate how smart you are. I've always told you that you should major in something more important than child-hood education."

Ari pulled her hand away. "And I've always told you there is noth-ing more important than childhood education. You've just never believed me."

"Ari, that's minor stuff, nothing to break up over."

"Childhood education is *not minor stuff*."

"For God's sake, Ari, I'll be making hundreds of thousands of dollars. You'll be making pennies."

"I'll be making a difference," Ari said quietly.

"You'll be making *mud pies*," Peter shot back haughtily. The mo-ment he spoke, he squinted in a kind of discomfort, as if he knew he'd said the wrong thing.

Ari let the silence linger while they both absorbed the impact of their conversation. Finally, quietly, Ari said, "Listen to yourself. We aren't right for each other." She slid her engagement ring off her finger and handed it to Peter. Pushing herself off the bench, Ari rose. "I honestly, seriously, hand over heart, do not love you, Peter. I'm sorry, but it's true."

Peter's pale face flushed. He stood, too, one hand clenched tight, holding the valuable ring. "That's blunt. I'm sorry, too. Because I love *you,* Ari." He had tears in his eyes.

Ari wished she could cry, too, and she did feel like a terrible person, but she also felt as if invisible ropes were loosening, as if she was almost free.

"Peter, I don't think you even know who I am. You're in love with a fictional me, and—and I could never make you happy." Let him have that, she thought. Let him believe she would be a failure.

"No, Ari, I—"

Ari didn't wait for the rest of the sentence. She turned and ran.

Maybe she was a wicked, cruel, heartless person, but as she ran away from Peter, toward freedom, she wanted to throw her head back and laugh. She wanted to make victory signs with her hands and wave them in the air. With each step, the bonds of their relationship slipped, fell away, and vanished. She was released.

She surged toward her sorority house. She yelled "Hooray!" to her empty room. She was almost ready for the drive home. Her parents had already come to take most of the boxes of books, winter clothes, silly costumes, stuffed animals. She quickly showered, finished her last-minute packing, and in a kind of controlled frenzy, she finished loading up her old dark green Subaru Forester and hit the road.

It was a seven-hour drive to Boston. She left at three in the afternoon, which meant she'd be home by ten. Maybe eleven if she stopped to pee and get food. She found the eighties music station on her radio, which provided good emotional songs to cry and yell with, and she sang and screamed until her throat was hoarse. Her phone beeped constantly, but she didn't want to talk to anyone. She was exhilarated, and at the same time she felt guilty, sorry for what she'd done to Peter. For him it would be an insult and an embarrassment, but truly more a massive inconvenience than a heartbreak, and that eased her guilt.

As she crossed the state line and entered Massachusetts, the late spring light was slowly fading. She was leaving her past behind her, entering her future. She shook her hair back, a habit she had when beginning an exam. She sang along with Cyndi Lauper, "Girls Just Want to Have Fun," and Eurythmics, "Sweet Dreams," and Journey, "Don't Stop Believin'." She stopped for gas and coffee, and returned to her car full of caffeine and energy.

What would her mother think about this? Her mom had been so thrilled about Ari's engagement to Peter. She would be angry—no, she would be furious. Ari's father would hug her gently and tell her that it was good she made the decision now, and things would work out in the end. Whatever, her mother would be dramatic. For once Ari was ready.

Her family's home was in Wellesley, on a street of towering trees and sweeping lawns. Lights were on in the upstairs room of the house. Both her mother's and father's cars were in the garage. Ari pulled into the driveway, turned off the ignition, and sat for a moment.

She had been moving, putting miles between herself and Peter, driving fast, screaming along to the radio. Now, as the car went quiet, she felt how she was quivering inside. She was exhausted.

The porch light came on. The front door opened, and her mother stood there in her velvet robe. She was tall and slender, like Ari, with curly brown hair and large blue eyes. Ari's father, tall and smiling, stood behind his wife.

"Ari!" her mother called.

"Hi, Mom!" She got out of the car, slammed the door shut, and stretched. Her back hurt from sitting for so long. It felt good to walk, even for the few yards to the house.

Her mother was never the lovey-dovey kind of mom who hugged and cuddled and praised everything she did. In truth, her mother was a narcissist, and Ari braced herself, because her mother was going to flip out.

Ari hugged her mother. "Hey, pretty mama. You didn't have to wait up."

"Hi, Dad." She hugged her tall, unemotional father.

"What's going on?" Ari's mother could be scarily psychic.

"Let's go into the living room for a moment, okay?"

"What's wrong?" her mother asked.

Ari led the way into the living room. She didn't want to sit down so she stood by the fireplace, crossed her arms over her chest, and said, "I broke up with Peter. I told him I don't love him and I don't want to marry him."

Her mother blinked. "The wedding's off?"

She could always count on her mother to make her laugh. "Yeah, Mom. The wedding is toast. It's not going to happen. I'll probably never see Peter again in my life."

Her father crossed the room and hugged Ari. He hugged stiffly, because it wasn't in his nature to be emotional. He was so good at saving other people's lives and so bad at living his own. But he did hug her. "Are you all right?"

"Dad, I'm more than all right. I feel free! I'm happy, I'm out of a kind of prison—"

"What a dreadful thing to say." Her mother sank onto the sofa. "Sit down. Let's talk about this."

"Mom, I've been sitting in the car for seven hours. Sitting doesn't appeal to me right now. Besides, there's not much to talk about. I gave him back his ring."

"It was such a beautiful ring," her mother said mournfully. "Maybe you should have waited . . ."

"Mom, I tried for weeks to talk to him. I'm certain he sensed how I felt, but he wouldn't listen to me until I forced him to."

"He must be terribly sad," Ari's mother said. She stood up. "I'm going to call Barbara."

Barbara was Peter's mother. Again Ari laughed. "Mom, don't be ridiculous. Barbara probably hates me right now. Plus, you can't fix it."

"Ooooh," her mother moaned. "This is terrible."

"We need brandy," her father said. He poured three generous drinks and handed them out.

"Thanks, Dad," Ari said. She took a sip and then a gulp. The fiery liquid burned all the way down, casting an amber haze of protection around her. "Come on, Mom. It's not the end of the world."

Her mother drank her brandy slowly, wiping tears from her face. "I thought Peter was such a nice man. He was madly in love with you. And he was so *rich*."

Ari's father snorted. "Alicia," he said to his wife. "For God's sake."

"Mom, we're rich, too," Ari reminded her mother.

"Not like the Andersons are rich," Alicia said. "You could have had everything, Arianna."

"I have everything already," Ari said quietly. She yawned and stretched. "I'm so tired. That's a long drive. All I want to do is sleep."

"Then that's what you should do," her father said. "Go on up. I'll bring in your luggage and leave it outside your bedroom."

"Thanks, Dad." She kissed his cheek. "Don't worry, Mom. It will all be fine." She kissed her mother's forehead.

She left the room, crossed the hall, and went up the stairs. Her room was in shadow, the only light coming in from a high moon. She didn't bother to brush her teeth or take off her clothes, but fell onto her bed, pulled the comforter over her, and was asleep at once.

She woke the next day at noon. Her mouth tasted vile and she was desperate to pee. She stripped off her clothes in the bathroom, brushed her teeth, and took a long hot shower, washing her hair, closing her eyes to the steam and the sensation of becoming clean, becoming new. She found yoga pants and a long blue shirt in her closet and dressed. She wanted coffee. As she descended the stairs she heard voices. Uncle Cliff was here. She groaned. She prayed her mother hadn't called him to share Ari's momentous news.

But when she entered the kitchen, where everyone was sitting at the long oak table, she found them all smiling.

"Darling," her mother said. "We have the most wonderful news!"

"Hi, Uncle Cliff," Ari said. She kissed his cheek.

Her uncle Cliff was seven years younger than her mother, and he was still a bachelor. He sold real estate in the most expensive Boston suburbs, belonged to all the most exclusive clubs, and enjoyed tennis and good wine. He was dashingly handsome and could be charming, when he wanted to be. He radiated confidence and good humor. Ari found him shallow, but likable.

"Sit down," Ari's mother said. "I'll bring you some coffee and a plate. Cliff brought us pastries!"

Ari dropped into a chair. Her mother set a mug of coffee in front of her and patted Ari's shoulder. "Just wait!"

"Uncle Cliff," Ari said dutifully, "I'm all ears."

Uncle Cliff cleared his throat.

"I had a business lunch yesterday with Muriel Wheeler. She is vice president of the Gold Sand Resort Company. They have hotels in Jackson Hole, Palm Springs, and Sarasota. They want a hotel in Nantucket." He paused dramatically. "They want to buy Eleanor's property for fifteen million dollars."

"Dear heavens! That's fabulous!" Ari's mother cried, clapping her hands.

Ari asked, "But, Mom, what about Gram?"

Alicia said, "Don't you worry about Gram. Ari, it's like fate! Mother turns seventy on June third, and she's invited us to Nantucket to celebrate. In the meanwhile, I'm going to check out the very best retirement homes in the area. Not on Nantucket, of course, because of their hospital. They aren't set up to treat heart attacks and such. They have to have a helicopter fly over and take the patient to Mass General, and the trip costs sixteen thousand dollars. Besides, as she gets older, Mother will be happier here, near us. Cliff, did you get a text from Mother, too?"

"I did. I think we should all go over for a couple of days. Take cool presents. Send masses of flowers. Show up with cases of champagne."

Ari's father spoke up. "I'm not certain that Eleanor will want to sell her home."

"Oh, Cliff, don't be so negative," Ari's mother said. "She's *seventy*. She'll be grateful that we're thinking of her future. She's got to realize it's all downhill from here."

"Mom!" Ari cried. "That's an awful thing to say!" Overcome with emotion, Ari pushed her chair back and stood up. "I love Gram's house! It's been in her family forever. It should remain in the family forever."

"Ari, sweetie," Uncle Cliff said, as if she were six years old, "the house is falling apart. It needs more work than Eleanor can afford. It will make her sad to sell it, but also, she'll be relieved."

"*So* relieved," Alicia echoed.

"Well, I think you're all terrible people. Like ghouls at a funeral and Gram isn't even dead yet!"

Ari stomped from the room and flew up the stairs. As she went, she heard her mother say to her uncle, "Pay no attention to her. She broke her engagement to Peter yesterday. Obviously, she can't think straight."

Ari spent most of the day calling her friends, telling them her news. Meloni, her BFF, lived in Concord and drove to Legal Sea Foods at the Chestnut Hill mall to meet Ari for a long dinner. So Ari escaped any more arguments with her mother. At home, she talked briefly, politely, with her parents, said good night, and went to her room to watch YouTube videos on her laptop.

The next morning, Ari woke to the delicious aroma of coffee. It took a moment for her to realize she was not in her sorority house, but in her own bed at home, and another moment to realize her mother had brought her coffee.

She sat up, pushing a pillow behind her.

"Good morning, darling," her mother said, handing Ari the coffee and sitting down on the bed, close to Ari. Alicia was fully clothed in a pale lavender linen dress with amethyst earrings and bracelet. Her delicate makeup brought out the lavender tones in her blue eyes.

"Mom," Ari said. Her mother never brought her coffee. Alicia wanted something, and Ari could guess what it was. But she took the coffee and drank.

"'Thank you' would be the polite response," her mother said.

"Thank you. The coffee is delicious. But I'm not changing my mind about Peter."

"Really?" She put a soft hand on Ari's arm. "Can't you allow yourself a little time to think about it? All that you're throwing away? Sweetie, I don't think you understand. Many brides get cold feet before the wedding. What you're going through is absolutely normal. But even though you acted rashly, I'm sure if you consider how wonderful Peter is, what an excellent life the two of you will have together, you'll—"

"Mom, please stop. Don't you realize I've *considered* breaking off with Peter for months? I wanted to when we were here on New Year's Eve, but that was the wrong time—"

Alicia looked horrified. "It certainly was. That would have been cruel!"

"I know! So I didn't do it then. In January he went skiing with his buddies, and when he got back, he was stressed-out by his classes, plus we never had any private time to talk."

"But *why* break up with him? He's such a fabulous catch!"

"No one thinks that way anymore, Mom. Peter isn't a *catch* and I'm not a fisherman, fisherwoman, whatever. I don't love Peter. I've always cared for him, ever since we were teenagers, but somewhere along the way I realized I don't love him. I don't want to spend my life with him."

"Well, I think you've made a *dreadful* mistake!"

"Mom—"

Alicia withdrew her hand and stood up, trembling with anger. "All the things we've done for you, the privileged life you've led, and the education we've given you so you could do something with your life, something that would make us proud! And you want to run a daycare? For God's sake, Arianna Eleanor Paget, you're smarter than that! You're better than that! I thought when you got engaged to Peter you were finally doing something right. Now you go and throw it all away!"

Ari set her mug on the bedside table. Her mother's face was a dangerous pink. "Mom, please. It's all right. I think teaching little children is the most important job in the world."

"Well, I don't! Look at what teachers get paid compared to lawyers!"

"Then things should change."

"Oh, you think you're going to set the world to rights, do you? You think you're going to live in a house as nice as ours and wear nice clothes *and* change the world? How can you be so naïve?" Tears glittered in Alicia's eyes.

Concerned for her mother, Ari stood up and reached out to hug her. "Mom. Mommy. It will be all right."

Her mother shoved Ari's arms away so quickly and angrily, it was like a slap.

"I am so ashamed of you!" her mother said. She pivoted on her heel and left the room.

Ari sank back onto her bed, hugging herself. Her mother had always had a temper, but this was unusual, and it worried Ari. Naturally, Ari had had arguments with her mother all her life, but this was different.

As worried as she was, Ari was also angry. Did her mother expect her to marry a man she didn't love? And her mother was *ashamed* of her? Ari wanted to storm out of her bedroom and yell at her mother that *she*, Alicia, had never worked since she had married, she'd never sold an ice cream cone or baked a damn cookie or even volunteered, except for stupid clubs where all they did was hold galas. Her mother loved that sort of thing. No wonder Ari's dad always looked so tired. Alicia was probably disappointed in her husband.

Too bad Peter couldn't marry Ari's mother. They'd be a perfect match.

The ridiculous thought made Ari laugh. She quickly sobered up, thinking of her parents' marriage, which was so full of storms and distances.

Ari kept to her room that day. She unpacked, carried winter clothes, duffel bags, and old school books up to the attic. She had long, emotional talks with her friends on the phone. She napped. In the late afternoon, when she knew her mother would be having a little cocktail with her father, Ari pulled on running gear, slipped out of the house, and went for a run. She pushed herself, glad to focus on her muscles, breath, pace, all physical and clear. Back home, she hurriedly made herself a peanut butter and jelly sandwich. She took it and an apple up to her room. She showered, pulled on a fresh tee and boxer shorts, and ate her dinner in bed while watching a gory mystery.

At some point in the evening, her father knocked on her door.

"Come in," she called.

He peeked his head around the door. "Just checking to see if you're okay."

"I'm fine. Just unwinding from the past month. It's such a pleasure to eat in bed and watch junk."

"Good, then." Her father started to shut the door.

"Dad?" she called.

He opened the door a bit. "Yes?"

"Are *you* okay, Daddy?"

Her father looked surprised. "Of course I am, Ari. Don't worry about me. I think it's just fine that you broke your engagement with Peter. Your mother will get over it. She'll be okay." With a smile, he withdrew, closing the door firmly.

Ari sighed and shook her head. She could never understand why her father loved his tempestuous, irritable wife, but it was reassuring each time she was reminded that he did. Her father was such a gentle man, a brilliant surgeon, although somehow vague during the rest of his life. Perhaps he saw so much misery and illness that the rest of life with all its difficulties and stresses seemed just fine to him. Certainly Alicia was beautiful, and she could be loving and fun. Maybe her mother was less stressed, more cheerful, when she was alone with her husband.

In a few days they would all go to Nantucket. Ari was looking forward to seeing her grandmother, but dreading the moment when her mother suggested Eleanor sell the bluff house.

Three

They were all coming. Her son, her daughter and son-in-law, her granddaughter. For a moment, Eleanor was breathless. Also, slightly unsettled. When the family was here for Christmas, Alicia constantly batted away at Eleanor like a cat with a toy mouse, trying to make Eleanor agree to sell the house.

This house.

Eleanor sat on the deck, watching the sun slowly rise. The sky faded from black to the palest silver, and along the horizon, a stripe of peach appeared, reflecting in the water, which was also awaking from the dark. Then the burst of brilliant light. It was always a splendid display, and different each time.

Eleanor usually rose early, usually pulled her L.L.Bean robe on over her nightgown, and went out to the porch to watch the day break. It took longer than you would think, as if the sun were being coy or having second thoughts. Eleanor curled up on a wicker chair and admired the lawn, now freshly green with spring, the low wall of privet hedge protecting her property from the walkers' path, the wooden landing with steps leading down to the beach, the long luxurious beach itself, and then the blue ocean, forever.

It was in her will that when she died she was to be cremated and her ashes tossed into the sea. Not that she had plans for dying soon, but it was best to be prepared.

When she died, Ari would inherit this house. Not Alicia, not Cliff. She hoped Ari was strong enough to keep the house in the family.

As if conjured up by her thoughts, Eleanor's phone buzzed, and the caller ID announced that it was her granddaughter.

"Darling, hello," Eleanor said. "How are you?"

"I'm good, Gram. All done with college and exams—oh, and also all done with Peter. I broke our engagement."

"Are you all right?"

"Better than all right, Gram. I'm happy. I'm free!"

Eleanor laughed. "Good for you!"

"Yes, but poor Mom is miserable. No wedding, no parties, no new clothes. I've been phoning the hotel and the caterers and so on, canceling our arrangements. But I've stayed in my bedroom, because Mom gets so gloomy at the sight of me."

"She'll cheer up. It's spring, the sun is warm, the island is waking. Also, I've decided that for *this* birthday I'm going to *give* presents. I know there's some ancient silver up there that your mother would love to have, or sell."

"Cool," Ari said. "Gram . . . I was wondering . . . Could I live with you for the summer? I need to work and I could make good money on the island. Plus, I could do grocery shopping and chores for you, and meet guys—it would be a whole new world!"

Eleanor was so happy she thought she was going to have a heart attack. Really, why hadn't anyone told her how *emotional* old age made you? Maybe what her instincts had been telling her was that something *wonderful* was in her future.

"Gram, are you still there? I mean, I'd understand of course if you didn't want me—"

"Ari, I would love to have you live here with me in the summer. You can have the downstairs bedroom so you can sneak out or sneak someone in when I'm upstairs sleeping."

"Gram! What a scandalous thought!"

"Don't tell your mother I said that."

Ari laughed. "I'm so excited! This is awesome. I wish I could come tomorrow but I'll come with everyone else for your birthday in a few days. Gram, you are the best!"

They said their goodbyes. Eleanor sat with her phone, looking out at the water. The sun had ascended while she'd been talking, and now it lit up the whole world.

Eleanor sighed deeply and went into the kitchen to make coffee and a bowl of cereal with blueberries. Blueberries were supposed to help keep your mind sharp and your heart healthy. She ate them at the kitchen table, scrolling through the news on her iPhone. It was useful, this instrument. She could flip past whatever bored her, unlike watching the news on television where the newscasters chatted and laughed as if they were at a party instead of discussing important events. Still, Eleanor thought, those newscasters probably understood that part of their job was to present cheerful faces to the audience sitting at home with their hair standing on end as they learned of another day in the world news.

She rinsed out her cup and bowl, tucked her phone in her pocket, and went upstairs to dress. She would shower later. She planned to work in the attic today, so she would *need* a shower later. She had a pair of ancient corduroy jeans that no longer fit around her waist, but who would see her today? She looped one of her husband's old ties around to use as a belt—the zipper was broken. She buttoned an overlarge blue shirt over it. Put on her socks and sneakers. Took a last gulp of coffee and went up the stairs.

Eleanor had always enjoyed the attic. It was a high-ceilinged, open barn of a space, with two windows at each end, looking out at the houses on either side, with no glimpse of the water. She liked that it didn't have a view of the ocean. It made the attic feel like its own private world.

Large furniture loomed everywhere, perfect for hide-and-seek. Her grandparents' steamer trunks, empty now but still with buckled leather straps and funny old labels: CUNARD WHITE STAR, EIFFEL TOWER, ROMA. Three hope chests sat around with their lids up, mostly emptied by someone needing blankets or sheets or dress-up clothes. One chest held a pile of gorgeous, delicate linen tablecloths trimmed with lace and embroidery. No one wanted those anymore, just as no one wanted silver, china, or crystal. Too much work. But the world moved in cycles. Someone would want these someday.

A matching sofa and chair, both covered in hideous, scratchy gray wool, sat near the window, heaped with chintz material. For curtains? Clothes and hats for the local theater company? A dress Eleanor had worn in a party in sixth grade curled over the back of the chair. It was made of white polished cotton covered with pink roses. It had a pink satin sash that tied in a big bow in the back. Her mother had made her a matching headband with a bow at the side of her head. Black patent shoes, white socks. Oh, Eleanor had thought she was beautiful, the most beautiful girl on earth. These days, no one would wear the dress; no one would even use the fabric for curtains.

Turning away, she found the antique dresser with two brass handles missing. She opened the drawers and discovered the quilts her grandmother had made. She lifted them out in her arms, hugging the plump, colorful bedding to her chest. She thought she remembered a time when quilts were out of favor. People used electric blankets, which Eleanor had abhorred; you could feel the wires running the length of your body. Then, duvets, also not Eleanor's favorites, with the duvet covers that after washing had to be stuffed with the duvet, which never went in agreeably but bunched up down at the bottom. You had to struggle with it for hours to get it in properly. When her husband was alive, he was always cold in the house when they came down for Christmas or Easter, so they slept together beneath a down comforter, which made Eleanor so overheated she had to sleep nude, with both bare feet sticking out.

Mortimer. Eleanor had been married to him for forty-six years. He was five years older than Eleanor. She'd met him when she was twenty-one, a student at Wellesley, spending the summer on the island with her family. Eleanor had been troubled about her future. Her one love, what her parents called her *hobby,* had been sewing. The New York fashion world emphasized hippie clothes and glamour dresses made of synthetic materials that Eleanor disliked. Her parents were appalled when Eleanor told them she wanted to be a seamstress of some kind, and really, Eleanor didn't quite know what she meant. Her mother had a seamstress named Minnie who came to the house to alter her clothes to fit her perfectly.

That August in Nantucket, Marsha Richard had called to ask Eleanor to make up the fourth for a game of doubles tennis. Her tennis partner was Rocky Colby, a regular summer visitor and Marsha's beau. Rocky's friend, Eleanor's partner, was Mortimer Sunderland, a tall, slender, dark-haired man. He was extremely handsome, and Eleanor expected him to flirt with her, but Mortimer concentrated on tennis as if it were a game of chess, taking his time to consider the arc of the ball before reaching out to slam it back just over the net. He was older than Eleanor, and quiet, cautious, giving little away. After the game, the four sat on the patio drinking Anchorages, half iced tea and half lemonade, and while Eleanor couldn't keep her eyes off him, she assumed he didn't like her because he spoke so little.

To her surprise, later that day Mortimer phoned to ask her to dinner. Now, here in the attic, she could still recall how her heart had thumped at the sound of his voice. She drove herself crazy trying to decide whether to wear a dress with a plunging neckline—*sexy*—or a more conservative dress—*elegant*. Should she wear her hair down—*sexy*—or up—*elegant?* Mortimer seemed to be a closed door, and she was determined to open that door. At least a little.

At the same time, Eleanor was deeply disappointed in herself. How could she be so physically attracted to this man who was absolutely and exactly who her parents would have chosen? She wanted to be a rebel, or at least rebellious. She wanted to fall in love with the wrong person, someone dangerous, maybe with a motorcycle. And here she was, trembling with excitement to see a man as conservative and sophisticated as her father.

The evening turned out to be almost dull. They ate at the yacht club, where so many of their parents' friends stopped at their table to say hello that their conversation was superficial, almost forced.

Mortimer looked dashing in a white shirt with yacht club cuff links and a navy blazer, and he seemed as drawn to Eleanor as she was to him. It didn't make sense. She'd heard about Mortimer. He was a *catch*. She was certain this would be their only date.

At one point, Mortimer leaned across the table and touched her cheek lightly. She was so surprised and pleased she couldn't remember what she'd just said that made him react affectionately. She gazed into his eyes, completely smitten. Then he said, "Sauce. It's gone now." She put her hand to her cheek, blushing with embarrassment.

But he must have liked her. When he drove her home, he asked her for a date the next night. He waited until the third date before he kissed her—back then it was some kind of unwritten law.

During that summer, Mortimer snowed her—that was what her friends called it in her day. He asked her out almost every night, he sent her flowers, he brought her home to dinner with his parents. Eleanor discovered that Mortimer had been brought up to believe that the guiding principle in life was duty. He was a very serious man, but in those early years, he was also a very sexy man, knowing how to focus and pay attention. Mortimer was an accountant in an established insurance company, a man good with statistics and percentages, so Eleanor knew that he wasn't fooling around when he told her he liked her a lot, and after dating three months told her he loved her, and after dating six months, he asked her to marry him. She said yes.

They had had the extravagant wedding both their parents wanted. She was a virgin and Mortimer was patient, gentle, and sometimes funny in bed, so that as she turned their small rented Boston apartment into a home, she discovered she was eager for the evening and the night. She had fallen in love with the man she married.

Mortimer continued working as an insurance investment manager. They bought a large house in the right neighborhood, using loans from their parents for the down payment. Eleanor gave Mortimer a daughter and, seven years later, a son, and sadly, as the years went by, the passion of the early months of marriage flickered and died. Eleanor was overwhelmed with her babies. She had help from her nanny, but she had responsibilities to help her husband, too—dinner parties, cocktail parties, joining the proper clubs. Mortimer worked even more assiduously at the insurance company, and he left for work each morning with an eagerness he didn't have when he was alone with Eleanor.

Still, Mortimer had been a diligent father, blocking out time to be with his family as if referring to an invisible chart. Every June he took them on a vacation for two weeks. To London. Paris. Florence. Alaska. Brazil. He arranged special tours and went along with Eleanor and their two children, his presence serious and watchful, making it obvious that he wanted his children to learn more about the civilized world and not giggle with each other about penises on statues. When the family returned home, Mortimer went back to work in Boston, and Eleanor brought their children to the island, where they were wild with joy at being liberated. They rode bikes, raced around with friends, bought candy, swam and swam and swam beneath the hot summer sun. They stayed up too late, they went days without eating broccoli or Brussels sprouts, they camped out in a tent in the backyard, they played outdoors after nine o'clock when the sky was dark and they could run free.

As the children grew older, Eleanor talked with other summer mothers who were concerned about problems their adolescents could cause. They worried about alcohol and pot, but not the harder drugs, which weren't as prevalent then. They worried about unwanted pregnancies, and car accidents, especially car accidents. Every summer at least one group of kids drinking beer would end up in a car crumpled on the Milestone Road where the long, straight ten miles tempted the driver to get up to a hundred miles per hour, even though the speed limit was thirty-five. No one was killed in the accidents, but there were some spectacular injuries.

Alicia and Cliff always whined that it was a drag on the weekends when Mortimer came to the island. He insisted on playing tennis with them on Saturday, and sailing with them on Sunday, and both nights eating at the yacht club, where he always commented on their manners. Mortimer told Cliff that his hair was too long. He told Alicia that she was getting fat—he told her that at the dinner table in the club dining room, and Alicia had politely excused herself and gone to the ladies' room, returning with eyes red from weeping.

Other men and women liked Mortimer, and sought him out. The men mostly wanted insurance advice, and the women wanted to flirt, because Mortimer really was unusually handsome. Alicia and Cliff seemed perplexed at their father's popularity, when he was so unlikable to them.

During that period of their marriage, Eleanor found it stressful having her husband around, especially on the island, in her family's house. She tried to enforce her husband's rules while at the same time allowing her children to have fun. She'd let them drink Cokes even though they had sugar. She told them that if they ever got drunk to call her and she'd come get them and not lecture them. She didn't want them to drive drunk, and as far as she knew, they never had. It was an enormous responsibility, raising children, and taking care of teenagers was a roller-coaster ride.

Gradually, Eleanor fell out of love with Mortimer. She cared for him. She was grateful for him. Mortimer seemed to find his excitement in the numbers at work. Eleanor, who'd always loved books, read every night of the week.

Those days could never be called difficult. No, Eleanor was spoiled, and she knew it. Furthermore, she had no burning desire to do something exceptional with her life like many of her friends wished. She didn't have artistic cravings, she couldn't sing, didn't want to teach (what could she teach?), had no strong political leanings. She had a really lovely life, with darling children and wonderful friends and a handsome, kind, trustworthy husband.

Did she miss him now? Maybe not a lot. He'd never been in the house often in the summer. He'd never enjoyed walking on the beach during a wailing wave-crashing storm and he'd been hopeless at cooking outside on the grill.

One thing she knew for sure: Mortimer would absolutely approve of Eleanor selling the house.

The thought saddened her. She went down to the kitchen, brewed a cup of utterly boring chamomile tea, took it with her to the dining room, where her jigsaw puzzle was laid out, three-fourths done, and settled in. The colors and shapes calmed her, as always. She pretended that she forgot the chamomile tea.

Four

The slow boat docked early, at four forty-five. One by one, the trucks and cars from Hyannis rumbled over the noisy metal ramp onto the island. Ari's parents were in their black BMW. Ari followed behind in her Forester, her car packed with duffel bags, suitcases, and boxes of books she needed for the summer. They drove to South Water Street, past the town buildings and shops, past the Dreamland movie theater and the library's garden, over the bumpy cobblestones of Main Street, and onto Washington Street and the road to 'Sconset.

It was early June, yet some late daffodils lingered along the long straight stretch to the small village on the eastern side of the island. The sun sifted through the budding trees, casting a lime glow in the air. Milestone Road was busy with plumbers, contractors, electricians, carpenters, all going to and from 'Sconset in their trucks. Bicyclists lazily pedaled along the bike path, occasionally passed by someone in bright blue spandex and a pointed helmet. Nearer to the village, several people were walking their dogs, and there was the picture-perfect little town, its main street canopied with the lush green leaves of stately trees. They slowed to twenty-five miles per hour, went around the small rotary and past the post office and the

Sconset Market, along the idyllic antique Front Street, and finally around and onto Baxter Road, where grand hedge-hidden mansions looked out over the Atlantic.

Ari's dashboard lit up as her phone buzzed.

"Hi, Mom, I'm right behind you," she said.

"Of course you are," her mother replied. "Now remember. First we celebrate Gram's birthday, and *tomorrow* we mention the offer for the house."

"I know, I know," Ari grumbled, adding, "but I'm not sure Uncle Cliff will obey your instructions."

Her mother's exasperated sigh came through loud and clear. "Cliff never did play by the rules. Oh, here we are, and unless Gram has taken to driving a convertible, Cliff got here before us."

"He said he was flying in and renting a car," Ari reminded her.

"I don't blame him." Her father's voice rumbled in the background. "No one likes to be dependent on someone else for a ride."

Her parents parked in the driveway, behind the convertible. Ari could imagine her mother's smirk at blocking her brother in. Ari pulled over to the side of the road, half of her car resting on the verge. The roads were narrow here, narrow all over the island.

Ari got out of her car and stretched, breathing in the fresh sea air.

"Come on, come on," her mother called. "We should go in together."

Before Ari could reach the front door, it was opened, and her grandmother stood there, smiling and already tanned.

"You're here!" she called.

"Mother," Alicia said, "you haven't been using the sunblock I gave you. Look at that brown spot on your face! It's bigger than ever."

"It's lovely to see you, too," Gram responded, ignoring her daughter's remark and hugging her.

Ari stood back, watching them.

Ari's mother was slender and attractive, with her brown hair frosted monthly to keep streaks of blond brightening her face. Her mother worried a great deal about her looks. She went to an exercise class three times a week. She ran three times a week, and had convinced her husband to build a home gym in the basement with a treadmill and weights and a television on the wall just like the one Gram had installed in her Nantucket basement.

Ari's mother wore one of her Nantucket-appropriate dresses of small green and pink checks complete with a pink silk scarf and a handsome and expensive Nantucket lightship basket hanging over her arm, Queen Elizabeth–style. Gram wore white slacks—a sure sign of summer—and a long denim shirt with the sleeves rolled up. The top two buttons were undone so everyone could see the colorful beaded necklace Ari had made for her in fourth grade. Gram's style was looser, freer, and even though she weighed more than Alicia, she was more attractive. Alicia's goal seemed to be flat, front and back.

Ari's father wore khakis and a navy blue crew neck sweater. Ari wore white jeans and a black cashmere sweater. The first week of June in Nantucket could be cold.

Ari had to admit it. All in all, they were an attractive family. Her mother deserved some gratitude for making all those home-cooked meals with lots of carefully sourced veggies and lean meat and never very much sugar. Ari reminded herself to thank her, if she ever found a moment in her life when she wasn't mad at her.

They filed into the house, through the large hall, and into the long living room with the floor-to-ceiling windows overlooking the ocean.

A man was standing by the windows. He turned to greet them all. "You're here at last!"

Ari saw her mother's shoulders tense up.

"Hi, Uncle Cliff," Ari called, and walked the length of the room to kiss his cheek. He was square-jawed and ruggedly handsome, with his thick dark hair and muscular frame. He played squash, indoor tennis, and basketball all winter when he wasn't down in Florida boating and swimming. He had a smooth tan and a flashing white smile. Ari was sure he'd had his teeth professionally whitened.

Uncle Cliff gave Ari a one-armed hug. He strode across the room to kiss his sister on the cheek, and whispered something in her ear.

Alicia gave her brother a grateful smile, and Ari knew at once that Uncle Cliff had not yet revealed the offer for the house.

So for a while, they could all be in a good mood.

Maybe not for long, though.

"I'll bring in our luggage," Ari's father said. "Hello, Cliff. Good to see you."

Uncle Cliff shook hands with Ari's father. "Good to see you. I'll help with the luggage." As he picked up his sister's Louis Vuitton suitcase, he pretended he could scarcely get it off the ground. He said, "I see you're traveling light, as always."

Ari's mother retorted, "I never know what the weather will be on this island."

Ari's father snorted out an ironic noise. Cliff grinned.

Eleanor moved into the group. "Come sit down on the patio. It's still slightly cool, but I've made coffee. You all know where the Scotch and vodka are."

Ari's father and Uncle Cliff bumped into the house with the luggage. The family bustled about, wandering off to use the bathroom, pouring coffee or drinks. Alicia returning to the living room to lift a cashmere throw from the sofa and wrap it around her shoulders. "Still a bit cold," she said with a smile to the others. Finally, they were all seated on the white wicker furniture around the patio table.

"It's gorgeous here, Gram," Ari said. "Today the ocean is almost a mirror."

"So your crossing was good, then?" Eleanor asked.

"A bit bumpy," Alicia said. She was leaning forward, pouring just a smidgen of milk into her coffee. "Really, I don't know how you tolerate it, the entire *trouble* of getting to Nantucket. Being at the boat early or missing it, dealing with the *racket* of other people's dogs and screaming babies and teenage boys with their donkey laughter."

To Ari's surprise, Eleanor didn't answer right away. She stirred her own cup of coffee, staring out at the ocean, thinking.

"You know what," Eleanor said abruptly, but calmly, "let's get right to the point of this visit, okay?"

Ari's mother drew back, as if insulted. "Mother, it's your birthday party. You invited us. Oh, dear, have you *forgotten* you invited us?" She put her hand to her throat, shocked, worried. Pretending.

Ari looked down at her hands. Her mother and grandmother often participated in these squabbles. It didn't disconcert Ari. She had plenty of similar squabbles with her mother, and had decided it was a mother-daughter tendency. When the silence continued, Ari glared at Uncle Cliff. It was so like him to hang back during difficult moments, even if he was the cause. Ari had heard her mother and uncle arguing about their mother.

"Mother loves you more than she loves me," Alicia had complained, "but I'm the one who has given her a grandchild! I'm the one who visits the most often, so that Mother knows she's not alone in the world."

"Mothers always love their sons more than their daughters," Uncle Cliff had answered lightly. "It's a male-female thing. In the genes."

Now Eleanor replied, her voice gentle, "Of course I haven't forgotten, darling. I'm not quite senile yet. I've made reservations for us tonight at Le Languedoc." She sipped her coffee. "But I'm guessing there's another reason for the visit. It's seldom I get to have all of you at once."

Ari glared at her uncle, mentally urging him to speak up. *Not* speaking up was a kind of lie, Ari thought.

After a few more moments of uncomfortable silence, Ari said, "Gram, I apologize, but there is another reason we're all here. I think Uncle Cliff should be the one to tell you because he's the one who knows the most about it."

Alicia sent Ari a quick smile of gratitude.

Cliff shifted uncomfortably in his chair, gathering himself like a peacock getting ready to display his tail feathers. "Mom, of course we're all here to celebrate your birthday. It just so happens that something has presented itself at the same time. Almost the same time."

"Go on." Eleanor tilted her head slightly, encouragingly.

Cliff cleared his throat. "I ran into an old college friend, Muriel Wheeler, who is vice president of the Gold Sand Resort Company. They're looking to expand their base. They'd like to buy this house and the surrounding land, and Muriel told me they're willing to pay fifteen million dollars."

Ari watched her grandmother. Eleanor's expression didn't change, but the light went out of her eyes.

"My," Eleanor said. "That is a lot of money."

Emboldened by her mother's calm, Alicia leaned forward. "It is, isn't it? Mother, if we split it three ways, that would be five million dollars for each of us. Oh, of course we would use our share to fund Ari's graduate school tuition." When her mother didn't respond, she added, "Or, we could split it four ways, and Ari could have an equal share. We would still come out with almost four million dollars each."

"Yes," Eleanor softly agreed. "But you wouldn't have this house. This water view."

"It's a gorgeous view, Mother," Alicia said. "But frankly, the house . . . needs work. It must be difficult to keep it up, especially at your age. Phillip and I have been talking, and we *worry* about you, Mother. Out here on the bluff alone in the winter. And going up and down the stairs—you could *fall.* Or if you, heaven forbid, had a heart attack, it would take so long for the ambulance to get here, and the Nantucket Cottage Hospital doesn't have facilities for serious heart events. You would have to be medevaced by helicopter to Mass General in Boston. That would be terrifying!"

Eleanor smiled. "You are kind to think of my health."

Ari spotted the flash of anger in her grandmother's eyes. *Oh, Mom, shut up,* she thought.

"Yes, we *do* think of your health. We do worry about you. That's why"—Alicia rustled around in her purse and brought out several glossy brochures—"Cliff and I, and also Phillip, have visited several retirement communities on the mainland near us. There are some *darling* cottages! The community would take care of the outside, the roof and painting, but you could have the inside exactly as you want. You would have your own kitchen but you could go to the communal dining room to meet friends for meals, or you could have your meals brought to you. *I* would like that myself!" Alicia laughed. "Here, Mother, take a look." Alicia tried to hand the brochures to Eleanor.

Eleanor did not reach out to take them. "Actually, I am very happy here. I'm not afraid of falling, and I think I possess the most beautiful view in the world."

Ari knew what was coming. The more her grandmother remained cool, the more heated her mother became.

With a shaking hand, Alicia laid the brochures on the table. "If you won't think of yourself, think of us."

"Go on," Eleanor said quietly.

"First of all," Alicia said, "we *do* love you and *we* are aware that you are entering a more . . . difficult stage of life. You and I have talked on the phone about the people we know who've recently gone in for hip replacements or even open-heart surgery. It's a *fact of life* that people sixty-five and older are prone to accidents, falling down the stairs, loss of stability, not to mention becoming forgetful and setting the house on fire."

Eleanor raised her eyebrows. "You've been reading some extremely depressing literature."

Alicia soldiered on. "Also, you know that *I'm* getting older. I want to enjoy life while I can."

"Which means buying a ten-thousand-dollar purse."

Alicia held her head high. "Well, yes. And taking cruises . . . Phillip and I have been longing to go on some cruises. I've never really seen the world . . . and Phillip has been working so hard. I want so much to help him escape his work and relax."

"What is it with these cruises?" Eleanor asked.

Alicia jumped right on that. "Mother, you should go with us! In a separate stateroom, of course. Ari could come, too. Why, just think, all of us together, maybe on the *Queen Mary 2*. I've heard women need to wear *gowns* for the balls and the men wear tuxes! We could go to the Mediterranean. To Norway! To Hawaii! Where have you always wanted to go?"

"Darling, I've always wanted to stay right here," Eleanor said.

"How would you do that?" Uncle Cliff asked sternly. He moved to sit on the edge of the wicker settee so that he could be next to his mother and also on a higher level. "This house is falling apart. Mom, be reasonable. The plumbing has to be replaced. The wooden steps to the beach are in bad shape. If a step broke and someone fell, you could have a lawsuit on your hands. Your furnace is a hundred years old."

"Not quite a hundred," Eleanor murmured.

Cliff said smoothly, "You're out here alone all winter. No one else lives on the bluff or nearby. Frankly, Mom, never mind that this house is a wreck, I'd think you'd be bored silly out here by yourself. If that's not the way to become an eccentric old bat shuffling around in five sweaters over a bathrobe, I don't know what is."

Ari was weak with relief when her grandmother burst out laughing.

"What an elegant image you have of me!"

Alicia said in her most soothing voice, "Of course that's not how we envision you. You are much too classy for that. But really, how can you afford to keep this place heated in the winter? We know how the wind batters the house."

Eleanor closed her eyes and leaned back in her chair.

"Enough, children. I'm going to shuffle off to my room now. My poor weak mind needs to rest. Our dinner reservation is for eight. I'll see you around seven forty-five. It's only a short drive."

Ari watched her mother shoot Uncle Cliff a worried look. Eleanor never shuffled and her mind was far from weak, so she was being sarcastic, and when she was sarcastic, hot anger was never far away.

Uncle Cliff offered his hand. "Let me help you up."

"Oh, Cliff, for God's sake," Eleanor snapped, and slapped his hand away, rising in one smooth, graceful movement.

The family sat in uncomfortable silence as Eleanor made her way into the house. Uncle Cliff started to get up and open the door for his mother, but obviously thought again and stayed put.

When Eleanor was out of earshot, Alicia murmured, "That went well."

Uncle Cliff said, "That's the way it would always have gone. Mom would never have jumped for joy at the proposal. Let's give her some time to process the idea."

"I suppose you're right," Alicia agreed.

Ari stood up. "I'm going to my room to start unpacking."

"Oh, that's right!" Alicia rose and took Ari in her arms. "Ari, you are our secret weapon. You can work on her this summer in your own adorable way to convince her to take this offer."

"Don't put me in this position, Mom," Ari said.

Her mother smiled her most angelic smile. "Darling, you were born in this position."

That night at Le Languedoc at the birthday dinner for Eleanor, the family was slightly subdued. Stiffly polite. No one wanted to bring up the Gold Sand Resort offer for Eleanor's house, but of course it was all anyone could think about. Ari tried to keep a conversation going.

"Dad, tell me how many operations you did last week. And what kind? And how long did they take?"

Her father looked astonished at her question. Usually no one paid much attention to him. He glanced over at his wife.

"Oh," Alicia had said, "we don't want to talk about all that medical stuff while we're eating."

"I'd love to know," Eleanor had said, leaning forward eagerly. "Phillip, you perform so many miracles with your skills and you never talk about it."

Ari's father brightened. "Well, Eleanor, it *is* rather exciting. Over the years, we've advanced so much in surgical techniques. We now have minimally invasive surgery, with computer-assisted spinal navigation. We can travel in and out of the spine on a computer—"

"Really, Phillip," Alicia said. "This is a bit too much information.

Mommy, you can talk privately with Phillip if you're really interested." She aimed her lovely blue eyes at Ari. "And *you*! You're now a college graduate. The world is yours. What are your plans?"

For just a moment, Ari had almost reverted to the monster child that lived within her, who would have said, *I've only told you a million times and you've only said you wished I would do something classier.* Instead, Ari smiled. "I'm going to work here all summer and pile up money for living expenses when I go to grad school to study early childhood education."

Alicia returned the smile. "I do hope your father and I can come up with the money for tuition. We're fairly wiped out after paying for four years of college."

Fortunately, the waiter arrived to set their entrees in front of them, and Ari became fascinated with her salmon en croûte.

The delicious food and wine helped lull the family into a semblance of tolerance. When the waiter brought out the birthday cake with eight large candles—one to grow on—that Uncle Cliff had called in and ordered, a kind of magic happened at their table. Eleanor blew the candles out in one powerful breath, and everyone clapped, including all the other diners, which especially delighted Ari's mother, who nodded at them all with aristocratic pleasure. Uncle Cliff had also ordered a bottle of Dom Pérignon that was the perfect accompaniment for the chocolate truffle cake.

"I feel as if I've been drugged," Eleanor said when she set down her fork and patted her mouth with her napkin.

"I feel like I've gained ten pounds," Alicia said.

"Mom, you're beautiful," Ari said, squeezing her mother's hand. At that moment, full of good food and wine, everyone seemed beautiful.

Eventually, Uncle Cliff, in his artful way that assured that everyone saw what he was doing, gave the waiter his credit card and then signed the check. They all rose, still feeling rather glowy with each other, and went down the stairs, out onto the street, and into their two cars. Eleanor had ridden in with Ari, but whispered to her, "I'll ride home with your parents and Cliff. We're all too cheerful to fight now."

When they arrived back at Eleanor's house, Uncle Cliff suggested a nightcap, but it had been a long day, and everyone wanted only to sleep.

Five

When Ari woke, the room was full of light. Had she overslept? She glanced at the clock. Five after seven. Good. Now she could hear movements in the hall and the light murmur of voices. She sighed, wondering how this day would go. She rose, showered and dressed, and joined the rest of her family, who were in the kitchen drinking coffee.

"Good morning, everyone," Ari said, going to the coffee machine. She kissed each member of her family on the cheek before pulling out a chair and sitting at the kitchen table.

"Don't get too comfortable," Uncle Cliff said, with a wicked grin. "It's First Saturday."

Years ago, when Ari was just a child, Eleanor had decreed that the first weekend the family was together on the island, they would breakfast at the Downyflake, where they enjoyed sinfully hearty breakfasts of bacon, eggs, pancakes, and hash browns. After that, they went as a family to one of the island's museums—the Whaling Museum, the Maria Mitchell Aquarium, the Museum of African American History, the Nantucket Shipwreck & Lifesaving Museum, the Lightship Basket Museum, or one of the many historic homes. Ari's grandfather had been keen on history. He always knelt down to Ari's level to point out the seahorses or a ship made from shells. Ari's father and her uncle Cliff were good-natured about it, because, after all, as Eleanor always said, they shouldn't be like New Yorkers who never went to the Empire State Building. It was only Ari's mother who sighed and pointedly stared at her watch. Alicia would always rather have been shopping.

This year, everyone wanted to keep Eleanor happy, so they piled into two cars and headed off for breakfast. Eleanor drove her ancient Range Rover because, she said, it held a lot of people, but really, Alicia muttered, it was because she liked to be in control. Ari's father, Phillip, happily rode with Eleanor.

Cliff asked Alicia to ride with him and she agreed, because she liked having time alone with him. Alicia was seven years older than her brother, and when she was in her teens, Cliff had played endless practical jokes on her. Putting sand in her bed and hanging her underwear out the window had been the least of it. Now they were both adults, but Alicia had been jealous of him when he was the darling little boy and she was jealous of him now because he was so wealthy and wouldn't tell her the truth about how much money he had.

Ari drove her Subaru, because she wanted to stay in town and look for jobs, and finally, after sorting out their rides and going back into the house for a cellphone or a shopping list, they were on their way from 'Sconset into town.

The Downyflake was a Nantucket institution, and Ari always experienced a jolt of pride when the year-rounders called out greetings to them from their tables. Because Eleanor had taken up permanent residence in the bluff house, she was no longer a "summer person." She'd moved up a rank, into a "washed-ashore." As a teenager, Cliff had hung out with some of the year-round guys and now the president of the bank and the foreman of a huge construction site waved at Cliff. The family sat at the round table to enjoy sausages, eggs, bacon, and, for dessert, a Downyflake doughnut.

"This is carb overload," Alicia said, as she had done every time they ate at the Downyflake.

"We've got to fuel up to have energy to walk around," Eleanor reminded her, as she always had.

"If you don't want to eat your doughnut, I'll take it," Cliff told his sister, as he always had.

"Mom, you look beautiful," Ari said.

"Thanks, Ari. What do you think, Phillip?" Alicia asked her husband.

As always, Phillip's mind had floated off to his medical thoughts. "Hm?" he asked.

Ari saw a shadow pass over her mother's face, and not for the first time she wished her father were more demonstrative with her mother.

Alicia gave her brother her doughnut. She never ate it and he usually snatched it anyway. They finished their breakfasts, paid their bill, chatted with the waitstaff, and left the restaurant in good spirits. Everyone, even Alicia, left the Downyflake happy.

They decided to drive into town and tour the Whaling Museum. It always had new, fascinating exhibits. Once inside the distinguished brick building, they gathered together to admire the whale skeleton hanging from the ceiling in Gosnell Hall, the beautiful scrimshaw exhibits, and the view from the roof of the museum. Uncle Cliff took Ari into the shop, which he'd done since she was three, and asked her to choose something she'd like him to buy for her. Not for her birthday or Christmas, but because it was the beginning of summer, and he loved her. This year, Ari chose the new book *A Thousand Leagues of Blue* by Betsy Tyler. Ari's mother drifted in and bought a linen tote printed with a design of a tall ship, and Eleanor, who seldom bought things—she really had all she needed—fell in love with an adorable ceramic whale butter dish.

With their loot in their hands, they all left the museum and walked out into the summer day, blinking in the bright sun. Now, according to tradition, they were free to scatter until this evening, when Alicia and Phillip and Cliff would prepare a lobster dinner for them to enjoy on the deck at the house.

Ari said, "I'm going to the Hub to see what jobs are available. See you later." She blew a kiss at them and hurried off. It was a blissful summer day and the town had never looked more inviting. All the shops in the quaint clapboard and brick buildings were open for the season. The windows were sweet with stripes and pastels, straw hats and sandals. Already parents were leading their children from the Nantucket Pharmacy, ice cream cones in hand. The Hub, on the corner of Federal and Main, sold souvenirs, magazines, and coffees to go. Outside was a standing bulletin board, covered with dozens of flyers for summer roommates, babysitting services, a Jeep for sale, paddleboard lessons, lost keys, and the opening of the local theater's new play.

Ari was just beginning to search for job offers when she heard her name called.

"Ari, it's me! Michelle!" A blonde with a sensational figure jumped up from a bench and hugged Ari. Michelle Hathaway had been in most of Ari's childhood education classes at Bucknell. She'd never been a super-close friend, but they'd gone shopping together and gossiped at parties. Michelle was always fun, and Ari was delighted to see her.

"What are you doing here?" Ari asked.

"We've rented a house on Nantucket for a couple of weeks every summer for years. This year, the parents *bought* a house here so we can stay as long as we want. How cool is that?" Michelle linked her arm through Ari's and pulled her along. "Let's get some coffee and I'll tell you all about it."

They went across the cobblestone street, up past the Bartlett's Farm truck with its bushels of tomatoes and lettuce, and into the pharmacy. A few stools with red vinyl seats were empty at the counter, so they sat and ordered.

"Doesn't it feel *the best* to have all that *structure* behind us?" Michelle asked, spinning her stool this way and that like a kid. "I feel like I've been let out of prison."

"I don't know . . ." Ari began, but Michelle chatted on.

"I'm glad I have the entire summer to be *free,* because you know my wedding is in September."

Ari pretended to twirl a Hercule Poirot mustache. "And, ma'mzelle, what do you mean by '*free,*' eh?"

Michelle laughed. "Well, I'm not going to have sex with another guy, but I'm certainly going to . . . flirt."

Next to Michelle, a portly gentleman drinking coffee and doing the *New York Times* crossword puzzle cleared his throat meaningfully.

Michelle rolled her eyes. "You and Peter are tying the knot this summer, right?"

"No," Ari replied, with what she hoped looked like a wry smile. "I broke up with him. I truly don't love him and I told him so."

"Oh, honey, how sad! I'm so sorry! I was hoping you and I could do silly wedding stuff together."

"Don't be. I'm fine. Peter's fine," Ari said impatiently, uncomfortable with other shoppers staring at her. She caught the attention of the soda clerk. "Can we have our drinks to go, please?"

"When did you break up? Was it *terrible?* Where's your ring?" Michelle snatched up Ari's hand. "Did you give him back his ring?" Without waiting for an answer, Michelle continued, "I guess you had to." She extended her hand in front of Ari's face. "I'd rather kill Josh than give back this beauty."

"Our drinks are here," Ari said. She put down enough cash to leave a good tip and slid from her stool. "I need to go back to check out the job postings."

As they strolled along the sidewalk, Michelle asked, "Do you have a place to live this summer?"

"I'm living with my grandmother, out in 'Sconset. She's got a huge house, and it's right on the bluff."

"Wow. Perfect."

"I know. Plus my grandmother is wonderful, fun to be with."

Once again, Ari wandered over to the Hub, looking at the bulletin board with its sheets of flyers, Michelle following in her wake. On a yellow piece of paper was an ad for someone wanting a counselor at a kids' summer camp.

Ari took out her phone and snapped a shot of the ad. She turned to Michelle. "Do you know Cal Marshall?"

"No," Michelle answered vaguely. She was busy jumping up and down and waving at a guy in a car trying to turn from Main onto Federal. Just when the car would start to go, another clutch of people would stroll slowly out onto the crosswalk.

The car was a convertible, Ari thought enviously. And the guy in the car!

He was blond, with a profile off a Roman coin. Classically handsome.

"Beckett!" Michelle called, her hands on either side of her mouth to channel her voice. "Becky-Beck! Whoo-hoo!"

Becky-Beck? Ari snorted. "Michelle, is that your fiancé?"

"Oh, God, no," Michelle answered. "He's my brother."

The crosswalk emptied and Michelle's brother steered his car around the corner. As he did, he swept his eyes over his sister and Ari. When he saw Ari, he smiled.

She smiled back. For a moment, time stopped, as their eyes met. A kind of *dazzle* swept through her. Beck felt it, too, Ari thought, because he didn't take his gaze from hers, he didn't stop smiling, and he didn't drive away until the car behind him honked its horn.

"He smiled at you!" Michelle yelled. "Did you see that? He likes you!"

"That's your brother? Wow, Michelle, he's . . ." Ari had no words.

"Do you want to come for dinner tonight? He's not seeing anyone—well, not exclusively."

Ari forced herself back to reality. "I can't tonight. Some other night, maybe."

"Maybe tomorrow night?"

"Michelle," Ari said, laughing, "I hope you have five children just like you."

"Oh, I hope so, too. That would be so much fun!"

They exchanged cell numbers and parted. Ari walked to her car and sat for a moment, grinning at the little buzz she'd gotten from seeing Michelle's brother.

"Stop it," she told herself. She called the number for the children's camp.

"Cleo Marshall," a woman announced.

"Oh, hi, my name is Ari Paget. I'm calling about the position at the children's camp?"

"Wonderful! Where are you calling from?"

"Um, I'm on the island right now, on Main Street, actually."

"Okay, well, do you know anything about our camp?"

"Only what I saw on the flyer at the Hub."

"Would you mind if I ask how old you are?"

"No, not at all. I'm twenty-two."

"Do you have any experience with children?"

"I just graduated from Bucknell with a major in childhood education."

"Sweetheart, you sound like perfection. Could we meet? Is now okay? I'm at Our Island Home. Are you familiar with it? It's just off lower Orange."

"I know where that is."

"Come over now. I've got break time."

"I'll be right there."

As she made her way through the narrow streets, Ari imagined a tall, wide, take-charge woman with double chins and salt-and-pepper hair chopped at her ears.

She drove past Marine Home Center and into the parking lot of the long, low building facing the salt marsh and the calm blue waters of the harbor. She'd never been here before, but she knew this was where people came when they had reached the assisted-living stage. Ari couldn't imagine Eleanor ever needing assistance. Eleanor liked her privacy, and she was only seventy, so it wasn't time even to imagine that yet.

Ari got out of the car and headed toward the electric doors of the gray-shingled building.

A young woman exited the building. She wore white polyester pants, sneakers that lit up with each step, and a top printed with red, yellow, and blue balloons. Balloon earrings hung from her earlobes. Her hair was chin-length, dark, and wavy. Her eyebrows had obviously seen some care; they were like raven's wings, accentuating her big brown eyes. When she smiled, her white teeth dazzled.

"Hi," the woman said. "Are you Ari?"

"Um," Ari said. "Yes. I'm looking for Cleo Marshall?"

"You've found her. Thanks for coming over. Follow me, we'll sit on a bench that faces the harbor."

Ari trailed behind the other woman as she went behind the building toward a patio with benches. The day was warm and bright, but no one was on the patio.

Noticing Ari's look, Cleo said, "We brought some of our patients out here in the sun this morning, but it's almost lunchtime—they eat early, get tired easily. We'll bring another group out in a while. You're pretty. Sit here." She plopped down on a bench and patted the seat next to her.

"What a great view," Ari said. She was trying to figure out Cleo's age without simply gawking at her.

"You're looking at my earrings. It's something I do to brighten the day for my sweeties. Also to help them know what day it is. Today is Saturday, balloon day. Tomorrow will be bunny rabbit day, Monday daisy day. And so on. It makes them smile, and a smile is like sunshine in there. Wait until you're old, you'll see. But you want to know about the camp. It's called Beach Camp, because much of the time is spent at the beach. Also, it's two words, easy to remember."

Cleo reached into her pocket and brought out a pack of cinnamon gum. She offered one to Ari and took one herself. "Can't let my sweeties have gum. They might choke on it. Okay, Beach Camp. Here's the deal. We have fifteen kids, ages five to nine, and three counselors. Teenagers sometimes volunteer to help out. My cousin Cal is the lead counselor. Camp starts at seven-thirty at the drop-off at Jetties Beach, rain or shine, and parents pick the kids up at four-thirty at the community school."

"That's a long day," Ari remarked.

"Yes, it is. Their parents work long hours. We have two vans to take the kids to the community school if it rains and also for lunch and rest time. Our director takes care of all paperwork and helps schedule special events like trips to the library or a play or a movie." Cleo broke into a bubbly laugh. "I tried having the camp come here on a field trip. I thought our patients would enjoy seeing all the darling children, but unfortunately some of the older ones rather frightened the children. There was some screaming. Crying on both sides. Dogs work better. They're less judgmental."

Cleo's laugh was contagious. Ari could envision the scene. "I can understand that."

Cleo got herself in control. "Here's the deal, Ari—it is Ari, isn't it? Beach Camp is a special camp. It's free, which means we give out full scholarships. Our director organized it two years ago to help the children of parents who work all day in the summer but don't have the resources to pay for daily camp." Before Ari could speak, Cleo continued. "Don't worry, the counselors get paid. Beach Camp has a committee that fundraises to pay for counselors and supplies." She named an hourly wage that was higher than the minimum daily wage in Massachusetts but lower than many other jobs paid.

"Okay . . ." Slightly disconcerted, Ari realized Cleo was studying her, sort of scanning her—judging her.

Cleo nodded, as if she'd decided something. "I know. I know. You can make a lot more money waiting tables. Working at the camp is a long day with unruly little children. You have to have a special personality to do that. And frankly, you don't look like you match the job."

"Why?"

"Well, for example, look at your teeth."

"Um, that's impossible right at this moment."

Cleo laughed. "Oh, you're funny. I mean, they're so straight and white. Braces in adolescence, right? You're so healthy looking. And your clothes. Your sunglasses. Ralph Lauren, I'd bet. Not everyone can afford to pay over a hundred dollars for a pair of sunglasses.

Personally, I buy them in bulk at the Christmas Tree Shops and I'd advise you to do the same. If you take the job, you'll lose your sunglasses a lot."

How old was Cleo? Ari wondered again. Not that much older than Ari was. Ari said, just a bit sassily, "*Your* teeth are straight, too."

"Annnnd just like that, you've got the job!" Cleo announced.

"What?"

"We need someone at Beach Camp who can take it and give it right back. We've got three or four sixteen-year-olds who help out, but sometimes the camp kids can be troublesome. Obstinate." Cleo stood up. "I've got to get back inside. I think you're cool, Ari. I hope you like the kids. Here's the address of our office. It's on Amelia Drive. I've texted your name to Poppy so she's already checking you out. If you can go over there and give Poppy any other info she needs, that would be great." As Cleo set off, she said over her shoulder, "Poppy's good with computers but not so good with people. But you'll like her. And she'll like you."

As Ari walked back to her car, she almost wished she could talk to Peter. She always talked important things over with him, or she had until the past few months. She sat in her car, pulled down the visor, and redid her lipstick. What would Peter say? That Cleo Marshall was eccentric. That it was a wonderful, altruistic idea to have a free camp for children whose parents had to work, but was that what Ari really wanted to do? Wasn't she here to enjoy herself, to give herself a break from finishing college exams and starting more coursework in the fall? Peter would say she shouldn't even think of starting at that camp unless she was willing and ready to work for the entire summer. And that was true.

She drove down lower Orange, through the rotary, and turned right on Amelia Drive, past the Meat and Fish Market, and Annye's Whole Foods, and Life Massage, and turned right into a small parking lot next to a two-story building. A sign for BEACH CAMP in large block letters was nailed above a blue door. Ari knocked, opened the door, and walked in.

A lovely woman in her forties sat behind a desk. Her long brown hair was piled in a messy bun, she wore blue-framed glasses over her brown eyes, and such a pretty shade of lipstick that Ari wanted to ask her what it was.

The woman rose and held out her hand. "You're Ari. I'm Poppy Marshall. Cleo told me you were coming. She's my cousin. Have a seat."

Ari shook the other woman's hand and settled in a chair facing Poppy's desk.

"You're a Marshall, too."

"Oh, yes. There are several of us involved with Beach Camp. Calvin, awful name, for the camp he goes by Cal, is our cousin. He runs the camp. This is his third year and he's excellent and very chill. Now, I need some information from you, and you have to sign some forms."

As they went through the paperwork, Ari noticed how the office walls were covered with framed and slightly wrinkled drawings of flowers. Red flowers, obviously poppies.

Poppy noticed Ari noticing. "I run a preschool in Arlington. Massachusetts, not Virginia," she explained. "I have about seventy skillion paintings my kids have given me, so I brought some down here." She took Ari's papers, slapped a staple through them, and put them in her in-box.

"You know where Jetties Beach is, of course," Poppy continued. "Be there Monday morning, a little before seven-thirty, so you can introduce yourself to Cal and he can fill you in on the day's plan." She tapped something on her desktop. "It's supposed to be sunny all day Monday, so it will be an easy day. Here, take this folder, we give it to all parents and counselors. And have fun! It's nice to meet you, Ari. Welcome aboard."

For a moment, Ari would have sworn a big yellow light shone right out of Poppy, surrounding Ari in a glowing warmth. Poppy was truly beautiful, and Ari liked her immensely.

She left the office feeling slightly high with happiness, and the feeling stayed with her as she drove to the Stop & Shop. She went up and down the aisles, filling her cart with food she knew Eleanor would like, and also with a small Tupperware box to hold a sandwich and a plum for Monday. Her 4Ocean non-plastic water bottle was in her luggage at Gram's.

She carried her groceries to her car and headed out to 'Sconset. She couldn't wait to tell her family about her new job.

That evening, as the family had done almost every year before, they celebrated the arrival of summer on Nantucket with a lobster dinner prepared by Alicia and Phillip. Cliff set the table, bought and poured the wine, and Ari was in charge of putting small porcelain ramekins of melted butter in front of each plate.

They sat out on the deck because the air was warm and the wind was low. Uncle Cliff regaled them all with inside info on the tastes of Boston celebrities whose homes he'd sold. Ari's mother watched Cliff adoringly, eager for this kind of gossip, Ari's father carefully and maddeningly dissected his lobster as if performing an operation, and Eleanor gazed out at the ocean, occasionally tuning in to the talk. Ari cleared the table and tidied the kitchen while the rest of the family gathered inside around the dining room table to play Clue.

Ari had told them about Beach Camp when they first sat down to dinner. Her mother had reacted predictably.

"Ari, couldn't you find a job in a clothing store? That would be so much more fun."

Uncle Cliff had smoothly intervened. "Sis, stop it. You know Ari's all about childhood education."

Alicia sighed and focused on her food.

Eleanor had patted Ari's hand. "It sounds just the thing, darling. Tell us more tomorrow."

Ari smiled and nodded. Her parents and her uncle were leaving tomorrow, so she knew there would be no time to talk about Ari's job. They played the game in high competitive spirits, because Eleanor had kept track of who had won all the times before. At eleven o'clock, Ari's father and Uncle Cliff wanted to watch the news. The three women said good night and went off to bed.

Sunday morning, the family went, all together, as was their custom on the first Sunday of summer, to church. Ari sat between her mother and father as she had for years, admiring the Tiffany stained glass windows and the carved wooden pillars. Being in St. Paul's felt like coming home to Ari—the hush, the rituals, the music, the congregation turning toward each other as they said, "Peace be with you."

Afterward, they walked to the yacht club for a buffet lunch. Ari's mother was in her element here, greeting old friends, making dates for tennis, lunch, and committee meetings. Eleanor also was surrounded by friends returning to the island for their traditional Nantucket summer, and Cliff moved from table to table, shaking hands, laughing, flirting with almost every woman there. Ari was glad to sit quietly next to her father.

"So," Phillip said, after sipping a tall Bloody Mary, "are you all right, Ari?" When she hesitated, he clarified, "About Peter, I mean. Sad thing, breaking an engagement."

"I'm fine, Dad." Ari put her hand on his. "Please don't worry. I don't know if I was ever seriously in love with Peter. We were close because we'd met in camp and again here on the island and at university. It seemed kind of destined, but all last year I was filled with dread. I don't know why I let it go on so long. I guess I didn't want to disappoint Peter . . . and Mother was so happy about it all."

"If you think you've done the right thing, then *I* think you've done the right thing," her father said.

"I love you, Daddy." Ari kissed his cheek.

Before they could say another word, Ari's tennis friends came flying over, like a flock of exotic chattering birds in their colorful summer dresses. Ari stood up to hug them. They discussed summer plans and plotted get-togethers for the days they all wouldn't be working. As Ari settled back in her chair, she saw Michelle and her family come onto the porch. There was her brother, Beck, with his broad shoulders and blond hair. Ari forced herself to focus on Michelle, and when she did, Michelle winked, as if she knew exactly what Ari was thinking.

Ari pretended she was fascinated by her family's conversation. A moment later, she saw Michelle walking toward their table.

"Don't get up," Michelle said, but of course Ari's father and uncle rose politely while Ari introduced them. "It's a pleasure to meet you all," Michelle said. "Ari, we're having a party at our house next Saturday evening. I hope you can come."

"I'd love that," Ari said. "Thanks."

As Michelle walked away, Ari's mother said, "How nice."

Ari rolled her eyes.

In the afternoon, they headed back to Eleanor's house. Ari's parents and uncle got ready to leave. After their dinner in town Friday night, the waiter had handed Eleanor a bag containing the rest of the chocolate cake. While the others bustled around packing up, Eleanor sat at the kitchen table, dividing up small triangles and slipping them into plastic bags.

"Honestly, Mother, I don't need to take that home," Alicia said.

"I'll eat whatever's left!" Ari announced, throwing herself down at the table and grabbing a fork.

"We've just had lunch!" her mother objected.

Feeling mischievous, Ari said, "I'll call this my English tea."

"Oh, *you*," her mother said, which was what she always said when she couldn't come back with an appropriate response.

An emotion like love, but also like pity, swept through Ari. Alicia looked tired, older and duller than usual. Her father looked tired, too, but he always did. Uncle Cliff, on the other hand, looked like he'd just slapped his face with an upmarket men's cologne.

"You people are so slow," Uncle Cliff moaned. "I've got to make my plane."

Ari's father stood up. "He's right, Eleanor. We need to go."

In an awkward bundle of hugging and saying goodbye, Ari's mother, father, and uncle went out the door and got into their cars.

Ari and Eleanor stood on the front porch, waving. It was very quiet when the other three were gone.

"Well, they're off!" Eleanor threw her arms high in the air. She wore a loose cotton sundress and sneakers. "We can relax! I'm going for a nice long walk. Ari, you're free to do whatever you want except go with me. I'm up to my chin in togetherness and need some time alone."

"I've got some texts and emails from friends I want to answer," Ari said. Also, she thought, she might just take a nap. She had to work tomorrow.

Six

Monday, after Ari took off for her first day of work, Eleanor drove into town to exchange books at the library. She went to the grocery store and the liquor store. Then, when her tide chart indicated the tide was at its lowest, she drove to the Jetties Beach parking lot, put on her waders, and tromped through the sand down to the water's edge. The jetties made a calm channel for boats entering Nantucket harbor. They were made of boulders and rocks stacked together like walls. Sometimes the tide was so high they covered everything but the top bit of the rocks. Sometimes the tide was so low a person could walk a few yards out into the water, and Eleanor knew of a special place past the third boulder where mussels gathered in colonies, clamped onto the rocks, ready to be picked.

There they were, waiting for her. Elongated and ebony-shelled, the mollusks clung together with streams of brilliant green seaweed flowing from them like mermaid hair. Eleanor took hold of a few and tugged and laughed when she found resistance. She had read up on mollusks and knew they did not feel pain or anxiety (although how had the scientists done that experiment?), so she felt no guilt wresting them away from the boulder and carefully placing them in her bucket. She didn't want the shells to break. Ari loved mussels, and it would be fun to present her with this treat for dinner tonight.

Water washed around her waders as she gathered the mussels. The tide was coming in. With her bucket almost full and the sun warm on her shoulders, she sloshed back up onto the beach and over the crunchy sand to her Range Rover.

She listened to 97.7 ACK FM as she drove home. It was important to keep up with the island news, plus she enjoyed hearing familiar voices talking about town events. A new play. The Select Board's report, every week during the off-season, every other week in the summer. She was especially pleased that in the past few years the policy-making group of the island had changed its name from the Board of Selectmen to the Select Board, indicating that it was not a completely male assembly. About time.

Back at her house, she unpacked her groceries, setting her bucket of mussels on a shelf in the refrigerator. She needed a few more things, so she set off walking to the Sconset Market, one of the most charming and old-fashioned establishments on the island. They sold everything a person needed for a perfect summer day: ice cream cones and delicate chocolate pastries, tote bags and tees, gourmet crackers and cheese, sunscreen, postcards, and paperback books. Near the shop, beneath the shade of several trees, were benches and bike racks.

Eleanor bought a fresh baguette for soaking up the liquid of the mussel broth, which she would steam with garlic and white wine. Outside, she settled onto a bench with a paper cup of ice cream and let her thoughts roam. She was glad Ari had chosen not to marry Peter, and she was sorry that Alicia was so angry about it all. Status was so important to Alicia. Alicia had been the sweetest, daintiest, prettiest little girl, the only person in the family who could make Mortimer smile. Alicia would run to her father when he returned from work, as if he were a warrior returning unscathed from battle.

"Daddy!" Alicia would fling herself at him, hugging his knees and begging for him to pick her up. Alicia always preferred pastel, full-skirted, twirly dresses and ribbons or headbands in her hair. The wisdom at that time was to give girls trucks and boys dolls. Eleanor had given Alicia overalls, an engineer's cap, and an electric train, but Alicia hated the overalls and never played with the train. Alicia's passions focused on being pretty and being loved. Eleanor knew that somehow some of that was her own fault. Had she not loved Alicia enough?

Fortunately, Ari had a passion of her own aside from love. Ari wanted to teach preschool. Eleanor envied her. Eleanor had been raised to play a good game of tennis and make frivolous conversation, saying nothing controversial that would embarrass her husband, because back then the husband was the center of a woman's world.

"Eleanor!"

She glanced up to see who had called her name. It was Silas Stover, who'd been a friend of Mortimer's. Eleanor had never been close to Silas's wife, Maxine, because Maxine was a keen golfer. The couples met at cocktail parties, shared the news of growing families and grandchildren, but when Maxine passed away two years ago, Eleanor and Silas had lost touch.

"Silas, how nice to see you," Eleanor said.

Silas was tall and solid, with thick gray hair and an old sailing injury that set his nose to one side. He wasn't handsome. He never had been. But he was clever and kind and it lifted Eleanor's mood to see him ambling toward her.

Silas lowered himself onto the bench next to her. "How are you, Eleanor?"

"I'm good, Silas. And you?"

Silas rubbed his left knee. "Oh, well, I've got a knee replacement scheduled for the fall, and I can't even count the twinges in my hinges, but as they say, if you don't wake up in the morning without something aching, you're dead."

Eleanor laughed along with him. She remembered what she'd always liked about Silas— he was a great conversationalist. As Mor timer and Eleanor grew older, Mortimer had become less talkative, as if he were saving his words up in some part of his brain. She told him that someday she'd slap him on the head and all sorts of words would come tumbling out. Mortimer hadn't thought that was funny. It seemed his sense of humor had atrophied, too.

Silas was still talking. "You live out here in 'Sconset, don't you, Eleanor? I seem to remember a cocktail party at your house, oh, it must have been eight years ago. When Mortimer was alive, anyway. Great house, great view. You still living there?"

"I am," Eleanor told him. "You know, it was built by my grandparents, and I lived there with my parents until they passed away, and now I've got a granddaughter to pass it along to."

"Grandchildren, aren't they a wonder? It makes having children worthwhile. Not that I don't love Belinda and Justin, but those adolescent years were holy hell. I say a prayer of gratitude every day that my kids turned out all right and when they visit with their kiddies, I'm like a dog rolling in—" Silas looked at Eleanor and laughed. "Let's call it moose droppings."

Eleanor laughed along with Silas, silently picturing the big man rolling on the ground. "I only have one grandchild," she said. "Ari. I adore her. She's going to live with me this summer and work."

"Good for you," Silas said. "Good for you. You have a big house and if you adore her, you won't mind having her around. Me, I've gotten used to living alone. I think I like it. I love when my grandchildren come but I enjoy it when they leave, too. The oldest one is eighteen, the youngest, thirteen. I find adolescents a mystery, but at my age, almost everything's a mystery."

"I know." Eleanor was busy eating a spoonful of ice cream.

"That looks good," Silas said. "That's why I drove out here. To have some ice cream. Sure, I could get it in town, but when Maxine was alive, we'd drive out here once a week to get ice cream and walk around the town, looking at the roses on the old fishermen's houses."

"You must miss her."

"I do. But she was wise, Eleanor. She told me not to become an old man in a cardigan shuffling around with the drapes drawn. She made me promise to enjoy myself."

Eleanor smiled. "That's lovely, Silas." She thought a moment, then said, "Mortimer had a heart attack and never gave me any advice about how to go on without him, but I'm sure he'd have said, 'Don't forget to change your status on the IRS forms.'"

Silas snorted with laughter. "Mortimer was always practical."

Eleanor wondered if she should feel guilty for making fun of Mortimer. She allowed herself another minute or two to sit on the bench with the sun on her shoulders and a companion to talk with as she scooped up the final dollop of ice cream.

"You know," Silas said, "Maxine and I had arguments all the time. She liked the bedroom cold, I like it warm. She thought I ate too much red meat. She was probably right about that. And back when the children were teenagers, well, for a few years it seemed if I said yes, she said no. I couldn't even seem to put on the right pair of socks. It was hard. But for a time after the children left, as we got older, we mellowed. Even when she served me that damned tofu for dinner, I didn't get so mad. We didn't get so mad. Now Maxine's gone aloft and my children are bossing me around."

"How are your children?" Eleanor asked.

"Oh, they're not in jail, and I'm always glad when they visit, but I'm always glad when they leave. My daughter fusses that I need to get my hair cut, start a diet and exercise program, and wear my hearing aids, which I hate—they make my ears itch. My son does something in computers, and he's always yelling on his Bluetooth or pounding away at his computer. His wife left him last year, and I can't say I blame her, but I feel sorry for their kids." Silas looked at Eleanor. "So tell me about your grandchild."

"Alicia's daughter, Ari. She's lovely. She just graduated from Bucknell."

"Is that right? How is that possible? How old is Alicia?"

"Alica's forty-six. She had Ari when she was twenty-four."

"And you had Alicia when you were thirteen, right?" Silas joked.

"Right," Eleanor agreed with a smile. "Cliff is seven years younger. I had two miscarriages in between. I'm glad he came along. We get along better than Alicia and I do, but I worry that Cliff isn't married yet."

"Maybe he's gay."

"I don't think so. He would have told me—he knows I would be fine with that."

A young couple rode up on their bikes, easily swung both feet to the ground, and walked into the market.

"Youth," Eleanor said. "I can't remember when I last rode a bike."

Silas nodded. "I can't ride a bike anymore, but I can do a lot of other things." He grinned playfully as he stood up. "I'd better get my victuals. It was awfully nice chatting with you, Eleanor. We should do it again."

"I'd like that." Eleanor stood up, automatically putting her hand on her back where it always pinged when she rose. "Goodbye for now." She headed away from the market and began her walk to her house.

Back home, she put the baguette on the counter, hung her tote bag on its hook, and went to the living room window to see what the ocean was up to. It was an odd habit, she knew, as if she expected to see a pirate ship or Neptune himself appear on the vast sheet of blue.

The sea was calm. She spotted a fishing boat in the distance. Restless, Eleanor decided to replace the lightweight puzzle boards where they belonged, with half of a lighthouse puzzle finished and two other boards with puzzle pieces turned faceup. They took up only one-third of the dining room table, so she and Ari could eat here if they wanted. Eleanor had had to pack them up and hide them under her bed before the entire family arrived Friday. Alicia thought doing jigsaw puzzles was a sign of dementia, even though Eleanor had forwarded Internet articles about how they helped the brain. Eleanor thought doing puzzles must be a bit like taking Valium plus a light hallucinogenic. She went into a kind of Zen zone when she worked her puzzles, and she could truthfully say that she felt her brain percolating, sort of lighting up with pleasure. Well, she would never say that to her daughter or son. They'd put her in an assisted-living home for sure.

Seven

At seven twenty-five on Monday morning, Ari parked her Subaru in the Jetties Beach parking lot, took a last swig of coffee from her go-cup, and checked her face in the mirror. She'd put on a ton of sunblock, pulled her hair back in a ponytail, and dressed in a bathing suit with shorts and a tee over it. She was ready for whatever the day would dish out.

She walked across the sand to the long pine Mobi-mat that was rolled out from the restaurant to the water. Today the tide was in and the boulders were almost underwater. A scrum of adults and children were at the end of the mat, parents checking in their kids and hurrying back to their cars.

A cute woman Ari's age was organizing a group of children all wearing matching red tees printed with a dancing duck and the words CAMP NANTUCKET.

"Hi!" Ari said. "Do you know where Beach Camp is?"

The other woman wrinkled her nose. "Over there," she answered, waving to the far left where another group of children and counselors wore miscellaneous ragged tees, shirts, and bathing suits.

"Thanks!" Ari said brightly, but the cute woman had hustled her charges away from Ari as if she were contagious.

Ari walked down the beach toward the other camp. A young man was talking to one of the parents while a small girl tugged on his leg. Ari waited until the parent headed back to the parking lot, and then she stepped forward.

"Hi. I'm Ari. I spoke with Poppy and Cleo Saturday—"

"Right! Hi, Ari. Welcome aboard. I'm Cal Marshall."

Cal Marshall was short and muscular, like a wrestler. Like his cousins, he had dark hair and eyes and a great smile.

"*Cal!*" The little girl tugging on Cal's leg tugged harder.

Three little boys ran up to Cal. "Come on!"

Cal waved his hands, palms down, in a slow-down gesture. "Hey, guys, meet Ari! She's going to be a camp counselor. Let's head back and get in our morning circle."

The four children yelled "Hi!" to Ari. They raced back to a group digging in the sand and building sand castles. Another counselor waited with them, a pretty woman with short blond hair, blue eyes, and a tee that couldn't hide her lovely figure.

"Hi," the woman said. "I'm Sandy." She held out her hand.

Ari shook hands. "I'm Ari Paget. Are you another Marshall?"

Sandy laughed. "There are a lot of them, aren't there? No, my last name is Spendler. This is my second year, so if you have questions, feel free to ask."

A young guy with spots and glasses stuck out his hand. "I'm Greg. I volunteer here sometimes. It's like herding cats."

Ari laughed and said hello.

Sandy took Ari's arm. "So the first thing we do here is have morning circle."

Cal was clapping his hands. "Sit down. Sit in a circle. That's right. No, Nita, you can't sit in the water. Come over right here."

With a lot of squealing and pushing and complaining, fifteen children seated themselves in the sand in a loose circle. Sandy pulled Ari to sit down next to her across from Cal.

"Who has the feather today?" Cal asked.

"I do!" A boy around six waved his hands eagerly. His tee was stained and too small for him, but his smile reached to his ears.

"Okay, Gabriel, you start our day off with our morning prayer."

In a high clear voice, Gabriel said, "Today I want to thank Tona-tiuh, the Aztec god of the Sun. Because of him, we have food and . . . my mother told me, but I forgot the rest."

"That was awesome, Gabriel!" Cal said. "Okay, camp, let's all thank Tonatiuh, who is giving us this sunny day."

Fifteen kids yelled their thanks so loudly that Ari was certain To-natiuh, reclining up in the sun, had no choice but to hear.

Next, they went around the circle, everyone calling out their names. When they came to Ari, Sandy spoke up. "This is Ari, our new camp counselor! Everyone say hello to Ari!"

"Hello!" Ari called back.

"What do you like, Ari?" Sandy asked.

Ari was comfortable with this kind of interaction. She grinned and threw her arms out. "I like tacos and pizza! I like books about dogs. I like kids. And I like the ocean best!"

The kids hooted and applauded in agreement.

She smiled at seven boys and eight girls as they introduced them-selves. The oldest child was a girl named Maria, the youngest, a boy named Casper. Ari tried to remember each child's name, but she knew it would come with time.

After the morning circle, Sandy, Greg, and Cal organized the kids for several games: Traffic Cop, Simon Says, Capture the Flag. This would be an educational summer for her, Ari thought, watching fif-teen children, some of whom didn't understand the rules, and several of whom didn't care about the rules but instead ran as hard as they could into another camper, shrieking and wrestling and screaming with laughter. Ari gently peeled the kids apart, helped make impor-tant decisions about who won, and consoled the youngest girl who kept coming to Ari to cry about a scratch on her arm. After the third time, Ari got it that this girl, Sheba, really wanted to sit in her lap.

When the children stopped caring about the rules of the game and threw themselves on the ground laughing and kicking, Cal blew his whistle lightly and told the children it was time to swim. They screamed with delight and splashed into the water.

Around noon, Cal announced it was time to go to the vans and to the school for lunch. Ari was amazed to see that it was after twelve. The counselors and kids raced toward the parking lot, where two well-used gray Honda Odysseys were parked next to each other. The words BEACH CAMP were painted in bright red six-inch-high letters. The kids had a free-for-all trying to get a seat next to their friends, and the noise level rose a few decibels, but finally they were all in with their seatbelts on.

"You ride up front with me, Ari," Sandy said, and they were off.

At the community school, the children were guided into the bathrooms to use the facilities and wash their hands. Afterward, they gathered in the classroom at the end of a hallway. Cal and Sandy handed a yoga mat to each child, who dutifully spread the mat out and sat on it cross-legged. An anticipatory mood rolled through the air. Ari thought the children seemed to be holding their breath. From the refrigerator in the room, Cal and Sandy brought out brown paper bags and handed them out to the children.

"What do you say?" the counselors reminded the children, who quickly responded, "Thank you."

Ari watched the children tear into their lunches. Peanut butter and jelly on whole wheat, a small cup of Pepperidge Farm Goldfish, three carrot sticks, a gingerbread cookie, and, in reusable bottles, water.

The counselors sat at their own round table at the front of the room, looking out at the kids, who were all too deeply involved with eating to talk to one another. Greg quietly left for the day, so it was Sandy, Cal, and Ari at the table.

"How do you like Beach Camp so far?" Sandy asked.

Cal was eating with one hand while texting with the other.

"I love it," Ari answered. "But I wondered . . ." She lowered her voice. "The kids in the other camp all had matching shirts. Wouldn't it help give the kids a sense of belonging—"

"I'm going to stop you right there," Sandy said, sounding rather terse. "Our kids are not from wealthy homes. Beach Camp has been operating for two years, and we've raised grant money to buy those two used vans you saw, and the yoga mats, and all the toys and balls, and Cal and I make all the food ourselves. Sure, matching tees would be awesome, but first we need to pay for gas and insurance for transportation, and necessary medical supplies like thermometers and Band-Aids and state and local paperwork—oh, and to pay our counselors, of course."

Ari felt chastened. "I hadn't thought about all the other expenses."

"Look." Sandy reached over and took Ari's hand. "I didn't mean to depress you. These kids are so lucky to have this camp. And to be clear, I need the money. I don't feel a pinch of guilt for taking my pay. You shouldn't, either. It's enough that you're helping these kids have a great summer so their parents don't have to leave them alone all day with the television while they work."

After lunch, the kids filed up one by one to put their trash in the basket. They returned to their yoga mats for rest and reading period. Some children curled up and fell asleep at once, others lay there mumbling to themselves, and others lay propped on their elbows, chin in hand, reading. The counselors took turns leaving the room for the bathroom and to check their phones. After forty-five minutes, Cal roused them—although they were almost all awake—and told them they were going to a special place today.

The special place was the State Forest, one hundred forty-three acres of black oak and pitch pine, with walking trails, grassy racetracks, and fallen trees made into hiding places. Since Nantucket was a sandy island with few tall trees and the sun relentlessly beating down, this forest was like a magical place with its shadows and bright spots. The kids went wild, running, calling out, tossing the balls Cal had brought. A sense of joy burst through the air like the birds that swooped from tree to tree.

Later, back in their schoolroom, the children sat at long tables working on art pieces to decorate the flowerpots they would eventually give to their parents.

For the last hour of the day, the counselors shepherded the children out to the community school playground. They ran screaming with glee as if set free, climbing the jungle gym, hanging from the monkey bars, whacking the tetherball back and forth. Then, one by one and sometimes in a bunch, the parents arrived to pick up their children.

"Goodbye!" everyone called. "Goodbye!"

All at once, it was very quiet.

"I'm exhausted," Ari said, immediately wondering if that was the wrong thing to say.

"You have no idea," Sandy agreed, sitting on a log in the playground.

Ari plopped down next to Sandy, sticking her legs out straight in front of her.

Cal sat down. "You did well today," Cal told Ari. "You fit right in."

"Thanks," Ari said. "Good to know. They're cute kids."

Cal pulled his phone from the pocket of his shorts and checked it. "The forecast is for rain tomorrow. We'll do some gymnastics on the beach and hit the library. Get a good rest tonight!"

They rose and headed to their vehicles waiting at the far end of the parking lot. Cal's car was a Ford pickup truck, old but in good shape. Sandy's car was an ancient white sedan, dented and scraped. A twinge of guilty embarrassment pinched Ari as she opened the door to her Subaru. She settled in, strapped on her seatbelt, and waved at Cal and Sandy as they all drove off. Cal waved back.

Eight

Eleanor was in the kitchen mixing herself a nice vodka tonic with lime and lots of ice when Ari rushed into the house.

"Hi, Gram! I'm going to unpack some groceries and then take a shower. I'll tell you about everything when I get—oh, my gosh, you have mussels! You are *amazing!*" Ari kissed her grandmother on the cheek and flew down the hall to her room.

When Ari came out of her bedroom, dressed in a light cotton sundress and smelling of citrus shampoo, her hair pulled back in a ponytail, Eleanor said, "Yes, we've got mussels for dinner and a salad and fresh peaches and ginger snaps."

"Oh! You're the best!" Ari kissed her again and flopped into a chair, tapping away at her phone.

With her drink in hand, Eleanor returned to her puzzle. Over the years she and her granddaughter had become comfortable with one another, neither needing to stop whatever she was doing to pay full-face attention to the other. Alicia thought this was impolite, but it worked well for Eleanor and Ari. Eleanor's mother had insisted you couldn't have civilized culture without polite conversation. Somehow this belief had jumped a generation and landed on Alicia, which made Eleanor feel extremely uncivilized when dealing with her daughter.

"Aha!" Eleanor found a puzzle piece she'd been looking for and rewarded herself with a sip of her drink.

Later they had dinner at the kitchen table—the dining room table was covered with puzzle pieces. Ari told Eleanor about Beach Camp and the sweet children and the busy day. Eleanor told Ari about picking the mussels and walking to the Sconset Market. Over the peaches she'd sliced and sprinkled with sugar and ginger snaps, a brilliant combination, Eleanor told her about her meeting with Silas.

"Gram, you have a beau!" Ari teased.

"Don't be such a romantic," Eleanor said. "It was completely accidental, running into each other. But he is a pleasant man."

"Are you lonely here, without Grandpa?" Ari asked.

A warning bell rang in Eleanor's consciousness. She didn't want Ari to feel she had to be a companion for her poor old Gram. She didn't want Ari's pity. "Oh, not so much," Eleanor responded cheerfully. "In the winter, maybe, but summer is always such a busy time for me." In fact, Eleanor thought, she was enjoying herself much more now that she could choose which invitations *she* would like.

"About all that, Ari, I wanted to tell you that I may not always be home around dinnertime. I'll always keep some casseroles or frozen dinners for you, and bread and so on, but you don't need to be back here for dinner every night. You're an adult now, and you should come and go from the house as you please."

"Thanks, Gram," Ari said, with a smile that showed her dimple. "I do hope I'll be having a few dates this summer, and I'll want to tell you all about them."

"Maybe not *all* about them," Eleanor answered with a twinkle in her eye.

After dinner, Eleanor and Ari did the dishes and tidied the kitchen. They streamed an old Hitchcock movie, and around eight-thirty, Eleanor told her granddaughter good night and went up to bed. She put on her summer pj's, striped pink and white cotton, which she had washed and ironed herself. She loved the feel of ironed pajamas. She brushed her teeth, creamed her face, reminding herself she had to buy new sunscreen, turned off the light, and slipped into bed.

Shadow leapt lightly onto the bed and curled up next to her. Eleanor wasn't tired, but she had books to read, and she didn't want to crowd Ari. The young woman would have calls and texts to make and posts to read on Instagram and Eleanor couldn't imagine what else.

Eleanor realized she should show some evidence of nightlife, too. She picked up her phone and checked the movies scheduled this week at the Dreamland. Most movies involved men with far too much testosterone armed with explosive machinery, or frenzied cartoons sure to drive children into states of hyperactivity. Concerts and plays were debuting in late June. She checked the library listings and found a few lectures she'd enjoy. It had been a long time since she'd simply ambled up and down Main Street in the evening, listening to the street musicians, stopping at the Hub to buy a magazine, sitting on a bench on Straight Wharf gawking at the fabulous yachts in the harbor.

Also, she reminded herself, she didn't *have* to go anywhere. Ari knew from previous summers what an introvert she was, happy with her own company. Eleanor didn't have to pretend anything at all.

She looked at the stack of books on her bedside table. Two novels, a biography, and a mystery. She chose the mystery.

She was only a few pages into her book when a light tap came at her door.

"Gram?" Ari stood there in a white tee and what looked like men's boxer shorts and flip-flops. "Can I talk to you for a while?"

"Of course," Eleanor said.

Ari crossed the room and slid into bed, effortlessly curling up against Eleanor so that Eleanor put her arm around her granddaughter just as she had years ago when they snuggled while Eleanor read her a fairy tale.

"What's going on?" Eleanor asked.

"It's nothing, Gram, really. I just feel so guilty, breaking up with Peter like that. I tried my best to do it nicely."

Eleanor said, "I don't think there's a way to break it off nicely."

"You're right. I know. The actual truth is, I never was *madly* in love with him, but he was so perfect, so the guy I should marry. And he loved me. I thought he loved me so much it would make up for the little bit I didn't love him, like I was thirty percent and he was seventy. I didn't mean to hurt him. He's such a nice guy."

"Oh, well, I always thought he was a bit of an asshole," Eleanor said.

Shocked, Ari sniffed and sat up. "You did?"

"Remember last summer, when he visited, and we sat down to dinner and he made an absolute spectacle of standing behind my chair and pushing me into the table?"

"He was trying to be gentlemanly."

"No, he was trying to show off. He was saying, 'Look at me, I've got the best manners of anyone in this room.' He was phony and performative. And I can scoot my chair into the table without help, thank you very much. I'm not decrepit yet. Do *you* think I'm decrepit?"

Ari had to laugh at her grandmother's indignation. "Not at all, Gram." Ari turned to the bedside table and took some tissues. She blew her nose loudly, then subsided back against Eleanor. "I never knew you thought that. You should have told me."

"Right," Eleanor said wryly. "You would have hated me forever."

"Mom liked him a lot," Ari said in a small voice.

"Of course she did," Eleanor answered.

They both laughed a little bit.

"You're a blue ribbon champion of a young woman," Eleanor said, then immediately corrected herself. "That makes it sound like you're in a competition. That's not what I mean. I mean you are extremely smart and capable and creative. You're beautiful, although these days that's not supposed to matter. Plus, you're right where you should be at this exact moment in your life. It's the beginning of a Nantucket summer. You've finished all your exams and graduated from college. That's impressive. You should give yourself some time to relax, to let go, to be free. You should *feel* free." Eleanor paused. "Oh, dear, I sound like I'm leading a self-help course, don't I?"

"I love everything you said, Gram."

"I'll say one last thing. Love is strange. I was madly in love with your grandfather, and after we had children, I wasn't very much in love with him but we were too busy to notice and then, as we grew older, I loved him again."

Ari said, "Thanks, Gram. I think maybe I was only fond of Peter. Certainly I was never madly in love." She stretched and yawned. "I feel better now. I should go to bed. I have to be at Jetties Beach at seven-thirty tomorrow. And I don't stop until four-thirty, so who knows when I'll get home."

"I might not be up when you are," Eleanor said. "But good luck with your job."

"Thanks, Gram." Ari hugged her tightly before bouncing off the bed and leaving the room.

Eleanor listened to the patter of Ari's feet on the stairs. It was delightful, having the girl with her, and it had warmed Eleanor's heart to have Ari confiding as she snuggled against her. She didn't worry about Ari. Her granddaughter was young, beautiful, smart, and kind. Ari would be fine.

With a sigh of pleasure, she returned to her mystery.

Nine

On Saturday morning, Ari made breakfast to share with her grandmother on the deck. Hot coffee, scrambled eggs, crisp bacon, and a colorful fruit plate.

They discussed the events of the past week, the lectures Eleanor went to, and Eleanor's adventure volunteering in the Hospital Thrift Shop where she had to struggle not to buy a gorgeous set of sterling silver fish knives and forks that had been donated.

"They were so elaborately made," Eleanor said. "The handles were shaped like fish and the blades of the knives were engraved. Beautiful objects, and completely useless."

"I'm proud of you for not giving in," Ari said. "You already have lots of silver."

"I know, I know, and I don't polish it as often as I should. But I do like beautifully crafted objects." Eleanor focused on Ari. "How do you like the camp?"

"I love it! Oh, if you could only see the children. There's this little boy named Jorge who is totally uncoordinated but determined. And Lila, she has a little scar on her face, I don't know what caused it, but she's embarrassed by it. When she sits in a group for a story or something, she puts her hand over it. They're all good sports, and they eat up personal attention."

"I'm glad you're happy there."

Ari frowned. "You know, one thing that bothers me so much is that all the other camps have tees with the camp name on it. Like Camp Nantucket. I wish we could have tees saying Beach Camp or something, to make them feel more like a group, and to make some of them feel less sensitive about their clothes. I mean, it *is* a camp, so they don't have to dress up, and it's smart to have children in old, stained clothes, but . . ."

"You can't change the world," Eleanor softly reminded her. A napkin fluttered off the table. "The wind is picking up. I'd better go off for my walk now. Leave the dishes for me, Ari."

"Don't be silly. It will take a minute. What are your plans for the rest of the day?"

"I'm meeting Sylvia in town for an early dinner and a movie at the Dreamland." Eleanor carried her plate and mug and silverware into the kitchen.

Ari followed. "What movie?"

"One of those aristocratic British things. I can't remember the title. I'll let you know if it's any good."

Eleanor went off to her room to put on her walking shoes. She kissed Ari on her cheek before she left. Ari dealt with the dishes. She went to her room to collect her laundry, but instead lay down on her bed and allowed herself to close her eyes. Spending five days with children was exhausting. Besides, she was going to a party this evening, and she wanted to enjoy it. She immediately fell asleep.

Michelle Hathaway's family's new summer house was an enormous trophy house out in Dionis. The unpaved driveway was long and winding, and when Ari arrived at the circle drive, valets were there to park her car on the grassy lawn with dozens of other cars. As she entered the open front door, a waiter held out a silver tray with glasses of champagne and directed Ari toward the stairs to the second floor. This was an upside-down house, popular on the island, with the bedrooms on the first floor and the living room on the second, higher floor, with views of Nantucket Sound.

The party was crowded near the high, wide windows and out onto the long balcony. Women in tropical prints and men in blazers gazed out at the water as they chatted. Ari strolled in that direction, pausing to admire the art on the walls. From another room, she heard music, and without thinking, she turned and walked into that room.

A young girl was seated at a baby grand piano. She wore a pale blue dress with ruffles on the hem, and her dark hair was gathered in a braid down her back and tied neatly with a blue ribbon.

Ari settled on a sofa behind the girl, wanting not to disturb her, and listened.

When the girl lifted her hands from the piano keys and sat still, Ari clapped.

"*Für Elise,*" Ari said. "Such a beautiful melody, and you played it so beautifully."

The girl swiveled around to face Ari. She had a winsome, clever face. She was probably eleven or twelve years old. "I *should* have played it beautifully after all the damn lessons they made me take." She stood up, walked to the sofa, and held out her hand. "Henrietta Hathaway. Hen for short. Why aren't you out there with the others?"

Amused, Ari said, "I heard your playing and was enchanted. I'm Ari, by the way, a friend of your sister's."

Hen's face brightened. "I know a secret about Michelle. She has a special drawer in her bathroom with thirty-two different shades of lipstick. I've counted."

Ari had learned from college friends how younger sisters were fascinated with their older sisters. She smoothly sidetracked. "How many lipsticks do *you* have?"

Hen laughed. "Me? I'm eleven. I'm not allowed lipstick. But I do have my ears pierced." Hen cupped her ears with her hands and leaned toward Ari.

"What lovely pearls, Hen!"

"I know. Beck gave them to me for my birthday. Beck is my brother. He loves me more than anybody else."

"What a lucky girl you are. I don't have a brother or sister."

"It's just you?" Hen looked horrified.

"Just me."

"Oh, that's sad."

"I know, but it's all right. I have a grandmother who lives here, and this is a secret, but she likes me best."

Hen nodded her head decisively. "Good. Everyone needs some-one who likes them best."

In a cloud of fragrance, Michelle floated into the room. She wore a violet slip dress and had her hair piled on top of her head. "Ari! Sweetie! I thought I saw you come in. Why are you in here?"

"I heard such beautiful music, I had to come in," Ari said. "Hen is quite talented."

"Hen is a child who has been told to stay downstairs," Michelle said. When Hen began to protest, Michelle approached her and put an arm around her. Very softly, Michelle said, "I know. Hen is a fas-cinating person. But the last time we had a grown-up party, she drank some of the cocktails and became violently ill. She vomited right in the middle of a crowd—"

Red-faced, Hen jumped up and fled the room.

"I'm sorry, Ari," Michelle apologized. "I didn't want to embarrass her, but she was so sick that night. Mom and Dad had given Hen her favorite dinner and let her stream a new kid's movie in her room. But she slipped out and took sips of all the 'pretty drinks' and had alco-hol poisoning. She could have died."

Ari said, "Frightening."

"Yes. But I'll keep a watch for her tonight. Now let's join the party."

People were still on the balcony, talking in groups. Michelle slid through the crowd, tugging Ari along with her to stand at the front, arms on the railing, gazing out at the view.

"This is spectacular," Ari said.

"I know!" Michelle agreed.

A couple of Michelle's friends joined them, chatted briefly, then kissed Michelle on both cheeks before leaving. In a kind of dance, people in gorgeous summer clothes approached Michelle, met Ari, and chatted enthusiastically, happily lifting flutes of champagne or gin cocktails from trays and sipping as they talked. The party with its blur of laughter, its display of beautiful people in beautiful clothes, the caviar in deviled eggs, the mini–lobster rolls, the chocolate-dipped strawberries, made Ari feel elated, high, optimistic, thrilled to be in the warm Nantucket air with luxuries all around her. A woman in a beaded dress pulled Michelle back into the crowd. Ari leaned against the railing and looked, not at the water, but at the people gathered on the balcony.

"Hey," a man said, leaning next to Ari.

Beckett Hathaway wore chinos, a white polo shirt, and a light-weight navy blazer. He had thick blond hair, the wide shoulders of a swimmer, eyes as blue as the ocean, and a magic smile. When Ari's eyes met his, her heart skipped a beat.

"Hey," Ari responded, just a little breathlessly. "I'm Ari Paget. Michelle and I were in the same childhood ed classes."

"Oh, I know who you are," Beckett said, grinning. "Michelle talks about you a lot."

Ari laughed. "Michelle talks a lot. Sorry, that sounded mean."

"Sounded truthful to me. I've grown up with her. Both my sisters are champion talkers."

"And you?" Ari asked.

"I'm more of a listener, I guess," Beckett said. "That's probably why I'm a therapist."

Ari jolted back. "*You* are a therapist?"

"I just finished a doctorate in behavioral cognitive therapy. I work with the East Coast Mental Health Group in Plymouth. Why are you so surprised?"

"It's just . . . *I'd* never be able to be in therapy with you. I wouldn't be able to confess my problems."

"Why not?"

Ari shrugged. "The truth? You're too handsome."

Beckett laughed. "I don't know whether to take that as an insult or a compliment."

Ari shook her head. "I don't know, either!"

Beckett twirled an invisible mustache and said in a fake Freudian accent, "Vhy don't you come to my couch and let me analyze you, my dear?"

Ari laughed. "I'm sure I could use it." She cocked her head and looked at him. Damn, her hormones were having a party. "But isn't psychotherapy more or less simply listening to someone talk about their problems?" Even as she said the words, she knew she was being antagonistic. It was a kind of protection, in case he wasn't caught in the same spell.

Beckett nodded. "That's certainly part of it." His look made her knees weak.

"So part of it is having the wisdom to give advice?" She wanted to pull him to her so much that she needed to keep him at arm's length.

His voice was gentle. "I'd say that part of it is knowing what questions to ask."

"*What* are you two doing? You look like you're talking about physics!" A redhead Ari didn't know and wasn't sure she wanted to know swept up to them, surrounding them with the fragrance of perfume and whiskey. "Beck, sweetie, will you be my partner for the doubles tennis at the yacht club tomorrow?"

"Sorry, I can't—" Beck said.

"You are not!" The redhead stamped her foot. "Beckett Hathaway, you are not working tomorrow. You are on vacation."

Somehow the redhead had managed to squeeze between Beck and Ari, so it was easy for Ari to lift an eyebrow in what she hoped was an ironic goodbye and slide away, back into the house. She found the table holding trays of cheeses, bowls filled with chopped ice and shrimp, crudités, and chocolates. She found several friends in the crowd. They discussed their plans for the summer. Some, like Ari, were working. Some, like Michelle, were swimming, sailing, playing tennis, and recovering from four years of college or seeing the grandparents before hiking around Europe. As the evening went on, Ari became subdued, smiling and nodding and listening, while wondering all the time why these particular people had so much and the kids at Beach Camp had so little.

She mouthed, "Drink," held up her glass, and drifted away from the group, heading not for the table set up as a bar but for Michelle, to tell her she had to go, and the party had been wonderful.

Before she could find Michelle, Beck approached her.

He said, "I've been looking for you."

"Oh?" She tried to look as if she didn't care.

"I'd like to invite you to go sailing with me tomorrow."

"Sailing."

"Yes. It's an activity that involves a boat with sails that zips around on a body of water." He grinned.

"I thought you were playing tennis," Ari said, immediately wishing she hadn't.

"I told Lynn I was working. And I will be until eleven, when I'll take you sailing."

"Actually, that would be great," Ari said. "I haven't been sailing yet this year."

"Okay, then. I'll meet you at eleven-thirty at the club pier. Don't worry about food. I'll have our cook make up a picnic basket."

"How *Downton Abbey*," Ari teased.

"I'm trying to impress you," Beck said, with laughter in his eyes. "How am I doing?"

"I'll let you know after I see how well you sail." Ari was proud of herself for being playful with this man, as if she'd managed to keep some wits about her while under his spell.

Driving home, she realized that now she had some news that would make her mother happy, even if only for a moment. She'd call her mother to tell her she had a date with Beckett Hathaway.

Ten

On Sunday morning, after Ari took off to go sailing with Beck Hathaway, Eleanor was taking herself on a health walk around the flowered lanes of 'Sconset. Actually, she was pacing, but she'd decided that if she had to pace, she might as well go outside and entertain the Fitbit her son had given her for Christmas.

The day was beautiful, a clear, hot day with blue skies and a calm sea. Eleanor was thinking about her granddaughter. Ari had worked at Beach Camp for a week now, and loved it. Ari enjoyed the children, liked the fresh air and sunshine, and seemed to get on well with the other counselors. She talked about them often, and Eleanor wondered, not for the first time, if Ari wished she'd had a sibling or at least a cousin.

Ari could have a cousin if Cliff would marry and have a child. Well, Cliff wouldn't even have to marry anyone to produce a cousin for Ari. Eleanor smiled at her thoughts.

She returned to her house, poured a refreshing glass of iced tea, and settled on the deck. The moment she sat down, her cell rang. Once again, she'd forgotten to bring it out here with her. This ancient Lilly Pulitzer sundress, like many others, had no pockets. She laughed at herself and went back into the house for the phone.

"Hey, Mom," Cliff said. "Guess what. I'm here on island. I thought I'd come out and put the air conditioner in your bedroom window."

Eleanor thought back. Yes, it was true: After Mortimer's death, Cliff had been the one to carry the air conditioner from the basement and install it in her room. So it was probable that he wasn't coming out to press her about selling the house.

"That would be lovely, dear," she said. "Will you be able to stay for lunch?"

"Sure. I'd like that. See you soon."

Eleanor went to the kitchen to see what she could provide for lunch. Cliff was never picky about his food, unlike Alicia, who, since she was a teenager, had shunned anything with mayonnaise or red meat. Now Eleanor took the egg carton from the refrigerator. She would make curried egg salad, one of Cliff's favorites. And yes, she had beer. She knew he liked a beer at lunch.

Well, Cliff had usually liked anything. He had been the easygoing child and the family darling. When he was a baby and a toddler, Eleanor had asked Alicia to help her by fetching a diaper or giving Cliff a bottle, because she thought this would make Alicia feel included. Instead, it had made her feel put-upon, that she had to wait hand and foot on the baby. Eleanor had tried her best not to show favoritism to her children, but when Alicia was thirteen and angry with Eleanor for simply breathing, Cliff was six and full of giggles and cuddles and charm.

On the other hand, Eleanor thought, silently arguing with herself as she had done many times before, Cliff could complain that Alicia had been their father's favorite. Mortimer expected more of Cliff than he did of Alicia. If Alicia made a B minus on a test, Mortimer praised her. If Cliff made a B minus, Mortimer demanded to know what Cliff had done wrong. Had he not studied enough?

The watershed moment had come when Cliff was fourteen. The family was sitting at the dining room table, eating dinner.

"Mom, Dad," Cliff said. "I've decided that when I'm out of college, I want to join the Peace Corps or Teach For America."

After a moment of shocked silence, Mortimer exploded. "What the hell is wrong with you?"

"Dad." Cliff spoke quietly, although his face and neck were turning red. "I want to help people. I want to do good in the world."

Mortimer shot up from his chair. "You don't think helping people protect their lives and property is doing good?" Mortimer demanded.

"I'm not saying that. I'm saying I want to help people who can't find work or even food or clean water."

"Then you're a fool. I have worked hard to make enough money to provide my family a comfortable life. You, Cliff, have never worked—"

"I tutored students—"

Mortimer made a swiping motion. "That's not work! You don't have any money now and you won't if you don't have a decent profession! Mark my words. If you continue on this path, you will get no money from me, not for college, not even left in my will."

"Daddy!" Alicia said, horrified.

"Mortimer," Eleanor said angrily.

Mortimer sat down again, but his fists were clenched on the table. "You're no son of mine," he growled.

Cliff shoved back his chair and left the table.

Eleanor wanted to go to her son, but she knew that would divide Cliff from his father even more. She was surprised, and relieved, when Alicia ran from the table to be with her brother.

Eleanor knew that in his heart Mortimer loved his son. Mortimer had been raised in a strict, unaffectionate family, and he'd been taught to value strength and tradition. In his family, men were tough and in charge and women were always in the home behind the kitchen sink or the vacuum cleaner. Eleanor's heart was divided between sympathy for her son and anger at her husband.

The next year, Cliff was sent away to an elite boys' boarding school. When he graduated and went on to college, he no longer had any interest in working for the Peace Corps. He was interested only in making money. He became a real estate agent in Boston, and did well. Was Cliff happy? He seemed to be. But Eleanor was afraid that Cliff's life was devoted to showing his father he could make a lot of money, too.

When Cliff was twelve years old, he'd broken his arm playing baseball. All that summer at the Nantucket house, Cliff had lounged on the wicker sofa on the deck, listening to Eleanor read aloud various tales of Sherlock Holmes by Arthur Conan Doyle. She read to him because he couldn't properly hold a book. She could have rigged up a cassette player so he could listen to a professional reader, but somehow she'd started, and it had been such a perfect way to be with her son. He'd loved the stories, and they had been together, sharing a time they'd always remember.

How Eleanor had loved Cliff when he was a little boy. He'd been so sweet, so earnest. But *of course* he'd changed. When he was a senior in his boarding school, he'd been tall and handsome, like Mortimer, with a kind of easy superiority in the way he carried himself. In the fall of that year, the head of the school asked Eleanor and Mortimer to come in for a talk. It seemed that Cliff had been driving—only seniors were allowed to drive—into Boston, where he bought bottles of expensive vodka and bottles of cheap rotgut liquor. He was so tall, so broad-shouldered, so blasé, that no one asked for his ID. They assumed he was over twenty-one, and he always had cash. Back at the school, Cliff would empty the bottles of Absolut vodka into flasks and jars. He would then pour the cheap vodka into the Absolut bottles and sell shots to underclassmen at vastly inflated prices.

Eleanor was heartbroken about this. Cliff was suspended for a month, but was allowed to finish the semester and graduate with his class. Mortimer had appeared angry and disappointed with his son, but when Eleanor and Mortimer were alone, he told her he actually was quite proud of Cliff's enterprising adventure and by the summer, Mortimer had turned the episode into a witty tale about his son's genius in moneymaking. That summer on the island, Cliff took a job on a boat launch and spent his free time with friends and girls. He grew taller than Mortimer and handsomer, too. He condescended to Eleanor, but clearly he had grown away from the sweet little boy and the ethically inspired boy he had once been.

Now Cliff was thirty-nine. He'd been a great comfort when Mortimer died, walking down the aisle after the memorial service with his arm around Eleanor's waist, supporting her. He had stayed in the bluff house for a week, doing business on his phone and computer, but also coaxing Eleanor out for walks on the beach and dinner at good restaurants. He hadn't talked about his personal life, and Eleanor was very curious about that, because he was then thirty-six and not married or in a serious relationship. But the week he was with her after her husband's death, Eleanor was overwhelmed with grief and couldn't think straight. That week their relationship changed, so that he was taking care of her more than she would ever take care of him again.

He'd been a truly dutiful son after Mortimer's death. He'd brought her up to Boston to see plays and eat at expensive restaurants at least once a month, but he'd never had a companion with him. And that worried her.

Once, during a phone call several months ago, knowing it was sometimes easier to discuss intimate things at a distance, she'd said, "Cliff, you know I'll love you no matter what. Just a thought: Are you gay? Because that would be cool."

She could almost hear him rolling his eyes over the phone. "No, Mom, I'm not gay. I would have told you. I date women, but I'm extremely busy."

"I worry that you're lonely," Eleanor had said, and she knew she was intruding a step too far into his adult life.

"You can be lonely when you're married," Cliff had responded, not unkindly.

How odd it was, Eleanor thought, to have grown children who've become people you don't really know. Or maybe it was this way only in her family.

Even so, Eleanor put on a fresh dress and brushed her thick hair into a loose bun. She made curried egg salad sandwiches with fresh strawberries and ice cream for dessert. By noon the summer heat was rising, but the deck was in shadows and the air was fresh and cool, so she put out placemats and cloth napkins in navy blue with white piping, not that Cliff would notice. His beer was cooling in the refrigerator. Eleanor no longer drank wine at lunch because it made her need a nap.

Cliff arrived wearing a pink rugby shirt—Mortimer would hate the color but it emphasized Cliff's tan.

"Hi, Mom," he said, coming into the house and giving her a big hug.

She did like the big hug, even if Cliff had ulterior motives.

"Let's get that air conditioner in before we have lunch," he suggested.

They went down to the basement. Cliff lifted the appliance as if it weighed nothing. He carried it up to Eleanor's bedroom, raised the window and storm window, and easily slid the air conditioner into place.

"Thank you," Eleanor said. "I think I'm beyond carrying air conditioners upstairs."

She expected him to say, *That's why you should move,* but Cliff only said, "I'll just wash my hands and we can have lunch."

When they sat at the table, Cliff did what Mortimer often did—focused on his food while maintaining a pretense of conversation that made Eleanor do most of the talking. She told him about Ari's job, and he said he was impressed, but he didn't pause to remember that once, years ago, he might have done the same thing. They agreed the new minister at St. Paul's was quite a find for their small island congregation. They reminisced about yacht club members who had passed away, and who among the current members had married, or had children, or grandchildren.

"Grandchildren are nice," Eleanor said pointedly. "Especially babies and young ones. I love Ari, but I miss being around little children."

Cliff didn't bother to respond. Instead, he pushed his empty plate away, wiped his mouth on a napkin, and settled back in his chair.

"I want to talk to you about something," he said.

"Oh, no, Cliff, please—" Eleanor objected.

"It's not about selling this house."

She took a deep breath. "All right, then. What is this *something?*"

"Do you think Dad enjoyed being a father?"

She was not expecting this. Her son's gaze was intense. She didn't want to lie. "Your father was very proud of you. He loved you very much."

"That's not what I asked."

Eleanor sighed. "Cliff, I know Mortimer was not a . . . a *fun* father. His own father had been serious and rather aloof. He was Mortimer's role model. Your father wanted to protect you financially, and provide a good life for you. Don't forget all the countries he took us to every summer. Few children have that experience."

Cliff finished his beer and spent a moment looking into the glass. Not meeting his mother's gaze, Cliff said, "You think he was glad he had children?"

"Cliff, yes! Don't ever doubt that. Mortimer was very glad he had children. You were the world to him. He just wasn't a very demonstrative man. But he loved you and Alicia with all his heart."

Cliff nodded. "Thanks, Mom." He stood up suddenly and walked to the end of the deck, where he stood staring out at the ocean for a few moments.

Eleanor sat quietly. These private conversations with her son were rare.

Cliff came back to the table and sat down. He looked lighthearted now, and Eleanor was pleased that he'd been able to ask her about Mortimer.

"Mom, there's something else I'd like to talk to you about."

"Of course, darling. What is it?" She smiled at him, her handsome, precious son.

"I'd like you to spend some time with me going over your legal and financial affairs."

Eleanor was too shocked to respond. Had his question about his father been nothing more than a way to soften her up for more talk about money?

Cliff continued. "For example, do you have a healthcare proxy? Someone who can make a decision about medical matters if you can't."

"Someone to sign the Do Not Resuscitate order," Eleanor said coldly.

Cliff didn't even wince. "Do you want to be an organ donor? Do you have a will? Have you provided someone with a durable power of attorney? Do you—"

"Enough, Cliff! That's enough." Her own son had played her. She felt betrayed.

"Mom, be sensible. For all I know, you have this all taken care of. If so, tell me. But you're like Dad, so secretive about financial matters. I don't even know if you have enough savings to live on for the next ten years. For the next five years."

"You said we weren't going to talk about selling my house." Eleanor's voice shook from anger.

"We're not talking about that. We're talking about the fact that you are a seventy-year-old widow living alone on a bluff facing the Atlantic. Come on, Mom. You must have friends who have made these sorts of decisions. What's going to happen if you get Alzheimer's? Parkinson's?"

"Has Alicia put you up to this?"

"No, Mom, but if she did, she'd be doing the right thing. You need to make some decisions while you can."

"Before I go gaga, you mean."

"Before you trip over the cat and fall down the stairs and can't reach the phone."

The image was so hideous and actually so possible that Eleanor scraped back her chair and stood up, trembling all over. "I'd like you to leave now."

"Mom, I'm sorry I upset you. I only mean the best."

She tried to keep her dignity. "Please leave."

Cliff stood up. He carefully picked up his dessert plate and coffee cup and carried them into the kitchen. Eleanor followed him, not carrying her plate for fear of dropping and breaking it.

"Mom," Cliff said. "At least do this. Talk to your friends. I'll bet they're discussing the same sorts of things."

Eleanor was on the point of tears, but she was damned if she'd cry in front of him, so without another word she left the kitchen, crossed the hall, and went up the stairs, praying she didn't trip over the cat.

She strode into her bedroom, slammed the door shut, and paced, muttering to herself. She wasn't *senile*. She didn't live in a fantasy world. Occasionally, she and her friends had talked about all those morbid but necessary subjects: wills, DNRs, power of attorney. After Mortimer died, Eleanor had decided to take care of all that unattractive paperwork for herself, but somehow she'd never found the time. She was too busy in the summer, and in the dead of winter, with the sky as dark as a coffin lid, she couldn't bring herself to organize herself for death.

She would do it. Tomorrow, this week. She would.

The fact that she had a will didn't mean she was going to die. It just kind of felt that way.

She heard Cliff's car leaving her driveway. She didn't want to spend this beautiful day thinking about the end of her life. She wanted to do something *positive!*

In a flash, she came up with a plan. She would make tees for the children at Beach Camp. Her tears vanished. She almost ran out of her room.

First, Eleanor made a mock-up from one of Cliff's old childhood tees she'd found wrapped around crystal in a box in the attic. She was excited about her idea, so she forced herself to be orderly as she searched all the drawers and cupboards in her mother's sewing room. Well, *her* sewing room now. First, she used the basic embroidery backstitch on her brilliant sewing machine for the letters. Each letter was about two inches wide. After sewing, she flattened the letters with a warm iron. She held up her first creation and studied it.

BEACH

CAMP

Not quite right. The embroidered letters were heavier than the cotton shirt. That wouldn't do.

Undeterred and seized with excitement for her project, she went into town, bought fifteen plain white tees in three different sizes, a pack of large-letter stencils, and three non-toxic, non-fading, non-bleeding fabric markers.

Back in the sewing room, she moved the sewing machine aside in order to spread the tee out on the wide table. She selected the letters she needed, laying them out so they touched a ruler, and picked up a broad-tipped red pen.

Or should it be blue? Blue was the color of the ocean.

No, red. It was more joyful.

She took her time filling in the letters. She didn't want these to look sloppy. After each letter, she sat back and took a breath.

It was nice, being in this small, quiet, warm room at the back of the hall. Unlike the chaos of the attic, the sewing room was extremely neat and organized. The closet held bolts of fabric that had been used for dresses or curtains. One side of the room was shelves with baskets devoted to knitting, crocheting, and needle-pointing. The long table where Eleanor sat held the sewing machine and a wicker basket lined with rose-printed muslin that contained dressmaker's scissors, pinking shears, a tape measure, and a pair of tiny gold embroidery scissors shaped like a bird with a long thin bill for snipping threads. On the shelf nearest her were a red cloth tomato stuck with straight pins with fat heads and a fabric tomato stuck with safety pins. In the far corner of the room was a dressmaker's dummy. Years ago, Eleanor had taken pity on the headless, naked dummy and wrapped one of her grandmother's shawls around it.

Eleanor's mother's mother had turned up her nose at store-bought clothes. Winifred had had a dressmaker who helped her create dresses, slips, and nightgowns that fit her measurements precisely. In the black-and-white photographs, Winifred always looked neat, even regal, with her long hair in braids fastened tidily to the back of her head. Eleanor had no idea what her grandmother looked like with her hair down.

Now here Eleanor was in the same room where her grandmother had been painstakingly pinned into a figure-fitting one-of-a-kind dress. Eleanor was making matching tees for her granddaughter's charges at Beach Camp.

It made Eleanor smile. She lifted the stencil sheet off the first tee. "Hooray!" she cried, for the words looked professionally done, all the letters equally dark, not even the smallest slip of red marring the letters.

Carried away with her success, she carefully made a few more. She wanted to do them all, but her hands got cramped and her neck hurt from bending. She stood up, put her hands on her back, and leaned backward, relishing the pull on her muscles. Time for tea? She glanced at her watch. Yes, she would finish the lot and then it would be time for a drink!

Eleven

Ari pulled into an empty space in the yacht club parking lot. As always, she checked her reflection in the visor mirror—fine. She looked fine. She dotted and swirled sunblock/moisturizer all over her face, especially on her nose. Her only makeup was a light touch of pink Burt's Bees balm. She'd pulled her hair back into a high ponytail. She wore deck shoes, navy shorts, and a white yacht club tee over her bathing suit, plus a red fleece tied around her shoulders in case she got cold. It was not yet the depth of summer, and the water was cool.

She walked through the parking lot and into the club, greeting old friends and acquaintances. She saw Beck waiting for her at the end of the dock. Board shorts, navy tee, deck shoes, and a red scalloper's cap with the long bill for sun protection and to keep the sun out of his eyes.

"Hey," she called, walking toward him. "Nice day for a sail."

"Hi, Ari." Beck leaned forward and kissed her cheek as any friend would. "The wind is fickle today. We'll see what happens."

They took the club launch out to Beck's sailboat.

"Here," Beck said as they got settled. "Wear this." He handed her a lightweight buoyancy vest. "Hen made me promise to make you wear it," Beck said.

Ari laughed in surprise. "Hen?"

"She likes you. And she's surprisingly good at getting her own way."

"She's a smart girl," Ari said, putting on the vest, and she was thinking, with a kind of envy, how close Beck's family seemed to be. That Hen even knew Ari was sailing with Beck—that Hen even remembered Ari—was surprising.

They cast off from the buoy and sailed across the harbor toward the end of the Jetties and around to the deeper waters of the sound running along the north shore of the island. Beck was an aggressive, playful sailor, letting the sails fill, tacking back and forth, completely concentrating on his boat and the wind. Now and then the boat rose and slapped down hard onto the rocking waves. Ari was glad she didn't have her grandmother's problem with motion sickness.

She leaned back on her elbows, lifting her face to the sun. The wind flipped her ponytail, and the boat splashed and the water sprayed, making fans of rainbows. She relaxed against the boat, listening to these sounds so familiar from her childhood as a boat cradled her in the ocean. She stopped thinking as the sun warmed her face and shoulders. She almost dreamed.

The boat slowed, turned, stopped.

Beck said, "Sorry to wake you."

"I wasn't asleep." Ari straightened, taking a deep breath. "But I was more relaxed than I've been in months." She looked around. "Oh, there's the Great Point lighthouse. We've come farther than I thought."

"Fifth point," Beck said. "I think this is good, don't you?" He headed the boat sideways to the land, dropped anchor, and slipped into the water. It hit him at chest level. "Damn! It's freezing! Hand me the picnic basket. I'll come back for you."

"I'm fine." Ari took off her life vest and dropped her fleece. She slid into the water with her clothes on. She did this often, knowing that in a few minutes the sun would dry them. The water reached up to her mouth, an efficient demonstration that Beck was taller than she was, although she was tall. She quickly pushed her way through the water, which got shallower with each step, to the beach. She could tell by the damp clumps of seaweed high on the sand that the tide was in, so when they were ready to leave, the water would be retreating. Then, probably, only her legs up to her knees would get wet.

Beck lifted a threadbare tartan blanket from the basket and flipped it out. Ari caught the other side and together they brought the blanket down to the sand. Beck anchored it with Tupperware boxes and two bottles of sparkling water.

"Water?" Ari asked, sitting cross-legged on the blanket. "No wine?"

"I don't drink when I'm sailing," Beck told her. "Well, I do when I'm with a bunch of friends in a bigger boat."

Plates, silverware, and cups were fixed with leather straps to the top of the basket, and cloth napkins rested between the tubs of food.

"Fancy," Ari remarked.

"Old family thing. I don't always use it," Beck told her. "Just when I'm trying to impress someone."

Ari laughed and took the plate he held out to her.

They ate awhile in silence. Chicken salad sandwiches, deviled eggs, apples. In the distance, sailboats skimmed the water. Waves lapped at the shore.

"It's nice here," Ari said. "I like the quiet. I work five days a week at a kids' camp. Fifteen kids, and the noise is astounding. But I like it. I want to own a daycare center someday, so this is good experience."

"Have you always wanted to work with little kids?" Beck asked.

"I have, actually. I'm an only child. When I was little, I used to line my stuffed animals and dolls up and teach them, read stories to them, put them down for afternoon naps." Ari laughed. "They were docile students. I didn't learn until practice teaching in college that kids also fought, disobeyed, and got sick all over their desks." She glanced at Beck. "Did you always want to be a therapist?"

"Ha. No, I had plans to be an infielder for the Red Sox. Seriously. I played ball in Little League and was a star. I spent every minute I could catching balls I forced my sister or parents to throw. I dreamt of being a professional ballplayer. That dream burst in middle school. Only in my dreams do I run faster and throw farther than anyone else in the world. I was seriously depressed for a few months. I felt lost. It sounds ridiculous now, but we're learning that adolescent brains are different from those of adults. And I wasn't truly in a depression. I could sleep, eat, go to school. I was just unhappy. I was even brokenhearted.

"Then a couple of things happened. My cousin, older than me, Jack Franklin, went to Afghanistan and came home with PTSD. His life was shattered. And a guy we know on the island, Joey Vaughan, got drafted to the Pawtucket Red Sox minor league. And the thing is . . ." Beck took a deep breath. "The thing is, Jack saw a therapist and got better. Joey couldn't handle the competition and started drinking. He got kicked off the team. Lived at home for a while, drinking and growing a beard, then drifted out of town. We don't even know where he is now."

"That's sad," Ari said quietly. Really, she didn't know what to say.

"It is sad. Joey was a good guy. I couldn't stop thinking about it. It was like a puzzle to me. So I took some classes. Then majored in psychology, then got a master's and doctorate."

"Do you want to be a psychiatrist?"

"Not at all. They solve problems with pills, and believe me, I'm glad that works. I have a friend who's bipolar. He was miserable, and not much fun to be around, until his psychiatrist prescribed lithium. Almost that fast"—Beck snapped his fingers—"he was better. He's having a great life now." Beck laughed. "Ari, you wouldn't believe it after hearing me talk so much, but I'm a good listener."

"I believe it," Ari said. "Sometimes in student teaching, a kid would get upset, red in the face, frustrated. If I took him to the back of the room and sat with him, and just listened, he would calm down. He found it hard to articulate his problem, but I know—I could *feel*—how my being there, quietly, *attentively,* helped him."

"Right. We're all so busy these days with our screens, we don't take time to turn off the electronics and sit with someone and quietly listen."

"My grandmother is good at listening," Ari said. "She's good at being quiet as well. She can sit and think over a problem and not speak until she's prepared her thoughts."

"My grandmother was that way, too." Beck took a deep breath. "Let's walk."

The beach was long and golden, the water translucent. Ari picked up some shells and found a rare piece of turquoise sea glass. They didn't speak, and Ari was glad. Beck was an interesting man with an interesting profession. She'd assumed he'd be lighthearted and fun, so she had to let their talk settle. It was as if she'd thought she'd spend the afternoon laughing as balloons lifted into the air. Instead, she'd discovered solid ground for her thoughts . . . and her soul. So curious, because he looked like a playboy.

As the sun drifted lower in the sky, they gathered the picnic basket and blanket and returned to the boat. Once again, Ari sat with her face lifted to the sun as Beck sailed them back to his buoy.

"I've had a really nice day," Ari told him as they waited for the launch to pick them up.

"Me, too," Beck said. "I'd like to do it again."

"I'd like that," Ari agreed.

They climbed onto the launch and were delivered back to the dock.

Beck walked Ari to her car. "So I'll call you," he said.

Ari smiled. "Or maybe I'll call you," she teased, because she *knew,* she sensed it, it was real—he was enchanted, too. She stood on tiptoe and kissed his mouth quickly.

On the way home, Ari pulled into the Stop & Shop parking lot. She stepped out of the hot sun into the cool store, grabbed a cart, and filled it up with fruits and vegetables. Grapes, strawberries, plums, broccoli, kale, carrots. Next to the grocery store was a liquor store. She bought two bottles of sparkling rosé. Then, walking toward her car, she saw something so strange she almost dropped her bags.

Her father was coming out of the liquor store. Wearing plaid Bermuda shorts, loafers without socks, and a rugby shirt with the collar turned up. Ari started to wave at her father, but he was getting into a convertible with a young woman who was absolutely not her mother. The young woman was driving, and her father said something that made them both laugh as they drove away.

Of course it couldn't be her father.

Ari leaned against her car and stared as the couple disappeared around the corner.

She must have been dazzled by the sun. It must have been a man who looked like her father.

Still, she took up her phone and called her house in Wellesley.

"Hello?" Her mother always answered as if she never knew who was calling. Ari thought her mother considered caller ID vulgar and never checked before she answered.

"Hi, Mom, just calling to say hello."

"Did you go sailing with Beck Hathaway today?"

"Yes, and we're going again next weekend." Ari could imagine the smile on her mother's face. Her good deed for the day. She kept chatting for a few minutes before asking, "Is Dad there?"

"No, sorry, darling. He got called in to the hospital early this morning for an emergency surgery. Something complicated, I can't remember. Don't worry, I'll tell him everything tonight when he comes home."

"Okay, then," Ari said, sounding too hearty for her own ears. "We'll talk later."

Ari got into her car, strapped on her seatbelt, and sat there, trying to think logically. That might have been a man who only looked like her father. Her father was as likely to have an affair with a young woman as he was to grow wings and fly. So, she had been wrong. That had not been her father.

Or, her father flew in to do emergency surgery at the Nantucket Cottage Hospital and the young woman was a nurse? Not likely, in those clothes. Plus, Ari's mother hadn't said he'd been called in to the Nantucket hospital. That might make sense if he were on island and listed as a summer emergency surgeon, but although her father had signed up when he was younger, in the past few years he'd decided they needed other younger physicians, and he'd wanted a vacation.

She drove back to her grandmother's house, chewing on her lip, unable to stop worrying. She could mention it to Eleanor, but Eleanor would laugh. Or worry—and Ari didn't want to make her grandmother worry. She decided not to mention it.

"Hello!" Ari called as she entered the house.

"Did you have a good day?" Eleanor was in the kitchen putting cheese and crackers on a plate. She handed a glass of sparkling wine to Ari.

"I had a great day!" Ari said. "How was yours?"

Eleanor said mysteriously, "Let me show you," and she left the table.

When she returned, she had a pile of T-shirts in her hand. They were all white, with the words BEACH CAMP printed on them in red.

"These are wonderful," Ari exclaimed, holding a tee up to look at it. "Where on earth did you get them?"

"I made them," Eleanor said.

"Get out of town."

"It's true. I made them today. Very easily, actually. Of course, I bought the tees. Three different sizes. Fifteen tees. The writing is done in non-toxic permanent marker that won't bleed in the wash."

"You certainly have a steady hand," Ari marveled. "No slipup anywhere. They look store-bought."

Eleanor laughed. "That reminds me of something my own grandmother said. We gave her a bouquet of hothouse roses for her birthday, and she said they looked pretty enough to be artificial."

Ari laughed with her grandmother. "I can't wait to give these out tomorrow."

Monday morning, Ari rose early, double-checked the weather—it was a gorgeous day—pulled on her shorts and tee, put her hair in a ponytail, and quietly went down the stairs to the kitchen. She chomped down a banana while the Keurig made her coffee, poured the coffee into her go-cup, scooped up the tote bag holding the tees, and headed out the door. In her car, she quickly dabbed sunblock on her face, slipped on her new, inexpensive sunglasses, and hit the volume to high on her radio.

She was excited about the tees for the Beach Camp kids. Eleanor had made five each of small, medium, and large. They might be too big for a couple of the younger campers, but over the summer, the children would probably grow into them.

The kids were already on the beach. When they noticed Ari, some of them came racing toward her, waving their arms and screaming. Ari intended on showing Cal the shirts before morning circle, but Cal and Sandy were already shooing the children into place. Ari joined them on the sand, settling the tote bag next to her, and waited while they went through their daily ritual.

Just before the circle disbanded, Ari raised her hand. "Do any of you have grandmothers who love you *so much*?"

The children yelled and clapped.

"Well, my grandmother loves to sew. She is sew loco!" Ari joked as she reached into the tote bag and took out one tee. She held it high so everyone could see the words: BEACH CAMP.

"I want one!" a kid called, and started to his feet.

"You can all have one," Ari told them. "Line up according to height, and I'll hand them out."

Several minutes of chaos ensued before Ari and Cal got the kids into line. She saw that some children would explode if they had to wait more than a second, so she handed the pile of large shirts to Cal and the mediums to Sandy, and Ari started with the smalls. Old shirts flew to the ground as the kids pulled the new tees on over their heads. The little ones puffed out their chests and strutted, gazing proudly down at the letters. The older ones smoothed the material carefully over their chests. One little girl, Sarita, sat in the sand, motionless, staring at the tee in her hands.

Ari knelt down next to Sarita. "I think your shirt will fit you."

Sarita nodded, almost sadly. "But if I swim, will the letters go away?"

"No, no. They are permanent." Ari stood and announced to the crowd that water would not fade the letters.

Immediately the children ran toward the water, but Cal called them back. "Games first!"

The rest of the day passed swiftly. Ari knew how important it was that Cal kept them on a definite routine. They played Magic Ball, sending it around in a circle, and tug-of-war, and held a contest to see how far each camper could jump. Finally they were allowed into the water, which was a crazy free-for-all. Then the minivans to the community school for lunch, and nap time and story time. Next, they rode in the minivans to the small Maria Mitchell aquarium near the town pier and saw seahorses serenely floating up and down in tall, narrow tanks, and the rare blue lobster. Outside, in the circle tank, swam the dogfish, which looked like small white sharks. After an appropriate amount of giggling and shrieking at the sight of what the sea held, the group was channeled back to the buses and back to the community school. Here they were instructed to draw some of the creatures they'd seen at the aquarium. At four-thirty, the parents arrived to pick up their children, and peace descended over the room.

Ari automatically joined Cal and Sandy as they tidied broken crayons, crumpled paper, and bits of plastic into the trash. Ari was hoping Cal would take the time to thank her for the tees, so she wasn't surprised when he suggested the three of them sit down for a moment. They gathered at one of the small round tables the children used, and Ari grinned at the sight of them balancing on the tiny chairs.

"Ari," Cal said, his voice serious. "We need to talk about those T-shirts."

"Okay."

Cal said, "You're new and we haven't discussed rules with you. It's not like we have an employee handbook. But we do have a list of needs and a plan for allocating money. Something as important as those tees should have been okayed by all of us before you handed them out."

"But . . ." Ari had learned a lot about compromise and conciliation during her student-teaching days, so she spoke with composure. "I was told that the camp doesn't have enough money for tees. It seemed so sad that they didn't have them. My grandmother made them, without even suggesting it to me first. My grandmother loves to craft. But, okay, I get it that I should have talked to you first, so I apologize."

"No need to apologize," Cal said. "We're grateful for the tees, of course, Ari. The children are thrilled, that's what's important. Please give your grandmother our thanks."

"I will," Ari said. "And I promise not to do anything without consulting you—the two of you—first."

"Good," Cal said, clapping his hands on the table. "Is there anything else we need to discuss? No? Then we're out of here." He rose and headed to the door, held it open for both women, and followed them out.

Ari settled into her car, feeling grumpy as she drove out of the parking lot. She wouldn't tell her grandmother about this rule of Beach Camp. Ari understood their reasoning, but she felt like one of the children who had just gotten her feelings hurt.

She was at the rotary when a buzz came from her phone in its clever dashboard mount. Beck Hathaway. She pushed "Accept."

"Hey, where are you?" Beck asked. His voice was low and easy. She could almost hear him smiling.

"On lower Orange, heading toward home."

"Turn around and come back into town and I'll take you to dinner."

"I'd like that, Beck, but the truth is, I'm exhausted. Playing with fifteen children under the hot sun has turned out to be more challenging than I'd anticipated."

"Maybe tomorrow?"

"I'm working tomorrow, too. Every day until Saturday. Plus, I want to spend some time with my grandmother."

After a moment's silence, Beck said, "So basically, your summer is booked?"

"Gosh, no, Beck! I'd love to see you. Maybe Saturday?"

"Saturday I'm spending with Hen."

"Really? What a cool older brother you are."

"She's a cool younger sister. We're going to see the new Disney movie. We're planning on buying the largest bag of popcorn. After, we're going to the Juice Bar for ice cream." Beck paused. "Want to join us?"

Ari laughed. "For a Disney movie and popcorn and ice cream? How can I resist? Yes, I'd love to join you."

"Good. I'll tell Hen. She'll be thrilled. I'll be in touch about the time."

"So what did you do today?" Ari asked. She realized she enjoyed talking to Beck, hearing his voice.

"I worked on a paper I'm writing for *Psychology Today*. Answered emails. Caught up on my office work. Oh, and I went for a long, bracing swim. Cleared my head."

"Cold water does wonders for the disposition," Ari echoed.

"It's not so cold this June. One of the benefits of global warming."

"Our poor planet," Ari said.

"Didn't you get the memo? It's illegal to worry on Nantucket in the summer."

Ari laughed.

Beck said, "Okay, then, I'll look forward to seeing you on Saturday. With popcorn and Hen."

"I look forward to seeing who is going to sit in the middle at the movie," Ari said mischievously. When their call ended, she realized she was in a much better mood than when she'd started the drive home.

At the rotary, she stopped to let a few cars pass. She was in the left lane, watching for her chance, when she saw her father in the same snazzy navy blue Porsche with the same young blond woman. For a split second, Ari thought it wasn't her father—he was laughing, relaxed, and the sun fell on the couple, lighting them up as if they were in the last scene of a romantic movie. But he turned his head slightly, and she knew that profile, that slightly prominent nose, the hair with its silvery touches of gray.

I'll honk and wave! she thought, with an insane kind of rebelliousness. *Let him explain to his mistress who that was who waved at him.* But the moment passed, the Porsche slid smoothly around to the Airport Road, and behind her a pickup truck honked impatiently.

This was the second time she'd seen her father with that particular woman. She couldn't simply worry about it with Eleanor, she had to *do* something. But what? Her thoughts tumbled anxiously in her head. She felt as if she were on a roller coaster or some kind of whirligig, and ten minutes later, when she pulled into Eleanor's driveway, she threw her car door open, leaned out of her seat, and threw up on the drive.

Twelve

Silas had phoned on Saturday to ask Eleanor to join him and friends going out on their yacht on Monday, and she had never been more grateful to have a reason to think about something other than her legal matters. She fussed around all morning, trying to find a bathing suit she could fit into, and then something comfortable, modest, and attractive to wear over it, which she knew was asking a lot from a piece of material.

Why was she worrying about the way she looked? Was she nervous about going out with Silas? That was ridiculous. She probably had indigestion. She wasn't worried about getting motion sick. There was almost no wind, and she was sure they'd be staying close to shore. Still, she was uneasy.

The June day was hot and clear, so she remembered to put sunblock in her beach bag. She brushed her long hair and left it down, because it was still lovely, but quickly changed her mind. She didn't want to look, as the British said, like mutton dressed as lamb. She clamped it to the back of her head, put on a light touch of lipstick, removed the lipstick, sighed, and put it on again. After all, it was Burt's Bees balm, which was good for protecting the skin.

Silas came for her in his rather rusty old heap of a Jeep. He actually came to her door, carried her beach bag, and helped her into the Jeep, which was quite gentlemanly of him and made her flush but not so much he would notice. Eleanor had intended to talk with him about his legal matters—wills, power of attorney, funerals, all that—but Silas was in a good mood, telling her the jokes he'd heard at his men's poker night. She laughed and allowed herself to enjoy the day.

They took the yacht club launch out to their friend's yacht. Eleanor swallowed her surprise when she saw how long it was, how its four decks towered above the water. She knew Clarissa and Chip "had money"—money was the number one topic of conversation on the island. But Clarissa had never flaunted it like Muffy did. An astonishingly gorgeous young man in crisp white shorts and a shirt with the emblem of the boat on its pocket held out his hand to assist Eleanor aboard, and a beautiful young woman in a similar uniform held out a tray with flutes of champagne and glasses of iced tea.

Eleanor chose the tea, and a moment later she felt Silas's hand on her waist. He guided her into the top deck where their hosts and a few other guests were seated in comfortable cushioned wicker chairs. Eleanor had never been so happy to see old people in her life. She was friends with Muffy Andover (she'd secretly made fun of the woman's name) and Muffy's husband, Mick, both with tanned faces wrinkled like a closed accordion. (Eleanor thought it was a wonder the boat didn't sink from the sheer weight of all Muffy's gold jewelry.) Their hosts, Clarissa and Chip Lourie, were pleasant and welcoming. When Clarissa leaned to kiss Eleanor on her cheek, she whispered, "I'd rather be reading a book."

"Not I," Eleanor whispered back. "This boat makes me feel like I'm living *in* a book!"

Another couple, Bonnie and Donnie Hamilton—who went to St. Paul's church and knew that people made fun of their matching names, but what could they do?—were the last to board. The yacht rumbled beneath them like a great sea monster waking up, and they headed out of the harbor and toward Great Point.

Eleanor relaxed. Everyone else was more or less Eleanor's age.

The men had potbellies, the women had dimpled thighs and upper arms, and they were all sprinkled with brown old-age spots, as well as white old-age spots, which Eleanor had never known about until recently. Eleanor was the only widow. Chip Lourie was a good ten years older than Eleanor, and weighed down with various ailments.

Clarissa yelled—because the breeze the boat caused whipped away their words—"Every year Chip predicts it will be the year he sells this old thing. Every New Year's Eve, we place bets on who will go first, me, Chip, or the boat." She threw her head back and laughed, and as Eleanor laughed with her, she admired her for joking about death. Eleanor would bet fifty dollars that Clarissa and Chip had all *their* legal affairs in order.

"How's your summer going?" Chip asked.

They talked about various galas to raise money for the many organizations on the island, and what neighbor's house had just sold for how many million, and how they'd spent their winter. Eleanor and Silas and the Louries were the only ones who didn't have winter homes in Florida and the others were aghast.

"What is there to do here in the winter?" Muffy asked.

"Read books!" Eleanor told her.

Muffy looked even more appalled.

Silas spoke up. "There are lectures and movies and great local theater and concerts held by the Nantucket Community Music Center, plus lots of dinners with friends."

Muffy nodded sadly. "I suppose you can always travel."

Bonnie saved the day. "We often visit our grandchildren."

"Yes!" Silas said. "For Christmas, and—"

He was interrupted by everyone else wanting to show pictures of their grandchildren on their phones. Clearly this was the favorite subject, and for a while Eleanor leaned back, tilted her face up to the sun, and relaxed.

"How is your granddaughter?" Clarissa asked Eleanor.

"Oh, she's lovely. Ari's twenty-two. She just graduated from Bucknell."

"Wonderful!" Clarissa said.

"She's working on the island this summer at Beach Camp," Eleanor said.

"What's that?" Clarissa asked.

Eleanor explained that it was a day camp for children whose parents had to work and couldn't afford babysitters.

"How divine!" Muffy clapped her hands together. "We must send them a check. Just think, we could make it possible for them all to take a trip to Boston to the science museum."

"That's a fabulous idea." Eleanor smiled and thought Muffy looked quite lovely in all her gold jewelry.

Muffy said, "I'll call you tomorrow."

The captain came onto the deck and announced, "We're almost at Great Point."

"We'll stop for a swim before lunch," Clarissa informed them.

They anchored. The rumbling stopped. Chip was first to dive off the boat, and then one by one, like a rather shapeless chorus line, the men dove into the water. Eleanor didn't dive, nor did the other women. They went down the ladder and eased themselves into the cold.

After a moment of dog-paddling, Eleanor's body went, all of its own accord, into swim mode. She remembered as she speared through the surface that as it went deeper, it got almost icy. But she was exhilarated, by the cold and the sheer sensation of swimming. She recalled her different strokes, and for a while caught her breath by treading water and watching her friends pass by her in a blur of color and splashes. She floated, her body cold, the sun hot on her face. It was slightly scary, letting her ancient body, with its weaknesses, surrender to the obliviousness of the ocean, which wouldn't care—wouldn't know—if she, a superior creature on this planet, sank or swam. She didn't have the strength to swim to shore, which was very far away. As a girl, she'd enjoyed the challenge, but now she knew she couldn't keep it up.

Still, she was the last one to climb the ladder attached to the boat, where the gorgeous young man held out his hand to heave her onto the deck. He immediately gave her a large and fluffy white towel. She could have cried with gratefulness. It wasn't just that she was too old to expose others to her body in its one-piece skirted (the skirt did no good) bathing suit, it was also that she was so cold. Her teeth chattered. Her skin was riddled with gooseflesh.

"Your lips are blue!" Bonnie called. She patted the cushion on the wicker sofa. "Come sit here and have a drinkie."

Eleanor wanted a hot shower and a nap. She would have settled for a hot cup of anything, but the glamorous attendant handed her an iced glass of something with a frivolous name and Eleanor sipped it. She discovered immediately that in spite of the ice cubes, the beverage warmed her with its fruity alcoholic content. But a stirring, unpleasant sense of unease was there, fluttering just under her skin. It had been there all day and she'd ignored it because she was having so much fun.

Maybe she needed to see her doctor.

While the swimmers warmed up, the crew came around with broiled oysters, fresh oysters, grilled shrimp, olives, and crisp radishes. Soon they were invited into the handsome teak dining room. They settled at the table, where they were served freshly caught seared sea bass with sinfully crisp French fries and salad. Key lime pie for dessert, with champagne. They sat around the long table and regaled one another with stories of what the island was like decades ago, when everything here was simpler and better. Eleanor rolled her eyes and caught Silas's grin and knew he was thinking what she was. How could anyone on this yacht complain about the present? There was something magical about being on a small vessel in the vast blue waters, and being there with good friends. She almost forgot about her silly little fear.

At around five, the yacht docked in the harbor. The beautiful boy helped her onto the pier, and everyone said goodbye, all looking as exhausted as she felt. Fifty years ago, they would have gone dancing, but that was fifty years ago.

Once home, she took a long, luxuriously hot shower, pulled on slacks and a warm cashmere crewneck, made herself tea, and settled on the sofa. Her skin was red and tender from the day in the sun and her head was totally empty of thought. She was relaxed and glowing.

The kitchen door slammed. Ari was home, and something smelled. Eleanor heard Ari running water at the kitchen sink, and then Ari appeared in the living room. Her tee had yellowish stains down the front, and she was wiping her face with a dish towel.

"Oh, my dear, are you all right?" Eleanor rose to go to her granddaughter.

Ari collapsed against her. "I saw Dad with another woman. At the rotary. In a convertible. He was smiling."

"I see." Eleanor led Ari to the sofa, settled her against the arm of the sofa, pulled an afghan up over her, and gave her a mug of tea.

Ari drank gratefully. She met Eleanor's eyes. "I've got to go back outside. I barfed in your yard. I should clean it up."

"Oh, never mind about that," Eleanor said, waving her hand. "The rabbits will be glad of a free meal tonight." She sank into a wing chair across from her granddaughter. "I wonder, Ari. Could you be pregnant?"

"What? Of course not! I haven't—I've only been here a couple of weeks. I certainly haven't had sex!" The moment she spoke, a chill ran through her. She said, "Wait." She counted on her fingers. "I . . . I had sex with Peter three days before I broke off with him. I didn't want to, but . . . he wanted to. I had just stopped taking my birth control pills. Oh, no—I haven't gotten my period this week. I wasn't paying attention to the dates. Oh, God, what if I *am* pregnant?"

Eleanor reached over and put her hand on top of Ari's. "If you are, we will deal with it one way or another. First, let's go into town and buy you a few pregnancy tests."

"I can't have a baby," Ari whispered.

"Let's be sure before we panic." Eleanor rose. "I'll drive to Dan's Pharmacy and get the tests."

"Thank you," Ari said meekly. The very thought of being pregnant terrified Ari. If it was true, did that mean she had to marry Peter? Would Peter even want to marry her? She certainly didn't want to marry him. And Beck wouldn't want to be with her if . . .

She didn't want to be pregnant. *Someday.* But not now. The time wasn't right.

"Do you want to ride in with me?" Eleanor asked.

"No, if you don't mind, I'd rather go out for a walk. I'm so nervous."

"Of course you are. Go for your walk—go for a run. I'll be back as soon as I can."

Eleanor found her purse, patted her hair into place, dabbed on a touch of light lipstick, and went out the door.

Thirteen

Ari stood paralyzed as her grandmother left the house. Ari was still wearing her soiled shirt, so she hurried to her room—suddenly she felt she needed to hurry—stripped off her shirt, pulled on some running shorts, a loose tee, and running shoes, tied her hair up in a high ponytail, and, not bothering to check her watch, ran down the drive and onto Baxter Road. She ran toward Sankaty Head, vaguely waving when someone waved at her. She ran up the path until she could touch the great white-and-red-striped lighthouse. She touched it, turned, and ran all the way back, past her grandmother's house, past all the houses with magical gardens, until she reached the small lanes leading to the Sconset Market and the rotary and the charming white 'Sconset bridge over the road down to Codfish Park. She bent with her hands on her knees, took some deep breaths, and ran back toward her grandmother's house and whatever news was coming to her there.

Eleanor's car was in the drive and she was back on the deck overlooking the Atlantic.

"You look like you've had a run," Eleanor said.

Gasping for breath, her chest heaving, Ari nodded.

Eleanor gestured toward the brown paper bag in the middle of the patio table.

"Maybe you should take a shower," Eleanor suggested.

Ari choked out a laugh. Only her grandmother could drive off to buy pregnancy tests and diplomatically refrain from speaking of them.

"Thanks," Ari said. "I will." She picked up the bag and hurried upstairs and into the bathroom. She wrenched off her shoes and clothes, did what was needed to take the test, and turned on the water for her shower. She was thoroughly soaked when she decided three minutes was up, and she reached out to pick up the small plastic tube of information.

She was pregnant.

She retreated into the shower, washing her hair, scrubbing her reckless body, weeping the entire time.

She was exhausted when she stepped out of the shower. She wrapped her hair in a turban of towel, pulled on her fluffy bathrobe, and went into her room to slide her feet into flip-flops.

Eleanor was in the kitchen making grilled cheese sandwiches. Ari stood in the doorway, glad for the comforting sight and smell. Clenching her fists to keep the fear from dropping her to her knees, she waited until she had Eleanor's attention.

"I'm pregnant," she told her grandmother.

Eleanor turned the burner down and with extreme care, put down her spatula. She let out a long sigh and covered her belly with her hand. "Okay," she said to herself, smiling. "Okay." She walked over to wrap her arms around Ari. "It's going to be all right."

Emotion swept over Ari, nearly knocking her to her knees. With her face buried in her grandmother's shoulder, she sobbed, "How can it be all right? I don't want Peter's baby. I don't want any baby. This shouldn't have happened. Mom will be so angry and humiliated, and Dad will be . . ." Ari remembered why she'd phoned her mother in the first place. "Is Dad going to leave Mom?"

Eleanor kissed the side of Ari's head. "We have a lot to deal with, but let's do it day by day. Remember, you are surrounded by people who love you. Sit down. Your sandwich is ready. You'll feel better once you've eaten."

Ari sat. She was surprised that she could eat, and that the sandwich was delicious. Eleanor sat across from her, eating her own sandwich, drinking a glass of dry white wine. She had given Ari soda water, and the fact of *that* hit hard.

"No more wine for me, I guess," she said.

"We'll see," Eleanor responded. "In my twenties, I had a friend from the Netherlands. When she was pregnant, she used to drink a small glass of a Dutch liquor called Advocaat every night. It had egg yolk in it. It's supposed to be good for the baby and the pregnancy."

"It sounds awful," Ari said.

"True. But I drank a little wine, now and then, when I was pregnant, and my children turned out all right." Eleanor smiled mischievously, adding, "More or less all right." She stopped smiling and spoke in a serious tone. "Ari, I don't need to tell you that this is enormous. Not to be unpleasant, but many first-time pregnancies miscarry. Also, you know there are options. You don't need to have the baby of the man you do not love. This is very early in the pregnancy, and you could have an abortion—I would come with you. It could go that way. It's your decision. Give yourself some time to think about this from all angles. Don't panic."

"Sorry. I've already started panicking," Ari said. But she was no longer crying. "The sandwich was delicious, Gram."

"Thank you," Eleanor said. "Would you like a pickle to go with it? And some ice cream?"

"That's awful," Ari said, but she at last smiled.

They spent the rest of the evening watching a James Bond movie in the surety that no character in the movie would get pregnant. Ari thought she wouldn't be able to sleep, but when she snuggled into her bed, she fell asleep at once.

———

For the rest of the week, Ari was grateful that the never-ending chaos of Beach Camp kept her from dwelling on the pregnancy. Most nights she spoke with Beck, who was in Plymouth. He talked in general about the sort of work he did, the sense that people these days had what he called "free-floating anxiety," suddenly hit by an anxiety attack brought on by the world news or a friend's accident or simply by living in this curious world. Ari didn't tell Beck she had a very specific reason to be anxious.

Friday night, Cal and his cousins were having a cookout for the Beach Camp crew. Cal asked Ari to come and to please bring her grandmother. Ari wore a blue summer dress and Eleanor wore a lavender caftan, and they were both lighthearted as they drove toward Sunnydale Lane. It was a warm evening with clear skies and a light breeze. Sometimes Nantucket could seem like heaven, an idyllic island with soft sea air, magnanimous old trees creating patches of shade, rose-covered arbors over slate walkways to historic homes. On the way they passed a Jeep carrying a laughing family with their black Lab sticking his nose out the window to catch the breeze, and a father on a tandem bike, with his young son pedaling like crazy, the mother behind, pulling a child's bike trailer. Summer evenings on Nantucket were very much *I'll think about that tomorrow.*

"Ah," Eleanor said when they turned onto Sunnydale Lane, "a new person's street."

Newly built modest homes set among slender saplings planted to take away the naked look of the landscape. Most houses wore shingles that were golden instead of gray, meaning they were recently built, because all old Nantucket buildings, even if only a year old, had turned gray from the weather.

Three cars already filled the driveway and more cars were parked by the curb. Ari neatly angled hers between a van and a Jeep. As they walked toward the house, they heard laughter at the back. They went around the side of the house to the backyard.

Cal was standing at the grill, turning hot dogs and flipping burgers.

"Hi, Ari," Cal said. He handed the spatula to Sandy, who waved, and walked toward them. "Mrs. Sunderland," he said. "It's such a pleasure to meet you. Thank you so very much for the tees."

"Please call me Eleanor. And you're most welcome. I admire what you're doing."

"Well, it's exhausting, but it's fun. And Ari is a star. The children are crazy for her."

"They certainly are," Ari joked.

Sandy, pretty in pink, arrived. "Ari! Hi! And you must be Mrs. Sunderland. Gosh, we love the tees. You're so clever. Would you like a beer? Or a soda? Sparkling wine? They're over here in the cooler. Or what else would you prefer?"

Ari and her grandmother followed Sandy to the cooler, where Ari poured sparkling water into her plastic cup and poured wine into Eleanor's.

"Hello, Ari." The woman was older than Ari, but not by much, and she was enchanting.

It took Ari a moment to recognize Cleo without her balloon earrings and clothing, but she remembered just in time. "Oh, hi, Cleo."

"I work at Our Island Home."

"Yes, I remember."

"Sometimes people don't recognize me." Cleo came close so she could speak softly. "I think some people are afraid I'm going to check their pulse or stick them with a blood sugar monitor."

"I know," Ari replied soulfully. "That happens to me all the time, too."

Cleo laughed so loudly, others looked over at her.

Ari introduced Cleo to Eleanor. A large handsome man with a bushy red beard joined them.

"Ari, Eleanor, this is my husband, Scott."

Eleanor and Ari shook his massive paw.

"So," Eleanor asked, "is this where Cal lives?"

"It's where Poppy and I live," Cleo answered. "Cal lives in the apartment above the garage."

Scott added, "I stay here when I get a chance to come down from Boston."

"What do you do in Boston?" Eleanor asked.

"I'm a lawyer for an exceedingly boring firm," Scott said.

Before Ari could ask what firm, Cleo chirped up. "Tell her how we met, Scott. You guys, it's such a funny story."

Ari listened with a smile on her face as Scott described in detail how Cleo accidentally smashed her ice cream cone onto his best shirt at the Harvard Square Brigham's that doesn't exist anymore.

Poppy, Cleo and Cal's cousin, came over to say hello. This evening her glasses had pink frames, Ari noticed.

"Oh, what a detail to remember!" Poppy laughed. "Of course, you're young. My eyes are only slightly bad, for reading, and I tend to be a little absentminded—"

"A *little*?" Cleo teased.

"I accidentally leave them down the corner of the sofa or on the kitchen counter. You know how it is," Poppy admitted. "So I just buy in bulk and have them all over the house."

"Poppy's divorced," Cleo explained. "I think her husband couldn't stand all those glasses everywhere."

Poppy wasn't bothered by Cleo announcing that she was divorced. "I wouldn't be surprised if that was the reason," she agreed with a grin.

Some of the younger volunteers joined their group and introductions were made. Ari thought her grandmother must be overwhelmed by all the new names, but Eleanor seemed to be having a wonderful time. Soon the food was ready. They piled hamburgers, potato salad, and coleslaw on their plates and strolled over to sit at the several picnic tables. Eleanor and Ari sat at a table with Cal, Cleo, and Scott.

"Oh, delicious," Eleanor said. "There's nothing like a burger grilled outside."

"I'm glad you like it," Cal said.

"Thanks for asking us," Ari said. "It's fun talking with your cousins."

"Oh, they're all right," Cal said, knowing Cleo and Scott could overhear, "but a bit boring, I find."

"Come on!" Cleo said. "I jumped off the roof of the boathouse up at the lake and hit my head." Leaning forward, she pulled back her hair to show her scar. "Sixteen stitches!"

"I stand corrected," Cal said. "You're a daredevil."

"I'd have to be, to marry Scott," Cleo joked.

"Hey!" Scott objected.

"Where do you go after the summer?" Eleanor asked Cal.

"Back to divinity school," Cal replied.

Ari was surprised. "You're going to be a minister?"

"I got my master's in divinity at Yale, but next year I'm going down to a seminary in New York to become an interfaith minister."

"What does that mean?" Eleanor asked.

"It means I can marry two people who don't belong to the same religion. A Muslim to a Catholic. An atheist to a Jew. A woman to a woman. Like that."

"Good for you, Cal," Eleanor said. "We need more people like you."

What an interesting family, Ari thought as they continued talking while the evening grew cool. She was glad Eleanor was having a good time, talking and laughing. But her thoughts flickered back to Beck. They had a date for a movie with Hen this Saturday.

Also, Ari thought, with a pang of fear, she was pregnant.

Suddenly restless, she picked up her empty cup and walked over to the cooler full of ice and drinks. She knew she was having a minor panic attack. She'd had those before finals in college, and she wasn't surprised to be having one now. So many things of huge importance were coming at her this summer like a flock of birds, blocking out her view of the future. Would her parents divorce? Should she tell Peter about the baby? Should she have the baby? She strolled along the edge of the yard pretending to admire the dahlias and daisies as the night sky dimmed to lavender.

Poppy appeared at her side. "I know this isn't much of a garden. I'd love to plant some annuals, but we're only renting this house, and we need to focus our money on Beach Camp."

"Do you have a garden in Boston?" Ari asked.

"Well, I have container pots in all my windows, but I live in a condo, fourth floor, so I can't actually have a garden. I had one when I was married, but after the divorce, I needed a temporary home. That was three years ago . . ." Poppy shrugged.

"Temporary homes can be wonderful," Ari said. "I've lived on a campus for four years. Never had to mow the grass or shovel the snow."

"Where are you going to live now that you're out of college?" Poppy asked. "Do you have a job lined up?"

"I'm going to B.U. for a master's in childhood education," Ari said, pushing all thoughts of being pregnant out of her mind. "I'm not sure whether I'll stay at home or get an apartment of my own. Where do you work, Poppy? I mean other than running the camp office."

Poppy leaned close. "I'll tell you but you have to promise not to judge me. I'm an accountant. I do people's taxes."

"Wow. You obviously like numbers."

"Love them. Stick me in an office with a pile of forms and I'm happy all day."

Ari laughed. "You have such a great family."

"I think it's fortunate that we're all cousins. We don't carry the childhood resentments that siblings do."

"It's impressive that Cal's going to be a minister."

"I suppose. But he's not the old hellfire and damnation sort of pastor. Our family, from our great-grandparents on, have always been interested in what they used to call 'good works.'"

"That's why you run Beach Camp."

"Yes. Unfortunately, all the money our family once had has dwindled over the years and we can't do as much as we'd like, but we do what we can." Before Ari could answer, Poppy laughed. "Oh, Lord, now I sound absolutely puritanical. Maybe I should talk about my sex life. Or Cal's."

Ari gazed down into her drink. "That's not my favorite subject these days."

"Oh?" Poppy said.

For a moment, Ari wanted to confide in this smart, kind young woman about her pregnancy, but no, Ari wasn't ready yet. "I just broke off with my fiancé," Ari said.

"Oh, dear. Is he heartbroken?"

Ari snorted. "He's certainly angry."

She was glad when Sandy came up to them, offering them plates of blueberry cheesecake. "Do either of you want coffee?" she asked.

"Thanks, Sandy, but I'm fine without it," Ari said.

"I don't need any, either, but thanks, Sandy," Poppy said. She turned back to Ari. "What are you doing with your weekend?"

"I'm spending time with friends," Ari told her, thinking of Beck and Hen.

Ari saw Eleanor approach.

"I hate to say this, Ari, but I'm beginning to fade."

The two women said goodbye to everyone and walked around the side of the house to Ari's car.

"I'm sorry to drag you away from the party," Eleanor said as they sat in the car, buckling their seatbelts.

"Did you have fun?"

"Yes, very much. I admire the Marshalls and their benevolence. They were interesting and fun, and even if Cal is a minister, he's not all pious and preachy."

"I agree," Ari said. She slid her car from between two other cars and began the drive back home.

Eleanor shifted in her seat to face Ari. "I'm grateful to be invited there. I don't get the opportunity to be around young people very often."

"We'll do it again," Ari promised.

"We should have them out to the house for our own cookout," Eleanor said. She leaned against the side of the door, pleasantly tired. "We'll invite them, and also I'll ask Silas and you can ask Beck."

"I've got to deal with a few other things first," Ari murmured.

Fourteen

The weekend went by too fast. Saturday was so much fun, seeing the movie with Hen and Beck, going for ice cream afterward, strolling around town people-watching. Ari was disappointed when Beck said he had to return to Plymouth for an emergency on Sunday, but he promised to call. Sunday it rained, and Ari was glad. She slept late, caught up on laundry and emails to friends, and made lobster macaroni and cheese for herself and Eleanor. As if by tacit agreement, they didn't talk about Ari's pregnancy or her father's affair.

At camp Monday morning, Ari had trouble concentrating. As she played water volleyball with the children, she was entranced by their silliness, their giggles, their whoops—their sheer pleasure in being alive. Each child, pale or dark or freckled, was beautiful, and Ari couldn't help wondering what her child would be like. Then she'd remind herself that the baby was Peter's, too, and she had to talk to him, and she had to talk to her mother about her father, and it was all so impossibly difficult she almost cried.

That evening, when she returned home from the camp, she told Eleanor she wouldn't have dinner. She needed to sleep. She fell into bed at six o'clock and didn't wake up for twelve hours. Her hair was

still sticky from yesterday's sandy water and she was wearing yesterday's clothes. It seemed to take all the energy she possessed to force
herself into the shower.

When, teeth brushed, hair washed, clothes fresh, Ari walked into
the kitchen, she found Eleanor there.

Ari managed to smile. "I'm sorry about last night."

"Nonsense." Eleanor handed Ari a go-cup of hot ginger tea and
a cinnamon bun wrapped in a napkin. "Tonight we're going to
Madaket to get takeout from Millie's and walk on the beach."

Surprised, Ari laughed. "Great idea, Gram. But what brought this
on?"

"I haven't seen the other end of the island for weeks."

Ari laughed. "You make it sound as if Madaket is miles away."

"Well, it is."

"Yeah, not even ten," Ari scoffed, but she smiled as she left the
house.

Ari drove home after camp. Her grandmother wanted to drive her
Range Rover and Ari wanted to fetch a sweater in case it got breezy.

"Here you are!" Eleanor was waiting by the open hatch of her car.
"I've put a bottle of lemonade in ice in the cooler. I've wrapped the
glasses in towels—it spoils the taste to drink lemonade out of paper
cups."

"You're the best," Ari said. She ran through the house to get a
sweater, left the house, and jumped into the Rover.

"Perfect evening," Eleanor said as she drove.

"Yes," Ari agreed, biting her tongue so she wouldn't say that actually it wasn't perfect for her.

They passed the golf course, Sesachacha Pond, houses grand and
modest, and all of the land bursting with green. Eleanor looked over
at Ari, who was relaxing against the window.

"How was your day?" Eleanor asked.

"Wonderful and exhausting," Ari said. "I love those children, but
I can't imagine how anyone has enough energy to be a mother
twenty-four seven."

"Most mothers don't have fifteen children," Eleanor reminded her.

"How's Silas?" Ari asked.

"He's fine." Eleanor smiled. "We went to lunch in town today and to a lecture at the library about whales and sharks and other things hiding down in the watery depths. Did you know that killer whales don't kill people? They kill other whales. Terrible creatures, actually, they prey on baby whales. And they're so cute with their black-and-white skins. Or is it hides? What is it with sea creatures?"

"I know whales are mammals because they have live births," Ari said. Oh, no, she secretly moaned, would her every thought be about birth?

They went through the residential area of town and turned onto Madaket Road. As they passed Crooked Lane, the street leading to the animal hospital, a blue convertible with a man at the steering wheel and a young woman in the passenger seat approached the intersection and stopped at the sign.

"Gram!" Ari cried. "I think that was Dad in the car!"

"I know." Looking in her rearview mirror, Eleanor saw the convertible turn toward town. Without hesitation, Eleanor braked, turned into the first empty driveway, did a pivot turn, and sped to catch up with the car.

Ari clutched her seatbelt. "Gram, wait, what are you doing?"

"I want to be certain I saw what I think I did." Eleanor's hands were clutched tightly on the wheel.

"If that really is Dad," Ari said, her voice trembling, "what are you going to do?"

"I don't know yet. I haven't had a chance to think it through. Don't worry, I won't cause a scene."

They followed the blue convertible as it wound through the narrow village lanes out past the Stop & Shop and onto Fairgrounds Road. The convertible turned onto Dionis Beach Road. Eleanor did, too, keeping her distance. She didn't want her son-in-law to spot her, and Phillip knew her car well, although the island was packed with Range Rovers.

"There," Ari said.

The blue convertible pulled into the drive of a sweet little Cape with blue shutters, a blue door, and window boxes spilling with pansies.

Eleanor brought her car to a stop at the end of the block, in the shade of an old maple tree. She turned off the engine, wanting to focus on the convertible and its occupants.

The man got out of the car, came around to the passenger side, and opened the door. The young woman smiled up at him as she stepped out. The woman wore a pink sundress. The man wore colorful board shorts and a navy blue polo shirt.

"It's Dad," Ari said.

"I never would have believed Phillip would wear board shorts," Eleanor said.

"What should we do?" Ari asked in a whisper. Her forehead was cold. The world was just a bit blurry.

Eleanor moved her hands from the steering wheel and put them in her lap. "First, let's take a deep breath. I need a few moments to make sense of what I saw."

Ari was fiery. "I know absolutely what I saw! I don't have to *think* about it! Grandmother, my father is messing around with another woman!"

Eleanor met Ari's eyes. "Why do you think that is?"

"*What?*" Tears rolled down Ari's face. "Grandmother, my mother is your daughter! Shouldn't you protect her? Why are you siding with my father?"

Eleanor reached out and touched Ari's cheek. "Sweetheart, I'm not siding with anyone. I do want to protect Alicia. I know very well she's my daughter, which is why I need some time to think about the best thing to do."

Ari sagged in her seat. In a small voice, she said, "I can't imagine that there even is a best thing to do."

"Let's think," Eleanor said. "Let's head back to Madaket and have tacos and lemonade on the beach. Looking at the ocean can be very helpful in times like this."

"How many times like this does a person have in her life?" Ari inquired.

"You'd be surprised," Eleanor said, steering the car to Madaket.

In the summer, the sun stayed high in the sky, beaming down slanted rays that made the sea splash with violet and silver. They ate the tacos—Ari was amazed at how hungry she was—and sipped the tart lemonade. They tucked away the paper holding the crumbs of food so the gulls wouldn't dive-bomb them for their own dinners. They walked side by side, a long way down the shore. Ari spotted colorful shells, picked them up, then flung them into the ocean.

Not until they about-faced to walk back to their spot did they speak.

Eleanor said, "Your father is a good man, Ari. Your mother is difficult. I know. She's my child. She was the sweetest little girl when she was young. We adored each other. As she got into her teenage years, though, she began to be angered by me, by everything that I said or did. Somehow we grew apart. I know it's normal for adolescents to disdain their parents, but usually when they're older, they become friends again. That didn't happen for us, although once you were born, we were closer."

"What about Mom and Dad?"

"Your father and I always got along. But if you mean how *they* were . . . your father was in med school and always studying and then working at the hospital and then starting his private practice. His family was very formal, starchy, and oddly your mother adored them. Phillip's mother, Emily, was the consummate do-gooder. She ran two or three volunteer organizations, and Alicia became involved." Eleanor stopped walking and gazed out at the ocean.

"Alicia made no secret that she preferred Phillip's mother to me. She became Emily's lieutenant for her organizations. She copied Emily in small but significant ways. Alicia had never been a good student. She always seemed to be content to get by with her good looks. But after she married, she became so . . . organized. She bought a briefcase like the one Emily carried, with a daily diary and color-coded folders for her appointments. She imitated Emily's manner of dressing. They both wore gold circle earrings, small, but heavy. Alicia began sitting with her legs together, angled to the side, like Kate Middleton." Eleanor laughed. "Oh, dear, listen to me rambling on this way."

"No, don't stop, Gram," Ari begged. "I love listening to you."

"The thing is, Ari . . ." Eleanor cleared her throat and gave herself a moment to choose her words. "My daughter was so loving as a child. But as she grew up, especially after she married Phillip, she became cold to me. I've never figured out why. When Emily died a few years ago, Alicia was desolate."

"I remember," Ari said softly. "I was sorry Emily died, but the truth? I always thought she was cold. I never had fun with her like I do with you. It seems her only words to me were, like, 'Sit straight,' 'Don't play with your hair,' 'Your skirt is too short.'"

Eleanor chuckled. "She was a bit of a harridan."

"She never wanted me to sit on her lap when I was little. It wrinkled her clothes. You always wanted to hold me."

Eleanor paced a few steps in silence. Then, looking straight ahead, she said, "So maybe we should give your father a break."

"I don't understand," Ari said, but in a way, she did. Her mother was not a natural hugger, toucher, kisser. Alicia was strict and fussy about how things looked. Still, Ari didn't want to hear her grandmother criticize her own daughter, especially when Ari might make her own mother into a grandmother. It was too confusing. It made her head hurt. "Please can we not talk about my parents and sex."

Eleanor said, "Of course."

Gathering their picnic blanket and basket, they walked back to the car. It was tough going, walking through heavy sand up a dune. Eleanor was too winded to talk. They rode home absorbed in their own thoughts.

Once inside, with the picnic things cleaned and cleared away, Eleanor said, "I think we should call your mother and invite her down for the weekend."

Ari groaned. "Mom will freak out. She'll go mental."

"Do you think we should do nothing, then? Keep it our secret? Perhaps ask your father?"

Ari shuddered. "I hate him. I never want to speak to him again."

"Sometimes . . ." Eleanor paused, considering her words. "Sometimes it's good to let things play out, and then, after a while, they just go away."

"No. No! He's cheating. That's absolutely gruesome." Ari burst into tears. She wiped them from her face, tossed her head, and said, "Okay, let's. After all, my parents usually come for most weekends in the summer. They didn't come last weekend."

They flipped a coin to see who would make the call to Alicia.

Eleanor won.

"Hi, Mom!" Ari said cheerfully when her mother answered the phone they had set to speaker.

"Hi, Ari. Are you having a good time?"

"Yes, it's all grand. I love the camp. The kids are adorable. Listen, Gram and I want you to come down and stay here for a girls'-only weekend. Maybe next weekend, if you're free."

Alicia was quiet for a long time. When she spoke, she nearly knocked Ari off her feet.

"Are you pregnant?"

"What? No! Don't be ridiculous! You always come down on summer weekends. Gram and I just want to spend some time with you."

"Why don't you want Dad to come?"

Ari huffed. Every conversation with her mother turned into a battle. "Because it's a *girls'* weekend. I don't see Dad wanting to stroll Main Street, trying on clothes with us."

"No, something's up. Tell me."

Ari looked helplessly at her grandmother. Eleanor took the phone.

"Alicia, my dear, you are always so perceptive. We do want to talk with you about something, but not over the phone." When Alicia didn't answer right away, Eleanor said, "It might involve the house."

Ari watched Eleanor's face, which softened into a smile. "Good, darling. Let us know when you can come and we'll meet your boat."

"Poor Mom," Ari said as her grandmother ended the call.

"I know," Eleanor said. She sighed. "If you don't mind, I'm going to retire for the evening. I have some favorite television shows to catch up with."

"Enjoy. I'll see you in the morning." Ari kissed her grandmother's cheek.

The week passed slowly. Ari forgot her worries when she played with the children at Beach Camp, and by evening, she was too tired to go out with friends. Beck called her every night, and they talked for hours, about their families, their pasts, their friends, and their plans for the future. Ari was torn. The sound of his voice made her feel so warm inside. She knew they were becoming attached to one another. She sensed that, for her, Beck was *the one*. But here she was, pregnant with another man's child, and she couldn't tell him. Not yet.

First, she had to talk to Peter. Summoning her courage, she called his cell number, which was still stored in her phone. It went to voicemail.

"Peter? It's Ari. Please call me. I need to see you. We need to discuss something important."

All she could do now was wait for him to return her call.

The fuzzy yellow tennis ball came rocketing over the net toward Ari. Ari gently tapped it back. It fell just over the net, and Beck, even with his long, quick, athletic body, couldn't get to it in time. She laughed, and Beck laughed, too.

"Game," he called. "I thought you hadn't played tennis in months."

"Oh, that was just luck," Ari told him.

Beck met her at the net to shake hands. They left the court to go to the brick patio. Ari collapsed at one of the tables, grateful that the staff had raised the umbrella and tilted it to provide maximum shade.

"Wow," Beck said as he pulled out the chair and sat across from her, "you're a clever player."

"Well," she rejoined, flirting, "I'm a clever woman."

The waitress, a lovely girl named Annette who came from St. Louis and was majoring in hospitality, came to take their orders. Drinks were an iced coffee for Beck, an Anchorage for Ari. Ordering gave her a chance to wonder why she felt so attracted to Beck. True, he was six two, had floppy blond hair and those amazing robin's-egg blue eyes, and he was broad shouldered and as handsome as—who was that poet? George Gordon Byron—Lord Byron. Ari resisted the urge to google him on her phone and compare the two. Okay, so Beck was gorgeous, and he was kind and funny, but how could she feel so much desire for him when she was pregnant with another man's child?

"What's Michelle up to?" Ari asked Beck.

"She's sailing today with some friends. Her fiancé, Brendon, and I think you know Dan and Filly."

Ari sipped her drink.

"Where's Eleanor?" Beck asked.

They talked about Eleanor, who was going to a party with Silas. Beck talked about his parents, who went to church religiously, a little laugh here. "We're all— I mean my parents, Michelle, Hen, and I are going to a croquet party this evening."

"Croquet!" Ari was amused. "I haven't played since I was a child. It still conjures up images for me of ladies with enormous hats and long skirts."

"And men wearing white flannels and straw boaters trimmed with a grosgrain ribbon." Beck leaned forward. "I'd rather spend this evening with you, but these are my godparents, so it's kind of an obligation."

"Oh, sure," Ari said lightly. He'd rather spend the evening with her? She couldn't stop smiling.

Beck read the meaning in her smile. "Maybe next time I'll be able to take you."

They gazed at each other, allowing the moment to last, caught in a glow of realization. They were becoming a couple. They were falling in love.

The waitress came by. "Is there something wrong with your meals?"

The moment was broken. "No, they're delicious," Beck told her.

He and Ari dutifully returned to their lunches, but Ari felt Beck nudge her foot with his own, under the table.

"Beck," she said, leaning back in her chair, "tell me about being a therapist."

"Ah." Beck's face grew serious. "I don't want to bore you."

"You won't bore me. Really, I'd like to know."

Beck sat very still for a moment. "You understand I can't talk about my patients."

"Of course."

"Okay. Well, on my part, what *I* do, what I've been trained to do, sounds really simple, but it's not. I'm a cognitive behavioral therapist. That sounds complicated, but one of the things I do is listen. Just listen. Don't smile—it's not that easy. Let's say I told you my grandmother just died. How would you react? Most people would say, 'I'm so sorry. I loved my grandmother, too,' and they'd talk about their grandmother. *I* ask them questions about their grandmother. I let them grieve."

"I see what you mean," Ari said.

"People need to be listened to. They need to be taken seriously. The process of venting is important. But it's not only that. I'm trained to catch the trouble spots, the signs that someone might need medication—"

"Can you prescribe medication?"

"No. But I can recommend that a patient see a psychiatrist for meds, while I continue the talk therapy. I can sort of listen between the lines. I can spot something significant bubbling up that the patient is trying to avoid. A lot of my patients see me short-term, when something like a divorce is taking place. Or a loved one died on an ordinary day in an accident. Others might be dealing with an old trauma that they've never discussed because they're ashamed, and getting it out into the light of day is a kind of healing."

"Wow," Ari said softly, impressed. "How do you deal with all the sadness and anger that you meet every day?"

"Do you mean how do I take care of myself emotionally?" Beck's voice lightened. "I go to the gym. I work out, and if the weather's good, I run. I hike. Hiking somewhere new is my best therapy for myself." With a crooked grin, he added, "Also, playing tennis. I need to play a lot of tennis with you."

"I'm up for that," Ari told him. "And I won't bill you for therapy."

After lunch, Beck walked Ari to her car in the parking lot. Cars were all around them, people slamming doors, yelling greetings, carrying tennis rackets and life jackets.

"This isn't the time or the place," Beck told Ari. "But I hate it like crazy that I won't see you tonight. I agreed to this family thing months ago."

Ari leaned against her car. Beck stood only a few inches from her. She longed to put her hands on his chest, to rise up on her toes and kiss him. "I understand. We have lots of time."

"I hope we have all the time in the world," Beck said.

Then, surprising her, he pulled her to him, bent down, and kissed her mouth firmly, right out there in the sunlight.

Ari was breathless.

"I had to do that," Beck told her. "And I'm going to do that again the next time we meet."

Ari felt as if she were absolutely glowing as she sank into her car. She waved at Beck and drove out onto the street, and she couldn't stop smiling.

Fifteen

Sunday morning, they agreed that Ari should pick Alicia up at the ferry while Eleanor waited at home. Alicia looked as cool as ice as she stepped off the ferry in her clamdiggers and striped linen sweater. Ari kissed her cheek and led her to the car, gathered her mother's luggage, and put it in the back. Her mother was aloof, as if waiting for something terrible to confront her, so Ari babbled about her Beach Camp job as they rode back to the house on the cliff. Her mother pretended to listen. Alicia wouldn't force her daughter to tell her what this important talk was about without Eleanor there.

The day was overcast, threatening rain, and windy, so Eleanor had made a small fire in the living room fireplace, where it glittered and gleamed like a casket of topaz. She'd prepared crackers and cheese, as well as her blueberry muffins, with sugar liberally sprinkled on the tops. When Alicia arrived, Eleanor rose from the sofa and welcomed her with a hug, which her daughter coolly returned.

"Mom," Alicia said. "I'm going crazy. Could you tell me?"

"Let's sit down." Eleanor had dressed in slacks and an old, familiar wool sweater.

Alicia sat, keeping an eye on Eleanor as if her mother could vanish at will.

Ari, in jeans and an old Bucknell sweatshirt, sat next to her mother.

"Now." Alicia's back was ramrod straight. "Tell me."

"Yes, of course," Eleanor said. "And we're sorry. I'm not even sure this is the right course of action."

"Mother, tell me." Alicia held back her anger.

"Ari and I have reason to believe that Phil is having an affair with a young woman on the island."

Alicia sat very still, not reacting. She cleared her throat. Calmly, she said, "You have reason to believe? What does that mean?"

Ari spoke up. "It means I have seen Dad with a young woman several times here on the island. I think Dad's having an affair."

Ari's mother's face became very pink. She put her hand over her eyes for a brief moment. "That is possible. There have been some nights when Phil hasn't come home. I let myself believe he was at the hospital. When we were very young, newly married, he used to sleep at the hospital." Her voice was trembling, but no tears appeared. "You know, Mother, this is your fault."

"*My* fault?" Eleanor's eyes widened. "How in the world do you get to that conclusion?"

Alicia said quietly, "You were such an irresponsible mother. You didn't give me proper guidance."

Eleanor said, "I don't understand."

Alicia looked agonized as she tried to explain. "I wanted to be a little princess, like Daddy thought I was. I wanted to be . . . precious, protected. You allowed me to have a Barbie doll so I thought that was how women looked. You never made us stop watching TV when we were teenagers so I didn't do well in my classes. You let Cliff have a dirt bike and he ended up with a cracked rib. You were like the Queen of Free Love. Your curfew on the island was midnight, and you didn't even enforce that. You let me run free. You told me I should marry whomever I chose."

"Not when you were fifteen, I didn't," Eleanor clarified.

Alicia cried, "You insisted I attend a coed college instead of Smith because, you said, it's more fun if boys are around. You said I should marry the man that makes me dizzy with love!"

"I'm completely lost," Eleanor said quietly.

"You were always, like, *ecstatic* if I brought a boy home to dinner, especially if he had a motorcycle and a dragon tattoo. But I was too scared to sleep with anyone, and then I met Phillip. Phillip made me feel safe. He treated me gently. And *you* thought he was boring!"

"I never said Phillip was boring," Eleanor said. She smiled, just a little. "Although, he is boring."

Alicia cried, "You see! I'm not what you wanted in a daughter. You wanted Janis Joplin and you got Jane Austen. You let us go to concerts where there were all kinds of drugs and slimy people. You were so cool, so lenient." Alicia fell back onto the sofa, tears exploding from her eyes, sobs wrenching her body. "Phillip isn't boring," she said. "*I'm* boring. That's why he's having an affair."

"Oh, my dear," Eleanor said. "I'm afraid I was trying to be a better mother than my mother was to me. My mother was a strict authoritarian. She had rules for everything. How to hold a fork. When to speak to an adult. Why I needed to improve my posture. I couldn't even seem to breathe correctly for her. She was mean. She made me feel trapped. I wanted to be a *happy* mother, a friend to you. I went through my life feeling like a disappointment to my mother. I wanted you to enjoy being with me."

Alicia wiped her face and calmed down. "You must have hated it when I loved Phillip's mother so much."

"I did," Eleanor said. "I still do."

"I'm going to make some cocoa," Ari said. She wanted to leave the room to let her mother and grandmother have some privacy, and because she needed to think her own thoughts. This would not be a good time to tell her mother she was pregnant.

But when she returned to the kitchen, she found that her mother's emotions had moved from sorrow to anger.

"Who is she?" Alicia asked Eleanor. "Is she an island girl?"

"We don't know who she is," Eleanor told her daughter. "She has a blue convertible. She lives on Dionis Beach Road."

Alicia whipped around to face Ari. "You saw her. Who is she?"

"Mom, I don't know her name. She's young, not as young as I am, but young—"

"Younger than I am, right?" Alicia ignored the cocoa. She rose and stalked over to the window, looking out at the sea and the gray sky.

Ari set the tray of cocoa on the coffee table. Eleanor gave Ari a slight nod as she took her mug. They had done what was necessary, and it was terrible. But they weren't the ones who had betrayed Alicia.

"Maybe you should call him, Mom," Ari suggested. "Maybe call and tell him you're on the island and you'd like to see him."

When Alicia turned from the window, her face was composed again, although her carefully blushed cheeks were tracked with tears. She was quieter now, and somehow shut off, somehow emotionally shielded. She returned to the sofa, picked up her cocoa, and sipped.

Ari and her grandmother waited.

"I'm not going to call him," Alicia announced. "I'm going on a trip."

"What?" Ari asked.

"Where?" Eleanor asked.

"I don't have to tell you." Alicia had regained her poise and slipped into her Queen of England mode. "I'm going on a fabulous trip. I'm going first-class. I'll be gone for weeks."

"Mom," Ari began.

Alicia arched an eyebrow and sweetened her voice, which meant she was totally furious. "Why shouldn't I go on a trip? My own mother won't discuss selling this rattrap of a house so that I can enjoy life. No, she sits here with millions spread around her and doesn't think of me. My husband is enjoying life with another woman and my daughter prefers to live with her grandmother. Where am I in this family? Who respects me? Who cares for me?"

"My darling," Eleanor said quietly, "don't make any quick decisions that you'll regret."

"Why not?" Alicia asked. "Everyone else does."

"Mom," Ari cried. "We love you!"

"I don't want to be with you," Alicia replied. "I don't want to be with any of you."

Ari was shocked. "But what if there's an emergency?"

"You're an adult," Alicia said coldly. "I'm going to use the bathroom and then I'll call a taxi." She went out of the living room and down the hall.

"Wow. I didn't see that coming," Ari said to her grandmother.

Eleanor smiled. "I didn't, either. But you know, I hope she goes through with this plan. It will do her a world of good and give Phillip the slap in the face he deserves."

"But what about me?" Ari whispered.

"How helpful do you think your mother would be, especially now?" Eleanor asked gently.

Ari smiled ruefully. "She wouldn't greet my news with cries of joy."

"Nor would she be delighted to know she would be called 'Gram.'"

Ari closed her eyes and leaned back against the sofa. It was almost a pleasure to focus on her father's affair. It took her mind off her own problem. She wasn't prepared to be a mother yet, not emotionally or practically. For a moment, she thought she was going to throw up again, right in the living room.

"Hey-ho!" a man called. The screen door slammed shut and Cliff strode into the living room. In his tennis whites, his skin tanned and blushed from the sun, his shoulders wide, his smile brilliant, he looked like the very model of a healthy, happy man.

"Uncle Cliff!" Ari said, shocked.

"Cliff? What are you doing here?" Eleanor asked.

Cliff looked affronted. "Excuse me. Do I have the wrong house? You do resemble my mother. I usually stop by on the weekends."

"Uncle Cliff," Ari cried, "we've got a terrible problem."

"Really?" Cliff asked, eyebrows arched.

Alicia returned to the living room. Her face was again perfectly blushed, her mascara darkened. "What are you doing here?" she asked Cliff.

"What are *you* doing here?" Cliff shot back. "Where's Phillip?"

"Probably with his girlfriend," Alicia said.

"What?" Cliff asked.

"My father's been seeing a woman on the island," Ari told him quietly.

"You mean, like playing tennis?"

"No," Alicia said. "They've seen him go into her house."

"Have you called him?" Cliff asked.

"Why, no," Alicia said sarcastically. "That never occurred to me." Her shoulders slumped. "Whenever I have tried to call Phillip, I only get voicemail. I haven't seen much of him this summer. He said he was working."

Cliff's pose of hail-fellow-well-met evaporated. He went pale. "That jerk!" Blinking, he looked at Ari and at his mother and back at Alicia. "What are you going to do?"

"I'm going on a trip," Alicia said. She was beginning to cry again.

Ari wept, too. Her mother hated being embarrassed. She always tried to look perfect, and now she stood before them shaking, with tears running down her cheeks, streaking her mascara, her shoulders slumped, nearly falling to the floor in her misery. Ari started to go to her mother, to hug her.

Cliff crossed the room. He pulled his sister to him, hugging her tightly, her face nestled against his chest, as if protecting her from the rest of the world.

"You know, Leeci," he murmured, "it's not the end of the world. Men do stupid things like this all the time."

Ari and Eleanor stared at each other wide-eyed. They'd never heard Cliff call his sister by a nickname before. They'd never seen him so tender before. With the age difference between them, Alicia had considered him a pest. In the past few years, when the family got together, Alicia was haughty and Cliff was devil-may-care. But they were adults now, and clearly they cared for each other.

"Listen," Cliff said to Alicia, "I'm taking you up to Boston to my apartment. We'll get drunk. I'll make some diplomatic inquiries and find out what the bastard is up to."

Alicia sniffed back her tears. "I want to go on a trip," she said, sounding like a child.

"Well, we'll go on a trip! First stop, Boston," Cliff said. "Come on, kiddo." He kept his arm around his sister's shoulders as he led her to the door.

Astonished, Ari and Eleanor watched them go.

"I always thought Mom disliked Uncle Cliff," Ari said, trying to puzzle it all out.

Eleanor spoke slowly, thinking it through. "Even when they were children, I never thought they were close. I do think Cliff idolized her when he was little. His sophisticated big sister."

"Maybe he's been waiting all his life to be her hero," Ari said.

"Yes," Eleanor agreed. "I think you just may be right."

"Let's go for a walk," Ari suggested.

"Yes, let's," Eleanor agreed.

The rest of the day they spent quietly, struggling with their own thoughts and emotions. That night they ate sandwiches and went to bed early. From her bedroom, Ari heard the sounds of *Masterpiece*. She was glad her grandmother had something elegant to soothe her thoughts and let her escape from reality for just a while. Ari googled topics about pregnancy and Planned Parenthood until her head swam and her wrists ached. She was exhausted. She'd never been so glad to fall asleep before in her life.

Sixteen

Monday, Beach Camp was fun, as always, but after the children left, Cal asked if he could talk with Ari privately.

"Sure," she said. They were in the community school building. Sandy and all the young volunteers had left.

"Let's just sit here," Cal said, sitting on one of the small round tables.

"Okay." She perched on the table facing him.

"I have an enormous favor to ask you. Please feel free to say no."

"Well, that's intriguing," Ari said.

"I always check the forecast at the first of the week. It looks like we're in for four solid days of rain."

"Okay. Sounds challenging." Ari knew how this happened during the summer, and she'd always felt so sorry for vacationing families who couldn't go to the beach, where the sand was soggy and the windy air cold.

"Exactly." Cal cleared his throat. "There are other camps, too, and they'll be going to the library and the museums, any place inside, and it will be a squirrel cage. So I wondered . . . someone told me your grandmother has a big house with three floors. I was hoping we could have a scavenger hunt there."

"Oh." Ari was stunned. It took a moment for her to process his ask. "Wait," she said, holding up her hand. "Let me think."

Quickly she envisioned her grandmother's house. It was large, and if you counted the attic, there *were* three floors. Fifteen children could roam up the front stairs and down the back stairs. Somehow they could shut off Eleanor's bedroom. Ari's, too. Those rooms were too personal for strangers.

Then she thought of the children. All those children, all day in the rain. On the one hand, she understood. Poppy's house was too small for a scavenger hunt for the camp.

On the other hand, it was a weird thought: fifteen children, maybe a volunteer, and Sandy and Cal, all relative strangers, roaming her grandmother's house. It was too intimate, too invasive.

"I don't know," Ari answered. "I need to ask my grandmother."

"Thanks for even considering this, Ari," Cal said. Leaning in, he hugged her—quickly, but firmly. She could smell summer on his neck and a faint trace of raspberry juice from their afternoon snack.

Ari worried about Cal's request as she drove home, and she worried about her mother and father, and she worried terribly about talking with Peter.

"Hello!" she called, walking in through the kitchen door. The delicious aroma of beef stew stopped her in her tracks. It was, she thought, the best part of this unnerving day.

"Hello, darling," Eleanor called back. "I'm in the living room. I made a stew. Look at the clouds. A storm is coming."

Ari kissed the top of her grandmother's head. "I'm going to take a shower, then I'll set the table. The stew smells heavenly."

Over dinner, Ari discussed Cal's request with her grandmother.

To Ari's surprise, Eleanor said, "Yes, why not? Not the attic, though. It's already too disordered and chaotic. Children would get lost in there and never find their way out. Also, as you said, not my bedroom or yours or my sewing room. But we've got two guest rooms and a bathroom with a hamper and that old painted standing cupboard. Shadow likes to hide in there. He knows how to open the door. We'll have to shut Shadow up in my room or he'll be terrified. How about the basement? It's got my exercise room and equipment."

"You're fabulous," Ari said.

"The house is fabulous," Eleanor told her. "It has seen many parties during its life. I think it will be glad to see one again."

At Beach Camp the next day, Ari told Cal her grandmother had given them the okay.

"That's great!" Cal said, spontaneously hugging Ari as gray clouds rolled into the blue sky.

Wednesday dawned cold and windy, with a sky threatening rain. They managed to give the kids some outdoor time in the morning, but by noon the rain was beginning. They had games organized in the community school room, and jumping jacks and other fun exercises to loud music. But Thursday the rain came down in buckets, hurled sideways by a howling wind, and by late afternoon, the children were antsy from being indoors. They drove them in the two minivans to the library, but another camp van was parked right in front of it. The foyer of the Whaling Museum was lined with adults and children trying to buy passes. Finally, they drove out to the Shipwreck and Lifesaving Museum, which was fascinating but small. Some of the children were too young to appreciate the roped-off ancient rowboats and fought to watch the video of the *Andrea Doria* sinking.

"Thank God we'll have your house for them to stretch out in tomorrow," Cal whispered to Ari.

Ari nodded uncertainly.

That evening, at seven-thirty, a knock came at the door. Eleanor had been informed that Cal and Sandy wanted to come over to hide the items for the scavenger hunt so they wouldn't have to do it in the very early morning.

Cal had showered and changed from his wet camp clothes and looked handsome in a pair of khakis and a blue shirt.

"Nice to see you, Mrs. Sunderland," he said, shaking Eleanor's hand. "It is awfully good of you to allow us to entertain the children here."

Sandy smiled and thanked Eleanor when Eleanor offered her hand.

"We've made maps of fifteen places which my grandmother and I think will make good hiding places," Ari said.

Eleanor handed out the maps and walked through the house with Cal and Sandy to show them exactly what she meant, in the second-floor guest bedroom, in the crowded closet, behind the muddle of deck shoes and waders. Beneath the bed. Behind the bureau, hanging from the wood filigree surrounding the mirror attached to the bureau.

The other second-floor guest bedroom was still reserved for Cliff, who insisted that one day he'd clear it all out. It was crammed with his tennis and sailing trophies, his stacks of CDs, spy novels, and old cameras, including a Polaroid from the high school days when he thought he'd be a photographer. On his desk were a massive computer and boxes of floppy discs, and boxes, *boxes,* of love letters from girlfriends and not-quite-pornographic photos of those girlfriends tucked into a manila envelope—Eleanor picked that up and took it to her off-limits room. Cliff's closet was hung with Nantucket red trousers in several sizes, and navy blue blazers he'd outgrown, and a sword— "A sword? Where did that come from?" Eleanor asked as she carried it out of the room and put it high on a shelf where no small hands could reach. Cliff had also saved stacks of magazines: *Nantucket Today, GQ, Esquire, Sailing.* Burgees and pennants covered one wall. Another wall was lined with shelves holding high school and college albums and photo albums and plastic boxes filled with tennis balls and a life vest that hadn't fit him since he was ten.

"Maybe he's planning to marry eventually and have children," Eleanor mused.

"Well," Ari whispered, "he's almost forty, so he'd better get busy."

Cal and Sandy found more hiding places: inside an Indiana Jones leather hat lying upside down on a shelf, in a pottery pencil holder Cliff made in sixth grade (why had he kept that?), boxes of old clothes meant to be taken to the dump someday.

Next, they went through the main level hiding objects—inexpensive items like Slinkies, yo-yos, plastic mermaids and ogres, small boxes of Play-Doh, a ball and jacks, a rope bracelet, a bag of marbles.

When they were done, Eleanor asked, "Would you like to sit down a moment and have a drink? Lemonade? Wine?"

"Yes," Sandy said. "Please."

"I'll bring some lemonade," Ari told them.

In the kitchen, she filled four glasses with ice and lemonade, set them on a tray, and headed to the living room. Just at that moment, her cellphone, tucked into her pocket, trilled. She'd turned the volume up in case Eleanor needed her when Ari was at camp. Now she sent the call to voicemail. Peter's voice roared from the phone.

"Ari, you're out of your mind. But fine, come up to Cambridge. I'll meet you for lunch Saturday at the Coffee House. You're paying."

Ari's heart kicked so hard she nearly dropped the tray. Forcing a smile, she set the glasses on the table, pretending she hadn't heard Peter's message. Eleanor continued to smile serenely.

Ari sat with them and took part in the conversation about the camp and each of the children.

"Fifteen children, and fifteen prizes," Cal said. "We'd like to give them an hour to search. Then we'd like to sit in a circle on the living room floor and talk about sharing, so that eventually every child will have something, even if he hasn't found anything."

"So wise," Eleanor said. "I will have lunch waiting for them. Probably mac and cheese and carrot sticks."

The next day, Cal and Sandy arrived at the house on the bluff with the excited children. The group entered the house through the mudroom, where they shed their raincoats and boots, then went into the kitchen and on into the living room, where Eleanor and Ari greeted them. Ari introduced her grandmother, who addressed the camp.

"Hello, children," Eleanor said. "Please sit in a circle on the floor so we can tell you how to begin the game."

As she spoke, she handed out small brown paper bags, in case they found two or more prizes. Ari hid a smile, thinking how cleverly her grandmother had dressed, with several strands of glittering beads and an enormous diamond brooch. Many of the children were slack-jawed at the sight of the room with its fireplace and owl andirons and the mantel with the old marble clock and heavy silver candlesticks. Ari and Eleanor had removed anything breakable. Still, the heavy antique mahogany table with winged lions for legs was startling and impressive, and on the coffee table, the enormous geode, cut in half to expose glittering amethyst crystals, caused much whispering.

Cal took over, splitting the teams in half, making sure the two boys who could be the most trouble were not on the same team, and started the search. Ari and Sandy went up to the second floor to keep an eye on the children. At first, the Beach Camp kids were quiet, awed by the size of the old summer house and its many rooms. Then someone on the first floor shrieked in victory, and the second-floor children went mad, racing into the bedrooms and bathrooms, crawling beneath beds, bumping into furniture, giggling and arguing and shrieking.

The greatest attraction of the day was the basement. A few years ago, Eleanor had had a room fitted out for exercising. One wall was mirrored. She had a small exercise bike, a rowing machine, and a shelf of rubber weights and bands, none of them very heavy. The boys mostly took over the bike and rowing machine, while some of the girls used the bands to tie around their waists in a bow so they could admire themselves in the mirror and others used them for a tug-of-war. After a fairly long, very noisy while, they were sent to the rest of the basement to find a brown paper bag with their name printed on it, and inside, pretzels and raisins. Then they were chan- neled back upstairs.

Later, the children ate macaroni and cheese and buttered green beans. Finally, they gathered their loot and raced through the still- pouring rain out to the vans. As they left, each child, prompted by Ari, Sandy, or Cal, shook Eleanor's hand and said, "Thank you."

Ari was last to leave. She had to meet the Beach Camp at the community room for story time and games.

"You were wonderful," she told her grandmother. "You really saved the day."

"I enjoyed it," Eleanor said. "But the moment you leave, I'm going to my room to take a nap."

Seventeen

Saturday morning, Eleanor was still in bed when her granddaughter slipped into the room and put a note on her bedside table.

"Good luck," Eleanor said, her voice croaking, because she hadn't had her coffee yet.

"Thanks," Ari said, and hurried away.

Eleanor lay for a moment, wondering what exactly *good luck* would mean for Ari, who was taking the six-thirty car ferry to Hyannis and making the short but crowded drive to Boston, where Peter was taking a summer-semester law review class at Harvard. The drive that should take ninety minutes could take hours, depending on the vacation traffic. Peter had not agreed to meet Ari partway, in one of the towns just outside of Boston. He'd insisted she come into Cambridge and meet her at a small café in Harvard Square.

What would Peter say when he found out Ari was pregnant? For that matter, what did Ari hope Peter would say? What did Eleanor hope would happen? She couldn't imagine.

Eleanor tried to still her thoughts and fall back into the oblivion of sleep, but no, she was awake. She rose, pulled on a loose sundress and no bra—the joys of not wearing a bra were extreme—dropped her cellphone into her pocket, and went out to the kitchen to fire up the Keurig. It was a sunny day. She'd drink her coffee out on the deck.

She sat in her favorite wicker chair for a while, soaking in the sun, savoring the day, the fresh air, the blue ocean extending farther than she could see. It was both a blessing and a relief to be at this place in her life. In spite of an aching back and fickle joints, she relished old age.

Her cell buzzed. It was only a few minutes after seven. Ari would still be on the car ferry. Without looking, Eleanor said hello.

"Eleanor. Do you know where Alicia is?" Phillip's baritone voice cracked with emotion. Anger? Concern?

"Good morning, Phillip," Eleanor said, giving her a moment to catch her breath. This was the last call she'd expected.

"Good morning, Eleanor. I apologize for calling so early, but I came home last night and Alicia wasn't here. She hasn't come home, and she didn't leave a note."

Eleanor caught her breath. Just when she thought she was free of decision-making, Phillip's call. Should Eleanor tell Phillip everything now, on the phone? She had always liked Phillip, and respected him. He had put up with a lot from his wife, who could be demanding and self-absorbed, as Eleanor knew only too well.

Eleanor answered with a question of her own. "You came home last night? Where had you been?"

Phillip was silent.

"Well, when did you last see Alicia?"

"It's been a while," Phillip said quietly.

"It's been *a while* since you've seen your wife?"

"Eleanor," Phillip said, his voice pleading.

"Phillip, you know I've always loved you, but Alicia is my daughter. You have hurt her, and that was cruel. Is cruel."

After a moment's silence, Phillip said, "Does that mean you won't tell me where she is?"

"I can tell you what she knows," Eleanor said.

"Do you want me to come to the island to talk?"

Her heart felt as if it were squeezed and cracking. "No, Phillip,"

Eleanor answered, and her voice was angry, "I don't want you to come to the island. Really, you only want to come so your girlfriend can comfort you."

"Eleanor—"

Eleanor gave in. "She's going on a trip. She didn't tell us where. You should know that Ari knows about your affair. *Your daughter* has seen you with your . . ." Eleanor couldn't speak the word. She clicked off the phone, using every ounce of restraint to keep herself from throwing the innocent piece of technology across the yard.

By luck—good or bad—Ari found a parking spot on Mass Ave near the Coffee House. She was sure Peter had chosen this because it wasn't in the heart of Harvard Square, where his friends might see her.

She sat in her car for a few minutes, calming her thudding heart, working out how to tell Peter. What if he said he wanted to marry her as they had planned, and have the baby and live together? That would make Peter happy, and presumably it would make the baby happy, too, to have both parents living together.

But she didn't love Peter. As each day without him passed, she seldom thought of him, and when she did, she shivered with dread at what she had almost done.

But . . . the baby.

Ari wanted to have this baby. He or she already felt like hers, part of her life, and Ari was pro-choice, but something about this baby made her choose to keep him or her. It just felt right. So wasn't she somehow obligated to marry the baby's father? After all, she had loved Peter once, and they had been friends since that moment on the rock in Lake Winnipesaukee. She did not want the life Peter intended to live, but she could slow him down from the fast track, just a little . . .

It was time. She got out of her car and walked to the coffee shop. Peter wasn't there yet, of course he wasn't—he would want to be late, proving he was more important than she was. She bought a cup of iced coffee and found a table in the corner. She wore a blue sundress, because Peter had always liked her in blue, and she hoped the color would work subliminally to make him feel kind to her.

Five minutes later, Peter strode in. Ari thought, *Good God.* Peter had already changed, his chin held higher, his shoulders straight, his comportment making it clear that he was very significant and very busy. His red hair had been parted on one side and swept over neatly and he wore chinos and a button-down shirt. He carried a briefcase instead of a backpack.

"Peter," Ari said. "Thank you for coming."

Peter yanked a chair out from the table and sat. "I don't have much time."

"Of course." Oh, help, she didn't love this man even a little bit. "Would you like a cup of coffee? I'm having iced coffee because it's so hot."

"Fine," Peter said.

She knew what he wanted her to do, so she did it. She was, after all, the supplicant here. She went to the counter and bought him an iced mocha grande and brought it to the table and set it before him.

"How are you?"

"Exhausted. This coursework is tougher than I'd anticipated."

"But you love it," Ari said with a knowing smile.

Peter nodded. "I love it."

For a moment, they were almost friends. But their eyes met, and Peter's gaze grew wary.

"Why did you want to see me?" Before she could answer, he announced, "Because I'm with someone else now. Lacey Harbuck. She's at the school, too, and she's got the same goals I have. She's gorgeous, and she's smart, and we can see a successful future together."

"Well, that happened fast," Ari said, not hiding her surprise. "Not even two months."

"When it's right, you know it," Peter said, jutting his chin out defensively.

Ari took a sip of coffee. How could she say this now? Should she not tell him, because he was clearly so together with Lacey?

But he should know.

"Peter, I'm pregnant," Ari blurted.

Peter froze. Defiantly, he said, "So what?"

"It's your baby."

"You can't prove that."

"Actually, I can. If I wanted to go to the trouble of getting a DNA test. You know I wasn't with any other guy, Peter." Before he could reply, Ari said, "I've missed a period and you know I was regular. I've taken some pharmacy tests. I haven't gone to a doctor yet, but I've got nausea, and I've been throwing—"

Peter leaned across the table, hissing. "For God's sake, Ari, I don't need the details. I'm sorry if you've been inconvenienced, but you know what to do. Just get rid of it. If you insist, I'll pay for half the abortion."

Without thinking, in a completely spontaneous action, Ari crossed her arms protectively over her abdomen. She waited until Peter sat back in his chair and calmed down.

"Peter, I want to keep the baby."

"That's impossible."

"No, it's not. I don't know why this happened, but somehow it seems right."

"You are not going to force me to pay child support."

"Stop that. I'm not going to ask you for any money at all. You don't have to even see him or her, ever, if that's your choice. But I thought it was necessary to tell you, to inform you that you will have a child walking on this earth."

"It will not be my child." Peter brought a fist down on the table hard, making Ari jump. Several other diners looked their way. "Jesus Christ, Ari, you are a curse on my life."

Ari said earnestly, quietly, "I don't mean to be a curse on your life, Peter. If I hadn't told you, that would have been wrong, wouldn't it?"

He gritted his teeth and didn't answer. But he valued being honest, so he spoke. "You did the right thing to tell me. But I am in the right to say I will not consider this my child. I will not legally acknowledge it. I never want to see or know about it. My wish is that you never have it. If you press, I will hire a lawyer to make a financial settlement for you. Otherwise, Ari, I hope I never hear from you or see you again."

Ari nodded. Peter pushed back from the table and walked away.

Ari drove back down Route 3 along the coast toward the Sagamore Bridge and Cape Cod. She realized she felt oddly empty. Not saddened by Peter's reaction, not angry, not anything at all. In a world where her father was having an affair and her mother blithely went off on a trip, and she was pregnant by a man she'd made love to out of sympathy because they were taking finals and she didn't want to upset him then—she had done what she'd thought was *right*—what *was* right? Did *right* even matter?

She had the obligation to decide. She was pro-choice and she'd helped friends go through interventions, friends who were adamant about not having a baby and who were relieved afterward. Now, this was her body—and her life. Could she go through life alone, as a single mother? In a way, it was a ridiculous question. She was educated, she had resources, she had a family who would help her. Well, Eleanor would; Ari wasn't sure about her parents. And families were made in all sorts of ways.

But what would this mean for her personal life? Right now, it was Beck who made her feel as she'd never felt before, but everything with him was new. A summer infatuation? In reality, Ari thought Beck had feelings for her. If they had all the time in the world, she was sure their mutual attraction would blossom into love. But if she was pregnant by another man, a man who would not claim the baby, what would they think? What would they do? She had less than two months on the island, and that wasn't enough time to create a serious relationship. Was it?

And what would she do about her own plans for her life? She was supposed to start working toward a master's in early childhood education at Boston University in September. According to her math, she'd be having a baby in February. Her plans had been to get an apartment near B.U., maybe share with a friend, take courses and do research. She could do that while pregnant. She could do that even if she had a baby. Couldn't she?

By the time she got to the car ferry, she was exhausted. Too tired to head up to the snack bar, she swallowed the last few ounces in her water bottle, put her seat back, and slept until the ferry docked at Nantucket.

The sky was still bright as Ari slowly drove her car down the ferry's ramp and onto solid land. As she passed through town, she saw people talking, laughing, buying ice cream, and she remembered that the world could be a beautiful place. Life could be good. At Main Street, she stopped her car at the crosswalk. A woman strolled across the street, wearing a baby carrier holding a plump little girl—Ari assumed a girl because the baby's fine hair stood up in a whale's tail, tied with a pink ribbon—across her chest. The woman looked dreamily pleased with herself and the baby was wide-eyed and happy, kicking her legs, waving her arms.

So that could be me, Ari thought. It was a happy thought.

The road to 'Sconset was two-lane, the speed limit thirty-five miles an hour, the fastest speed allowable on the island. Forests lined both sides of the road, with a bike path winding along on the south side. Bikers cycled along, women and men pushed baby carriages, and a woman rode a tandem bike with her young son at the back. The woman's dark hair streamed out behind her as they flew along, and her little boy pedaled furiously, a huge grin on his face.

I could do that, Ari thought.

When she arrived at her grandmother's house, she was delighted to find a chicken stew waiting for her in the Crock-Pot. She ladled a bowl for herself and went out to sit on the deck with Eleanor.

Eleanor was gazing at the ocean. She turned toward Ari with a smile. "How did it go?"

"He wants nothing to do with the baby. He said he'd pay half for the abortion."

"That is one possibility."

"I know, but, Gram, I've made up my mind. I want to keep this baby. I want to have this child. I know it's awkward and difficult, but I've decided, and I'm glad."

"If that's your decision, you know I will help you," Eleanor said.

"Thank you." Ari sank into her chair and gratefully spooned the rich, delicious stew into her mouth. "I've got to go one day at a time, and right now I'm ravenous. I forgot to eat lunch. I didn't know I was so hungry until I came in the house."

"Tell me more about Peter," Eleanor said.

"Basically, he wants nothing to do with the baby. Ever."

"He's still angry with you for breaking off with him."

"I'm not sure. He says he's already found someone he's serious about. Her name is Lacey."

"Well," Eleanor said, searching Ari's face, "you don't love Peter. So that's okay, isn't it?"

"Yes." Having finished every last bit of the stew, Ari leaned back in her chair. "It's great, actually. I had nightmares that he might want to be together again. I'm glad Peter's found someone else. Now I don't have to feel guilty for breaking off with him. I'm just tired. The roads were jammed. I listened to music, and that helped, but I'm glad to be home."

"I need to tell you, Ari, that your father phoned me, looking for Alicia."

Ari put her head in her hands. She loved her father, and she hated him for having an affair. "What did you say to him?"

"I told him his wife had gone on a trip. I told him you and I and Alicia knew about his affair. He wanted to come here and talk, but I hung up on him." Eleanor's voice was shaking. "I might not have been the perfect mother to Alicia, but I am her mother, and I'm angry and hurt for her."

"Yes," Ari said quietly. "Me, too."

"But this isn't a problem I can solve," Eleanor said.

"I know," Ari agreed. "I can't solve it, either."

They sat together quietly for a while.

"So!" Eleanor clapped her hands on the table and rose. "I've got *Masterpiece Mystery!* to watch."

"I'll tidy the kitchen and take a shower and be down in time to watch it with you," Ari told Eleanor. Rising, she picked up her bowl and started toward the glass door. Pausing, she turned to her grandmother and said, "Gram, thank you."

Eleanor looked surprised. "For what?"

"Everything," Ari told her, and smiled and went into the kitchen.

Eighteen

Monday morning, Ari set off for Beach Camp. The sun was bright, the sand hot, and the water cool. The children were adorable. The sun was shining and the day flew past.

As she drove home, her cell buzzed. Without looking at the number, she answered.

"Hey, Ari." It was Beck. His voice made her smile. "How're you doin'?"

"Doin' fine, Beck. How about you?"

"Oh, I'm up here in Plymouth, wishing I were on the island. Listen, I had a great thought. The yacht club's Mid-Summer Ball is this Saturday. Would you go with me? I promise I'm a decent dancer."

Her heart floated upward like a balloon. "That's a wonderful idea, Beck. I'd love to go with you."

"Want to put a table together? Like my sister and her fiancé, and Mickey and Sara Sullivan."

"Oh, yes. That'll be fun!" The Mid-Summer Ball was always a fantastic event, with fabulous dinners served before the band began to play every style of music while the dance floor filled with whirling skirts and navy blazers and laughing people.

"Good. I'll pick you up at six. Cocktails start at six-thirty."

"Oh, Beck, I can drive in from 'Sconset and meet you there."

"Not a chance that will happen. Ari, this is an official date, and I'm picking you up."

"Okay, then. I'll be ready."

When she clicked off her phone, Ari caught a glimpse of her face in her rearview mirror. She was smiling, as if she'd been lit up like a star.

Oh, dear, she thought, *what does it mean that the sound of Beck's voice made me happy?* When she was younger, she and her friends had scorned the Mid-Summer Ball because it was so old-fashioned and conventional. But right now, it seemed that a pretty dress with a skirt that swirled as she was held in Beck's arms was exactly what she needed.

Summer was here, and Eleanor's calendar was scribbled with dates for lunch, sailing, and dinner. She was glad. She knew this was good for her, happily reclusive as she was, so she went everywhere she was invited. This was good for Ari, too, Eleanor was certain. Ari needed some time alone. This Tuesday she'd had a girls' night out with friends, and tonight, Ari had gone out with Beck to a beach party. It was good, Eleanor decided, for both women to be busy, and let their subconscious minds do their back-of-the-stove simmering.

Eleanor was glad Ari was active, having fun, but soon her grand-daughter had to face serious changes because of her pregnancy. If Ari kept the baby, Eleanor worried that Ari's mother and father wouldn't want her to live with them in Boston. Alicia had experienced a long and difficult labor with Ari, ending in a hysterectomy. Alicia hadn't enjoyed having an infant to deal with, either. All that spitting up and crying and constant care—it had made Alicia miserable. Eleanor had gone up to Boston to help during the first month, but that only made Alicia crankier, having to live with her mother around. Finally, when Ari was seven months old and crawling, Alicia had hired a nanny.

No, Eleanor couldn't imagine Ari with her parents and a squalling newborn. Would Ari still take classes at B.U.?

Eleanor also worried Alicia wouldn't understand Eleanor's attempt to help—unless Eleanor agreed to sell the house and split the money among her daughter, son, and granddaughter. But Alicia was dealing with an adulterous husband, and money couldn't fix that. Could it? Ari would own this house when Eleanor died, but Eleanor had no plans to die for a good long time. It was a sad thought that only Eleanor's death would make Alicia happy.

She heard the clunk of her mailbox lid and walked out to pick up her mail. An electric bill, an invitation to a fundraiser, and a postcard from Martha, who was having the best time ever on the cruise. *Good for her,* Eleanor thought. She was sincerely happy Martha was having such fun, but she missed having her friend around to talk to about the very private matters she couldn't share with anyone else.

She walked slowly back to her house and was glad when the phone rang, interrupting her turbulent thoughts, and even more glad to hear Silas's voice.

"Eleanor," Silas said, "I should have asked earlier, but I'm afraid I just took it for granted—would you be my partner for the Mid-Summer Ball next Saturday? Please don't feel obligated."

"I'd be delighted, Silas," Eleanor said. "Are you putting together a table?"

"To be honest, I hadn't thought of that," Silas said. "I'd only gotten as far as asking you."

Eleanor said, "Well, we must put a table together. If we sit alone, people will gossip."

"A little gossip is a fine thing at our age," Silas said.

Eleanor laughed. "I'll call Sissy Hampshire."

"Good girl," Silas said. "Oh, damn, is it incorrect of me to call you girl? Or even a good girl?"

Eleanor laughed again. "As long as I can call you good boy."

"I'll try to earn that appellation," Silas said.

When they ended the call, Eleanor sat down on the overstuffed chair in a corner of the guest room. She hadn't gone to the ball since Mortimer had died three years ago. She tried to remember how dressy women were at the dance, and as she recalled, they were *very* fancy, wearing their best dresses and jewels. Most of the dresses had full skirts, which were such fun to swirl when they danced.

For a little while, Eleanor sat there, just remembering. Mortimer had always insisted on going to the various balls the yacht club held, but he had been an absolutely terrible dancer, stiff and as plodding as an overloaded mule. Eleanor couldn't remember her husband ever twirling her, not even once. But she could remember Silas dancing with his wife, Maxine, how perfectly matched they were, even daring to do the tango. Oh, Maxine had swirled her skirts a lot.

The image woke a memory. Up in the attic, inside a plastic wardrobe, hung "special" dresses she and, years later, when she was in college, Alicia had once worn. Eleanor wondered if she could squeeze into any one of them. Well, she could always alter one with her handy sewing machine. Humming the tune to "I Could Have Danced All Night," Eleanor went up to the attic.

For the rest of the week, Eleanor worked on a dress that Alicia had never liked, and altered it at the bosom and waist to fit her own figure. It was a pale gray satin knee-length dress, with a full skirt, a princess neckline, and a fitted bodice covered with a light layer of lace. Short sleeves made of lace did the most generous job of covering the wobbly part of Eleanor's upper arms.

When Ari came home from working at the camp, they talked about the Mid-Summer Ball.

"I'd be glad to alter a dress for you," Eleanor offered.

Ari's lips curved in a satisfied grin. "Don't worry. I have one that will be perfect."

"When you were little," Eleanor mused, "you spent hours going through the old photo albums. You were infatuated with my wedding dress, and my honeymoon suit and hat."

"I remember," Ari said. She clapped her hands. "Oh, please, let's look at the albums again."

Eleanor possessed many photo albums. She took them off the bottom shelf of the bookcase and sat with her granddaughter, gazing at the marvelous creations Eleanor had worn for her wedding and for formal dances throughout her life. The occasions for Alicia's wedding gown and party dresses filled another album.

"Men's clothes are so colorless compared to women's," Ari noted.

"It wasn't always that way," Eleanor said. "Men used to wear velvets and lace and chains of jewels."

"What caused the change?" Ari wondered.

"Let's blame the Puritans," Eleanor suggested with a laugh.

Saturday evening, grandmother and granddaughter posed together in the guest bedroom, which had the full-length mirror. They were getting ready for the Mid-Summer Ball and they were as silly as schoolgirls.

"What do you think?" Eleanor asked her granddaughter.

"I think you look absolutely beautiful!" Ari said, clapping her hands. "Now. You need jewelry."

"My pearls," Eleanor said.

"No, not your pearls. That's too conservative. You should go wild."

"Actually," Eleanor said, "what I'd like to wear is your necklace. And you can wear one of mine."

Ari was shocked. "Gram, I got this necklace from eBay. I think I paid maybe fifteen dollars for it. The flowers are plastic and the diamonds are rhinestones, plus it's kind of gaudy."

"Yes, but it hangs low, so it will cover my wrinkled chest." When her granddaughter looked unconvinced, Eleanor opened her sock drawer and lifted out the diamond and emerald necklace that had been her mother's. "This is what you should wear."

Ari squealed. "OMG, is that real? Gram! Why have you never worn it before? Here," Ari said, unfastening her eBay jewelry. "Put this on and let me try on that beauty."

Ari was wearing a simple green slip dress with spaghetti straps that fit her snugly.

"That's a very sexy dress," Eleanor said, "but I don't think the skirt will twirl."

"I've decided I don't want it to twirl," Ari said with a light laugh. "I want it to hug my curves. No one would ever expect that I'm pregnant when they see me in this dress."

"That's true." Eleanor sat down on the bed. "But you are pregnant, Ari. And you really need to see your physician."

Ari sat down on the bed next to her grandmother. "I know. I do know. But just for tonight, I want to feel carefree."

Eleanor nodded. "Well, then, let's see how the necklace goes with your dress."

Ari was wearing her long dark hair up in a chignon, with a few strands curling down on each side of her face. She sat still while Eleanor fastened the choker on her. She rose and walked to view herself in the mirror.

"Oh," Ari said.

"You look regal," Eleanor said. "Beautiful and elegant."

Ari touched the large square-cut emerald, the diamonds surrounding it. "I've never seen you wear this."

"I've never worn it. It was my mother's, and the occasion never arose. For my wedding, my future mother-in-law wanted to loan me her triple strand of pearls, and I obeyed. And it was a lovely look, those pearls. But really, I don't think women wear these sorts of jewels anymore. Too flashy."

Ari frowned. "I don't want to look flashy."

"You don't. Your hair is up and elegant. Wear small diamond studs in your ears and no other jewelry." Eleanor gazed at Ari's shoes. "Those heels are rather high."

Ari grinned. "Not changing the shoes, Gram. And before you ask, yes, I can dance in them."

Eleanor nodded. She went to her room to put on her gray satin pumps. It had been years since she'd worn them, and they were a little tight now. Her feet had spread somehow, and she had a bunion on her right foot that stuck out like a marble. The younger women didn't wear hose anymore, and Eleanor envied them because they didn't have to wrestle with hideous pantyhose, and felt sorry for them because they didn't wear, as Eleanor had when she was young, silk stockings and a garter belt.

As she sat on her slipper chair in her bedroom, easing on her shoes, she sat very still for a moment. She wondered how many women had been in this house, in this very room, over the generations of people who'd lived here since 1840. At moments like this, she felt such a *companionship,* an awareness of all of the people who had made love and fought and dressed for a party and laughed and lived and died. It made her feel better about her eventual death. She wondered if, when she got to heaven, the first woman of this house would greet her, saying, "I love what you did with the front parlor." It was a daft thought, Eleanor knew. Maybe she was getting senile, but she'd felt these invisible others since she was a child. It made her smile, and she could never tell anyone, but she wasn't convinced it couldn't happen.

Eleanor and Ari were still primping in front of the hall mirror when lights flashed. Two cars turned into the driveway. They glanced out the window and saw Silas stepping out of his freshly washed ancient Jeep and Beck emerging from his red convertible. The two men shook hands and talked for a while before walking to the door.

"I'm getting the giggles," Ari confessed. "I'm going out with my grandmother."

"Correction. You're going out with that very handsome young man," Eleanor said. "I just happen to be going out with a very handsome older man."

Someone knocked on the door.

"I'll get it!" Eleanor said. "Hello, Silas. You look quite presentable."

"That's the look I was aiming for," Silas said, and they both chuckled as he escorted her to his Jeep.

Ari paused by the open door, smiling at Beck, and he took her breath away.

Beck wore a faded madras jacket and a sky-blue tie that matched his eyes.

"I like your jacket," Ari said.

"It was my grandfather's."

Of course it was, Ari thought, opening like a flower to the sun. She felt beautiful and desirable and exactly where she should be. Why did the sight of Beck in a madras plaid jacket thrill her so? She wasn't that keen on madras. But Beck, the very presence of Beck, so tall, broad-shouldered, so handsome, thrilled her. The worn cuffs and slightly sagging cloth implied the jacket had belonged to someone in his family and had been passed down to Beck. She liked the idea of that kind of family. Well, she liked his family. She knew she would love Beck no matter who his family was.

"You look beautiful," Beck told her.

She couldn't stop gazing up at him, filling her eyes with the reality of Beck Hathaway. "So do you," she said.

Beck smiled. "If you keep looking at me like that, we'll never get to the dance. Come on." He took her hand and led her to the car.

At the club, Ari and Beck sat at a round table for ten. The other couples were all people Ari had met during her childhood summers. They'd grown up playing badminton and taking sailing and tennis lessons. Two couples were older, in their late twenties, like Beck, while Ari and her friends had just graduated from college. Tonight the division between old and young blurred. The conversation was witty, helped along by excellent wine, and in her heightened state, Ari thought they were all wonderful people. She was in the moment, completely happy.

Ari danced with Beck and with all the other men at the table. Beck danced with all the other women. Beck crossed the room and invited Eleanor to dance, and Silas came over and asked Ari to dance. Silas was one of those men whom you just liked on sight. He wasn't particularly handsome, but very charming. And he was an amazing dancer.

Ari saw her grandmother dancing with Beck and felt—really, there was no other word for it—she felt *blessed*. Maybe Eleanor would marry Silas. Maybe Ari would marry Beck. Then Rowena

Gates danced by with her husband, and Rowena was heavily pregnant, and Ari remembered with a sinking heart that she was pregnant, too. Still, Ari thought, she would remember this night.

At the dance, Eleanor sat with Silas on one side and the ever-perky Becky Dillard on the other. The ballroom was packed, the air fragrant with flowers and perfume, and people drifted from table to table, talking with friends. When dinner was served, either prime rib or lobster, depending on one's choice, the room was quieter, but when dessert was put in front of them, the musicians took their places on the bandstand and began to warm up. Women hurried to the restroom. Men huddled to discuss sports or the stock market. It was just as it always had been for Eleanor.

Until Silas asked her to dance.

Silas liked to dance. As Eleanor was twirled away from him and back, she remembered this about him, how smooth and enthusiastic a dancer he was. She wasn't quite sure she could keep up with him. It had been years since she'd danced and she didn't think she'd ever danced like this. She found herself laughing with pleasure.

A slow song came on, and Silas pulled Eleanor against him. She could feel his heart thudding, or maybe that was hers. His hand on hers was big and warm and sturdy. His hand on her waist was thrilling. Silas wasn't much taller than Eleanor, so it didn't hurt her neck to look up into his eyes. He was smiling, and he looked amused. Eleanor smiled back, and as the music slowed, she rested her head against his chest and let herself be swayed to the gentle rhythm of the song.

Beck and Ari moved past them, and Ari waggled her eyebrows and mouthed "Hubba-hubba" at Eleanor. Eleanor smiled back briefly and closed her eyes. It had been a long time since she'd been in a man's arms, and she'd never had a dancing partner like Silas. She didn't want to think about her darling granddaughter. She didn't want to think at all. She let herself be dreamily right there in the moment.

———

The party ended at one in the morning. People drifted out the door regretfully, not wanting to leave. Beck had taken off his jacket and rolled up his shirtsleeves.

"Want to walk on the beach?" he asked.

"Sure," Ari answered.

They drove to Surfside, where tonight the waves rolled in quietly, and the sea was calm. They took off their shoes and walked in the cool sand. They held hands and talked about the dance, the people they knew, the people who hadn't come. The moon was almost full, and the ocean looked silver, so they sat on the sand and stared out at the water.

Ari remained in a kind of enchantment. She leaned against Beck's shoulder as they talked.

She had to know. "Have you ever been engaged?"

"Not even close," Beck told her. "When I was working on my master's, I was a complete dork, reading constantly, attending lectures, figuring out how I was going to be the best therapist I could be. Before that, when I was in high school and college, well, I was the opposite. I don't mean I thought I was Don Juan, but I saw a lot of women, and the last thing on my mind was settling down."

Ari was stunned to feel a streak of jealousy move through her. All those girls and women he had been with . . .

Beck asked, "But you've been engaged, right?"

"Yes," Ari admitted. "To Peter Anderson. We've known each other all our lives. We met at a camp in New Hampshire when we were kids. We both went to Bucknell. Our parents approved. Peter is a good guy. He's at Harvard Law now." She told Beck about their wedding plans, the lodge they'd rented on the shores of Lake Winnipesaukee, his parents, her parents, everyone so thrilled.

"But during the last semester of school, I knew I didn't want to marry him. I couldn't. I did love him, but I never felt the way I feel . . ." Ari turned her head away. Suddenly she had tears in her eyes. "I loved him like a brother, or a friend," she said.

"You did the right thing," Beck told her, speaking quietly. After a moment's silence, he said, "I'm glad you broke your engagement. I'm glad for the chance to be with you."

Ari looked at Beck, allowing tears to fall. "I'm glad to be with you. But, Beck, I'm not sure what that means."

"Let's find out." He drew her to him and kissed her.

His hand was on the back of her head, cradling it gently. His other hand was on her waist. Ari placed both hands on his chest, feeling his heart beating through the fabric of the jacket and his shirt. They kissed for a long time, and it was sexual but also it was serious, a searching and a finding.

Beck pulled back. "Wow," he said quietly.

"I know." She kept her hands on his chest.

He smiled. "Ari, I've never made love to anyone on a beach, and I'm sorry to tell you I'm not going to now. It's the sand. It can sneak into places a person really doesn't want it."

Ari smiled back. "I know. But you can kiss me again, can't you?"

"I can," Beck said. And he did.

After a while, they rose, brushing sand off their clothes, and walked to his car.

Beck opened her door and kissed her thoroughly again, leaving Ari limp with desire. She sank into her seat and leaned her head against the back. The top was down on the convertible, and as Beck drove, Ari looked up and watched the stars watching them from the sky. They didn't talk. They didn't need to.

When they reached her house, Beck said, "I promised to go sailing with my family again tomorrow. Will you come, too?"

"Yes, please," Ari said.

They kissed again, lightly this time. Beck escorted her to the door. They kissed again. Ari wanted to melt right into Beck.

"Tomorrow," he said.

"Tomorrow," she agreed.

Ari turned off the light her grandmother had left on for her and went silently through the dark house. She dropped her dress right on the floor, kicked off her shoes, undid the gorgeous necklace, placing it carefully back in its case, and dropped on her bed, smiling as she fell asleep.

Something delicious woke her.

"Oh, Gram, thank you!" Ari scooted up against her headboard as her grandmother entered the room, carrying a tray with hot coffee and buttered toast.

"Last night was fun, wasn't it?" Eleanor asked, sitting on the end of Ari's bed, pulling her kimono up around her legs.

"You have no idea," Ari said. She looked at the clock. "Lord, it's almost noon. I'm going sailing with Beck and his family at one today."

"You have time to drink coffee," Eleanor said sensibly. "And to shower."

Ari was starving. "You had a good time last night, right?"

"Imagine, being my age, and dancing away until the band shut down."

"Silas is a good dancer," Ari mumbled, biting into the toast.

"He is. He's great fun to be with."

"Wow, Gram, do you have a boyfriend?"

Eleanor had a twinkle in her eye. "You know, I think I do."

"Oh! That's so exciting!" Ari almost tipped over her tray.

"No so exciting at my age, but terribly nice. I'd even say wonderful."

"That sounds like you kissed him."

"I did. And that's all you need to know. You need to get ready to meet Beck." Eleanor rose from the bed, leaned over to kiss Ari's head, and left the room.

The sun warmed Ari's shoulders as she sat on the Hathaways's schooner with Hen leaning against her. The boat skipped over the bouncing waves, the strong, capricious wind tangling her hair. Beck's father constantly shouted out orders to Beck and Michelle to trim the sheet or steady the rudder. Beck's mother had gone into the cabin to lie down.

Hen shouted to Ari, "Don't be afraid."

"I'm not afraid, sweetheart," Ari answered, and that was the truth. She was delighted to discover she was only slightly nauseous, and the sail was so exciting, she almost forgot about that.

They anchored near Great Point, on the Nantucket Sound side. Beck let down the rope ladder and all of the Hathaways dove off the boat to swim. Ari joined them, only slightly worried about the possibility of great whites in the water. The waves were cold and playful. After a moment of swimming against the tide, she turned on her back and floated, letting the water lift her up and pull her down.

Something from underneath her grabbed at her waist. She screamed, struggling, until she discovered it was Beck.

"Sorry," he said as they treaded water, facing each other. "Forgive me?"

"Of course," Ari told him. She hadn't been truly frightened.

"Let's kiss and make up," Beck said, and right there with his family all around and the ocean bobbing them up and down, he pulled Ari to him and kissed her. His lips were warm and salty and his torso touched hers. It was only with great willpower that Ari stopped herself from wrapping her legs around his body. They kissed so long that a wave rose over them, forcing them from the surface. For a few more moments, surrounded by briny, sun-scattered waves, they continued kissing, as if nothing could stop them.

They bobbed to the surface, gasping for breath and laughing.

Hen dog-paddled up to them. "Don't *do* that! I thought you were drowning."

Beck put his arm around his sister and kept his other arm around Ari. "This is what we were doing. Hold your breath. One, two, three." Hugging them securely against his sides, he dove under a rising wave. They were floating underwater, belly downward, their faces close and tinted green by the watery light. Beck tugged them against him and kissed Ari on her mouth and Hen on her cheek. They bobbed up to the surface, gasped for air, and Hen giggled and splashed in the water, looking triumphant.

"We were kissing," Hen yelled.

Michelle swam up. "Hen, you've been in long enough. Come on

out and warm up. You, too, Ari. We haven't had a chance to talk today."

They all swam to the rope ladder. Beck struck off toward the distance, swimming powerfully and fast. Mr. and Mrs. Hathaway were already back on board. Hen's mother held a fat towel in her hands as she reached out to wrap her youngest daughter.

"Your teeth are chattering," Mrs. Hathaway said. "Here, sit on my lap. You'll warm up soon."

"We'll make hot chocolate," Michelle said. She tossed Ari a towel and went down into the cabin.

Ari adored the cabin, with everything so tidy and compact. Bright red enamel cups, bowls, and plates were strapped securely above the gimballed two-burner propane cooktop. Michelle deftly took a pan from a cabinet, a box of hot chocolate mix from inside a hanging webbed hammock, and added milk from the mini-fridge above the sink.

"I'll take a beer," Mr. Hathaway called down.

"I will, too," Michelle said. "Want a beer, Ari?"

"No, thanks, I'd prefer hot chocolate with Hen."

Michelle laughed. "That's what you get for spending so much time with my brother. I tell you, the man is a seal."

"At least he's not a shark," Ari joked.

"Oh, Ari, no, Beck's not a shark at all," Michelle said, taking the remark seriously. "He's a really good guy. And I can tell he seriously likes you."

Ari said softly, "I seriously like him."

They smiled at each other, as if they had a secret.

When the hot chocolate was ready, Ari brought a cup up to Hen and to Mrs. Hathaway. Michelle brought her father a beer, kept a beer for herself, and handed a cup of hot chocolate to Ari. Beck appeared, climbing up the rope ladder onto the boat, water streaming down from him, his board shorts plastered against his legs. Ari couldn't help but admire every inch of his physique. There was no hiding bulges in a bathing suit, she thought, and glanced down at her own torso, her belly still as flat as always.

Beck toweled off and went down to get a beer. The family relaxed in the sun while Mr. and Mrs. Hathaway entertained everyone with tales of races they'd won or lost over the years. Ari did her best not to gaze longingly at Beck. She asked Hen about her summer events while they drank their hot chocolate.

As they sailed back to their buoy in the harbor, Ari was impressed at how the family all worked together, taking orders from Mr. Hathaway, who clearly was skipper of the boat. She wondered, had her own family sailed, would they ever have become closer, a better family? The boat skipped along over sun-tipped waves and the breeze made the sails flare like birds glad to be set free. Ari felt set free as well, somehow released from who she was in the past and who she was now . . . and who she was on her way to becoming.

The club launch puttered out to take them ashore. Once they were all on the boardwalk, Mrs. Hathaway invited Ari to come to their house for a light meal.

Before Ari could reply, Beck said, "Sorry, Mom. We've already made plans."

"I want to be with you!" Hen shouted, jumping up and down in front of Beck.

"Not tonight," Beck said.

"Awww." Hen pouted.

Mrs. Hathaway put her hand on Hen's shoulder. "Sweetie, you've got to come home and take a warm shower. You've got dance camp tomorrow."

"Oh, yeah!" Hen did a pirouette and hurried to the car.

Michelle was a few steps away from them, texting. "Have fun, guys," she called vaguely to Beck and Ari. She wandered off toward the parking lot.

"Let's go out to 'Sconset and get sandwiches at Claudette's," Beck said.

"Good idea. I'm too windblown to enter a restaurant," Ari told him.

"You look perfect," Beck said. "Although your nose might be a shade redder than your lips."

"Darn. I put sunblock on. Give me a moment." Ari went into the clubhouse and straight through to the ladies' restroom. She grinned at her reflection in the mirror. Her nose was sunburned, and so were her cheeks. Her hair had become a bird's nest. Her shoulders were red and hot to the touch. It was going to take a long shower before she could look normal again, but that didn't bother her at all. She was glowing from more than the sunburn.

They didn't talk as they drove out the Milestone Road to the small rotary at the entrance to 'Sconset. After ordering sandwiches and enormous sodas—they were thirsty after sailing—they walked down to the beach and sat in the sand, eating and looking out at the Atlantic.

"I love your family," Ari told Beck. "I wish my family were like yours."

"Oh, you only catch our good side," Beck told her. "I used to argue with Michelle twenty times a day when we were growing up. We'd get in some vicious hair-pulling fights."

Ari laughed. "That's hilarious."

"We played tricks on each other, too. Like I put sand in her bed and she put just the perfect amount of water in mine. When Hen came along, Michelle and I would compete to see who Hen liked better."

Ari sighed. "I wish I had a sibling."

"Yeah, I get it. As much grief as I got from Michelle, I love her. And Hen hung the moon."

"When I get married, I'm definitely having at least two children," Ari said. Boldly, she asked, "Do you want children when you marry?"

Beck said, "That depends on who I marry."

Ari felt his eyes on her face. Warily, she turned to meet his gaze. It was intense and questioning. Deep in her heart, she longed to say something, anything, to tell him how she felt, but the bossy good angel on her shoulder reminded her that she was pregnant, and Ari let the moment pass.

"I should go home," she said. "I've got Beach Camp tomorrow."

"I'll drive back up to Plymouth," Beck said.

They gathered their debris, stuffed it into trash barrels, and walked up the path to his car. As Beck pulled into Eleanor's driveway, he asked Ari when he could see her again.

"Anytime you want," she said, smiling. She leaned forward to kiss him thoroughly before sliding out of the car.

She found her grandmother in the living room, feet up on an ottoman and pen in hand as she worked on the Sunday *New York Times* crossword puzzle. Her cat, Shadow, sat on the arm of her chair.

"Ari! You are absolutely glowing!"

"It's the sun," Ari said.

"I don't think so," Eleanor replied.

There was a note of invitation in her grandmother's voice. Ari went around and sat on part of the ottoman. "Gram, I think I'm in love. Really, truly in love."

"With Beck?"

"Yes. Every time I'm with him, it just feels right. Plus, I love his family. We haven't made love yet, but I want to. I suppose I shouldn't be telling my grandmother this, but I really want to. But I don't want to rush things. Every moment with him is golden."

Eleanor leaned forward and took Ari's hand. "I'm happy for you, Ari. It's rare, a true love. But, my dear, you're pregnant. Have you made your decision? What if Beck doesn't want to be with you when you're carrying another man's child?"

Ari looked down at her grandmother's warm hand. The back of it was lined with wormy squiggles of veins and the long bones seemed almost to poke through her thin skin. Someday Ari's mother's hands would look like that, and someday, far in the future, Ari's own.

"You're older and wiser," Ari said softly. "I wish you would tell me what to do."

Eleanor shook her head. "That wouldn't be a good idea. It could end up dividing us. Besides, I don't know how you feel, what you want. It's your decision."

"I would never hate you, Gram," Ari said. She thought for a moment. "Things have changed for my generation. People are less serious about having a genetic heir to carry on. I have friends who want to adopt. I guess what I'm saying is that Beck might be willing to take on another man's child."

"You'll never know until you ask him," Eleanor said.

"You're right." Ari yawned. "I've got to shower and get some sleep. Beach Camp tomorrow." She rose, leaned over, kissed her grandmother's soft cheek, and took herself upstairs.

As she showered and prepared for bed, she intended to think calmly and logically about her dilemma, but she was so tired, she barely made it to her bed before falling asleep wrapped in her towel.

Nineteen

During the last week of July, the muggy intense heat of summer settled over the island. Eleanor's house didn't have central air-conditioning—they had never needed it until the last few years when summers became increasingly hotter. She did have a window air conditioner in her bedroom, so she was tolerably cool as she poured her coffee and buttered a piece of raisin toast. These mornings, Ari was already gone by the time Eleanor rose.

Ari.

Eleanor spent a lot of time worrying about her granddaughter, who seemed oddly irrational about her pregnancy. In Eleanor's day, the moment a woman got pregnant, she was examined by a doctor and put on all sorts of vitamins.

But that was a long time ago. Things change.

Still, with both of Ari's parents MIA, Eleanor felt she had some responsibility to her granddaughter. Eleanor struggled with her conscience to keep quiet and let Ari live her own life.

On Wednesday, Eleanor's phone rang.

"Eleanor," Silas said, "I'd like to invite you to my house for dinner Friday night."

For a moment, Eleanor was speechless. She gathered her wits and said jokingly, "Do you mean you want me to come cook dinner for you Friday night?"

Silas laughed heartily, and something in Eleanor released. Silas had a nice, warm laugh.

"Actually, in the past couple of years, I've come to be quite a chef. Not on par with Gordon Ramsay, but better than you'd expect."

"Then I'd be glad to come, Silas. What can I bring?"

"Maybe a bottle of wine? I have some wine, but you and I might end up wanting two bottles. Or maybe I'll concoct a never-before-heard-of cocktail and we won't need wine or dinner."

"This is beginning to sound slightly dangerous," Eleanor said.

"Well, maybe it will be," Silas shot back, laughing a fake pirate's laugh.

The timing was perfect. Ari left Friday after Beach Camp to drive up to Plymouth to visit Beck and go into Boston on Saturday for a day of museums and theater. To Eleanor, this indicated some level of intimacy between her granddaughter and Beck Hathaway, so she decided to give herself one weekend free of worrying about whether Ari would tell Beck she was pregnant, and why Alicia's husband was having an affair, and where in the world her daughter had gone on her sudden trip.

Of course, not having others to worry about meant that she had to decide what to wear Friday night. All her clothes were old. But she refused to rush out and buy something so glaringly new she'd seem to be overeager. Besides, it was summer. No one got dressed up except for galas like the Mid-Summer Ball. She had several sundresses that she wore to get-togethers. She chose a plain blue dress that went well with her dark hair and had elbow-length sleeves to hide her arm wobbles. She decided to wear sandals. At the back of her closet her pumps lingered. They had been tolerable enough at the ball. They seemed appropriate for church but not much else. Besides, her sandals were comfortable.

When Maxine was alive, the Stovers had lived in Monomoy, in a quite large house with a water view. Since then, Silas had moved to a smaller house on Fair Street. A gray-shingled Greek Revival, it had a shell drive where Eleanor parked her car, and a polished brass whale as a door knocker.

"Come in, come in," Silas said, greeting her.

"Hello, Silas," Eleanor said, almost shyly, handing him the bottle of wine.

"Thank you, my dear. Come on back to the kitchen."

Silas wore Nantucket red trousers and a navy blue rugby shirt. His feet were in sneakers. When Eleanor spotted those, she relaxed. Thank heavens she hadn't come in something silk with a gold necklace.

"Would you like a drink? Should I concoct a cocktail? My usual tipple is two fingers of Scotch, but you ladies don't drink that, I don't think. I'll open the wine with dinner—I've already made it, it's keeping warm on the stove—but I could open the wine now . . ."

He was babbling. Silas was babbling. He was nervous, or excited, or both, to have her here.

Eleanor laughed. "I'd love a glass of wine, and you must have your Scotch. What a nice house you've got."

Silas set about with the bottle of wine and a corkscrew.

"Thank you. It is a nice house. I bought it almost a year to the day after Maxine died. My children helped me choose the furniture, some new, some from the old house, such as my old desk I can't live without. But you know, although it's so much smaller than our old house, this house still seems too big to me. Four bedrooms? What do I need with four bedrooms? Well, I use one for a study, and one for me, and the children insisted I need two other bedrooms for when they come for summer or Christmas." He yanked the cork out, poured Eleanor a glass of wine, and handed it to her. "Here you are. How do like living in your great old barn?"

They sat in the living room, in club chairs with a coffee table between them.

"Oh, Silas, I love it. It's been part of my life all my life. I remember sleeping in a trundle bed in my parents' room when I was little. The wallpaper had a design with flowers, and I'd lie counting them until I fell asleep. Pink, violet, blue, orange—I never did like the orange." She laughed and sipped her wine.

"Tell me more. How was it when you were there with Mortimer and your own children?"

"My parents were still alive when we had Alicia. They had the second-floor room with the wide windows overlooking the ocean. Mortimer and I had to share the downstairs bedroom with Alicia when she was a baby. She slept in a wicker cradle." Eleanor cocked her head. "You know, it was a beautiful antique, that cradle, with a soft but firm cushion, and the cradle hung on hooks attached to the wicker legs so that we could rock it. It was the most soothing ivory color. Later, we found out that old paint had lead in it and that could cause lead poisoning in children. I felt sick with guilt."

"But your children are fine," Silas reminded her.

"Yes. Thankfully. When Cliff was born seven years later, my parents were living in Florida, so we had the whole house. Those were crazy days, especially when Cliff was older and had friends down for a week, and Alicia had her friends down, too, and the girls thought the little boys were animals." Eleanor smiled. "And they kind of were."

"Are you lonely living there now?"

"Oh, no. I've got the best bedroom so I wake up looking at the ocean. And I'm used to sleeping alone. In the latter part of our marriage, Mortimer took to sleeping in another room. He said it was because he thought his snoring bothered me. I secretly believed it was because my snoring bothered him."

They both laughed.

"Mortimer never cared much for our Nantucket home. Maybe because in fact it was *my* Nantucket home. He came down from Boston on most summer weekends, and for Thanksgiving and Christmas. He never enjoyed sailing or swimming or even walking on the beach. He loved cities."

"And you love the ocean."

"I do. The entire drama of the ocean, a new one every day."

"So the ocean is your companion."

Eleanor tilted her head, contemplating his words. "I've never thought of it that way, but I suppose it is." After a moment, she admitted, "But the winter winds have caused a lot of damage, and much of the plumbing needs to be replaced."

Silas laughed. "As we grow older, many of us have problems with our plumbing."

Eleanor smiled. She found herself liking Silas better and better as the conversation went on. They had another drink. When they went to the dining room, she saw that Silas had put out placemats and cloth napkins and what Eleanor thought of as Maxine's good china. Silas had made a beef stew with vegetables in a rich gravy laced with red wine. He set Nantucket Bake Shop rolls, warm from the oven, on a plate. He provided her own small block of butter in a porcelain ramekin like Eleanor used to hold crème brûlée, although how many years had it been since she had made a crème brûlée?

"I'm very sorry not to serve you a salad," Silas said, "but the truth is, I dislike salads. Especially that frisée stuff that gets stuck in my teeth. But lettuce in general is a mystery to me. My children tell me I must eat it, but I eat broccoli instead. There are carrots and green beans in the stew."

"But no lettuce in the stew," Eleanor said somberly.

"No. No lettuce." Silas shuddered.

The stew was excellent. The meat was tender, the vegetables plentiful, and the sauce so savory, she found herself dipping her roll in and munching it without the butter.

"Oh, good," Silas said. "I like to do that, too, but I didn't want to seem uncivilized."

"But now that I've shown my true nature, you're free to dip," Eleanor told him, and they both laughed.

It was a very friendly meal. They laughed often, about little things, and they talked about Maxine and Mortimer and the old days. Silas refused to allow Eleanor to carry her bowl to the kitchen. Silas fussed around in there, muttering to himself, and returned with two Klondike bars on a gold-rimmed dessert plate.

Eleanor laughed. "I love Klondike bars!"

After a while, they discussed their children and grandchildren, but not in depth.

"Frankly," Silas said, "I'm still exhausted from raising my son and daughter. I'd like to think I could be helpful in an emergency, but my grandchildren are still teenagers. Mountain and Ocean. Yes, those are their names. Mountain, male, plays drums. Ocean, female, is a Goth. Everything black and a nose ring."

"Mountain and Ocean?" Eleanor echoed, and she laughed so hard she had to excuse herself to go to the bathroom.

"Would you like some coffee?" Silas asked when Eleanor returned to the table.

"No, thanks. I'd be up all night."

"You women," Silas said. "Maxine was that way. Coffee or even chocolate, or a phone call after nine o'clock, and she was tossing and turning in bed all night."

"Maybe it is a gender issue," Eleanor said. "I've often had trouble with insomnia. Sometimes I wandered around the house. Sometimes I turned on the light and read." She laughed. "The light always woke Mortimer, so I bought him a sleep mask, but it caused a red mark on the arch of his nose so he refused to wear it. It's another reason he started sleeping in the guest bedroom."

They talked more about the eccentric problems of aging, laughing as they talked. When Silas's mantel clock struck ten, Eleanor told him she had to go home.

"Thank you so much for the delicious meal," she told Silas. "Next time, I'll cook."

Silas walked her to her car. "I'd really like to walk you home."

She laughed. "First of all, I live fifteen miles away. If you walked alongside me, I could drive only about five miles an hour, and we'd both be exhausted halfway there."

"Well, thank you for coming," Silas said. He leaned forward and kissed her cheek.

What was *that?* Eleanor wondered as something fresh and sweet and long forgotten sparkled through her from the slight touch of his lips. She liked Silas very much, and so, it seemed, did her body.

As she drove home, she realized she felt so much happier after the evening with Silas. She'd forgotten the pleasure of a companion with a sense of humor. Ari could be funny, but these days were not funny for Ari or for her parents.

As she went into her house and prepared for bed, Eleanor wondered when Ari would be away from her house again. She wanted to invite Silas for dinner. As she settled in bed, pulling the sheet up to her chin, reaching out to turn off her bedside lamp with a touch, she planned the menu. She thought she might start with a large bowl of salad, all kinds of lettuces, including frisée. She loved thinking of how Silas would react.

She slept late Saturday and woke to a silent house. No need to dress right away. No need to scramble eggs for her hardworking granddaughter. Eleanor rose, pulled on a loose, flowery cotton robe that made her look slightly unhinged, as if she were trying to appear like a young girl. But today she wouldn't see anyone—Silas would be playing golf with his chums all day.

Barefoot, she sauntered into her kitchen and made herself a large mug of coffee with plenty of cream and Sweet'N Low. She brought it out on the deck with her and sat in a lounge chair, facing the ocean. For a long while, she simply relaxed, watching the waves ripple in, the color of the water, the way the light changed as the sun moved.

But all too soon she began to worry. *Ari.* A mist of guilt and indecision hung over Eleanor's heart. Should Eleanor try to steer Ari in one direction or the other? Was she acting permissively by saying nothing? One way or the other, Eleanor was driving *herself* mad, she decided, sitting here with all these difficult dilemmas chasing through her mind. She needed to do something real. Something measured, absorbing, and optimistic.

She poured herself another cup of coffee and went into her sewing room. She had begun to make small, light quilts for the fifteen children of Beach Camp. They had so much appreciated their tees. Today she would try to finish the quilts. That would be something good she could put into the universe. Eleanor had always believed that all life was a battle between good and evil. All she could do now, as a woman of seventy, was to try her best to make some good new thing. The material was comforting and soft. She hoped it would bring comfort to the children.

Eleanor pushed back her chair, rose, and stretched. Her neck and back ached from bending over the sewing machine. She checked her watch—good, it was time for lunch. First, she showered and dressed and slipped on her beaded sandals.

She was standing in front of her refrigerator when her cell rang. She fished it out of her pocket.

"Hi, Mom," Cliff said.

Like all other mothers, she could sense—whether she wanted to or not—when her child was going to give her good or bad news. "Hello, darling," Eleanor said. "How's your sister?"

"I'm fine, thanks for asking, Mom," Cliff said sarcastically.

"Oh, dear, have I hurt your feelings?" Eleanor teased him right back.

"I'm calling to give you a quick update. I think it will cheer you up. Alicia and I are on a cruise from Boston up to the St. Lawrence River and back. And, drumroll, please, Alicia has met a man."

Eleanor pulled out a kitchen chair and sat down in it. "What on earth do you mean?"

"It means there is a group of professors traveling with us and one of them has become a good friend of Alicia's."

"I don't believe you."

Cliff laughed heartily, sounding much like his father had. "I'll text you photos. I'm texting them to Phillip, too."

"What? Wait, Cliff, think about what you're doing!" Even as she spoke, her phone pinged as it received the photos.

"Alicia is doing exactly what Phillip is doing. Having an affair."

"Really?"

"Don't sound so shocked. Alicia's beautiful and smart," Cliff said. "She can be charming, too."

"I know she can, but my head is spinning. Oh, Cliff, it would be so sad if Alicia and Phillip divorced."

"Mom, don't blame me. All I did was agree to accompany Alicia on this cruise. I didn't expect that she'd meet anyone. Besides, if it makes you feel better, I don't think she's slept with him yet."

Eleanor put her hand to her forehead. "I really don't need to know the details. But if Alicia's happy, I'm glad."

"I'm happy, too, Mom," Cliff said.

"What does that mean? Did you meet someone, too?"

Cliff laughed. "I'll be back on the island in a few days and then all will be revealed."

"You always did like to torture me, Cliff," Eleanor said sternly.

He laughed again. "I still do." He hung up.

For a long while after the call, Eleanor sat at the table, staring into space. How had her family become so careless, so separate? But then she remembered that her son was actually spending time with his sister, so that was a good thing, something she'd never have expected. Eleanor had never had an affair during her marriage to Mortimer, and she was sure Mortimer had never had an affair, either. He was strikingly handsome, and Eleanor was always aware of women flirting with him, but he was also honest, cautious, and more fascinated with his work as an insurance executive than with people. And he loved Eleanor and his family and his marriage.

Eleanor had always believed Phillip loved Alicia. But Phillip was having an affair, and now so was Alicia, and Ari was pregnant by a man who didn't love her and whom she didn't love. Eleanor's universe had tumbled over.

She was growing gloomy, sitting there with her chin in her hand. She forced herself up from her chair. She would go for a proper mind-clearing walk.

Twenty

Ari told Beck not to meet her ferry because he had to work Friday afternoon. She drove her trusty Subaru onto the rumbling car ferry and after it docked in Hyannis, she drove up Route 6 and over the Sagamore Bridge, up the coast to Plymouth, and finally to his house on Pilgrim Trail Road.

Beck came out his front door the moment she pulled into the driveway. He opened her car door and pulled her up into a passionate kiss.

"Wow," Ari said. "I'm happy to see you, too."

Beck laughed. "Come in. Wait, I'll get your bag." He shouldered her duffel and kept an arm around her waist as they walked up to the porch and the front door.

"It's not my ultimate house," Beck told her. "I'm concentrating on building my practice here. I wanted something clean, in good shape, and close to town."

"It's really nice," Ari said. She would have said that if Beck had led her into a canvas tent. She was determined to talk to him about her pregnancy and her mind was jittery and unsettled.

"Be my guest," Beck quipped, opening the door.

The house was small and seemed smaller, because almost every wall had a bookcase crowded with books. All kinds of books, serious psychology books, Western mystery books, Greek tragedies, Shakespearean plays, thick tomes on physics and quantum theory. The furniture was more or less Pottery Barn, in muted tones of gray and blue. It all looked comfortable and tidy.

"I'll put your bag in Hen's room," Beck said. With a smile, he glanced at Ari. "In case you want to sleep in there tonight."

"Beck, I—" Ari wanted to tell him that she was pregnant *right now* but he led her into the kitchen.

"Sit," Beck said, pulling out a chair. "You have now entered Beckett Hathaway's House of Fish. All of the fish is just out of the ocean."

Ari laughed. "Did you catch it?" Ari asked as she settled in a chair.

"I plead the Fifth," said Beck. He handed her a glass of prosecco. "Welcome."

Ari raised her glass and sipped the tiniest amount possible. She'd done research on drinking during pregnancy, and according to an article from Harvard, drinking in late pregnancy was bad, but during the first three months was not dangerous if the mother didn't drink much or often. Ari was determined to make this glass last the entire meal. She could say that she was feeling rocky after the crossing, and that was true. At every moment, she wanted to interrupt him, to tell him, but Beck had clearly gone to a lot of trouble for this meal.

First, baked oysters in spinach and cheese. Next, Beck quickly sautéed scallops in butter, and Ari thought she'd never eaten such sweet scallops in her life. Finally, clam chowder thick with bacon, onions, potatoes, cream, and clams. Beck sliced a newly baked baguette from a local bakery to dip into the chowder. Ari moaned as she ate. The small green salad served on the side plate was a perfect companion to the chowder. In the past month, she either couldn't bear to eat or she couldn't stop eating.

"You're not drinking your wine," Beck said. "Would you like a glass of water?"

"Please." Ari put down her spoon. She clasped her shaking hands beneath the table. She couldn't avoid it any longer.

"Thank you," she said when Beck set the glass, filled with water and lots of ice cubes, at her place. She drank deeply, with her eyes closed, saying a little prayer that the next few moments wouldn't be too horrible.

"I have to tell you something, Beck," she said, her voice trembling.

Beck smiled slightly. "Okay."

"I'm pregnant."

Beck rocked back in his chair as if punched. "Wow."

"I know. I'm sorry I didn't tell you before. I guess I've been hoping it would all, somehow, disappear. And, Beck, I like you so much . . ." She bit her lip. "I'm trying not to cry. I know it's not fair if I cry."

Beck asked, "Do you want to tell me who the father is?"

Ari nodded. "Peter Anderson is the father. I told you about him. He's been the only serious man in my life. I was going to marry him this summer. It happened three days before I broke off with him, at the end of May. I knew I was going to break off with him, but he was so stressed, I couldn't tell him then. I'd only just gone off my birth control pills . . ."

Talking had settled her, calmed her. She took another sip of water and crossed her arms on the table, gently pushing the empty bowl of chowder away.

"He was, understandably, upset when I ended it. Angry. Hurt. I came to the island to stay with my grandmother, having no idea I was pregnant."

Ari looked down at her hands. "I met you before I knew. I sailed with your family and had dinner with you and I did know by then, but I hadn't really processed it. Plus, so many people come to the island and have summer romances and then it's all over in September." Ari looked up and met Beck's eyes. "I'm falling in love with you, Beck, and it's the absolutely wrong time. I've messed this all up. I'm so sorry."

Beck looked at her steadily. "Have you told Peter?"

"Yes. It was awful. I drove to Boston two weeks ago and told him. He was angry. He wants nothing to do with a child, if I go through with the pregnancy, but he said he'd pay half for an abortion." Ari's lips quivered in a weak, wry smile. "That's so Peter. To pay for exactly half of something."

They were silent for a moment.

"Are you going to have the baby?" Beck asked.

"I am," Ari said, and burst into tears. "I don't know why, but I am. I love children. I know I'll be a good mother. It's not so very strange these days for a woman to have a baby on her own and raise it on her own. Lots of single women do it."

"Do your parents know?"

"Ha. My parents. No, they don't know. They're having their own problems. My grandmother Eleanor knows. I'm sure she'll help me somehow. I'll have to postpone my work toward a master's degree. As for the rest . . . I haven't figured it all out yet." She looked at Beck, desperation in her eyes. "I'm sorry, Beck. I'm so sorry. It was like nothing I've ever known, meeting you, being with you. I know I should have told you sooner, and stopped seeing you." She dropped her head in her hands and cried.

Beck didn't reach to touch her, and she was glad. It was too confusing. She willed herself to stop crying. After a moment, she wiped her eyes and looked at him.

Beck was looking at her, not with anger, and not with pity. "This is a lot to deal with. It's certainly not how I thought this weekend would play out."

"I know. I'm sorry."

"Ari. You must know I have feelings for you, too. I don't want to rush any decision. I'm having trouble getting my mind around this. But you are here, now, and I have tickets for the ballet tomorrow. There's no reason we can't spend this weekend together as friends. As for the future . . . let's not think about it. Or, rather, of course we'll be thinking about it, but let's . . ." Beck gave a short laugh. "As a therapist, I'm bungling this. As a man, I'm completely at sea." He grew serious. "Because to be with you would mean to act as father to another man's child."

"To my child," Ari whispered.

"So here's the plan. We're going to be good friends this weekend. Tonight we'll watch my favorite television series, *Q.I.,* which stands for Quite Interesting. It's a sort of quiz show where the panelists get points not for having the right answer but for having an answer that's quite interesting. It's funny, and it's smart. Tomorrow we'll go to Boston as planned, see the museums, have dinner, attend the ballet."

"That's a good plan, Beck." Ari took a deep breath. She had done it. She had told him. She had told him two things, actually, two enormous, significant things: that she was pregnant, and that she was falling in love with him. She was relieved that they could be friends for the weekend. She was glad, and sad, that she slept in Hen's bedroom that night.

Their day in Boston was perfect. At breakfast they were stiff, uncomfortable with each other, but by the time they were in the city, the awkwardness had passed. Beck was such an amiable, intelligent companion. He wore a lightweight navy blazer that set off his blue eyes. Ari wore a flowered summer frock that flounced when she walked and her amethyst necklace and earrings. It was fun to dress up after being in the sand and water five days a week. She saw people turn to look at him, or maybe, also, at her. He looked a bit like Prince William back when he had hair, and she looked like Kate Middleton. Kind of.

They toured the Museum of Fine Arts, and then, such a change, the Museum of Science. They had a delicious meal at the Atlantic Fish Company. They talked about everything—their families, their school years, their friends.

But when they were seated in silence at the Boston Ballet, Ari was miserable. She wasn't moved by the swelling music or the exquisite performance of the dancers. She only wanted to leave the auditorium and run away from Beck's car all the way to Logan Airport, where she could take a bus to Plymouth and a taxi to Beck's house, and settle in her own car and drive herself back to Hyannis and take the car ferry home.

The logistics of travel would drive a Gothic romance heroine mad, Ari thought, with an inner smile. She was sitting here being too dramatic. Probably because she was pregnant.

Probably because last night she had told Beck she was pregnant.

Tonight Ari and Beck sat side by side in the middle of a center row. She knew he was aware that her knee could so easily have touched his, and he could have so easily taken her hand, but that didn't happen. She could feel how uneasy he was now, in the dark, so close. She knew that this weekend they could have made love for the first time, and become lovers. They could have talked about the future. Well, they had talked about the future. Now they were thinking about the future. Separately. It was a relief when the ballet ended.

They listened to a local radio station on the drive back to Plymouth. It was after midnight when they returned to his house.

"I would ask if you'd like a nightcap," Beck said with a smile. "But . . ."

A nightcap, Ari thought, and immediately an image flashed into her head, from a beautifully illustrated version of *The Night Before Christmas:* "And mamma in her 'kerchief, and I in my cap, / Had just settled our brains for a long winter's nap . . ." It was all there, in the picture she'd studied as a child—the warm house, the children snug in their beds, their mother in a ruffled cap, their father in his stocking cap with a pom-pom on the end. If she could wave a wand, that would be her and Beck and this thimble-size baby inside her, and another child, one of theirs, together. But she had no magic wand. She was foolish to imagine such a sight.

When she looked at Beck, she knew he saw the longing in her eyes, the desire, but she said, because she had to, "No, thanks, Beck. This was a wonderful day. I'm glad I spent it with you. I'm sorry I can't . . . spend the night with you."

Ari wanted him to take her in his arms and say, *I don't care if you're pregnant, I want to marry you and be with you forever because I'm wild with love for you.*

Beck said, "I enjoyed being with you, Ari. Have a good sleep."

He didn't kiss her good night. She walked down the hall to the guest room in total misery, but when she was in her light summer pajamas, tucked between the cool cotton sheets, she fell asleep at once.

She slept late the next morning. She showered, dressed, and found Beck at his desk in the third bedroom he used for an office.

"Good morning," he said. "Would you like some breakfast?"

"Just toast. I can make it."

"Nonsense. I'll make it. You're my guest."

She followed him into the kitchen and sat at the table. He made fresh coffee and sat across from her. He wore board shorts and a rugby shirt. The hair at the back of his neck was damp from his shower. She wanted very much to touch him.

"What time does your boat leave?" Beck asked.

"I'm on the one-thirty back to the island," Ari said.

"I should have driven down and picked you up." Beck stared at her steadily. "I'll do that next time."

Ari's breath caught. "Next time? Are you saying there will be a next time?"

"I hope so." Beck crossed his arms and leaned forward on the table. "Ari, nothing in my life has prepared me for, well, *you*. I really need time to let it sink in, not just that you're going to have a baby in—when—February? Of course, I need to think about that. But what has happened between us, how I feel about you—it's all been sudden, hasn't it? I think I fell in love with you the moment I saw you on the island with my sister, in front of the Hub. I saw you and I thought: 'There she is.' But I think I need time, *we* need time, to get to know each other better. Especially because an innocent child will be involved. I don't know if I can do this. You probably don't know what is right for you, either."

Ari reached over and softly clasped his warm, muscular arms. "Thank you, Beck. You are so smart, so good, and I want you so much . . . in so many ways."

"Let's see where the summer takes us," Beck told her.

"Yes." Regretfully, she took her hands away from his arms. She rose, went into the guest bedroom, and slung her duffel bag over her shoulder.

Beck was at the front door. He was already holding it open. He smiled, a small, melancholy smile, took her bag from her and carried it to her car, put it in the hatch, and went to the driver's-side door where she waited.

"A thought," Beck said. "Talk to your friends. Your closest friends, not only your grandmother, but your friends."

"Yes, I'll do that," Ari said.

He bent to kiss her mouth, lightly, quickly, before standing straight and stepping back. He smiled, but his eyes were troubled.

Ari was trembling. Automatically she got into the car, pulled the door shut, adjusted the seat, strapped on her seatbelt, checked the rearview mirror, and started the car. Beck stood steadily, his hand lifted in a gesture of farewell.

Ari slept for the two hours and fifteen minutes it took the ferry to cross the sound and dock in Nantucket. She drove home in a stupor, feeling hungry and exhausted and guilty and cranky.

The house was quiet. "Gram?" she called. A movement from the window caught her eye and she saw Eleanor with the garden hose, watering her flowers. The summer humidity had made her salt-and-pepper hair fly up in wispy twists all around her head. *That's how women become thought of as witches,* Ari thought. Eleanor turned and saw Ari at the window and smiled like an angel.

Ari unpacked while Eleanor finished the watering, then they both sat on the deck with glasses of sweetened iced tea, more ice than tea.

"How was your visit?" Eleanor asked.

"I told him I was pregnant," Ari said. "The first night I was there, he had prepared a gourmet meal and served prosecco. I didn't drink it, and . . . I told him." Ari explained Beck's reaction, the strange day in Boston and at the ballet, Beck's kindness, and his hesitation.

"I'm glad he needs to think things over," Eleanor said. "You haven't been together long—"

"What can I do?" Ari asked.

Eleanor thought a moment. "A man would have to be crazy or maybe slightly mental to say 'Oh, my darling, I'll marry you and be the father of your child' when he's known you only for, what, two months?"

"I know," Ari agreed.

"So, we wait," Eleanor said, her voice kind. "I have some news as well. No, it's not about Silas. It's about your mother. Cliff called me to say he was with her on a cruise to the St. Lawrence River."

"That's nice."

"Wait. Cliff told me your mother has a . . . boyfriend."

"What?"

"He doesn't think they've . . . slept together yet. But she's happy. I don't know any more than that."

Ari rubbed her eyes. "Am I dreaming?"

Eleanor said, "It's confusing, I know."

"It seems like my family is flying in all different directions," Ari said.

"I'm here," Eleanor told her. "I'll always be here. And I think you're tired."

"I slept on the boat."

"Still, you need to get away from your thoughts. And it's very hot and humid outside. Let's go into the library, turn on the air conditioner, and watch something by Alfred Hitchcock. *Rear Window*. Or *The Birds*."

Ari nodded. "Anything but *Vertigo*. I'm having quite enough of that as it is."

"Do you feel well enough to continue working at Beach Camp?" Eleanor asked.

"Oh, absolutely, Gram. I really enjoy it, and after a good night's sleep, I'll be fine."

"I'm so glad. I was thinking, Ari . . . I've been checking the weather forecasts and it looks like we've got a nor'easter coming our way. Maybe Cal and the others would like to have Beach Camp here again this week."

"Wow, that's so nice of you."

"I enjoyed having the children in my house, Ari. I miss hearing their laughter, their sweet voices."

Ari studied her grandmother. "Do you get lonely out here, in the winter, when you're by yourself?"

"Not lonely," Eleanor answered. "And not bored. I have my routines and my friends. And of course I have my memories. If I want, I can look at photo albums, or the holiday videos Cliff made during the last few years. But seeing those small children . . . it makes me more optimistic about the future. About everything, really. And Cal. I like Cal and his family. They are making a difference in the world, and if I can help by having Beach Camp here on a rainy day, I'd love to do my own small bit."

"You're wonderful, Gram."

"Maybe I'm just old and wise," Eleanor replied, smiling.

Twenty-One

That week it rained every day. The air was humid, hard to breathe in. Eleanor was delighted to have the children from Beach Camp over again. When everyone was there, they had arts and crafts in the dining room. Then, when Gabriel asked if they could watch television, Eleanor said it was time to go outside and play in the sprinklers. With her hair whizzing around her head in the humidity, she looked like an enchantress, and the children were fascinated with her.

"But if we go out, we'll get wet!" Sarita cried.

"Yes, and when you run through my sprinklers, you'll get wet, too," Eleanor told her. "Now take off your shoes and leave them under your chair. That way when you come in for lunch, you'll know where to sit. If you want to, take off your shirts. I'll have towels waiting for each of you when you come back in."

The boys elbowed each other to get out the door first. The girls followed, some happily, some reluctantly. Eleanor had hoses with sprinklers set out on three sides of the house. She'd bought a clever toy she'd found online that was a ball you could jump on and the hose would shoot a rubber frog up in the air. Cal, Sandy, and Ari, wearing raincoats, supervised the three groups of children, who shouted and laughed in the rain and the sprinklers.

When they finally came back into the house, chaos reigned while the adults got the children dried off and dressed in their dry tees. In the dining room, they found lunches on paper plates. Peanut butter and jelly sandwiches. Chips. Grapes. Juice. Next, they all crawled under the table to sit with eyes closed while one child hid on the ground floor. After playing fifteen games of hide-and-seek, even the largest boy was yawning.

"Now, children," Eleanor said. "It's rest time. Let's go into the living room—"

"I want to stay under the table," a child yelled.

"Me, too!" cried another child.

Eleanor gave Ari a helpless look.

Ari was stern. "No, this is not the nap room. This is the lunch and arts room."

Eleanor added, "Once you've settled down, I'll give each of you a surprise that I think you'll like very much."

The children scrambled into the living room and dropped to the floor, wriggling and giggling. Eleanor opened the dining room sideboard and brought out a pile of small, colorful quilts. She saw Ari glance questioningly at Cal, who gave Ari a thumbs-up sign.

Eleanor leaned close to Ari and whispered, "I phoned Cal to get his permission." She spoke in a stern voice when she spoke to the children. "Close your eyes," Eleanor said. "Don't open them until I say so."

She walked among the children, stopping at each one to take a light quilt from the pile and place it gently on a child. The children were restless but for the most part kept their eyes tightly closed, except for the few who peeked through their lashes.

"Now," Eleanor said. "You may sit up for a moment and look at what you have."

"What is it?" a child called out.

"It's a quilt," Eleanor told the group. "It's like a very soft, light

blanket. For when you don't need covers to be warm, but you'd like
to have something over you."

"Me," a little girl shouted. "I do! I have to have a sheet over me to
go to sleep."

Eleanor nodded at the girl. "Look at your quilts. You'll see that in
the very middle is a white square. After you have your rest, we'll sit
at the dining room table and use magic markers to make your initials
on the quilt, so you'll know it's your very own."

"Can we take them home?" a child asked.

"Not until the last day of Beach Camp," Eleanor told them.
"These will stay with Cal and you can use them every afternoon for
your rest time."

"Mine is pretty," Sarita said.

"Mine is, too!" another girl called out.

"Mine is too short," a boy yelled, lying flat on his back and pulling
his quilt so that his toes peeked out.

"Then curl up like a snail," Eleanor suggested.

All the children immediately curled up. After a few "hush" sug-
gestions from Cal, the children were quiet. Some slept. One little girl
held the quilt as she lay on her side, moving the fabric around so she
could study each patch.

That Friday night, Eleanor went out to dinner with Ari and Cal. She
didn't want to go, because she was right in the middle of a mystery
by Julia Spencer-Fleming, but she knew Cal was trying to thank her
for her day with the children and she didn't want to hurt his feelings.

Cal took them to Fifty-Six Union. Eleanor had to wear her hearing aids, as she did whenever she went out in a group, but she had
calmed her hair down and combed it over her ears. She wore a
peach-colored sundress that showed a triangle of wrinkled skin
across her chest, but she was so hot during these summer days and
nights, vanity didn't matter.

Ari wore a sundress, too, in turquoise, which suited her perfectly.
It had a low-plunging neckline that exposed just a bit of the white
skin of her breasts against the dark tan she'd gotten over the sum-

mer. Her long dark hair was up in a high ponytail, and she wore dangling turquoise earrings. What a beauty she was, Eleanor thought.

Cal wore black trousers and a white button-down shirt with the sleeves rolled up. Eleanor could imagine him behind a pulpit, blessing people, but she could also imagine him with an eye patch and a parrot on his shoulder. Or in a gypsy caravan, or on one of the long boats on the British canals like the one she just saw on *Father Brown*.

All through their very excellent meal, Eleanor focused on Cal and his family and Beach Camp. In fact, Eleanor realized when her butterscotch parfait arrived, they hadn't really included Ari, and when they had, Ari was quiet, responding and laughing only when necessary. Eleanor knew she was troubled. Another week had passed. Another week when Ari's parents were split up, spending time with other people. Another week for Ari's baby to grow. Ari's parents should know, Eleanor thought, with an increasing sense of urgency. They should know now. They should be given time to consider how they could help Ari, and their grandchild. Eleanor could understand Ari's reluctance to talk to them. But Eleanor had no such reluctance.

"Gram? You have such a strange look on your face. What are you thinking?" Ari asked.

Eleanor rolled her eyes. "So sorry. I think it's just getting a bit late for me." It was only a quarter past ten, but she'd found she could play the old-age card whenever she wanted.

Cal called for the check. They walked out to the parking lot, where their two cars awaited. Ari had insisted that she drive Eleanor to and from her house. Cal helped Eleanor into the passenger seat of Ari's Subaru and walked around to the driver's side. Ari had already settled herself and was fastening her seatbelt.

"Thanks again, Cal, we had a wonderful time," she said, waving.

Ari steered the car carefully from the parking lot and turned onto South Washington Street.

"Did you have a good time?" Ari asked her grandmother.

"I did. I like Cal a lot." Eleanor saw her granddaughter's face caught in a flash of lights. Ari looked pensive, even sad.

Eleanor asked, "Have you heard from Beck?"

"Yes. He's texted several times. He's busy at the clinic. He asks how I am. But he's not coming down this weekend."

"Ah." Eleanor sat quietly for the rest of the ride, her mind churning with thoughts and possibilities. As Ari slowed the car to the twenty miles per hour required by 'Sconset, Eleanor asked, "Have you considered where you want to live once you have your baby? For that matter, where do you want to have your baby?"

"I think about it all the time," Ari said.

"I think your parents should know," Eleanor said slowly. "You're three months along now. True, you're not showing yet—"

"I'm looking a little chubby," Ari said.

"Well, you're going to look chubbier. You'll be showing soon. Some of the summer people leave in a week to return home to get their children ready for school. Have you asked Cal how long camp lasts in the summer?"

"No. I haven't even thought of that. I don't know why, Gram, but I seem to be in a stupor. I haven't even told my best friend. You're the only one who knows. Well, you, Peter, and Beck."

Eleanor said, very carefully, "You know you're welcome to stay here as long as you want. But you need to discuss this with your parents. And you need to remember how different the island is in the winter. Have you decided whether you'll take the courses you signed up for in childhood education? Because that means you'll need a home base in Boston. And childcare in the spring semester."

"Oh, Gram," Ari cried. Tears ran down her cheeks. "I'm a mess!"

"You're not a mess," Eleanor said. "But you are in a mess, for sure. I'll help you. I'm not saying don't worry, because you should worry, or at least make a plan, but I'll help you. I'm going to invite your parents and your uncle here for a meeting."

"But you don't know where Mother is!"

"No. But I can text her. Or email her. I'll work it out."

Ari turned into the drive and cut the engine. Her shoulders shook as she sobbed. "I'm so scared," she whispered.

"Yes, I know," Eleanor told her. She patted Ari's back gently. "You'll be fine. Right now you need to get some sleep."

Monday, after Ari had left for camp, Silas knocked on Eleanor's kitchen door. She knew he was coming. He'd promised to bring pastries from the Sconset Market. She'd promised to make fresh coffee.

"Good God, but this is an old white elephant, isn't it?" Silas remarked as they settled on the deck.

"It was in my grandmother's family," Eleanor said.

"And you live here year-round? How do you stay warm in the winter?"

"Oh, I manage. I keep space heaters in my bedroom and bathroom. Often, I make a fire in the living room, but I'll confess lugging in the wood and kneeling down to put it on the grate is becoming a bit of a trial."

"I'm sure. I had one of those gas-fired fake wood things installed in my fireplace. Works like a dream. And I don't have to clean out the ashes."

Eleanor was silent, thinking. "Did my children put you up to this?"

Silas looked puzzled. "Up to what?"

"Oh, Silas, they want me to sell this house."

"And you don't want to because . . ."

Eleanor made a little *humph* noise. "Because they're pretending I'm too old to keep it up, too old to live here alone. I know it's because they want the money."

Silas scanned the roofline. "The trim needs a new coat of paint."

"Yes, I know."

"You wouldn't have to give them all the money. You could buy a house in town."

"I never thought of that," Eleanor said. "I thought it was straight into the retirement home with me and stewed peas and mystery meat for the rest of my life."

Silas laughed. "You're far too young for that. If you lived in town, it would be easier to get to the library, to the grocery store, to the bank. You know I sold our house when Maxine died. It was hard, at first. Frightening, even. But now I'm delighted with my house in town."

Eleanor was silent, thinking. Before she could stop herself, she blurted, "My granddaughter's going to have a baby. By herself."

"Go on," Silas said.

"She's not quite three months pregnant, so she hasn't really come to her senses about it all. The father of the child wants nothing to do with it or her. Her parents are going through a rough patch, and my daughter never did care much for babies."

"So you think Ari might live with you?"

"She might."

Silas cleared his throat. He looked up and down the bluff edge, at the bluff path leading past all the glorious summer gardens and trophy houses.

He asked, "How many of these houses are occupied in the winter?"

"Well, none," Eleanor told him, feeling defensive. "But the village has quite a few year-round residents."

"Any young people?"

Eleanor leaned forward. "Silas Stover, are you trying to aggravate me? Because it's working."

Silas chuckled. The sound woke something almost forgotten inside her. That baritone, satisfying laugh . . . She leaned back in her chair. "Oh, Silas, isn't it hard, deciding to sell a house that's been in the family for five generations?"

"Not if you look toward the future," Silas said. "It seems to me that your children aren't as enchanted with this house or this island. That happens. It happened to me. So there they are, off into their future, which doesn't include coming to this house for the beautiful summer months. The thing is, what about *your* future? You're an active, lovely, smart woman. Whether you help your granddaughter when her baby comes is one thing, but you know she's not going to live with you forever. You wouldn't want that. She certainly wouldn't want that. So how do you see your future?

You've got a good fifteen or twenty years before you toddle off into assisted living."

"I love this island," Eleanor said quietly.

"I understand. So do I." Silas shifted in his chair. "And you know, I'm seeing more of it than I ever knew was there. I've joined a birding group and we go to the damnedest places, secret hollows and hidden forests. I take a lot of the Maria Mitchell science tours. It's good for my health, the walking. Good for my soul, too."

"My soul is fine," Eleanor snapped.

Silas laughed heartily.

That was a wonderful sound, Eleanor thought. "Silas, how much did you pay for your house on Fair Street?"

He named a sum that seemed both exorbitant, when compared with houses in the real world, and manageable, compared with what Eleanor thought she could get for this house.

"I don't know," she mused. "I have so much *stuff* in my house. It would take me a decade to sort through it all."

"There are special estate companies that will look through your *stuff* and give you an estimate for it all and come pack it up and take it away," Silas said. "That's what I did."

"My children might want some of it . . ." Eleanor said weakly.

"Let them have first choice," Silas said.

Eleanor stood up and paced along the deck. "This view. This endless blue sea."

"Yes. It's unique. It's awe-inspiring. But you know, Eleanor, grandchildren and great-grandchildren are awe-inspiring, too."

Eleanor returned to her chair. "Why, Silas, you're a sentimentalist. I never would have dreamed of you that way."

"Nope. Not sentimental. I speak the truth, madam."

Eleanor felt something move inside her, an iceberg melting, a clear stream flowing. She felt cool and clear.

She fought it off, this sense of hope, this sense of wonder. "You know, Silas, I never want to get married again. I like living alone. I have a cat, and I have my own routine, and I don't want to cook when I don't want to."

Silas put back his head and laughed a long time, which Eleanor thought was rather rude of him, even though she knew she'd been rude herself.

When he got himself together, he said, "I will never propose to you, Eleanor, I promise. I like my independence, too."

"Well, then," Eleanor said, "I will consider selling this place. I'll see if I can find a realtor I can trust."

"How about Jeff Townsend? He was the realtor for my house." Silas rose. "I've got to get back to town. I've got a board meeting for the Coastal Foundation."

Eleanor rose, too. They carried their mugs into the kitchen and Eleanor walked Silas to the back door. He opened it and turned back. "Just one thing," he said, as if he were Columbo. "The house next door to me is for sale."

Twenty-Two

Ari knew she'd been off her form today at Beach Camp. She tripped over a beach ball instead of catching it. She'd spoken harshly to a child—who was shoving a smaller child, but still. And worst of all, when she was guarding the outside line in the ocean so the children wouldn't go past her, she'd peed in the water. No one seemed to notice, but she was embarrassed anyway, even though she knew the children peed in the water all the time.

With her tingling, sore breasts, her uncomfortably tight waistbands, and her constant desire to sleep, she was ever more aware of her pregnancy and ever more confused.

Determined to be cheerful, Ari decided as she drove home to stop at her favorite farm stand, Moors End. She'd pick up some corn for this evening, and berries and fresh lettuce, and flowers, too! She turned onto Polpis Road and turned left when she came to the farm stand driveway. It was still Old-Nantuckety, with a cash-out table inside a wooden shed with only two walls. Large cardboard boxes of just-picked vegetables sat around on tables. Fresh flowers were displayed in mason jars filled with water. Beyond the shed were rows of herbs and the greenhouses and farther out were fields of flowers and growing corn.

Standing by the boxes of corn were her father and a woman.

The sight hit her like a punch in her chest. For a panicky moment, she couldn't breathe. Then she walked past the other shoppers and stood next to her father. He was busy looking down at the corn while the woman held out a hemp bag.

"Hello, Daddy," Ari said. She could hardly get the words out. She was shaking uncontrollably.

Her father straightened, looked at her, and stepped back. He wore a blue rugby shirt with the collar turned up like a frat boy, board shorts, and leather loafers without socks. For a moment, he looked like a stranger to Ari.

He said, "*Ari*. My goodness." He looked surprised, almost frightened.

Ari's fingertips were numb. She couldn't catch her breath, but she said, "Are you going to introduce me to your 'friend'? Why don't you bring her home and introduce her to Eleanor, and to Cliff, oh, and to *your wife?*"

"Ari," her father said, reaching out to steady her. "It's okay. It's going to be all right."

Ari twitched away from his touch. She was shaking so hard, her teeth were chattering.

Unbelievably, the woman spoke. Her head high, a gentle smile on her face, she said, "Ari, my name is Bemi. Your father is famous for his surgical skill—"

"How can you even speak to me?" Ari's heart jumped hard in her chest. She was hyperventilating, and her vision was hazy. All she could clearly see was the woman's shorts and blue halter top. "I am his *daughter*. He is *married*. And you are a—home wrecker!"

By now the other shoppers were looking at them, but Ari didn't care. Tears streamed down her face.

"Ari—" Her father had tears in his eyes, too.

"I'm a traveling nurse," Bemi said, speaking quickly. "I'm here only for the summer to help with the expanded population. I'm leaving at the end of September."

"Who cares?" Ari spat. "You've done your damage! My father is

destroying his marriage and breaking our hearts because of *you!*"
She had never hated anyone more in her life. She'd never been so
angry. She hoped her words hurt the other woman, because the
other woman was hurting her, and all of Ari's family.

Bemi put her hand on Ari's father's arm. "I'll wait in the car."

Ari caught her breath, taking in shivery gulps of air, as if she'd
almost drowned. She was aware of other people watching her in a
kind of hushed audience.

Her father said softly, "Ari, we can't talk here. Please. I love you. I
love your mother. I just . . . if you'd let me speak with you someplace
else . . ."

The pain of hearing her father's voice struck like lightning through
Ari. She was amazed she could stand.

"What could you possibly say? Why would I even want to hear
your words? I *hate* you." Ari turned to walk off. She stopped. She
looked back at her father. "Oh, and my mother is on a cruise with
her new boyfriend."

"Ari—" Her father held out his hand.

She tossed her hair like a mean girl in high school and said, "And
I'm *pregnant.*"

She felt triumphant as she walked to her car. She slid into the Subaru, closed the door, yanked on her seatbelt. The inside of the car
felt like shelter to her, like protection from her father and his girlfriend and all the people watching. Still, she knew she should calm
down before driving. She fished a tissue from her backpack and
blew her nose. She wiped her face and dug her fingers into her palms,
trying to stop her shivering. She didn't know who she hated more at
that moment, her father, weird Bemi, or herself. Why hadn't she
been cold and cutting? She'd behaved horribly. Couldn't she have
handled it better? Her anger melted as she was drenched with burning shame.

Ari carefully pulled around the lot to the exit sign, checked for
oncoming traffic, and headed toward her grandmother's house. She
screamed as loudly as she could while she drove.

Ari pulled into her grandmother's driveway, turned off the engine, and just sat for a while, staring at nothing. Her breath came out squeaky and hoarse and she wasn't certain she could walk. She took a long drink from her water bottle. She wiped her face and put on a touch of light lipstick. More deep breaths. As she got out of the car, weirdly, her mother's voice came to her, saying, "Be a big girl now," as she had said to Ari when she was a small child getting a vaccination.

Finally she crawled from her car. She felt weak, a hundred years old. The image of her father's face today—so worried, so surprised, so *guilty*—flashed before her repeatedly. It made Ari feel furious at her father, and it made her feel sad for him.

She found Eleanor sitting in the living room. Two tumblers of iced peach tea sat on the coffee table.

Eleanor said, "Your father called me."

Ari sank onto the sofa opposite her grandmother. "You know I saw him."

"Yes. He wants me to tell you that he's tremendously sorry, sorry about everything."

Ari wanted to make a sarcastic reply, but she was too tired. "The woman—Bemi—isn't even pretty."

"Your father says he's not going to see Bemi anymore. He wants to talk with your mother. He wants to know where your mother is. I told him I didn't know and I wouldn't tell him if I did."

Ari sat back in surprise. "That must have been quite a phone call." She thought a moment, her mind whirling. "I hope Mom is in love with that guy she met and she divorces Dad."

Eleanor was quiet for a long time. "I'm not sure you truly hope that."

Ari put her head in her hands. "I don't know." She sighed. "Bemi said my father is famous for his skill as a surgeon."

"Yes," Eleanor said. "I think he is."

"Does that *woman* think I don't know how talented Dad is?"

"Maybe she thinks you've forgotten that, gotten used to it."

Ari thought about that. "Do you think Einstein's wife thought he was boring?"

Eleanor laughed. "I'd bet Einstein's wife thought he was exhausting." She rose. "I'm going to fix myself a drink. I think you should take a nap. We've got chaos all around us and I'm sure you can't think straight. I certainly can't."

"I am tired," Ari admitted. She seemed always to be tired these days. "Thanks, Gram."

Her bedroom smelled of flowers. While she was gone, her grandmother had cut some of the Darcey Bussell roses Eleanor had grown in the shelter at the front of her house and put them in a vase. The roses sat on her bedside table, the leaves dark green and glossy, the roses crimson and old-fashioned, as if they were a part of the house. Of the family. Ari sat on the bed, pulled off her sneakers, and stretched out on the quilt. She loved this house, this room. If she lay on one side, she could gaze at the never-ending blue ocean, a body of salt water that during a storm could drive its salt into one small, fragile flower and kill it. But Eleanor had found a shelter for the rose. The bush was tucked into the one spot around the house where it could thrive. Ari thought of the baby, her baby, not even as big as a rosebud now, and how she was curled around it, protecting it, feeding and nurturing it. Had this last hour of anger and sorrow harmed it? She hoped not. She hoped it lay safe and innocent while the storm raged past.

She slept. Not long, because when her phone woke her, it wasn't yet dark.

"Hi, Ari," Beck said.

"Hi, Beck." Ari thought his voice was like balm. She was so relaxed from her nap, as if sleep had carried her anger away.

"I've been thinking of you, Ari," Beck said. "I'm sorry I couldn't get down to the island this weekend."

Ari scooted into a sitting position, cushioned by her pillows, and closed her eyes. Her entire body seemed tuned to the particular tone and resonance of Beck's voice. *Just this,* she thought. *Just now. Just always.*

"Ari? Are you there?"

"Sorry, Beck, yes, I'm here. I'm so glad to hear from you. How are you? What did you do this weekend?"

"Actually, I spent Saturday doing paperwork in my office. Sunday I picked up Hen off the boat in Hyannis and took her up to Boston for the day. We saw a matinee of *Hamilton*."

"Lucky Hen! She adores you."

"What did you do this weekend?"

"Oh," Ari said casually, taking a great deal of pleasure in saying this, "Cal took my grandmother and me for dinner at Fifty-Six Union. We had a wonderful time. My grandmother was quite charmed, I think."

Beck was silent for a moment. "I hope you'll spend this weekend with me. You know the yacht club is having another dinner dance, and the weather looks good."

Don't do this, Ari thought. *Don't get my hopes up.* "Sounds like fun," she said.

"If the weather holds, we can go sailing. Maybe with Hen."

Ari sat up straight. "Are you messing with me, Beck Hathaway?"

"I am most certainly not messing with you, Ari. I really want to see you."

"All right, then," Ari said, almost grumpily. "I'd like to spend the weekend with you."

After the call, Ari showered and put on clean clothes. The confrontation with her father and Bemi had somehow faded to the background, like a panel on those slowly revolving fantasy lamps on children's bedside tables. Now Beck was in the forefront—Beck was on most of the panels, she thought.

She found her grandmother in an unusually happy mood. They worked together roasting Brussels sprouts in olive oil and sea salt and preparing a huge salad that they ate with leftover meatloaf. Ari insisted on cleaning the kitchen, because she knew there was a television show Eleanor liked to watch. Later, she curled on the sofa, watching the show, too, keeping her grandmother company.

———

The summer days were hot and clear. Ari was glad for the routine of Beach Camp. Most evenings she spent with friends, idly shopping, enjoying dinner on the patio at the Boarding House, seeing a play or a movie. One friend, Peyton, remarked that Ari was glowing and voluptuous, and Michelle laughed. "That's because she's in love with my brother." Ari thought, not unhappily, *That's because I'm pregnant.* What Ari said was, "I'm in the sun five days a week, playing with children."

She hadn't heard from her father or mother, and neither had Eleanor. She replayed the event over and over in her head when she wasn't with someone else, so she was more sociable than she'd ever been before, and it was a perfect time for strolling outside, swimming, sailing, having a drink with friends.

"I will compartmentalize," she told herself, and tried to put her father and Bemi in a small ugly box at the back of her mind. It worked, sometimes, but never when she went to bed. Then, like a child, she remembered it all, and cried herself to sleep.

At the club dinner dance Friday night, Ari was certain from the way that Beck looked at her that he cared about her. They couldn't stop touching each other, holding hands, pressing their knees together under the table, and when they stood chatting with friends, Beck kept his arm around her waist, holding her against him. Several friends teased her about being Beck's date *again*.

"Don't you have to go to Boston or something?" one friend asked.

"Yeah, give us a chance," another friend said.

Ari laughed, feeling smug. *Girl, you are riding for a fall,* she told herself, but when Beck held her against him during a slow dance, his chin resting against her hair, she felt safe. At home.

They spent Saturday afternoon sailing with Hen. Ari was content to lean back in the sailboat and watch Beck show his little sister how to trim the sails, come about, tack, and jibe. *He would be a good father,* Ari thought.

Sunday afternoon they went swimming at Sesachacha Pond, where the water was separated from the ocean by a sandbar. The beach was small, but they found a place at the far end to put their towels and cooler. They entered the clear blue water together, swimming side by side, and floating. Beck's body in his navy blue board shorts was long and lean and muscular. He had a scar along one upper arm from a bike accident when he was thirteen. He swam up to her, put his arms around her waist, and together they treaded water. Ari had never been quite so completely exposed to a man, with her wet hair plastered against her head and her face free of makeup. Beck kissed her on her mouth. Their legs slid together as they slowly kicked back and forth. They sank below the surface, still kissing. When they came to the surface, they grinned at each other and swam separate ways. Far away, children splashed each other, laughing. Ari rolled onto her back and floated as the water rocked her and the sun warmed her face.

Afterward, Ari drove them to her grandmother's house so they could shower and dress. Eleanor wasn't home—she was off with her new friend Silas, playing golf (playing golf? Eleanor played golf?)—but Ari and Beck took showers separately, dressed separately, and emerged clean, combed, and ready for Ari to drive Beck to his ferry.

All weekend, Ari had wondered what Beck had decided. Could he continue to share his life with a woman pregnant by someone else? Was he ready to be a parent?

When they drove near the ferry terminal, Ari pulled her car over to the side of the Harborside Stop & Shop, where there was never a place to park, but which was wide enough for her to park behind cars for a moment. Swarms of families, college kids, and older people strolled onto Straight Wharf where the Hy-Line was docked.

"I'm sorry I can't walk you to the boat," Ari said. She would not mention their relationship. She would not.

Beck turned toward her, his eyes warm. He took her hand in his, and for a moment, he looked at their joined hands.

"Ari." He looked very serious. "This was a great weekend. You know I wouldn't have brought Hen sailing with you if I thought I wouldn't . . . see you again. Hen adores you. So do I. I think you know that. But I really need to think about this, about us. It's huge. It's important. Life changing. Please give me some more time."

Tears spilled down Ari's cheeks. She wanted him so much. Not only physical want, but spiritual and personal and everlasting. She knew it was too soon to make a decision. But she was pulled toward him like a compass toward true north.

She gathered herself. Sniffed back her tears. She wouldn't beg. "I adore Hen, too," she said, with a mischievous smile.

He nodded. He got out of the car, reached into the backseat to get his duffel bag, smiled at her, and walked away.

In August there was almost always a hurricane or tropical storm kicking up near Florida that brought high winds and crazy waves to the island. Monday, Beach Camp followed its usual routine, but Tuesday the wind arrived, not quite gale force, but strong enough to turn the ocean wild.

Under Cal's direction, they took the Beach Camp kids to the south side of the island, where the waves were the most spectacular. Cal, Sandy, Ari, and two of the volunteer counselors who showed up that day formed a line about three feet from the spot where the waves hit the shore. The children were allowed to play in the foaming, leaping waves, but not to pass the safety line the adults provided. The wind came hurtling toward the land, causing the waves to explode, and the air was full of spits of salty water. The children screamed with joy. They threw themselves into the surging waves. They struggled to see who could stay upright as a row of breakers rushed in. They invented a brilliant game of building sand castles as fast as they could, and watching the waves surge relentlessly toward the castles, demolishing the buildings and scattering the sand everywhere. They cheered madly and built more mounds of sand as high as they could, only to dance and yell triumphantly when the waves knocked them down.

"They really are little beasts," Ari yelled at Cal.

"We all feel that way in a storm like this," Cal shouted back.

It was true, Ari thought as she drove home at the end of the day. People loved the energy and wildness of a storm on the ocean. Well, people safely on the land felt that way.

If she thought of her own life, she realized she was on no kind of land. And her world was stormy. Uncontrollable. She hadn't heard from her mother or her father or Uncle Cliff. She knew she was in love with Beck, and she thought he was in love with her, but that gave her no harbor. Her waist was swelling beneath her loose shirts, and soon those shirts would be too tight. In her email were forms from the university requesting enrollment information, course selection. Would she want a room in the dorm? Ari laughed at that, and wept a bit, too.

More than anything, she wanted a nap.

When she arrived home, she thought, with a kind of jolt: *Home? Is this home?* It was her grandmother's house. Her anxiety kicked in, offsetting her exhaustion.

She found Eleanor at her desk in the small alcove off the kitchen. Here she kept and paid all her bills and handled necessary correspondence.

"Hello, darling," Eleanor called, standing up to hug her.

"Gram," Ari said, "could I talk to you?"

"Of course. Let's get some iced tea and sit on the deck."

They bustled around together in the kitchen, dropping ice cubes into glasses (Eleanor didn't own a fancy refrigerator with an ice maker—that would be one step too nouveau riche), pouring the cold tea from the pitcher on the top shelf of the refrigerator, Eleanor adding sugar, Ari adding nothing. The familiar everyday motions calmed Ari.

Eleanor slid open a door onto the deck and quickly closed it.

"We can't sit on the deck," she told Ari. "Too windy." Eleanor sat at her usual place at the kitchen table.

Ari brought her glass of tea over and took a nearby chair.

"Now," Eleanor said. "Tell me."

"I'm in love with Beck," Ari began, and then it all came out in a rush. "I think he loves me, I'm sure he does, but I've told him I'm pregnant, and he says he needs time to think it over, because of the baby, so here I am, like an untethered boat on a stormy sea, and I don't know what to do! Apparently both my parents are gallivanting through life with their brand-new lovers, so I can't even *find* them to ask if I can live with them, and Uncle Cliff is no help at all. I want to start my courses for my master's, and I could do it this semester, it's over in December, and the baby won't come until February, and—" Ari burst into tears. "Oh, Gram, I'm going to have a baby!"

Eleanor sat quietly, smiling gently.

"I'm scared," Ari confessed. She took a paper napkin and began tearing at it with her fingers. "I'm afraid of the pain—I've heard the pain is unspeakable—and I don't know how to take care of a baby, and I don't know where I'm going to live, and from what I've heard, I won't get any sleep for a year, and I'll be dumpy and unattractive and—" Ari was sobbing now, caught up in the full throes of her fear. "I won't be able to take courses for my master's, and Beck won't marry me and, and—"

"And you'll end up living in a trailer down by the river," Eleanor said.

"What?" Eleanor's words shocked Ari out of her frenzy. She met her grandmother's eyes, and suddenly they both began to laugh.

"Is it hormones?" Ari asked.

"Probably. Also, your life is a bit of a mess." Eleanor picked up a spoon and stirred sugar into Ari's tea. "Drink up. Sugar helps. And I'll help if I can. First of all, you are in a mess, but you're going to have to wait for Beck to make up his mind. It's no small responsibility to take on some other man's child as his own."

"Oh, I know, I know," Ari agreed and began crying again. "I don't know how I could have been so stupid. But I can't just *wait* for Beck. I refuse to be a pitiful maiden needing a big strong man to rescue me. I'm determined to take online classes from B.U. this fall and next spring, too. I'll live with my parents—they'll *have* to let me stay there. I'm their daughter. This will be their grandchild." Ari's heart jumped as a new possibility occurred to her. "What if they get divorced?"

"You could always stay with me," Eleanor said quietly. "I'd love helping you take care of my great-grandchild."

"You would?" Ari was so startled she stopped crying. "Gram, that's fabulous! You're so kind! I love you! Thank you!" Jumping up, she seized Eleanor in a hug and kissed the top of her head.

"Don't be silly," Eleanor told her. "Sit down. Calm down. Take things one day at a time, right?"

"Right, but the summer is almost over. Beach Camp has only one more week left."

"Beach Camp is a wonderful gift to all those children and their parents. You should be proud of yourself for working there when you could have made much more money elsewhere."

"Thank you, Gram." Ari blew her nose into her shredded napkin. "Maybe I'll never marry. Maybe I'll live here with you and we'll be all alone in the winter with gale force winds shaking the house and the waves crashing."

Eleanor said, "Maybe I won't be living in this house this winter."

Ari was startled. "Are you going to sell the house?"

"I don't know," Eleanor said. "I might. I have to think about it. Like Beck, I don't like to be rash about important matters." She stood up, pausing to let her blood pressure join her. "I haven't had dinner yet. Have you? Let's just have tuna salad sandwiches and watch television."

"Gram," Ari said, almost sternly, "what has gotten into you?"

"Ari, my darling girl," Eleanor said, "whatever I'm doing is related to what has gotten into you."

Friday was the last day of Beach Camp. Elementary school would start soon. Cal had to go to New York to begin his courses at the New Seminary. Sandy was packing up to move down to Florida to work for a hotel in Miami. Cleo would continue to work at Our Island Home, traveling up to Boston on her days off to spend time with her husband. Poppy would also commute.

Ari had thought about having a farewell party for the counselors at her grandmother's home, but during the final week of camp it was clear that everyone was in a hurry to get back to real life. Friday, after the last parent had picked up the last child, Cal and Sandy hugged Ari and thanked her, but didn't, as she'd assumed they would, suggest they all go for a drink.

"You were wonderful!" Sandy told Ari. "The best ever counselor. The kids adored you."

"I adored them," Ari said. She was almost in tears.

"Maybe you'll work with us again next year," Cal said.

"Maybe," Ari replied. She hadn't told them she was pregnant, and she suddenly realized that they probably had separate parts of their lives they didn't share with her.

"Don't look so sad," Sandy told Ari, taking her hand. "We'll email and text. We won't lose touch."

"Thanks. I had such a good time," Ari said. "I think Beach Camp is wonderful, and so important for the children. I'd like to be part of it somehow . . . I'm not sure how, just yet."

"We've got the whole winter to plan," Cal said. "Really, Ari, you're part of the camp now."

What does that mean? Ari thought, because no sooner had Cal spoken than a car drove up to the curb and honked lightly. Cal and Sandy jumped into the car, waved at Ari, and drove away.

Ari walked to her Subaru and sat down. For a few moments she didn't drive, she only relaxed into her seat, feeling the waves of emotion about it all—Beach Camp, those children, *her* growing baby, her grandmother, her crazy parents . . . and Beck. Would she have a future with Beck?

Twenty-Three

Eleanor hadn't liked computers and the Internet immediately. She still fought with her television. But Cliff had shown her how to search real estate sites on which she could view the interiors of houses. She could contemplate in privacy the details of a possible house she could relocate to and be comfortable.

The house next to Silas did look tempting.

Friday morning, after Ari went off to Beach Camp, Eleanor put on what she considered a sensible dress, and her grandmother's pearl drop earrings, and drove into town to visit her lawyer.

His name was Dirk MacIntosh, a nice Scottish name that made her trust him. He had been a friend of Mortimer's and he'd done all their legal work. He was older now, of course, and limited himself to working in his office only three days a week.

"Come in, come in," he greeted Eleanor as she waited in the firm's reception area.

He held the door open for her. Once inside, he indicated a leather club chair facing his desk. "So good to see you Eleanor."

"So good to see you," she told him, and it was. It was comforting to see that his thick red hair was now white and his white eyebrows had thickened into a Groucho Marx joke. He'd put on quite a bit of weight. Well, hadn't they all? "How is your family?"

They chatted amiably for a while, as if this was a social visit. Then Dirk said, "Eleanor. What can I do for you?"

"I want to revise my will," Eleanor said.

Eleanor arrived back home in the early afternoon, hugging her secret to herself like a present. She'd had lunch in town with Silas and argued about whether science fiction movies were harbingers of things to come or just plain silly. After lunch, she'd walked with him to Fair Street, and down the narrow, one-lane street to his house. They strolled around the outside of his house and the outside of the house next door. The good news for Eleanor was that there weren't too many trees. She was worried about feeling hemmed in, claustrophobic, after having such a wide-open view for so many years of her life. She could imagine, because Silas told her it was how *he* felt, that she might feel safe in this neighborhood, near neighbors and a short walk to the library, so that as she grew older, and less mobile—although, Silas insisted, that wouldn't happen for years and years—it would be less of a problem to buy groceries and medicine and such.

"You know," Silas told her, "when you borrow books from the library, the volunteers will bring them to you if you request it. Think how guilty you'd feel if they had to drive all the way out to your house on the cliff, especially on a stormy day."

Eleanor nodded, busy thinking.

"You'll miss seeing the ocean, though," Silas said. "No going around that."

"True," Eleanor replied. "But look at the yard. They've planted dozens of blue hydrangea. I could add blue cornflowers and delphinium and iris for the spring, and larkspur and of course periwinkle low in the bed . . . Look at their back porch! Morning glories are absolutely covering the latticework. Silas, I think I'll have enough blue."

After Silas walked Eleanor back to her car, she drove home full of excitement and not a little anxiety. Change was hard for everyone, but vast change was terrifying.

A strange car was in her driveway.

Phillip was leaning against it, his arms crossed in front of his chest.

Eleanor parked on the curb. She certainly didn't want to block him in. She took her time gathering her purse, emotionally preparing herself for the oncoming battle.

The problem was that she'd always cared for her son-in-law. She'd admired him for staying with Alicia, who could be, and no one knew this better than Eleanor, demanding.

When Alicia and Phillip were young, with their new baby daughter, in a new home with new neighbors, Eleanor spent weeks with them, helping take care of Arianna—she was Arianna back then and for years afterward, before she insisted on shortening her name. Phillip was doing surgery at Mass General, and he came home tired but ecstatic. Phillip would stride into the house, searching out his wife, and sometimes he was so ebullient he would pick Alicia up and spin her around.

"I saved someone's life today!" he'd say.

"Tell me everything!" Alicia would reply.

Eleanor would sit in the corner, holding Arianna, while Phillip described the surgery, telling her about the patient and the family. Alicia would gaze at him as if he were a hero, which, in a way, he was.

When did that change? Why? By the time Arianna was three, Phillip was busier with paperwork and Alicia was no longer thrilled by Phillip's successes. They were expected. Arianna was in a neighborhood playgroup, and Alicia spent time with the other mothers, who were gossipy and fun and wanted to take clothes to the Pine Street Inn or have a bake sale for the preschool. Eleanor was often invited to stay with Alicia's family, probably because she prepared dinner and played with Arianna while Alicia was at a meeting or out doing good works.

When Arianna started kindergarten, Eleanor was not invited over as often. Mortimer was five years older than Eleanor, and slowing down. A range of irritating health problems bothered him. Arthritis. Shortness of breath, coughing, and fatigue. Eleanor tried to make healthy meals, but Mortimer preferred his Scotch and his cigarettes to salad and fish, even though it was against the doctor's orders. As she thought about it, Eleanor realized her marriage was going through a difficult time just when Alicia's was. Mortimer retired, played golf, drank at the club with his pals, and lived in his leather recliner watching sports. He didn't want to join Eleanor when she went down to Nantucket to check on the house in the fall and spring, and he was cranky all the time when she made him come down in the summer.

Actually, it made Eleanor smile: *What time could do.*

She'd loved Mortimer when they married, and then they'd muddled through the middle of their years with Alicia and Cliff—and Cliff had been active, to say the least. By the time Eleanor was sixty and Mortimer was sixty-five, they had both slowed down, but by then they were good companions, rubbing along together like a pair of yoked oxen. When Mortimer died three years ago, Eleanor had been lost. Alicia and Ari and Cliff had come down to Nantucket for much of the summer, but Phillip had been too busy working to come to the island.

Now, here was Phillip, fifty years old—no, wait, he was forty-nine. He would turn fifty in September. Eleanor allowed herself to sit a moment with her head leaning back on the headrest. Current wisdom dictated that fifty was a dangerous age, especially for a man. It was probably true that Phillip had less energy for the long hours of standing on his feet, focusing on his surgeries. Also, he was starting to lose his hair. His only child, his daughter, had graduated from college and hadn't really lived at home or needed him or adored him for four years, and Ari was only going to become more involved in her own life. And his wife. Alicia. She was only forty-six, but the dreaded fifty was headed her way. She wanted some glamour. She wanted some . . . space. She'd baked cupcakes and chaired committees and centered her life around her home. No wonder she wanted to go on a cruise.

And now Cliff said Alicia had met a man on the cruise to Canada? Eleanor thought the durability of a shipboard romance was pretty unlikely. But in her heart, Eleanor hoped Alicia and Phillip would get back together. Hopefully they had some lovely companionable years ahead.

She stepped out of her car and walked up her driveway.

"Phillip. What a surprise."

"Could I talk to you for a few moments, please, Eleanor?"

She looked at her watch, even though she knew what time it was. "Ari will be home soon."

"I'd like to talk with her, too."

"Come in, then," Eleanor said, not smiling. He had betrayed her daughter. He had broken her beloved granddaughter's heart.

It was just after four o'clock. Over the weeks the sun had slowly changed position and now the deck was totally in shade.

"Would you like some iced tea?" Eleanor asked.

"That would be great. Thank you."

They took their glasses out to the deck and sat in chairs across from one another at the table.

Phillip put his hands around the glass and looked steadily at Eleanor. "I've botched it all up and I want to apologize."

"You should be talking to Alicia and Ari, not me." Eleanor stared back. The truth was, she loved Phillip as if he were her own child. She respected him for his work. Over the years, she'd watched him grow from an enthusiastic young man into a distinguished medical specialist. He'd given her daughter and granddaughter stability, a handsome house, and more important, he'd provided them with love—great, abiding, forgiving, admiring love—as they went through life. Ari would not be the person she was if not for Phillip. Eleanor had to remember that.

"Yes, and I will apologize to Alicia if I can ever find her." A note of anger threaded through his words. More softly, he said, "I hope I can talk to Ari today."

Eleanor said gently, "That's for Ari to decide."

Phillip surprised her by saying, "You know my parents are dead."

"Of course I do," Eleanor replied, insulted. "I went to their funerals."

"And my sister lives in Australia now," Phillip said.

"If you're trying to imply that you have no family—" Eleanor began.

Phillip interrupted, "I don't need to *imply*—"

"It's a fact. I know. And I'd think that would make your wife and child all the more precious to you."

"They *are* precious to me. But they are so connected to you and this house and Cliff that they don't actually feel . . . all mine." Phillip's face was growing red with emotion.

"But, Phillip, that's the way all families work," Eleanor reminded him.

"Is it?" Phillip asked. "How many Christmases has *my* family spent here? How many summers? I'll tell you. Every Christmas. Every summer."

Eleanor twitched with annoyance. "I had no idea that was a problem for you."

"I didn't say it was a problem. But look—Ari told me she's *pregnant*. I'm sure you knew about this before I did."

"That's true. You learned about it when Ari spotted you at the farm stand with your . . . whatever you call her."

"I don't call her anything anymore." Phillip stood up and paced the room, hands shoved into his pockets. "That's over. I've broken off with her. It was never a long-term thing, anyway."

"But it *was* a *thing*," Eleanor said.

"Yes, it was. And I regret it terribly. But honest to God, I didn't think it would hurt Alicia. I didn't think Alicia would even notice. All she talks about, all she wants, is for you to sell this damned house and give her a couple of million, and do you have any idea how that makes me feel? That I can't give my wife what she wants?" His voice cracked. "I work all the hours God sends me."

"Yes," Eleanor said, nodding. "I know you do."

"Yet Alicia and Ari, and probably you, think I don't spend enough time with them."

"Mortimer felt that way, too. That I didn't appreciate how hard he worked. I can remember being stuck in this house during a week when it rained constantly almost every day. Alicia wasn't upset, but Cliff was bored crazy, so he tormented Alicia, and I resented Mortimer because he wasn't there to help." Eleanor nodded to herself, remembering those days. "So I do understand, Phillip. A bit."

"Thank you for that," Phillip said. He collapsed in a chair. "So much has happened in such a short time. Alicia went on a cruise. And Ari told me she met a man."

"I can't speak for Alicia. She hasn't called or emailed."

Phillip hung his head. "I wish I could turn back time."

Eleanor said, "No one can do that."

"Eleanor, do you think our marriage is coming apart?"

"I really don't know. That's for you and Alicia to work out." Eleanor stood up. "Ari's here," Eleanor said. "I hear her car. I'll leave you two alone."

She met Ari just as she was coming into the kitchen. "Your father's on the deck."

Ari frowned. "What should I do?" she asked.

But Eleanor quickly left the kitchen. She understood how Phillip felt. She was not going to tell Ari what to do.

Ari slid the glass door open and stepped out onto the deck. Her father stood only a few feet away from her. Her familiar, weary-looking father. She ached to hug him, to feel him holding her tight, patting her back, telling her it was all okay. At the same time, she was angry at him, and disappointed in him, and in many ways he had become a stranger.

She was just beginning to say, "So where's *Bemi?*"

But her father spoke first. "Are you really pregnant, Ari?"

His concern, putting her first, the warmth of his voice, the question, made tears come to her eyes. She couldn't speak, she could only nod her head.

"Well," her father said, "that's kind of cool."

"Really? Do you think so?" Ari was smiling and crying at the same time. No one had told her it was kind of cool, and it *was*.

"I do. What's the due date?"

"Late February."

Her father pulled out a chair for her. "Let's sit down. Do you want me to get you some iced tea?"

"No, Dad, I want you to talk about you first. Are you leaving Mom? Do you love Bummer? Sorry, I mean Bemi. I just called her Bummer in my head."

"I've broken off with Bemi. I want to speak with your mother, but she doesn't answer her cell when I phone." He sat, and Ari sat across from him. "I've been a fool, Ari. I want to apologize to you, and to your mother. I suppose I wanted to feel young and free—you'll understand better after you have your child."

My child. Ari hadn't thought of it as a child, but of course it would be an infant, and then a toddler, and then a child. Her own child.

"Does your mother know?" Phillip asked.

"No, not yet." Before her father could ask, Ari said, "And Peter knows. It is his baby, but we've talked, and he wants no part of any of it."

"That's all right," her father said. "It seems like half the world is single parents these days, and they're all doing a good job, as far as I can see."

"Are you going to divorce Mom?" Ari asked.

"I hope not. I hope she'll forgive me. I think she's more likely to if it's true that she's met a man on her cruise."

"What? That doesn't make sense."

"I mean she'll be more likely to forgive me if she's done something I have to forgive."

"That is so weird," Ari said softly. "I feel like our family is coming apart."

Her father was quiet for a while. They heard a gull call as it flew out over the ocean. A breeze rustled the bushes. The sunlight was slanting. Fall was on its way.

"I understand how you feel. I could explain to you why I . . . spent time with Bemi."

"Please don't," Ari said, shuddering. "You said it's over."

"It is. I'll never see her, never be in contact with her again. I hope I can be forgiven by you and your mother."

"And by Gram?"

Her father took a deep breath. "Ari, I care a great deal for your grandmother, but all I care about is Alicia and you forgiving me. You are my family."

Ari was too shocked to answer. She was confused, and then she thought she began to understand, a little. She supposed families were like drops in the ocean, the most inner point enfolding parents and children. Grandparents, aunts, uncles, and cousins made up an outer circle ringing around them, with beloved good friends form-ing another outer ring, and through the years, more rings would grow.

"But, Dad," Ari said, a thought occurring to her, "Gram has no one else."

"She has her son," Phillip reminded her.

"Oh. Right. Do you think Cliff will forgive you?"

"I don't think Cliff is angry with me. Well, he would be if I have hurt you, and I know I've hurt you, and I'm endlessly sorry. I want to make amends, somehow. I want you to forgive me before your baby's born."

Ari smiled. It was so nice, the way her father was talking about the baby. As if he or she was already part of the family.

"Listen," Phillip said, "your uncle is on the cruise with Alicia. I got the cruise information from him."

"You did?"

"Cliff and I talk a lot. About a lot of things. He has a few secrets, too, you know."

"Like what?"

"I'm sure you'll find out soon. But here's the deal. Your mother's cruise ship docks in Boston Harbor this afternoon. At four o'clock."

"Okay . . ." Ari was surprised that her mother was returning so soon. Like the end of summer, it was always a shock.

"I think you and I should go meet her boat."

"What?" Ari felt as if she were on a Tilt-A-Whirl.

"She'll be much more likely to forgive me if you're with me," her father said, smiling.

Ari was stunned. Her father could be *charming*. Was being charming. She flashed on the times he'd seemed like a prince to her—a prince, not a king, because a king was always burdened with responsibilities. For her sixteenth birthday, her father had taken her and ten of her girlfriends on a private cruise of Boston Harbor with its many fascinating islands. An enormous picnic was set out for them on the boat, and there had been sparkling fake champagne, and an extravagant birthday cake. Her mother had been along, too, looking pretty as always, but Ari's friends had clustered around her father, who entertained them with historic Boston legends.

"Your father is so *nice*," one girl said, and Ari had been pleased and proud.

In the past years, when she was away at Bucknell, Ari hadn't seen much of either of her parents. She loved them both, of course, but they weren't nearly as interesting as any one thing she might be doing on any day. Her life was the song. Her parents were background music.

"I don't know, Dad," Ari said, looking at her watch. "I'm not sure we can catch a fast ferry to the Cape to rent a car and drive to the airport."

"We won't take a ferry," her father said. "We'll fly."

"Wow," Ari exclaimed.

"We'll get a taxi to the harbor, surprise your mother, and we can all go home. I mean to our Wellesley house."

"But what about Gram?" Ari asked.

"I don't think she needs to come with us," her father said.

"I don't want her feelings to be hurt," Ari told him.

"Nor do I. But Eleanor and I had a good talk. I think she'll be happy just knowing we're going to try to work things out with your mother. With my wife."

"Okay . . . How soon should we go?"

"As soon as possible, I think, don't you?"

"Right." Ari stood up. "I'll go tell Gram, and get my phone, and, well, we have everything at our Wellesley house."

Her father smiled.

Eleanor sat in her second-floor bedroom with the windows open to the fresh salt air. She didn't intend to spy on her granddaughter and her son-in-law, but the breeze carried their words up from the deck.

When she heard Phillip say that they didn't need to take Eleanor to meet Alicia, a strange pain stabbed Eleanor right in her heart. She was dismissed. A moment later, the pain disappeared, replaced by a lovely sense of *release*.

The truth was she needn't go with them. Really, it was between Alicia and Phillip, and Ari, too. Eleanor wasn't necessary, which meant she was free, as free as any mother who worries is, and was there any mother on earth who didn't worry?

Maybe she would be able to spend more time with Silas. Or more time talking to Jeff Townsend, the realtor, about houses in town.

Ari burst into Eleanor's bedroom.

"Gram, I've been talking with Dad and he says Mom's boat docks this evening, so we're flying up there so we can meet her!" After a moment, Ari said, "You'll be okay here, won't you?"

"Of course," Eleanor said. "I think your plan is wonderful. I have commitments tomorrow, so don't worry about hurrying back. Enjoy yourself. I hope it all goes well."

"Oh, Gram!" Ari seemed too excited to say more. She flew across the room, kissed Eleanor's cheek, and hurried out of the bedroom.

Eleanor overheard them talking, and the sound of the back door shutting. Two car doors slammed. She leaned back in her chair, listened to the car pull away, took a deep breath, and relaxed.

Twenty-Four

Ari's breath was ragged as she sat in her father's rental car, driving to the small Nantucket airport. She had seldom spent time alone with her father in the past few years, and especially after her confrontation at Moors End farm stand, her emotions were all over the place. Plus, she was pregnant and hadn't really organized her life to deal with that. How could she, without knowing about Beck's feelings? They needed more than three months to really know each other.

It was a relief when they arrived at the airport. She stood next to her father while he returned the rental car and bought tickets for the next flight to Boston. At this time of year, planes flew often between the island and the mainland. They were lucky. They had to wait only fifteen minutes before boarding a JetBlue. During the flight, Ari simply leaned back and closed her eyes for the forty-five-minute trip. The rumbling of the plane was familiar, even comforting, and she didn't have to make conversation with her father.

After they landed, they caught a taxi to the Cruise Atlantic pier on Boston Harbor. The ship was small compared to the towering luxury fleets at the far end of the harbor. Ari and her father got to the boat just as it was anchoring in its slip. Passengers waved from the upper decks to the small crowd waiting near the dock.

"I'm excited," Ari told her father. "It sort of feels like Christmas."

"We'll see," her father said, adding wryly, "It might be more like Halloween."

After that, they waited silently as dozens of passengers disembarked. Ari didn't see her mother, and as more and more people came down the ramp and greeted one another, hugging and laughing, Ari worried. For all they knew, her mother had stayed in Canada, traveling through all the enormous provinces with her new lover.

Suddenly, there she was. Alicia wore a blue summer dress and a wide straw hat with a blue ribbon. She looked rested and happy. Cliff was at her side, talking to her.

Behind her mother came a rather professorial sort, wearing tortoiseshell glasses, a rumpled linen sports coat, and a slightly raffish straw fedora. As Ari watched, the man leaned forward and said something to Alicia and Cliff and they all laughed.

Then Alicia caught sight of her husband and daughter waiting onshore. She stopped, surprised, causing the line of passengers behind her to also stop, bumping into each other. Ari waved and waved, and her father did, too. An extremely familiar look came over Alicia's face—Ari called it her mother's "Good grief, what now?" expression.

Cliff spotted Ari and her father and waved. Quickly, he looked away, scanning the dock. He spotted someone and broke into a wide smile, a happier smile than Ari had ever seen on her uncle's face.

Her mother and uncle continued down the ramp and quickly were lost in the crowd.

"She might ignore me," Ari's father said. "But she would never ignore you."

Her father's words made Ari feel sympathy for him, while at the same time she said, "If I were my mother, I'd slap you."

"Yes, you're right. I deserve that."

The crowd was thinning out. Ari spotted her uncle walking in the opposite direction. A pretty woman was waiting for him, and Cliff swept her up in his arms and kissed her for a long time. If Ari hadn't been waiting for her mother, she would have dashed down the pier and forced her uncle to introduce her to the woman.

She caught sight of a straw fedora headed in the opposite direction. Was her mother going off with the professor fellow? Ari's heart sank. Would her mother do that? Would she simply walk away from them?

A cluster of chattering women came toward Ari and her father, parting around them as if they were telephone posts, and then there was Alicia.

"This is a surprise," Alicia said. Her cheeks were very red.

"MOM," Ari cried, hugging her. "I'm so happy to see you."

"Alicia," Phillip said. He had tears in his eyes. "You look so beautiful. I'm sorry I never told you how beautiful you are."

Alicia looked at her husband with such sorrow in her eyes that Ari had to look away.

"That is what you're sorry for?" she asked. "You've been lying to me all summer. Are you going to keep lying now? Because if you are, I am leaving you. And I warn you, I have someplace to go."

"I'm going to take a little stroll up and down the pier," Ari said. She hurried away, hoping to give her parents some privacy for this discussion. Her uncle and his woman friend were no longer in sight.

As she walked, she remembered all the times in the past four years when she had learned that Peter was sleeping with someone else. The first time it happened, during their freshman year, she was confused more than upset. When Peter came to her full of apology, she quickly made up with him but soon was beginning to wonder if she was only agreeing to be with Peter because it was what she was used to. It wasn't so much a matter of forgiving as it was of habit.

During her four years of college, she met quite a few handsome or interesting or charismatic guys. Actually, it was *college,* and they were all around, everywhere. Now that she thought about it, a sort of strange balancing had existed in her relationship with Peter. It was as if his being with another woman made it possible for her to have a relationship with another man. And this was only natural, everyone said. But Ari had concentrated on her studies. She did go out with other men, but she never was serious with anyone but Peter.

Here, now, leaning against a pole on the long pier of Boston Harbor, Ari realized she had never in her life felt anything like what she felt for Beck. Whatever she'd had with Peter had been a matter of familiarity, the deep ease and freedom of a normal and reliable environment when so much of their lives was difficult and challenging.

They had been good friends. They had been kind lovers. Ari thought she would always be fond of the memory of Peter while at the same time she didn't care if she ever saw him again.

The way he'd reacted when she told him she was pregnant made her nearly weak with relief that she hadn't gone through with the wedding. That he was already in a relationship with someone else reassured her. The truth was, Ari thought, she would rather live out her life as a single mother than married to Peter just because he was the biological father of her baby. Oh, what a sad marriage that would be.

Slowly she strolled back down the pier, pausing to admire the great cruise ships in port, searching to find her mother and father. When she caught sight of them, she saw that they were arguing. As she watched, she realized a kind of force field kept her parents together so that even as they fought, they were two halves of a whole. They were joined not only by the laws of marriage and the passage of time and the parenting of a child but by an invisible yet unbreakable bond that held them together even as they struggled to be apart.

Ari put her hands on her belly. Here was another invisible bond. She hadn't asked or reached for this baby growing inside her. She hadn't knowingly chosen to begin this new person. She was well aware that whoever it was curled up like a little fox in a nest would bring her pain and joy and anxiety and as many arguments, if not more, than she'd had with her parents. She knew that it would change the course of her life and the core of her existence. She wasn't completely happy about this. She was completely terrified.

And she couldn't wait to see her baby's face.

This time when she checked, she found her parents in the middle of a crowd. Her mother was pressed against her father. They were holding each other tight, as if they would never let the other leave again.

When they reached the rental car, Ari's mother stiffened. "This is a rental car," she said.

"It is," Ari's father said. "We picked it up at the airport when we flew in from Nantucket."

The three of them were standing near the trunk of the car.

"You flew in from Nantucket," Alicia said, frowning.

"We did," Phillip said calmly.

"You were on Nantucket." It was a statement and a warning.

Ari stepped a few feet away as if she was suddenly fascinated by the sky.

"I was there to speak with Eleanor and with Ari," Phillip said. "We'll drive the rental car to Wellesley and then Ari can return it to the rental dealer in Hyannis when she returns to Nantucket."

"Are you returning to Nantucket?" Alicia asked her husband.

"Not unless you go with me," Phillip said.

That seemed to satisfy Alicia. She got into the front seat of the car, Ari got into the backseat, the child's place, and her father sat in the driver's seat. Ari could tell by looking at the backs of her parents' necks that they had somehow exited the zone of happy endings and gone backward into the muddle of the situation.

It was a long drive to Wellesley, with lots of traffic and stoplights.

"Who was the woman waiting for Uncle Cliff?" Ari asked.

"That's for me to know and you to find out," Alicia said smugly.

"Mom!" Ari kicked the back of her mother's seat.

"Don't act like you're ten years old," Alicia said.

I could say the same to you, Ari thought, but kept quiet. She wanted her mother to be in a good mood.

In this part of Boston, cars were double-parked everywhere. Taxis and delivery trucks honked. Lights turned red with diabolical timing. Ari's father had to concentrate, checking his side mirror and rearview mirror constantly.

The silence grew uncomfortable. Alicia asked, "How is Mother?"

Ari spoke up. "She's really good. I think she might even have a boyfriend."

Alicia craned her head to look at her daughter's face. "Eleanor has a boyfriend?"

"Yes," Ari said. "He lives on the island. His wife died a few years ago. They were all friends. Silas Stover."

"I remember Silas Stover!" Alicia said with a lilt in her voice. "He's nice and very well-off."

"Oh, Mom, stop it."

"Stop what?" Alicia said innocently.

"You think Eleanor is going to marry Silas and sell the house."

"Did I say that's what I was thinking?" Alicia began to rummage around in her purse. "Where did I put my lip balm? I think I've gotten addicted to it. If I don't wear it constantly—oh, here it is." She pulled down the visor and looked at herself as she carefully applied the balm.

They rode a few moments in silence. Finally, Ari said, "I'm fine, thank you. Three and a half months pregnant now. I finished my job at Beach Camp and I'm planning to take courses online for the fall semester." She could see in the visor that her mother's lips tightened.

"So you told your father, I hear." Alicia sounded displeased.

Phillip spoke up. "Yes. We haven't been able to organize any plans but I think Ari should live with us and have the baby at Mass General."

"I'm going to stay with Gram," Ari said.

"That's wonderful!" Alicia said.

"That's not going to happen," Phillip stated firmly.

"Nantucket has a perfectly fine maternity unit," Alicia told him.

"She needs to be at Mass General in case there's a problem."

"You say that simply because you work at Mass General," Alicia said.

"That may be true, but it's also true that our maternity department is one of the best in the country. Also, that will make it easier for Ari to get home as soon as she can."

"Home?" Alicia asked with iron in her voice. "For the last four years Ari has either been at school or on Nantucket. You and I have started a whole new life. You are working and I've made commitments to several charitable organizations, not to mention our social obligations. How do you expect me to take care of Ari? Do you remember how weak I was after Ari's birth? I had to have a hysterectomy, I had to have so many stitches, and I lost so much blood. I went into shock. I had to stay at the hospital for a week! What if something like that happens to Ari?"

"If something like that happens to Ari," Phillip said calmly, "then it will be good for her to be at Mass General." He smiled at his wife. "And when she comes home, we can help take care of our first grandchild."

Alicia went so still she looked frozen. Then she burst into tears.

"Phillip, you know I'm not a natural mother, especially not with babies." Alicia turned her head awkwardly to face Ari sitting behind her. "I always loved you, I always kept you clean and cuddled. I tried to nurse you but you had colic for three weeks and cried constantly and I cried constantly, too. When my mother came up, she was like the great maternal goddess who knew exactly the right thing to do with a baby. You have to remember that I had placenta previa and I almost died. I had to have a total hysterectomy. I struggled so hard to have what they called natural childbirth because that was what the best mothers did back then. It was like I was in some kind of torturous childbirth competition. But then you were breech, I almost died, and when I returned home from the hospital, I was exhausted and in constant pain. I have always loved you, even in the middle of the night when you woke me. But you made me feel like a failure."

"You've told me all this before," Ari said quietly. "I can apologize but I don't think it was my fault. I wasn't *trying* to lie the wrong way. I think you've been a wonderful mother. And I totally understand how you feel about babies. Some people are just that way and it doesn't mean they are good or bad or anything. But anyway, I don't want to live with you and Dad. I want to live by myself."

"How will you be able to afford that when you won't be able to work?" Alicia asked.

"For God's sake, Alicia," Phillip snapped. "Give the girl a break. Maybe she'll live with her grandmother. Or if she wants to be in Boston, I'll pay her rent for a year."

Alicia continued to cry. "Have you never thought that I might want to have a second house in the mountains?"

Phillip looked at his wife sternly. "Have you never thought that *I* might want a house in the mountains? I prefer the mountains to the ocean, you know that."

"If my mother would just sell her house, we would have plenty of money for Ari and for a second home for us." Alicia blew her nose heartily into her embroidered handkerchief.

"If we sold *our* house in Wellesley, we would have plenty of money for Ari and a second home for us," Phillip said.

"You can't mean that!" Alicia cried. "We've made that house so beautiful. Everything is perfect in every room. We deserve some comfort as we get older! Plus, our house is wonderful for entertaining."

"But it's a lot for you to maintain," Phillip argued. "Think of the freedom you would have to do other things if we lived in a condo. Not only would we have more free money but you would have more free time to do what you want. To do what we want."

"What sorts of things?" Alicia was tempted, Ari could tell by the sound of her voice.

"Well, for example, to visit first-class resorts in the mountains and look at what kinds of houses are available."

Alicia didn't respond.

"And we could take some cruises," Phillip said.

"But why would you want to do that?" Alicia asked. She folded her arms over her chest and stared out the passenger window. "And when would you have time? You are always working."

They were on Route 9 now, always a congested highway, with a few cars ahead of them when the light turned red. When Ari was driving this route by herself, she either blasted music or used the time to make quick calls on her cellphone. It was as if the engineers had designed this particular part of the road to be especially frustrating so that drivers were caught in a cage of other cars, all with their motors rumbling. It provided the perfect environment for arguing.

Phillip suddenly turned to glare at his wife. "Why am I always working? It's not enough to pay a mortgage on a house that we really can't afford and also pay for our daughter's college tuition and also and most insanely to pay for all of the galas you say we have to go to in order to help charities and especially to pay for the gowns you only wear once to attend the damned galas. Do you remember when I got out of med school and started at Mass General and was working all hours of the day and night, how we promised ourselves that when we got older, we would have time to spend with each other?"

"I remember," Alicia answered softly but did not turn her head to look at her husband.

"So we had a wonderful life and a beautiful daughter and summer vacations on Nantucket, but it wasn't enough for you. You wanted a bigger house and a flashy car and bigger diamonds and membership at country clubs. You wanted Ari to be sent to the best summer camp where she would meet the best people even though she could have spent all summer on Nantucket. I worked harder, you spent more time with your wealthy friends, and less time with me. The past year, you've spent more time finding out who the best caterers and florists are for Ari's wedding and reception dinner than you ever spent with me. I could probably make a time chart to prove it."

"I wanted our daughter's wedding to be magical," Alicia whispered.

"So we had to organize a sit-down meal for two hundred people up at the lodge on the lake," Phillip said.

"And Ari has gone and spoiled it all," Alicia cried. "Even though we've canceled everything, we still have to pay the twenty percent deposit. It's in the contract."

"Don't worry. I've paid it," Phillip said in resignation.

Sitting in the backseat, as if she were still a child, Ari burned with indecision. *I'm still here,* she wanted to say, but she knew her parents weren't thinking about her now. They were caught up in an argument they probably should have had years ago.

The stoplight turned green. The lines of cars began to inch forward. From behind them, an impatient driver leaned on his horn. Phillip gunned the car and shot through the yellow light just before it turned red.

Alicia still had her head turned away from her husband and she didn't speak. But Phillip, as if invigorated by his traffic triumph, declared, "Alicia, I have tried to give you everything you want."

Now Ari's mother did turn to stare at her husband. Her expression was both angry and sad. "Well, it seems *I* haven't been giving *you* everything you want."

From her witness box in the backseat, Ari saw her father's face flush.

Phillip cleared his throat. "Yes, that's true, but you would be surprised at how little I want. I suppose I was looking for someone's admiration. For someone who wanted my company, just my company. Who laughed at my jokes, who listened with interest to the way I had saved someone's life that day, as if that was a significant thing to do. I'm getting older, Alicia, and it takes more of my concentration and strength to manipulate tools, instruments that I never would have dreamed of which have been invented while I've been in practice. I have had to take courses! Now I watch and learn from younger surgeons how to work with lasers and television screens. It takes a toll on me now to stand for several hours at a time. And when I'm off duty, I want to relax and watch a movie and eat pizza with my hands. I don't want to be glamorous, Alicia. I want to be comfortable."

They had turned off Route 9 and were now in a maze of roads leading to their Wellesley house. The style was French provincial and the landscaping was elaborate. Alicia had hired gardeners to shape the evergreens into geometric topiaries, as if she were Marie Antoinette. Ari had lived in this house all her life, or all of the life she could remember. She could remember how her mother had worried and fretted over exactly what wallpaper to use and how she had been almost frantic to change the kitchen countertops from tile to granite. Alicia worked hard to keep the house uncluttered. She had a cleaning lady who came twice a week, but she was almost obsessive about where the silver pitcher should sit on the sideboard and the magazines should be placed on the table in the family room, as if the house would explode if magazines were left in the living room. Ari thought of her grandmother's house, which had gatherings of shells on the windowsills and books clustered on tables near wing chairs and notes and letters scattered around the house.

They pulled into the driveway. When Phillip turned off the engine, the silence inside the car was stark.

Ari spoke quickly. "I'm going to make a quick pit stop. Then I'm driving back to Hyannis. I'll take a boat back to the island. I have a lot of things left there. I'll need them wherever I am, Nantucket or Boston. Also, I want to take a few days to laze around on the beach and enjoy the island and my friends."

Alicia brightened. "How is Beck?" She turned around to smile at Ari and her face was mottled with emotion.

Ari wanted to give her mother hope but she had to be truthful. "Beck is fine. We are really good friends. He knows I'm going to have a baby. I like him a lot, Mom, and I think he likes me, but we've only known each other three months. I'm a lot to take on."

"He would be a lucky man to get you," Alicia said.

"Thanks, Mom."

Phillip reached into the trunk of the car and hefted out the suitcases Alicia had taken on her cruise. Ari started to follow but her mother put her hand on her arm and they stood outside for a moment on the green lawn.

"I'm sorry your father and I had to argue in front of you," Alicia said.

Surprised and reassured by her mother's concern, Ari asked, "Mom, did you really sleep with that professor dude?"

"Why shouldn't I?" Her mother tossed her head and her warmth vanished, replaced by her cool façade. "Your father had an affair all summer."

"That doesn't answer my question," Ari said.

"I know," Alicia replied with a smile.

Ari sagged from the weight of her emotions, from the sight of her mother being playful. Suddenly, she loved her mother. She understood for a moment how it was for her, so full of dreams, and so different from Ari, her own daughter. "I'm sorry, Mom. I hope you guys work it out."

"Thank you, Ari." Her mother turned away and walked toward the house.

Ari followed. She rushed to her room, selected a few things to take back to the island with her, and ran down the stairs to the front door. She needed to hurry in order to return the rental car and catch the last boat to Nantucket.

She had no idea where her parents were now in this expansive house. "Goodbye!" she called. "I'll talk to you tomorrow from the island."

From the back of the house, her father called, "Safe trip!"

Ari had to adjust the seat of the rental car because her legs weren't as long as her father's. She strapped on her seatbelt, found a radio station with eighties rock, and returned to the road, happy to be away from her parents.

Twenty-Five

Eleanor was tucked away in her bed with Shadow curled up next to her feet when she heard the kitchen door open and quietly close. She was reading a delightful mystery that she didn't want to put down but she knew if her light was on, Ari might feel the duty to report to Eleanor what had happened with her father and mother. Eleanor had a hunch that whatever had happened was not a complete happy ending but scene seventy-seven of a family drama that would continue for quite some time. That was only natural. But Eleanor was tired and she had a busy day tomorrow, so she put her bookmark into her book, turned off her bed light, and snuggled down into bed.

The next morning, she woke and dressed and left the house before Ari was up. Now that she had set certain things in motion, she was eager to get on with them.

First, she met Silas at the Downyflake for breakfast. Over a Tex-Mex omelet and delicious coffee, Eleanor gave Silas a brief summary of the turbulent events of the weekend. In return, Silas told her about his daughter, who was getting a divorce, and his son, who worked compulsively, leaving no time for pleasure.

They had an appointment at ten-thirty with Jeff Townsend, the realtor who'd worked with Silas. He took them both through the house next door to Silas.

"It's charming," Eleanor said, "but isn't it awfully small?"

Silas said, "Some hotels would be small compared to your 'Sconset house."

Jeff said, "It is actually fairly large if you look at the floor plan. Because it's an older home, the rooms are small—you know how Nantucket houses are. If you wanted to, you could knock out a wall here and there and have one or two bigger rooms."

"The en suite bathroom is nice," Eleanor admitted. She rather admired the new and newly conceptualized standing bathtub with its graceful curves.

"Absolutely," Jeff hastened to agree. "That's a definite plus in this old house. All new plumbing in the bathrooms and kitchen. The kitchen has granite counters!"

Eleanor rolled her eyes and turned away. "Just what I've always wanted."

But after they'd seen the basement, the cleanest basement Eleanor had ever been in, and walked around the house, and the realtor had pointed out that the house had all-new windows and storm windows, Eleanor told Jeff she wanted the house and would call in a few hours to discuss money.

When Eleanor got home that afternoon, she found Ari still in her pajamas, lounging on the sofa in the family room, watching television, surrounded by popcorn crumbs.

Eleanor laughed. "It looks like you've had a lazy day."

Ari began brushing the loose kernels off the sofa and into her hand. "Oh, man, I am such a slob," Ari said. "No wonder no one wants to live with me."

"It sounds like you're indulging in a nice, deep vat of self-pity." Eleanor perched on the end of the recliner and had a momentary flash of longing to lie back in the chair, pull the lever that would lift her feet up, steal the remote control from her granddaughter, and watch a British mystery series. She'd already had such a busy day. But she loved her granddaughter above all things, so she said in a grand-motherly tone, "What's going on?"

"I don't even know where to start." Ari twisted the tie on her bathrobe.

"Tell me about yesterday. How did your father and mother get along?"

"It was kind of crazy, actually. Mom got off the cruise ship with a man but they were too far away for Dad and me to get a good look at him. Anyway, Mom left him when she saw us and Mom and Dad had a momentary Hollywood ending. But on the drive home, they started arguing about everything. They talked about their marriage, but they also talked about me." Ari began to cry. "Basically, Dad thinks I should have the baby at Mass General and Mom doesn't want me at home with the baby because I was such a terrible baby and apparently traumatized her for life."

"You were not a terrible baby," Eleanor murmured.

"I can't understand my mother," Ari cried. "She was such a good mother, especially when I was in high school. She loved taking me shopping. She loved coming to the college for parents' weekend. But now that I'm out of college, she's kind of freaked out at the idea of having me live at home again. Also, she still has her heart set on you selling this house. I love this house and I know how you love it."

Eleanor was quiet for a moment, ordering her thoughts. "First of all, let's talk about your mother. You need to remember that she was very much her daddy's little girl. She was spoiled and always wanted the best of the best and to be popular. Once Cliff was born I know she felt jealous of all the attention I paid him."

"Okay," Ari said. "I can understand that."

"So," Eleanor continued, "and I'm just guessing here, while you were growing into an adult, your father and mother were edging up toward that terrifying milestone, the age of fifty. Lots of people go a little crazy around that age. They start wondering if they've accomplished as much as they assumed they would when they were younger. They start noticing a few gray hairs on their heads, a few extra pounds that just won't go away, and a kind of restlessness to do something different."

"Well," Ari said, "Dad certainly did something different."

"Think about it," Eleanor said. "For decades they spent their life taking care of others. Your father saved lives and made very good money but he certainly didn't become a millionaire. Your mother devoted her life to you and if you don't believe that, you will understand when you have your own child and she's two years old and sick or nine years old and has just fallen off her bike. Your mother really deserves a little escape, a little glamour. And the hard truth is that taking care of a newborn baby isn't glamorous."

Ari nodded. "Okay, I get that. But whenever I've been home during the last four years, I've always made my own meals and sometimes made dinner for the three of us. I don't know why Mom thinks I would be such a burden. I've done my own laundry since junior high!"

"You're going to have a lot more than laundry when you have a baby," Eleanor said gently. "But more than that, there's a kind of psychological freedom that comes when your children are grown up. When they can take care of themselves."

"But I can take care of myself," Ari insisted. She'd never sounded more childish.

Eleanor looked at her watch. "I believe it's an appropriate time for me to have a nice, healthy Bloody Mary." She rose and said, over her shoulder as she went into the kitchen, "I'll be right back."

While she fixed her drink, she also made a cup of hot chocolate on her Keurig. The day was warm, but Ari couldn't have alcohol, and hot chocolate was always helpful.

When Eleanor was seated across from Ari again, she said, "Let's start with the basics. How much of your salary from Beach Camp did you save?"

"Thanks for the hot chocolate." Ari had recovered her poise. "I've saved almost all of it. I never intended to be a parasite. I'd planned to get an apartment in Boston while working on my master's. I've talked with several friends about sharing a place. Of course, that's not going to happen now. Also, I'm sure you know that my grandfather on my dad's side left me a small trust fund. I can live on that for at least a year while I work toward my master's. Then I can get a job, maybe at a childcare center so I can take my baby with me. And you offered to let me stay here with you."

"Yes, and I would love that," Eleanor said.

"I did a lot of thinking after I left Mom and Dad at the house. I've always known I could support myself. It's just that so many things have been happening so quickly."

"Oh, my sweet girl, I don't mean to criticize you," Eleanor said. "This has been a whirlwind of a summer for us all." She had much more to say, but she felt they had both exhausted themselves and needed to let their brains and their hearts rest. She put down her drink. "Get dressed. Let's go for a walk on the beach."

Ari stood up, stretching. "That's a good idea. Although it can't change anything."

"It can change the way you feel about things," Eleanor reminded her. "A walk by the sea is always good for the soul."

Twenty-Six

It had always been Eleanor's custom to have her family at the Nantucket house for the Labor Day weekend. Here it was, and here they were.

Eleanor and Ari had slipped out to Bartlett's Farm early in the morning, before the rest of the family arrived. They'd bought pounds of potato salad, broccoli salad, fried chicken, vegetable curry, and edamame pasta with mushrooms and walnuts. They'd brought them home, lugged them in, and put them in Eleanor's own serving bowls. It was raining off and on, which was fine with Eleanor, because Phillip usually grilled a salmon or steaks, and even though Alicia and Phillip had reunited, Eleanor didn't want him swanning around her kitchen and deck as if he belonged again. He might belong to Alicia, but Eleanor was not so forgiving.

Actually, her family might not be so forgiving after she made her announcement.

Cliff knew, of course, but he only knew part of it, the part he liked.

They were gathered in the living room. Alicia and Phillip sat holding hands, like young lovers. Ari joined them on the sofa. Cliff sat in the chair Mortimer had always preferred, looking dashing in his white ducks and navy blue Brooks Brothers shirt. Alicia had had her dark hair cut and styled in a careless bob. It suited her. Phillip wore Nantucket red pants and a blue rugby shirt. He had not yet been able to meet Eleanor's eye since he entered the house this morning. Ari was wearing a lavender sundress that set off her tan. Her dark hair was curled up in a rather Parisian chignon.

She knew that Eleanor was going to make an important announcement, but she didn't know what it was.

Eleanor wore a new dress that seemed to startle her family and startled *her* from time to time. She'd ordered it from a catalog and was amazed at how her entire reflection changed in the mirror when she put it on. It was a bright blue batik "cold shoulder" dress, meaning that it had sleeves that left her shoulders exposed, and a slice of her upper arms, where what she called her flags waved the most. It was the most daring thing she'd worn in years, perhaps ever. She wore her long hair down, pulled back with a silver butterfly barrette, and lipstick and earrings. Her family thought she'd gone mad, but Silas liked her in the dress. A lot. It might be a sign to the others that she was changed.

She entered the living room and sat in her chair. Cliff smiled smugly and poured her a flute of prosecco.

"So," Eleanor said, "here we are. Alicia and Phillip, I'm so glad to see you together again. Ari, you know how I feel about you. Cliff, you look ridiculously smug, so you might as well tell the others."

Cliff couldn't wait. "Mother's sold the house! Gold Sand bought it for fifteen million dollars!"

Everyone gasped. For a moment, they all froze with shock.

Then Alicia absolutely flew out of her chair to kiss her mother. "Oh, Mother, thank you!"

"Wait, wait," Eleanor said. "I have more to say."

"Almost four million dollars, Phil! Four million for each of us! Mother, you can buy a home near us!"

"You won't want me near you after you've heard what I have to say," Eleanor told her daughter. "I've spoken with my lawyer, and I'm dividing the money into five, not four parts—"

"Oh, you're counting Phillip, too, of course!" Alicia said. She glanced at her husband. "That's *eight* million for you and me!"

"No, Alicia. Let me speak." Eleanor felt a blush of excitement rise up her neck and onto her cheeks, not unlike the blush she'd felt yesterday when Silas kissed her. "I'm giving three million each to Cliff, Alicia, and Ari, and keeping three million for myself. I'm going to buy a small house in town, on Fair Street. If I live prudently and keep receiving my annuities, I'll be fine for the next twenty years."

"But the other three million—" Alicia looked as if she wanted to bite something.

"The rest of the money," Eleanor said, "is going to Beach Camp. I'm establishing the Eleanor Sunderland Beach Camp Foundation. Cal Wallace, his cousins, Poppy and Cleo, and I have met with a lawyer and are in the process of drawing up papers. We're going to buy a small building on Amelia Drive that will be the headquarters of the camp."

"You don't mean it," Alicia whispered.

"Poppy Marshall will be the full-time office manager, working from Amelia Drive and from Boston, where she lives in the winter. Cleo and her husband will live in the apartment above the Beach Camp offices. After Cal is ordained as an interfaith minister, he will live on Nantucket. He'll direct the camp and begin a fundraising and development campaign."

"Have you lost your mind?" Alicia was no longer whispering. "I'm your *daughter*. Don't I mean anything to you?"

"Alicia. You are married to a surgeon. You have one child, who is grown. You will have three million dollars to take all the cruises you want. You mean a great deal to me, but so do the children whose parents work two jobs just to keep living in a basement and eating. They are the ones who need my money."

"They are the ones who have your love," Alicia shot back.

"If you measure love with money," Eleanor said calmly, "then I'd say I love you as much as I love those children, and the children who will come after them. Besides," Eleanor added, "I have something special for you."

Eleanor reached behind a lamp on the side table and brought out a black velvet box. She handed it to Alicia. "This is for you."

Alicia quickly opened it. "Oh," she gasped. The emerald and diamond necklace lay glittering in the satin. "Mom, you used to take this out and show it to me when I was a little girl. I always wanted it." Alicia rose from the sofa to embrace her mother. "Thank you. Thank you."

"It was my mother's," Eleanor said. "Your grandmother passed it down to me. I don't know how much it would bring if you sold it—"

"I would never sell it," Alicia swore. "It's part of our family."

"No one else has anything like it," Eleanor said. "It's special. Like you."

Alicia nodded, tears in her eyes.

"Put it on," Ari suggested.

Alicia shook her head. "No. I want to look at it." She touched the gems with her fingertip.

Cliff coughed into his hand. "What realtor are you using to buy the office on Amelia Drive?"

Eleanor burst out laughing. "Oh, my children!" Calming down, she said, "I want to use you, of course. Now, I'd like to toast with champagne. Cliff, will you get it from the refrigerator? Ari, will you bring glasses?"

Ari said, "Gram, I think you're absolutely magnificent."

Eleanor replied with a quirk of her mouth, "It's easy to be magnificent when you have fifteen million dollars."

Ari and Cliff went around the room, giving everyone a glass of champagne. Eleanor raised her champagne flute and opened her mouth to toast, when a knock came at the front door.

"Did you invite Silas?" Alicia asked.

"No," Eleanor answered, puzzled. "Labor Day is only for family."

"Well, this is family, for sure," Cliff said, with a dazzling smile. He went to the door.

"What is he talking about?" Eleanor asked the others.

The group heard Cliff say, "Judith. Just in time."

Cliff returned to the living room with a beautiful blonde at his side. She was about thirty years old, extremely poised and posh-looking, wearing a floaty red dress that didn't disguise her rounded belly.

Eleanor nearly dropped her glass.

Phillip, always proper, came to his feet as the lady entered the room.

"Everyone," Cliff announced, "I'd like you to meet my wife, Judith. Judith Crosby, now Judith Sunderland."

Eleanor was speechless.

Alicia smiled smugly. "Hello, Judith."

Eleanor stared at her daughter. "You know Judith?"

"I don't know her," Alicia answered, very pleased with herself. "But I know about her. Cliff told me about her on our cruise."

With a cry of joy, Ari jumped up from the sofa and ran across the room. "Aren't you the quiet one!" she said to her uncle. Ari embraced Judith in a warm hug, then stood back to look at her. "And aren't you gorgeous? And you're pregnant! I am, too! You are the answer to my dreams!"

"Really," Cliff interjected dryly, "she's the answer to *my* dreams."

Ari insisted, "I mean *we* can discuss gas and swollen feet—"

Eleanor rose to her feet. "Perhaps another time. Judith, I'm so happy to meet you. And, I admit, I'm shocked. When did you marry my mischievous son?"

Judith crossed the room with grace, her head held high, while Cliff followed, looking a bit like an adoring puppy. "Two weeks ago," Judith said, answering Eleanor's question. She held out her hand and Eleanor took it, and they didn't so much shake hands as simply hold hands for a moment, in a kind of tactile understanding.

"But how did you meet?" Ari asked. "How long have you known each other?"

Cliff put his arm around Judith's waist. "Judith is a lawyer specializing in real estate. I've worked with her for almost a year. She's brilliant and clever and unnervingly patient. Never play poker with her."

"We've worked together on real estate sales for months, but this spring—" Judith looked at Cliff and blushed deeply.

"This spring we took our relationship to a new level," Cliff said very formally, sounding much like his father, and he turned stoplight red.

"But why didn't you tell us you had a girlfriend?" Ari asked.

"We wanted the time to be right," Judith answered.

"Plus, this family had so much stuff already going on," Cliff added.

"This family will always have something going on," Phillip murmured.

"Did you tell Judith's family?" Eleanor asked, trying not to sound childish.

"We did," Judith replied. "We flew out to Jackson Hole in July to tell them—"

"Your family lives in Jackson Hole?" Alicia asked, eyes wide.

"They don't live there full-time but they have a house there," Judith told her.

Alicia looked at Phillip. They shared a smile.

Eleanor took Cliff's hand and for a moment they were a circle of three. Three and a half, counting Eleanor's growing grandchild. "I'm extremely proud of you, and happy for you both." She paused and said with her own mischievous grin, "Well, maybe happier for Cliff than for you, Judith. You do know you have a rogue on your hands."

"I'm never a rogue when I've got Judith, Mom," Cliff insisted.

"He wasn't a rogue at all when we went on the cruise together," Alicia said proudly. "He talked about Judith all the time, at least all the time he wasn't talking *to* her on his phone."

"Sit down," Eleanor told the couple. She sat. "Tell us everything."

"Congratulations, Judith and Cliff," Phillip said formally.

"When is your baby due? You look about two months further along than I am," Ari said.

"What legal firm?" Phillip asked.

Eleanor leaned back in her chair, sighed deeply, and simply listened and watched. Now she understood why Cliff had asked her if his father had enjoyed being a parent the day he came to the house earlier in the summer to put Eleanor's air conditioner in the window. She saw how her son beamed when he looked at his wife, and when Cliff turned to Eleanor with a proud "Hey, Mom, look what I've done!" expression, Eleanor raised her glass to salute him. From a nearby chair, Alicia leaned forward to describe in detail how Cliff had told her first about Judith. Eleanor listened with joy in her heart for her children, her son and her daughter, who had kept secrets from her, as if they had become the very best of friends. But when had this happened? When had they become so close? Eleanor hoped it wasn't simply because they were allies, trying to get her to sell the house. She thought maybe it was because with Phillip's infidelity, it was the first time in his life that Cliff was able to take care of his older sister.

That evening, after all the good food and champagne and chat and laughter, when Alicia and Phillip were tucked away down the hall in a second-floor guest bedroom and Cliff had gone back to the hotel with Judith and Ari was off somewhere with Beck, then, finally, Eleanor slid into the welcoming comfort of her bed. She was exhausted.

Shadow slunk out from under the bed, leapt up onto her quilt, and regarded her with exceeding disfavor. He wasn't a fan of crowds. He'd been ignored and he was cranky about it.

"I know," Eleanor told him. "It's just for tonight."

Shadow's eyes told her that she was not forgiven. Still, he curled up next to her ankles and purred.

"Now I can't change positions," Eleanor told him. "You always get so offended if I move after you've gotten settled."

Shadow didn't twitch an ear.

From her bedside table, her landline rang. It was her best friend, home at last!

"I'm back!" Martha said.

"Oh, I'm so glad," Eleanor told her. "I got your postcards. It all looks amazing."

"It *was* amazing, Eleanor. Truly. Our cabin was out of this world, the entire ship was luxurious. You've got to come over. I bought a *chapeau* when we docked at Nice, and gorgeous shoes in Italy, and we drank the most heavenly wine in Santorini—oh, I can't wait to show you the photos."

"I can't wait to see them," Eleanor said. "I'm so glad you're home."

"How are you?" Martha asked. "Did you have a pleasant summer?"

"I'm not sure that 'pleasant' describes it," Eleanor said, unable to hold back her laughter. And she told Martha about meeting Silas and Phillip's affair and Alicia's cruise and Ari's pregnancy and Cliff's surprise marriage and Judith's pregnancy and the Eleanor Sunderland Beach Camp Foundation. Finally, she told Martha that she'd sold the bluff house and was moving into town, next door to Silas.

Martha was speechless for a moment. Then she said, "Damn, I wish *I'd* been here this summer!"

Beck had come to the island for his family's Labor Day party, too. Later, after darkness fell and Hen was playing Clue with her parents, Michelle slipped out to see her fiancé and Beck slipped out to meet Ari.

They sat at Brant Point, where the small round lighthouse blinked as boats and ferries rounded the corner into port. Ari was still wearing her lavender dress, and Beck wore white tennis shorts and a red and white striped button-down. They sat in the sand, leaning their backs against the white lighthouse, their knees pulled up to their chests as they watched the lights of boats twinkle in the slightly moving water.

"I have to leave tomorrow morning," Beck said.

"Most of my family leaves tomorrow, too," Ari told him. "Beck, I want to tell you something."

"Let me tell you something first," Beck said.

"Okay."

"I've been invited to join a practice in Boston. It will be the same sort of work, with more patients and more office staff."

"But your patients in Plymouth—"

"I'll go down to Plymouth once a week to see them." Beck shifted in the sand to focus on Ari. "This is an important move for me. I'm working on a paper with another behavioral therapist, about the consequences of videogames on children. We're headed into a new world with all our electronics and we can't go backward."

Ari turned her face away from Beck. She palmed a handful of sand and let it drizzle down her fingers.

"Ari, listen. I want you to come with me. I want to marry you. We don't have time for a big wedding, but we can have a small one, whatever you want, and—"

Ari looked back at Beck. Enough light shone from the town, boats, and stars for her to see his face, his eyes. "Beck, are you sure? Marriage is huge. With your move, your new clients, marriage might be too much."

"I think it will be damn fabulous," Beck said with a grin. "I was always my best at a football scrimmage. Lots going on, plotting moves, kicking up our energy, and—"

"You think our marriage will be like a football scrimmage?"

"Yeah, maybe, just the first few months. We'll have to find a place to live, not too far from B.U. so you can take courses. Find a good ob-gyn for you and a pediatric doctor for the baby. Plus, we'll be dealing with so many relatives. Hen and Mom and Michelle will go crazy organizing baby showers."

"But the baby—"

"The baby is mine. I will be the baby's father. I could be, after all, if I'd slept with you on our first date."

"I'm kind of stunned." Ari was wide-eyed. "I didn't know you could be so . . . impetuous."

"You don't know a lot of things about me. I don't know a lot of things about you. But I know how I feel when I'm with you."

Ari smiled. "How do you feel when you're with me?"

"Like I'm right where I should be. Ari, this world is crazy, and I'm crazy about you. I want to be with you."

"You sounded like Humphrey Bogart just then," Ari said, joking to hide her emotions. She was afraid to believe this was real. 'Kid, this world is a crazy place . . .' I'm sorry, Beck, this is all so *much*. And I need to tell you something that's happened . . ."

"Is it more important than the fact that I love you?" Beck asked.

Ari took a deep breath and let go of her fear. Happiness streamed through her. "Nothing is more important than that. I love you, too, Beck."

Beck pulled her to him and kissed her for a long time. They kissed and kissed while the sand whispered as it shifted beneath them. They talked, about how soon they should get married, and if they married on the island, Hen could be the flower girl and have the best dress, and Michelle could be a bridesmaid because Ari's best friend would be the maid of honor. They spoke of how they had to tell their families before they told their friends, and whether they wanted an apartment in Boston or a house in one of the nearby suburbs. As they talked, the stars grew brighter, and fewer boats passed, and the last car ferry blew its horn and slid into the harbor.

"We should go," Beck said.

They stood up, brushing sand from their clothes.

"Come home with me," Ari said. "Spend the night with me, Beck."

"What about Eleanor?"

"Her house is big. Everyone else is on the second floor. We'll sleep on the first floor in a room far away from theirs."

"Let's go."

Because they had arrived separately, Beck drove his convertible behind Ari as she headed toward her grandmother's house. They parked in her driveway, held hands, and crept into the house, to the bedroom at the far end, the one Eleanor had jokingly given Ari at the beginning of the summer.

"What did you want to tell me?" Beck said as they turned the covers down and slipped off their clothes.

"Nothing important," Ari told him. "Just, when this house is sold, which will be soon, Gram is giving me three million dollars."

"That's nice," Beck said, but he seemed not to have heard her, because he slid into bed and pulled Ari into his arms.

Twenty-Seven

For the last time, Eleanor's family had gathered at the bluff house, this time to go through the house, choosing and marking what pieces of furniture or art or attic treasures they wanted to claim for themselves.

Eleanor had sat out on the deck during this process. She'd already chosen the furniture and other items she wanted in her new house on Fair Street, including the small unpainted wooden cradle that her mother, Eleanor, Alicia, Cliff, and Ari had slept in. She wanted to keep that for Ari's baby, just as she had also packed several boxes of heirloom toys and baby clothes and taken them to her new home. She wanted those to give to Ari's baby and she felt slightly confused and even guilty because she didn't want to allow Cliff and Judith to have them for their child. Okay, maybe she'd give Judith and Cliff some. Maybe half. She very much liked Judith.

Eleanor's family had left thirty minutes ago, thanking her for her generosity, hugging her, and reminding her of the days and times they would come to pick up their treasures. Alicia had cried at the realization that this was the last time she would be in the old island house, but Alicia could be dramatic . . . and, as always, complicated. At some point during the day, she had made a small calendar of the

coming week, marking exactly what hours and what day each relative would return with a moving crew to haul out the larger pieces of
furniture. Not surprisingly, she had earmarked the first day for herself.

Eleanor had had several sleepless nights wondering if she was
doing the wrong thing. Now that Ari was going to give Eleanor a
great-grandchild and Cliff and Judith were going to give her a new
grandchild, Eleanor wondered if it wouldn't be right to keep the
house for these new children to enjoy. That thought had led her
down the path of regrets: Had Phillip really wanted to spend time in
the mountains? Had he felt pressured to spend his summers here?
Had Eleanor been selfish and shortsighted?

Well, she couldn't go back in time. Phillip had always seemed content when he was here. Excepting, of course, this past summer,
when he might have been possibly a great deal more than content,
and had hurt Alicia and Ari. Had Alicia learned any kind of lesson
this summer? Had Phillip?

Silas had asked if he could take Eleanor out to dinner or come to
her house for a drink but she had told him that for this last night she
wanted to be alone, and he'd understood. When she moved into her
new house, there would be plenty of days and nights to share a drink
or a meal with Silas.

And truly, it was done. Legal papers had been signed. Eleanor's
name had been mentioned twice in the local newspaper's report of
real estate transactions. It was the end of an era, but as her ebullient
son said, it was the beginning of a new era. Eleanor was, just a little
bit, frightened. The walls of this house were as familiar to her as her
own skin. And wasn't she some kind of a traitor, to leave these walls,
this house, knowing that very shortly, crews with diggers and growl-
ing tanklike machines with shovels would arrive to knock this house
down into crushed and useless pieces?

When was the time in a person's life that she could relieve herself
of *all* responsibility? How did people feel when they moved into
assisted living? Were they glad for the freedom from obligation?
Probably. Still, Eleanor was sure that when the time came for her to

move into assisted living, she would need her doctor to put her on some pretty heavy tranquilizers.

But *now.* She was here now and the September wind off the ocean carried a shiver of fall. Her hands were cold. The deck furniture was cold. Who was taking the deck furniture, Alicia or Cliff or Ari? No matter, they were the ones who knew when to come and what to take.

Eleanor went into the house, firmly closing the sliding door. It was cold in the house, too, of course. She had a custom of not turning the furnace on until October 1. Ridiculous, really, ridiculous, all the little rules she had made for herself in this house. She could forget the rules. She could remember the house in all the photos taken over the decades. Soon the house would be gone.

But the ocean would always remain.

Twenty-Eight

It was November, a month Eleanor always liked. The cranberry festival was over, cold winds swept the beaches, and the ocean reflected the gray of the cloudy sky. It was dark at four o'clock. It was a time of rest, Eleanor thought, for the island and for families, before the great celebrations of Christmas and New Year's Eve. She could settle down with Shadow and a thick saga of a book. She could join her friends for a relaxed dinner out. She could dig out her wool sweaters, her flannel sheets and pajamas, her winter hat and gloves.

Today was going to be a different sort of day, and Eleanor was slightly nervous. Not about her family. She had spoken with her family last night and knew that all was well.

Ari and Beck were renting an apartment while they looked for houses. Ari was taking two courses at Boston University—she was going there, taking the MBTA Green Line right to the campus and climbing the stairs to her class. She told Eleanor she'd never felt more fit.

Alicia and Phillip were in the process of selling their Wellesley home, which was listed for more money than they'd imagined, and searching for what Alicia called a "pied-à-terre" in Boston. During the early fall weekends, they had been driving up into Vermont and New Hampshire, looking at homes in the mountains and staying at luxurious hotels with gorgeous walking paths. They'd even started trail riding with a group. When Eleanor spoke with them, they both seemed very happy.

Cliff and Judith bought a handsome home in the posh suburb of Belmont. They'd hired a decorator to furnish the house, from the living room drapes to the omelet pan in the kitchen. Eleanor thought this was slightly odd, because she considered her home as her nest. She couldn't imagine snuggling down on a sofa without first feeling the fabric and the give of the cushion. Of course, she'd said nothing. She didn't want to be considered a bothersome old lady.

Well, she might be old, but she was also extremely cool.

All by herself, she had created an organization, the Eleanor Sunderlund Beach Camp Foundation. During September and October, she'd met with Cal, Cleo, and Poppy, and together they'd met with the bank president and their lawyers to officially create the foundation as a nonprofit, with salaries and benefits for the director and her staff. They'd purchased the building on Amelia Drive that housed the current office, and they'd turned the upstairs of the building into two apartments where Cleo and Poppy could live in the summer.

Cleo would be the official director of the foundation. Eleanor was the president of the board. And she'd been able to invite exactly whom she liked to sit on the board. Silas, of course. When Muffy Andover learned that Eleanor gave three million dollars to Beach Camp, she'd immediately given three million five hundred thousand, so Eleanor asked her to be on the board and she accepted. Donnie Hamilton joined, and so did Beck Hathaway's sister Michelle and a young schoolteacher, Lois Brady. Eleanor was glad to have some young people on the board. If foundations survived on wisdom, wealth, and work, the two young women could do a lot of the heavy lifting. Finally, Martha had joined the board, mostly so that she and Eleanor could gossip about everyone afterward.

This was their first official meeting, held in a conference room at the bank because construction workers were adding bathrooms and kitchens to the headquarters on Amelia Drive. It would take only five minutes to walk from her house to the bank, so Eleanor allowed herself to finish reading the chapter in her delicious novel, and then had to hurry around to get ready. She had her agenda printed out. She'd emailed it to the others, even to Martha, who had finally agreed to join the technological world. Eleanor quickly showered, dressed in a plain but expensive gray dress, and put on her pearls. She thought the president of the board should wear pearls. If she were female, of course.

All right, she was slightly nervous. She'd never chaired a meeting before. The idea of using a gavel sent her into hysterics of laughter, so she still wasn't certain how she'd rein someone in if arguments took place. They needed to appoint officers today, and because Muffy spent the winters in Florida, Eleanor thought Muffy should be president and Eleanor vice president, so that Eleanor could do all the work, which was what she wanted to do. But of course, she'd have to see what the others thought.

Eleanor scrutinized her appearance in the mirror. No lettuce in her teeth. Lipstick on straight. Her thick hair was behaving nicely now that the humidity of summer had left. On the whole, she thought she looked just fine.

Alicia had thought Eleanor was too old to start an organization, but Ari thought Eleanor was awesome, and as she slipped into her coat, pulled on her gloves, and picked up her folders, Eleanor admitted to herself that she agreed. She did think she was awesome.

Epilogue

"I feel very strange about this," Eleanor confessed when she was finally buckled into the car with Silas.

It was Easter and they were on their way out to Tom Nevers Head, where Cliff and Judith and their son, Hastings, were hosting a family get-together.

When Eleanor's grandson was born, she had been thrilled to meet the infant, but when she was alone with Silas, she'd said, "Hastings! What kind of a name is Hastings! Hastings Sunderland! That poor child."

Silas had laughed. "Come on, don't be so critical. After all, my name is Silas Stover and I turned out fine."

"But really, what are they going to call him? Hasty? Haze?"

"Whatever they call him, he is a beautiful baby boy, with all his fingers and all his toes," Silas said. He was in the driver's seat, fastening his seatbelt.

Eleanor leaned over and kissed his cheek.

"What's that for?" Silas asked. "Not that I'm complaining."

"That's for being such a sweetheart," Eleanor told him. "You're right, he really is a darling little baby."

Now here she was again, on Easter Sunday, relying on Silas to keep her cheerful.

"Silas, do you think I'm becoming grumpy?"

"Eleanor, do you think I'm going to answer that question?"

"Silas, you are a wise man." Eleanor lay back against the car seat and watched the trees flow past.

The last few months had been too chaotic with the birth of two new babies and everyone moving houses for the family to gather all together.

Alicia and Phillip had sold their beautiful mansion in Wellesley and moved into one of the handsome brick condominiums on Boston Harbor, so close to the cruise ship piers they didn't need to take a taxi.

Ari and Beck had bought a charming house only three streets away from Cliff and Judith because they thought it would be so much fun for the cousins to be able to play together.

When Eleanor heard this, she felt oddly wounded, disconcerted. Lucky for her, Silas was her Rock of Gibraltar. They'd talked and talked about how hard it was to be getting old, to turn from welcoming host to dependent guest. Eleanor might never again hold a family reunion in her own home because, first of all, she simply didn't have the space. But thankfully, Cliff and Judith had bought a summer home in Tom Nevers Head, a beautiful development far from the center of town, near the Atlantic Ocean, an enormous modern house with a yard large enough for them to set up a badminton court. Judith had turned out to be a jewel, keeping Cliff on his toes, working part-time in the law office, and now on maternity leave, and the whole time having what she called simple little family get-togethers with clever finger food and lots of interesting cocktails. Eleanor admired her immensely.

Alicia didn't seem to mind or notice her sister-in-law's competency, probably because she and Phillip had gone on a Christmas cruise in the Caribbean and were planning a cruise on the Baltic in the spring. She did save the month of February to be around when Ari had her baby. All had gone well for Ari, who had the baby at

Mass General just as Phillip had insisted. Afterward, Beck, Ari, and little Maisie Eleanor Bertha Hathaway went home, to their cozy house on Lincoln Street. Alicia and Phillip had moved in with them for three weeks. Eleanor was delighted to learn that Alicia had discovered new heights of happiness when she met her granddaughter. Alicia had spent her free time buying little Maisie a complete wardrobe and a room full of stuffed animals and toys that the infant was too young to appreciate.

And then there was Beck's family, such a big family. Beck's younger sister Hen was baby crazy and when Ari's mother and father left after three weeks of helping out, Hen and her older sister, Michelle, moved in to help cook and do laundry for three weeks.

The very surprising thing was that when Eleanor and Silas *finally* were asked to move into the Hathaways' guest bedroom to help with the baby girl, Eleanor discovered she didn't have the same energy she'd had when she was a grandmother to Ari. She loved the baby, but it exhausted her to carry all the laundry down to the basement and back up again. Also, Ari and Beck were trying to become vegetarians and would eat only fish and cheesy things, which Eleanor cooked even though she thought if ever there were a time when a young woman needed a nice, healthy steak, it was now.

When, at the end of March, Eleanor and Silas returned to their Nantucket houses, Eleanor had stayed in her L.L.Bean long fleece robe for three days. The March meeting of the foundation was canceled because of weather—the winds were too strong for everyone to get to the island by plane or boat—so Eleanor had lived like a teenager, eating odd foods at odd times of the day. Potato chips and guacamole for dinner with vodka in V8 juice. At least the guacamole and V8 juice were healthy. A pint of ice cream for lunch one day, and part of a Mrs. Smith's cherry pie that she found in her freezer for dinner another night.

She and Silas spoke on the phone several times every day, and Silas brought her groceries, but they both admitted that it was a pleasure to live by their own time schedules and their own desires. One day Eleanor lay in bed watching reruns of *Monk* all day. Next door in his house, Silas did the same, and at night, on the phone, they discussed their favorite episodes.

Finally, Eleanor was rested. She answered her friends' messages, went out and bought her own groceries, and walked on the beach in her down coat and hat, loving that absolutely no one else was there, for who would be crazy enough to walk on the sand when the wind was blowing with almost gale force and the sky threatened to unload its burden of snow at any moment. She found books at the library and lay about reading and eating crisp apples, which she thought was a step, even if small, in the right direction.

Now, suddenly, it was Easter and Eleanor and Silas were going to a part of the island they knew little about. It was on the south side of the island, near the Atlantic, and sequestered from the town traffic and tourists.

When Silas and Eleanor pulled into Cliff and Judith's long white gravel driveway, they were both impressed. The house was large and beautiful, with romantic balconies and wide decks and lush green lawns surrounding it. Evergreen trees bordered it all. Eleanor had no idea how much money Judith had, but she liked to think that the money she had given Cliff had helped buy this secluded paradise.

Cliff walked out onto the wide deck and waved. "Ahoy, maties!" he called.

"What a beautiful place this is!" Eleanor said, kissing her son on his cheek.

They entered the long open room with its many windows and a fireplace burning brightly at one end. Eleanor was glad to see it, for it was still very chilly on the island.

Phillip rose to greet Eleanor and Silas, and Alicia turned from the refrigerator to call hello. Beck was walking back and forth in front of the fireplace with his daughter on his shoulder, who was wailing so hard she hiccuped.

Ari ran to hug Eleanor and Silas. "Don't worry, she just nursed and Beck is trying to get a nice big burp out of her and then she'll sleep for a couple of hours." Before Eleanor could respond, Ari added, "You'll have plenty of time with her after dinner."

"I'm so glad," Eleanor said, amused and pleased to remember the times in her life when there was no other topic in the world than her infant.

Judith sat in an armchair, nursing little Hastings. "I'll be finished in just a moment, and then Lydia can take over."

"Lydia?" Eleanor put her hand to her temple. Was she really becoming senile?

Judith explained, "Lydia is my niece. She's fourteen and baby crazy, so she'll take care of the babies while we have a nice grown-up meal."

"Let me show you the upstairs," Phillip suggested.

Eleanor and Silas followed Phillip up the winding steps to the second floor, where the bedrooms and bathrooms were located in a sort of fan around the central room, the playroom, thickly carpeted and scattered with soft toys. At one end sat two colorful toy computers, and slightly above them, hanging on the wall, was a small color TV.

"TV for the babies?" Eleanor was appalled.

"I know," Phillip said. "Alicia was worried, too, but the truth is the world has moved on since we were young, or even had young children. Screens are everywhere and they're not going away. The computers are basic, and sweet, actually. If a child hits the letter 'F,' for example, a fish appears on the screen. Let me show you."

Eleanor sat on the adult-size sofa, watching these new electronic marvels. The world has moved on, Phillip had said, and he was right. She didn't pretend she was also moving on, in a very different direction, but while she was here, she didn't want to be left behind.

"Maybe after dinner," Eleanor said, "you could show me how the computers work."

Phillip glowed. "I would love to. I know Ari and Beck are buying a computer like this for little Maisie."

They toured the bedrooms then, each room in a different tone of blue, the wide beds inviting, the bathrooms en suite, the linens crisp and expensive, the closets spacious.

"Why do they have six bedrooms?" Eleanor asked.

"Oh, because they'll have guests, of course. You met Judith's parents and sister at Ari and Beck's wedding. They'll be coming to stay in the summer, and Ari, Beck, and Maisie will come often. And Judith's friends, of course, and Cliff's."

"I'm absolutely dizzy," Eleanor said.

Silas quickly took her elbow to steady her.

"I'm all right," Eleanor told him. "Could I walk out on one of the balconies and see the view?"

Phillip opened the sliding glass door and Eleanor stepped out onto the balcony. The railings were white and more than strong enough for Eleanor to lean on as she looked around at this part of the island that she'd never seen before. Green lawns, evergreens, wild scrub oak and vines, beach plum bushes, seagrass, and sand plain extended to the blue ocean, peaceful today. Here and there the view was dotted with the roofs and chimneys of other houses, as if they lived in a village. It was a most comforting view. Some really unbearable rock music was blasting from a house to the east. Three boys on bikes raced down one of the lanes. A crow made a scream of exasperation—Eleanor thought it was because of the horrible music—and flew from its perch on a tree and out of eyesight. *This is the world,* Eleanor thought. *It's been going on all the time and I never knew it.* She hoped that was the way it was with heaven.

"Judith says dinner is ready," Phillip said.

They all tromped downstairs and into the dining area—the house was open-plan, so there was no formal dining room, although the table had been beautifully set with an Irish linen tablecloth and napkins, and a centerpiece of daffodils and tulips and iris, all from the local florist. Bowls of steaming casseroles, vegetables, rice, and couscous filled the table—no lamb or ham now that Beck and Ari were fully vegetarian.

"I've never tasted such divine bread," Eleanor said. "Where did you find it?"

Judith laughed. "I made it. I'll give you the recipe."

Eleanor asked, "You made it? When did you have time?"

"Oh, I get up early. And Cliff took care of the baby all morning."

Eleanor stared openmouthed at Cliff.

Her son gave her a naughty and totally happy grin.

While they ate, the conversation flowed. Ari asked Judith how her parents were and how Judith's grandmother, who was eighty-nine and in an assisted-living community, was faring. They discussed Beck's family, his parents and Hen and Michelle and her wedding, including the groom's family and Michelle's bridesmaids, and after a while, Eleanor sat back in her chair with her second glass of wine and just listened.

For a real family reunion, she thought, someone would have to hire the event room at a hotel. And she wouldn't be the one in the middle, making the arrangements. And truth be told, that was fine with her.

Silas sat next to her. When the others, the younger ones, rose to take their plates to the sink and bring out several fruit pies, he leaned over and whispered to Eleanor, "Are you okay?"

She squeezed his hand. "I'm a bit overwhelmed," she confessed. "All these people. I was thinking we'd have to hire a hall to hold a family reunion."

"Did you include my children and grandchildren in your plans?" Silas asked.

Dear Lord, Eleanor thought, *that would double the guest list.* "I did!" Eleanor told him, lying. She'd found that at her age lying came easily, and her conscience didn't bother her one bit.

Cliff went around pouring flutes of Veuve Clicquot, and everyone moved from the table out onto the deck. It was cool, but comfortable in the sun. They talked about baseball, and books, and jokes, and then they found hilarious posts on their phones and passed their phones around as people used to share photos of her grandbabies. The babies began to cry, and Ari and Judith went into the house, returning with their children wrapped in light blankets. Then the babies were passed around to adore, and they were both very sweet babies.

At last Eleanor yawned. "This has been the most delightful Easter ever, but I need to go home and take a nap."

Everyone rose—Ari and Beck with their baby, Maisie, and Cliff and Judith with their little Hastings, and Alicia and Phillip—such a large family. They hugged and said a million goodbyes, and finally Eleanor and Silas were seated in the car.

"Wait!"

Eleanor looked out her window. Ari was running toward her. Eleanor rolled down the glass.

"Gram, this is a secret, please don't tell anyone," Ari said, leaning in through the window, huffing and puffing and whispering, "but could Beck and I and the baby stay with you for a month this summer? I know your house is small, but we'd only need the one bedroom, and we'd be out of your way much of the day, but I miss you SO much, Gram, I really want to be around you, not having deep, meaningful discussions about life, but just . . . watching a *Masterpiece* mystery with you and eating ice cream. Beck could go visit his family with the baby, and of course I'll go sometimes, but sometimes I want to stay with you."

"Ari!" Eleanor felt herself tearing up. "Nothing would make me happier. Oh, what a gorgeous idea!"

"Good then. We can text about dates." Ari dipped her head in and kissed Eleanor's cheek, and turned and ran back to the house.

Silas put the car in gear and carefully maneuvered over the white gravel, between the tupelo trees, and out to the main road. "Are you okay, Eleanor?" he asked.

Reaching over, Eleanor took his hand. "I've never been better in my life."

About the Author

NANCY THAYER is the *New York Times* bestselling author of more than thirty novels, including *Girls of Summer, Let It Snow, Surfside Sisters, A Nantucket Wedding, Secrets in Summer, The Island House, The Guest Cottage, An Island Christmas, Nantucket Sisters,* and *Island Girls*. Born in Kansas, Thayer has been, for the last thirty-five years, a resident of Nantucket, where she currently lives with her husband, Charley, and a precocious rescue cat named Callie.

nancythayer.com

Facebook.com/NancyThayerBooks

Instagram: @nancythayerbooks

About the Type

This book was set in Garamond, a typeface originally designed by the Parisian type cutter Claude Garamond (c. 1500–61). This version of Garamond was modeled on a 1592 specimen sheet from the Egenolff-Berner foundry, which was produced from types assumed to have been brought to Frankfurt by the punch cutter Jacques Sabon (c. 1520–80).

Claude Garamond's distinguished romans and italics first appeared in *Opera Ciceronis* in 1543–44. The Garamond types are clear, open, and elegant.